About the author

Writing has always been Maureen's hobby and passion and she particularly loves stories that contain a murder, mystery, crime, psychological or supernatural element and has always wanted to invent a new detective duo who don't always comply with the 'letter of the law', but choose *right* over *wrong*, which doesn't always side with the *victim* of the crime.

Having previously penned six other novels, lockdown presented the author with the perfect opportunity to write *The Adnegveill,* the first novel in a series of novels introducing Steal and Wright: two detectives, polls apart in personality yet as one in their search for 'true justice'.

In her career, Maureen has worked as a librarian and volunteered as a radio presenter for Hospital Radio, which afforded her lots of insight into people's thoughts when she asked them why they picked a particular song that held such special memories for them.

Therefore, in *Steal & Wright,* she has also put some songs in that go with particular characters' past, present, emotions or memories, because, sometimes, music touches the parts of our emotions that no words can.

STEAL AND WRIGHT: THE ADNEGVEILL

Maureen Farenden

STEAL AND WRIGHT: THE ADNEGVEILL

Vanguard Press

A CIP catalogue record for this title is
available from the British Library.

ISBN 978-1-80016-419-2

Vanguard Press is an imprint of
Pegasus Elliot Mackenzie Publishers Ltd.
www.pegasuspublishers.com

First Published in 2022

Vanguard Press
Sheraton House Castle Park
Cambridge England

Printed & Bound in Great Britain

1
The Three Rings

The woman scrubbed inside the large circular mug with the scourer until every tea stain was removed before wiping it dry and carefully placing it back on the mug stand, when the doorbell rang.

Looking up, she stared out the kitchen window into the large, well-manicured garden with a stillness that engulfed the huge old-fashioned room before continuing to wipe down the sink and worktop. Turning round, she surveyed the room with her distant blue eyes.

Everything was as it should be. The doorbell rang again… and she waited.

She was in no hurry. She wanted to enjoy the quite moment. To savour the feeling of complete emptiness when the doorbell rang for the third time, and she smiled.

Slowly, she walked into the big Victorian hallway to see the shadowy outline of a man and woman through the coloured-glass front door, where she caught sight of her reflection in a large hallway mirror opposite.

It had been a long time since she had stared inside herself but today, she felt brave. She wanted to see what had become of the girl with a dream. The girl trapped deep inside the shadow of the woman staring back at her.

It hurt to see how time had aged her once-soft pure-white complexion of youth into the thin-lined, pale face of a forty-three-year-old woman with grey flecks of hair consuming her once-thick luscious long dark hair tied tight in a bun. Straightening her plain dark blue buttoned-up cardigan that covered the matching shapeless blue trousers encasing her thin undernourished frame, she smiled into the mirror again, when, for a brief moment, the girl returned. She opened the front door.

'Mrs Anne Kay?' the man asked.

7

'Yes.'

'My name is Inspector Steal and this is my colleague, Sergeant Wright.'

'How can I help you, Inspector?'

'We have been asked to check on your husband, Mr Jason Kay, who appears to be missing?'

The inspector waited. He liked to savour the moment when he confronted a suspect for the first time.

Steal was a tall, thin man touching fifty with short, grey hair; dark, deep-set eyes and expressionless face and clothes. Steal loved his job.

'Please, come in, Inspector,' she said, opening the door wider before leading them into the large, dual aspect sitting room opposite the kitchen.

'What a lovely, bright room,' smiled Sergeant Wright, staring out of the huge French windows into the garden that circled the entire room, encasing it in sunlight, which bounced off the expensive furniture and large marble fireplace in the centre.

Sergeant Liz Wright was the opposite of her partner. In her early thirties, she emanated warmth with a breezy, bright smile, open face, long blonde hair and trendy coloured waistcoats to lift her dull official work clothes.

The three stood in the middle of the room where the sunlight encased them in a halo of warmth, whilst each of them played the game.

Steal and Wright waited for the first sign. But the suspect was an expert in signs.

'Please, take a seat.' She smiled, opening her arms wide in front of the large cream soft sofa before sitting down opposite them on the accompanying sofa.

The silent moment between them was sharper than a knife when Steal began the game. 'When was the last time you saw your husband, Mrs Kay?'

'Oh, five days ago, Inspector,' she replied without a flicker of emotion.

'Five days, that's a long time. Were you not worried?'

'No.'

'That's a rather strange reply for a loving wife?'

'And you would be an expert in the art of loving wives, Inspector?'

'I think Inspector Steal meant that he was surprised that you hadn't reported Mr Kay missing when his colleagues and associates at work had,' interjected Wright, wary of alienating their prime suspect.

'My husband never involved me in his work or family finances, Sergeant. He liked to keep his home life separate. Sometimes, he would be away for several days without contact. I wasn't concerned because to me it was normal.'

'Was he worried about anything recently regarding his business affairs, etc.?'

'Like I said earlier, Sergeant, Jason never discussed business with me.'

Wright looked right inside the suspect's eyes but couldn't see the sign… when Steal asked, 'Was yours a happy marriage, Mrs Kay?'

'There are many kinds of happiness, Inspector; I am sure that you have experienced it in your job, but to answer your question, no, it wasn't a happy union.'

Steal and Wright sat in silence. They were used to lies, but honesty…

Mrs Kay savoured the moment. It was the first time in sixteen years that she had dared utter the words that would release her from the two shadows inside herself. It felt good. 'I hear the shock in your silence, Detectives, but you are both professionals so I didn't see the point in wasting your valuable time by pretending any more.'

Steal was puzzled. His instincts told him that she was guilty, but of what crime? Her manner was distant and almost unreal, yet he felt a strange sympathy for her. 'Why did you marry Jason Kay?'

'Because my father told me to, and I was a good daughter.'

Wright looked into her eyes again, and for a second thought that she saw the sign. 'We live in the twentieth century where choices are our own. Why didn't you walk away?'

'In your world, you have many choices, but in my world, there were none. Money and power controlled my father and my father controlled me. My husband was bought and I was sold in the name of business.'

'What was the contract?' Steal asked.

'Jason Kay was a man who wanted power and status and my father wanted his legacy to continue through a man, not a woman. Jason was the son he wanted and I was the price of my mother's failure.'

'So if your husband was dead, then you would be a very rich widow?' noted Steal.

'If that were the case, Inspector, then half the residents of the village would be rich widows.'

'Who else would benefit from your husband's death?' Wright asked.

'That is a question that I'm unable to answer, Sergeant. You will have to ask my husband's legal advisors, for as I stated earlier, I know nothing of my father's or Jason's business matters, except when I was exchanged in the name of good business.'

'If you do have any contact from your husband, then please call me on this number,' said Steal, handing her his card.

'Of course, Inspector,' she said, showing them to the front door.

Steal turned round and asked, 'Are you remotely interested in whether your husband is dead or alive, Mrs Kay?'

'I will have to come back to you on that one, Inspector,' she replied, closing the door.

2
Fourteen Days Earlier

Jason Kay stood upright at the top of the long, winding staircase. Stretching out his left hand upon the dark, highly polished banister, a long, lingering grin ran across his face whilst he surveyed the large Victorian hallway below.

Slowly, he walked down the stairs running his hand along the banister until he stood in the middle of the hallway. Turning his body towards the large mirror on the wall, the grin grew bigger as he checked his reflection.

Everything was as it should be. His tall, well-toned body donned an expensive grey suit, crisp white shirt and red silk tie. The face was smooth and chiselled with perfect white teeth and dark, deep-set brown eyes. The hair was cut short at the temples with a hint of grey but thick and dark on the top. For a man in his mid-forties, he was in prime shape.

Turning round, he stared into the large Victorian kitchen where his wife, Anne, stood at the top of the breakfast table with her head bowed and hands clasped in front of her while he ran his eyes over the contents on the table.

There was one china plate with two boiled egg cups perfectly placed in the centre with the silver spoon positioned beside the cups. Two slices of thickly buttered white bread cut into eight pieces lay on another plate to the left and a large, circular china mug and saucer aligned to the right. Salt and pepper in the centre of the table with the empty china teapot and milk jug. On the cooker was a saucepan filled halfway with cold water, three extra-large raw eggs and glass timer placed exactly in the centre.

Everything was as it should be.

'I'll be back in thirty minutes,' he said, noting that the time on the large iron clock hanging on the wall above the arguer was exactly seven am.

Reaching for his long, camel-coloured cashmere coat hanging on the coat stand near the mirror, he opened the front door and stepped outside onto the large, crazy-paved entrance porch when the heat of the early morning sun encased his face.

His eyes looked down the immaculate, long, shingled driveway leading to the huge iron gates at the front entrance before circling the perfectly cut lawns on both sides.

A tiny smug smile crept across his face when he lifted up his right wrist and set the timer on the expensive gold Rolex watch for exactly thirty minutes.

Stepping onto the driveway, he breathed in the air of indivisibility.

'Good morning, Mr Kay,' smiled the elderly man standing in the front garden of the large white house opposite.

'Lovely day, Mr George,' he replied, tipping his head towards his neighbour before strolling down the long wide private tarmac road whilst secretly eyeing up every large gated house on either side. As he arrived at the sign *'Welcome to Tree Top Village'*, his watch bleeped three times.

The walk had taken exactly seven minutes.

Tree Top Village was the perfect place to live with its selection of exclusive cafés, restaurants, wine bars, two small but well-stocked food shops, the post office, newsagent, chemist, butcher, baker, solicitor's office, accountant, estate agent, local undertaker, private care home plus a mixture of exclusive individual boutique home furniture, clothes, garden and emporium shops.

'What a lovely, bright spring morning it is today, Mr Kay,' said the well-dressed woman in her late fifties as she passed him in the doorway of the newsagents situated in the centre of the village.

'Indeed, it is, Mrs Platt.' He smiled.

'I hope Anne is getting better and able re-join the council soon?'

'All is as it should be, Sylvia. But I will pass on your good wishes.'

The newsagent, Ronald Phelps was ready with the newspapers. 'Not much good news in them today, Mr Kay,' he commented.

'At least the sun is shining, Mr Phelps.' He smiled before turning round and walking out with the *Financial Times* and *Daily Mirror* folded under his right arm.

Walking back through the village, Jason Kay smiled at everyone whilst wallowing in the respect afforded to him as a prominent member of Tree Top Village.

Arriving back at the village welcome sign, his watch bleeped three times, and he noted that the time was exactly 7.23 a.m.

Seven minutes later, he was stood at the gate staring down the gravelled path at the large Victorian, six-bedroomed house. It was the largest in the road. Built in 1864 and named Treetop Mansion, it dominated the sky and set the standard for the residents of Hill Top Crescent.

Every day, rain or shine, wind or snow, Jason Kay made the walk…

Opening the front door, his watch bleeped three times… he noted that the time was exactly seven thirty a.m.

Taking off his coat and hanging it back on the coat rack, he walked with the newspapers under his arm towards the kitchen where Anne stood, waiting, at the top of the table; staring blankly ahead with her hands crossed whilst he ran his eyes over the table, again.

The three eggs were on the plate. The tea pot and milk jug were full. The saucepan and timer washed and put away.

Everything was as it should be… Then, his eyes turned to the ceiling in the corner of the room above the arguer and his face went sour.

Anne knew that look as she too slowly turned her head and saw it.

Feeling her entire body go into lockdown, she watched as his right hand evolved into a solid white fist—when the doorbell rang three times and the voice shouted, 'Jason, I need to speak to you right now.'

'Clean everything away,' he ordered, throwing the newspapers onto the kitchen table and knocking over the teapot and milk jug before turning round and answering the door whilst Anne washed and cleared the table before taking a long wooden-handled broom from inside the tall kitchen cupboard and reached up to the ceiling above the arguer to brush away the cobweb hiding in the corner.

How did she miss it? She had checked everything three times!

Placing the broom with the cobweb on the floor, she wanted to stamp the life from it, but when she looked down and saw how small

13

and helpless the creature was, she opened the kitchen door into the garden. 'At least you will feel the light for a moment,' she said, setting it free.

'What the hell is going on?' the man asked, waving a large brown folder in the air.

'Keep your fucking voice down,' snarled Kay, grabbing the folder and pulling the man inside whilst checking that the nosy neighbour, Henry George, wasn't looking.

'Did you think that I would sign that?' said the man.

'Shut up and go into the study,' commanded Kay, checking that his wife was still in the kitchen before following the man into the study and locking the door.

Whilst Kay locked the door, Anne stood frozen in the kitchen. She had recognised the voice.

Once it was a voice of comfort, but that was a lifetime ago; now, the voice was as hollow as the man who owned it.

But why such rage and why now after all the years of silent compliance?

A sudden bravery erupted inside her, and for the first time in sixteen years, she broke the rules and tiptoed across the hallway to the study door, careful not to get too close to the edge of the carpet touching the thick dark varnished wooden door that muffled the voices inside whilst her entire body shook with fear. Yet, Anne knew she had to take the risk… that this was the chance she had been waiting for.

Simon Dodd paced the study floor. His entire body on fire with a burning rage that even unnerved Jason Kay, the man who feared no one.

The body wasn't as tall and well-toned as his adversary, but hidden beneath the slightly ruffled high-street black suit, white shirt and blue speckled tie was a man who, if he took some care and pride, could be quite handsome.

The face was pale and jaded with wrinkles around his dull, lifeless green-brown eyes that were almost hidden beneath a messy pile of curly brown, grey hair. Aged in his mid-forties, he was not a man in his prime, but a man who had never reached it. 'You got what you wanted, Jason. There's no need to do this. I won't let you,' he threatened.

Jason looked down onto the large, dark green, leathered-topped mahogany desk where the file sat between them. Stretching his back, his cold black eyes scanned the study. It was filled with expensive dark brown leather furniture, wall-to-wall purpose-built shelves and rich velvet curtains pulled back from the impressive coloured glass windows that looked out onto the vast and perfectly tended garden; it was the centre of his kingdom where he would sit at the desk in the huge high-backed brown leather throne, ruling over his subjects with an iron heart.

'You don't tell me what to do, Simon, I tell you.'

'This isn't legal. How did you get that hypocrite Pritchard to sanction it?

'Pritchard didn't take much persuasion. He knows all about self-preservation.' Jason smirked.

'I won't be a pawn in your evil games any more. You've used my firm to further your sickening ambitions for the last time. It's my company for Christ's sake, not yours.'

'You mean your father's company. You're only a figure head. Your father set the rules and gave me complete control when he died. I can do whatever I want, when I want, and you can't stop me. I can easily get another solicitor. You're nothing without me behind you so stop fucking whining and sign the document.'

Simon wanted to choke the life-force from the man who had replaced him.

His father, James Dodd, wanted a son like him, cold and ruthless, instead of a son with dreams beyond being a dull solicitor. James Dodd picked a man in his own likeness and threw his real son into the abyss of no man's land.

'I won't do it,' retorted Simon when Kay roared out loud and Anne's heart stopped…

Even through the thick wood-panelled door, the sound of his laugh terrified her… for it wasn't the laughter of lightness, but of the darkness that always followed it.

'It's already done, Simon. Everything has been arranged and if you don't counter-sign the document by mid-day next Wednesday, then I'll make sure you lose everything.'

Anne waited for the eruption, only to hear silence.

After all the years of emptiness, she didn't think that her heart could be broken for a second time.

Whatever evil document Jason Kay had hidden in that file, she knew that if Simon sanctioned it, then it would be her who would pay the price... and she had only nine days to find out what dark secret her husband was hiding.

3
Lunsford Police Headquarters

'Sergeant Wright,' yelled Steal from his office where his desk piled high with files of unsolved cases.

'You'd better get in there quick, Liz, before he blows up.' Her colleague Sergeant Jack Stone smirked.

'Very funny, Jack, the joker of Lunsford.' She laughed, giving him her usual once-over look of hidden approval.

Jack Stone was a grade below Sergeant Wright, but his big head and cocky attitude, even though irritating at times, was a tonic. Working with Steal wasn't. Jack was three years younger than his colleague, with a cheeky grin, thick read hair, tall, but well-toned physique donning a tight-fitting silver/grey suit with long pointed black shoes.

Liz knew that he fancied her which secretly she liked, but she was ambitious and so romance wasn't on the agenda. Solving a big murder case was, and even though her boss, Steal, wasn't the most cheerful of partners, his reputation for always getting his man was well-known, and so when he shouted, she jumped up.

'Did you hear me, Wright?' scowled Steal, banging his fist on the table again.

'Yes, Inspector,' smiled Liz. He might be a bad-tempered ornery sod, but no one, not even the grumpiest man in the force, was going to dampen her enthusiasm for life.

'Better get to, Liz,' laughed Jack, checking his mobile for any texts from the many female admirers he imagined wanted to bed him.

'What's Steal's first name?' she asked, curious that even though she had been assigned as his partner for the last six months, no one would tell her.

'If you find that out, then you're a better detective than anyone at Lunsford. It's been the best-kept secret for last twenty odd billion years,' grinned Jack when Wright calmly walked into Steal's office where he purposely ignored her whilst continuing to read the open file in front of him; a tact that he did with all fresh eager detectives, yet she wasn't intimidated. Six months working alongside the inspector had taught her two very important lessons.

    1) He never called anyone by their first name.

    2) He never did or said anything without a reason.

And so, Sergeant Wright waited patiently for the comment that she knew would eventually come. The opening words which would lead them to Jason Kay.

'A strange answer, Wright?' noted Steal, finally looking up.

'What answer?' she queried, desperately trying to fathom what was inside Steal's head for if she could think like him, then all her dreams of being the best female murder detective on the force would come true.

The inspector smiled. He may be the most difficult and bullish boss on the force, but Sergeant Liz Wright wouldn't have lasted five minutes as his partner if he hadn't seen that spark.

The moment she stepped into his office eight months ago and dared to say the words no other officer would—'I want to be the best detective I can be and then better than the best; you, Boss'—he knew that she would do.

A solitary man who appeared to have no family or friends, Steal preferred to work alone, but when he read Wright's file and noted that she excelled in every exam or task undertaken and that whenever she got a bit too cocky for her boots, her fellow colleagues would joke "They call her Liz Wright because she's ALWAYS RIGHT", it aroused his curiosity and so he dug deeper until he found something even more intriguing.

He checked his black notebook and read out, 'I will have to come back to you on that one, Inspector.'

Smiling, Wright knew instantly that Steal had seen it. That this case was not as straightforward as it appeared.

Inspector Steal had an ability that no other detective she had ever worked or studied under for the last nine years had; to travel deep into the abysses of a killer's mind and unravel the evil hid beneath.

Wright didn't need to check her notebook. The answer Mrs Anne Kay gave to Steal's question, "Are you remotely interested in whether your husband is dead or alive?" puzzled her too. She said, 'If Mrs Kay were innocent, then why answer with a statement that indicated her guilt?'

'Precisely,' acknowledged Steal, tapping his finger on the file. 'Mrs Anne Kay is a guilty woman, but of what crime? Jason Kay disappears for five days and his wife isn't concerned? No husband goes out to work for days at a time without bothering to check back home at some point. Even if he didn't give a shit about his wife, a man like Kay would want to know exactly what was going on in his empire, Kay Corporation. Yet, his personal assistant Miss Diane Moffatt, employees, the legal team, solicitor, estate manager at Hilltop Mansion have heard nothing from him for five days…? And where is his mobile phone and laptop? According to Miss Moffatt, he took them everywhere with him.'

Picking up the file, Steal marched into the main office and announced, 'Listen up, team' — holding the file up in the air — 'the file on Jason Kay is no longer just a missing person's case, but now a murder case too, so get to it, everyone.'

Within seconds, the entire office burst into life.

Police work is ninety percent tedious and boring. Dealing with petty criminals, drunks, mouthy youths, endless statements to write up and file etc. etc. so when a prime murder case lands in the department's lap, everyone, including the forgotten filing clerk in the basement, explodes inside with high oxygen energy.

Jack ditched his female admirers to erect the crime board in the middle of the office whilst Wright felt her hand tremble with a mixture of fear and excitement.

Steal passed her the file and she bellowed out, 'You heard the boss; get to it, team,' watching her work colleagues rush around the room setting up phone lines, computers and every other piece of equipment needed like drug addicts on a high.

Finally, she had attained what she had dreamed of all her life since the age of ten; the murder case of all murders to solve.

4
Kay Corporation

Steal and Wright cast their eyes up into the sky where Kay Corporation towered over them from a glass dome. 'How the mighty like to look down upon the minions,' said Wright.

'You're not a fan of a poor man making good, Sergeant?' said Steal with a sneaky grin.

'It depends on how that poor man dug his way out of the shit pile of poverty,' replied Wright, who had done her homework on Jason Kay who, on the surface, appeared to be admired and loved by everyone.

A self-made man, he enthused an easy charm that beguiled everyone around him, and yet his wife would have to get back to them about whether or not she cared if he was alive or dead?

Glancing down upon the hive of busy ants below from the circular glass lift taking them to Jason Kay's penthouse office on the twentieth floor, Steal and Wright could feel the power of Kay's kingdom emanating from inside the floating taxi.

Stepping out of the lift into the vast circular glass office, they could see the entire world unfold before them. The woman glided effortlessly across the room from the door in the far left-hand corner towards them.

'I'm Mr Kay's personal assistant, Diane Moffatt,' she said in a crisp, almost too-perfect English accent, her mouth housing gleaming white teeth.

Aged in her mid-to-late thirties with long legs, slim model hips, shapely bust, shiny brownish blonde highlighted hair neatly tied up in a pony tail, tight fitting black trousers, red high-heeled shoes and white crisp shirt with her face showcasing immaculate makeup; she was the perfect personal assistant to epitomise everything about Kay Corporation.

'You must be Inspector Steal and Sergeant Wright? Please, come this way.' She led them across the office to a large glass desk dominating the middle of the room whilst pointing to two small-backed grey leather chairs in front of the desk before slipping her slim body and long legs into the large high-backed black leather chair behind the desk with the world outside floating all around it.

Steal and Wright sank into the chairs like the tiny ants that buzzed below the lift, noting that Miss Moffatt towered over them from the other side when an uneasy silence stirred within them.

It was their job to find Jason Kay's killer, but once in a decade or two a case comes along that they won't rejoice in solving.

Yes, Lunsford Police Force will celebrate putting Kay's killer behind bars, but when the press cameras stop rolling, a little part of them will wither because sometimes catching killers can be a two-edged sword of victory.

The world sees the self-made millionaire Jason Kay as a shiny example of a good man rising up from the ashes of poverty that never forgot his roots and so generously supported many worthwhile charities, but their gut instincts told them that there was something more sinister behind his disappearance.

'Have you discovered anything, Inspector?' Miss Moffatt asked with her concern notably sincere.

'Our investigation is ongoing, Miss Moffatt, but I can inform to you that we are now treating the disappearance of Jason Kay as a possible murder investigation,' replied Steal, unmoved by her apparent concern because everyone involved in Jason Kay's life was now a suspect on the crime board.

'Murder…'

'I'm afraid so, Miss Moffatt,' interjected Wright, checking her notebook. 'I understand that it was you who telephoned the police station to report Mr Kay missing?

'Yes, Sergeant, he was due to telephone the office just before close of business at around six o'clock that day to check on any urgent matters so when I didn't hear from him, I rang his mobile, but the line was dead. I then tried to contact the hotel where he was staying overnight, but they said that he hadn't checked in. It was then that I became concerned and telephoned the police.'

'Why didn't you telephone his wife at the family home?' questioned Wright.

Miss Moffatt smiled that perfect smile and replied, 'Jason never involved Mrs Kay with his business matters and everyone, including myself, were instructed to never bother his wife at home.'

'I don't quite understand, Miss Moffatt,' commented Steal with that cool, detached and slightly puzzled expression he used to unnerve the suspect that Wright new so well.

'Understand what, Inspector?' queried Miss Moffatt, feeling her lips quiver when Steal pulled out his notebook and glanced over it before fixing his eyes dead centre with hers.

'It appears rather puzzling that you were so concerned about your boss being missing that you contacted the other staff and legal team at Kay Corporation, plus his solicitor, a Mr Simon Dodd; his estate manager at Hilltop Mansion, Mr Eric Finch, and even his personal physician, Dr Stuart Pritchard, and yet not his wife?'

'I presume that you've interviewed Mrs Kay, Inspector?' Miss Moffatt asked without a hint of a quiver on her lips.

Wright interjected, 'Your point being, Miss Moffatt?'

'Just that Mrs Kay is a rather plain mousy woman who has spent her entire life being sheltered from the harsh realities of the world.'

'That's a rather cruel comment about your boss' wife,' sneered Wright.

Miss Moffatt slipped back into the high-backed throne and smiled when she confessed, 'I can smell your contempt, Sergeant, so I'll save you the time of digging any further and tell you the facts. There has been a mutual agreement between Jason Kay, his wife and myself for the last six years. He chooses a mistress more suited to his desires and she doesn't have to be bothered by him in the bedroom.'

'And what do you get from this "mutual agreement"?' inquired Steal, noting that Wright was beginning to allow her personal feelings to cloud the investigation.

'Look around you, Inspector' — opening her arms wide — 'I live and work in a powerful rich world where the only price I have to pay to belong is a quick bonk under some silk sheets a couple of times a week.'

Fuming Wright couldn't help herself when she asked, 'How does it feel to realise that your meal ticket may turn out to be a corpse?'

'Don't pretend to me that you got where you are in the male-dominated police force because of your supreme detective skills, Sergeant,' countered Miss Moffatt.

Steal coughed towards Wright who bit her lip… whilst he checked his notebook again and queried, 'I take it that the main beneficiary from the estate of Jason Kay on his death would be his wife as there are no children and it appears that Mr Kay was an only child with no living relatives, and can you also confirm for the record that as his mistress, you wouldn't benefit from his estate on his death?'

'I don't know anything about Jason's personal finances except that he agreed to pay me three hundred thousand pounds if I stayed with him as his mistress for ten years, but with the added clause that I get nothing should the agreement be dissolved by either party before then. So, you see, Inspector, I lose three hundred thousand pounds if Jason is dead and with regard to Mrs Kay, you should contact the family solicitor, Simon Dodd, who deals with all the family's legal matters pertaining to the personal estate.'

Closing his notebook, Steal stood up. 'I think that we're done for now, Miss Moffatt, but rest assured Sergeant Wright and I will be back.' He walked to the lift with Wright and stepping inside, he turned to her and said, 'A good detective doesn't have time for personal rage, Sergeant,' while hiding a sly grin.

'Yes, Boss,' she muttered, angry at herself for allowing a suspect to rile her.

Steal's mobile rang. 'Yeh. Good. We're on our way back. Make sure that the warrants are ready.'

They stepped out of the lift and Wright noted that invisible spark of glee in his eyes when a vital clue had just been uncovered.

He announced, 'Jason Kay's mobile has turned up.'

Back in the office, Miss Moffatt pulled out the secret second mobile she had hidden inside her expensive designer Gucci gold bag. She located the number in her contacts and pressed dial.

'They've just left and it's now officially a murder investigation, so the game has begun…'

5
Fourteen Days Earlier

Simon Dodd stood in the hallway, desperate to make that short walk across the floor into the kitchen where he could see her standing with her back to him at the sink.

On the rare occasions over sixteen years that Jason Kay summoned Simon to Hilltop Mansion, he tried to make that walk, but never could… He hated himself for being a coward, but still he could never cross that small yet vast void that had become his tormenter.

Anne Kay could feel his eyes penetrating through her back when she turned round and locked hers into his, only to discover that every time it would be the same…

Her eyes begging him to make the first step, that never happened… and so she would turn round with her back to him and cry the dry tears of despair.

Once the tears were real and filled with an anger that encased her whole body, but now she had no more anger left, just a hollow emptiness as dry as the tears.

But today was different as she watched him pull his foot up into the air and force it down onto the black-and-white stone-tiled floor towards her when the study door opened and the coward shrivelled back into his pitiless lair.

'What the fuck are you still doing here, Simon?' admonished Kay, glaring over at his wife while she watched the front door slam shut and her husband march across the hallway towards her with his right hand locked into the fist… when the mobile rang inside his trouser pocket.

'Have I got to do everything my fucking self?' he yelled into the phone then cut the line dead. As he was stepping closer to Anne, it rang again. 'Fuck it. Set the extraordinary urgent shareholders meeting for precisely three hours from now.' He pushed his face into Anne's; she felt his fist sink into her stomach.

The doorbell rang just then, three times. 'What the fuck now?' he shouted, pulling his fist out. 'Today's your lucky day, my little bird.' He sneered, noting from the corner of his eye that the cob-web was gone. 'Get back to your cage,' he ordered, straightening himself up before answering the door. 'What do you want, Finch?' He growled whilst Anne slowly pulled her body inwards without a hint of fear or pain showing on her face.

'Sorry to disturb you, Mr Kay, but I thought you should know that the swimming pool pump has blown and needs replacing.'

'Why are you bothering me with this petty detail? It's your job as estate manager to deal with such matters.'

'Yes, sir, but the pump required for your pool can only be ordered from a company in America and they won't sanction the purchase and delivery until you confirm my order yourself, it being a rather expensive item,' he replied in his usual compliant dead-panned voice that hid a simmering hatred for the man who stole Hilltop Mansion from his real employer.

Erich Finch was a man in his early fifties with a bald head and weathered face encased in blotchy red skin evolved from decades of drinking too much alcohol. His eyes were dead and he had a body that was part-muscle from thirty-five years of outdoor work and part-fat from over indulging in the demon booze.

His late father, Alan Finch, was the original estate manger when Hilltop Mansion was owned by Anne Kay's father, Reginald Price; who wasn't a particularly kind man, but was a saint compared to his present employer, Jason Kay.

Erich had worked at the Hilltop since he left school at fifteen and became estate manager when his father died of a heart attack twenty-five years ago, aged fifty-eight.

He was a carbon copy of his alcoholic father whose mother left them when he was just five years old and so, his life had been one long bottomless pit of empty and drunken lost dreams... except for his constant regard for the little girl who never had a chance, just like him.

Eric would quietly watch over her, hoping that one day he could save her and so in turn save himself in one last act of selflessness before he followed his father into the drunken well of oblivion.

'Put the paperwork on my desk and I'll sort it out when I get back,' instructed Kay.

'Yes, sir,' nodded Erich, smiling that secret smile from under his eyes between him and Anne who smiled back.

When Eric saw, from his lodge, Simon Dodd slam the door behind him in rage, he knew that Anne would need him.

Shutting the front door in Eric's face, Kay turned round to see Anne walking back up the stairs to her bedroom located across the vast landing directly opposite his.

Satisfied that the bird was back in its cage, he locked the door behind him and slid into the soft black leather seat of his £150,000 silver-grey sports car before dialling on his mobile. 'That shrivelling shrimp Dodd was here bleating that he won't sign the document when you assured me that it was sorted and a done deal?'

'Everything is in place. In nine days' time, it will all be yours, Jason.'

'You'd better be right, Pritchard.' He drove off in a cloud of simmering fury.

Dr Stuart Pritchard sat in his office swallowing his own fear, knowing that if anything went wrong, it would be him, and not Jason Kay, who'd lose everything.

A small, fat man in his mid-eighties with balding white hair and grey, wrinkled face and pompous manner, Dr Pritchard enthused a medical superiority beyond his knowledge.

A failed surgeon and GP, he set up his own private practice, primarily specialising in mental health forty years ago, realising that the world was full of people willing to pay a small fortune for the elusive answer to happiness.

In poor physical health, he too was now seeking that halo of happiness in the Caribbean sun for himself.

Sitting up straight in his weathered brown leather chair, Pritchard buzzed through to his secretary, Olive Bence. 'Get me Simon Dodd on the line, now.'

Watching the beast drive off in his silver chariot from her bedroom window, Anne knew that this was her chance. She crawled underneath the bed and pulled out the hidden mobile stuck to the mattress.

Dialling the number, Anne felt the courage evaporate from her when she breathed in to feel HIS hard white knuckles penetrating deep inside her stomach… then said, 'I need to see you…'

The voice at the other end replied, 'I'll meet you at our special place in thirty minutes.'

It had been a long time since Anne had been to their special place, but when the voice answered, her heart lifted.

Opening the bedroom window wide, Anne shouted up into the bright blue sky, 'The bird is ready to fly again…'

Eric looked up at the window from the swimming pool to see her smiling down upon him. He felt his heart jumping for joy and hope for the first time in twenty-five long, dark years.

6

Staring at the crime board, Steal and Wright began to piece together the life of Jason Kay.

Jack had done a good job laying out the pictures of each suspect like a deck of cards with red lines drawn between and across them that appeared to look like a muddled maze, but was really an invisible path joining each card together like a tarot reading with hand-written notes with a black marker that would eventually lead them to the killer.

'What did you get from Kay's mobile, Stone?' Steal asked.

Jack's vocal cords began to crumble at his breakthrough moment showcasing a pivotal piece of evidence where an elderly lady found Kay's mobile dumped just inside the entrance of the public park near Kay Corporation and handed it into the local police station. 'Nothing, Boss. It had been wiped clean, but whoever did it knew what they were doing because the tech team couldn't retrieve anything.'

'What about fingerprints?' grunted Steal, annoyed but not surprised. Whoever murdered Kay was a lot smarter than any ordinary killer.

'None, not even the old lady's, who wore gloves when she found it.'

'Find out who the makers of the mobile are and send it off to them. I may not be a technological wizard, but you can bet your next month's pay packet that there will be some sort of spyware setup by them inside their latest must-have gadget for them to use and sell on.'

'I don't think that they will admit that, Boss,' trembled Jack.

'Then threaten them with a ton of shit search warrants about their company finances and see how cooperative they suddenly become, Sergeant.'

'Yes, Boss.'

'And when you've done that, get back to Tree Top Village and dig out what gossip the upmarket villagers and neighbours have on both Jason Kay and his wife.'

'On it, Boss,' nodded Jack, feeling the adrenaline rush through him at the chance to go out into the field and do some proper detective sleuthing.

Steal grunted, 'Where are the warrants for Hilltop Mansion, Kay Corporation and accountant, Timothy Gibbs, plus Kay's solicitor, Simon Dodd, and Dr Pritchard?'

'On your desk, Boss,' the voice shouted from the back of the office.

Steal glanced over, 'Good, hmmm?'

'Constable Rita Clark, Boss,' she said with a nervous smile.

Rita Clerk was a shy, plump woman in her late twenties with mousy brown short-cropped hair and spotty skin who melted into the invisible army of assorted admin staff at Lunsford that no one above the rank of Sergeant noticed, but couldn't do without.

Whilst the detectives went out with their shiny badges pretending to solve crimes, it was the dedicated army of invisible admin staff like Rita who empowered them with the animation. Without the long, intensively laboured phone calls, photocopying pictures of the victim, suspects, phone records plus old police files dug up from the basement and endless assorted paperwork done by them then the crime board of suspects would be practically empty.

Steal and Wright stood in the middle of the office surveying every tiny detail of the crime board in an attempt to see through the maze of clues.

In the middle was the main card of the deck; a picture of the corpse, Jason Kay, with red lines floating out from his smiling face, leading to all the people in his life that were now suspects on a board game of murder.

Prime Suspect No. 1: The Wife — Anne Kay

Suspect No. 2: The Mistress — Diane Moffatt

Suspect No. 3: The Solicitor — Simon Dodd

Suspect No. 4: The Accountant — Timothy Gibbs

Suspect No. 5: The Doctor — Stuart Pritchard

Suspect No. 6: The Estate Manager — Eric Finch

Suspect No. 7: Board Members — Kay Corporation
Suspect No. 8: ?????? — The Wild Card

Steal scratched his head before turning round and walking back into his office with Wright behind.

'What's up, Boss?' she asked, knowing that when the inspector scratched his head, it was a sign that something about the case puzzled him.

'Why was Jason Kay's mobile found in the entrance of the public park near his office and why wipe everything off it?'

'The killer must have dumped it there?' surmised Wright.

'If you've just murdered the most powerful overlord of Kay Corporation, why dump his mobile so close to the office and in such a public location whilst taking great care to make sure that his laptop and corpse disappear into thin air?'

'Because it's a red herring, Boss,' said Wright, when a big grin crept across her face as the penny dropped and Steal gave that tiny little smirk that made her want to leap into the air like a little girl who'd just won a prize at the fair.

He never gave away praise to his fellow colleagues, but that smirk meant more to her than passing the sergeant's exams first time with distinction.

Tapping his fingers on the pile of warrants upon the desk, Steal was hot to trot. 'Let's get to it, Wright,' he said, picking up the warrants and thrusting them into her hand on his way out.

Wright asked, 'Where to first, Boss?'

7

Fourteen Days Earlier

Anne opened the tall cupboard where the broom and vacuum were stored. She pulled out a tiny folded black plastic step ladder used to reach the top kitchen cabinets and shelves, then rushed back up to her bedroom where she opened the window and signalled over to Eric by the lodge, who knew exactly what to do.

Collecting a tall steel ladder from the estate shed, he slipped it under the window when Anne climbed down with the plastic step, giving him a kiss on his right cheek before running down the gravelled garden path to the back fence.

Unfolding the plastic step at the far left-hand corner of the fence, she carefully climbed over it, landing on a large dead oak tree trunk at the other side.

Standing on top of the crumbling trunk, she breathed in the air of freedom, then slowly surveyed the beautiful meadow of wild flowers, trees and stream whilst listening to the soothing sound of bird song and rustling wildlife hiding amongst the greenery and flowing water that transported her into another world.

It was a world where a little girl would play for hours with the magical animals that had become her friends and dream of a future as free as the birds that flew in and out of the meadow, like winged angels in a fairy tale.

It had been a lifetime since she had last dared step onto the tree trunk, but now the winged angels were calling to her again.

Running along the edge of the stream with her hands outstretched, feeling the life-force carry her along, suddenly the dark years floated away down the water when she saw the well and the outline of a ghost sat on the circular stone seat encased around the well.

The ghost looked up and smiled. 'Hello, Anne.'

'You came, Dotty?' she said, feeling the warm tears of pure joy trickling down her pale cheeks.

'Of course, I came. I never thought that we would ever meet here again,' she said, standing up and stretching her arms out wide.

Anne ran into them and they sat in silent peace on the damp stone seat, with their hands clasped around each other, looking out into the wilderness whilst savouring their precious minutes together.

Dorothy Short, nicknamed Dotty by her best friend, Anne, had grown into a pretty, petite at five-foot, freckled-face, forty-three-year-old woman with soft, almost wrinkle-free skin, and bright blue mischievous eyes encased by slinky strawberry blonde bobbed hair.

Wearing trendy light-blue tight-fitting jeans, red cashmere V-necked top and flat light-brown leather loafers, Dotty enthused a contentment and happiness with life that Anne dreamed of but never had.

'Do you remember when we were just eight years old and threw an old coin down the well whilst holding hands like we are now before closing our eyes and making a wish each?' said Anne.

Dotty laughed. 'I do, but we never told each other our secret wish.'

'That's because I never believed that mine would come true,' said Anne, letting go of Dotty's hand.

'I know, my dearest Anne. That's why I didn't tell you mine either. I knew that my life would be what I wanted it to be and that yours wouldn't and so couldn't let you share a future that was never to be,' said Dotty, clasping her friend's hand again.

'What did you wish for, Dotty?'

'I wished to be a successful businesswoman and that we would both grow old together as best friends.'

'Well, at least half of our wishes came true,' smiled Anne without a hint of jealousy.

Dotty's face crumbled. 'I'm sorry that I wasn't a better best friend. I'm a coward and not worth the love you still bestow upon me. I stopped answering your calls because I couldn't bear to see you so unhappy and not able to help you. I failed you, my dearest Anne. Can you ever forgive me?'

'There's no forgiveness to give. I couldn't escape and you couldn't save me.'

'Why did you ring me after all these months?'

'Why did you answer this time?'

'Because something inside me told me that you needed me now more than you ever did before and so I couldn't desert you for a second time,' said Dotty, feeling her eyes welling up with shame and regret.

Anne looked down the well which had dried up over the years and saw the old coins stuck in the mud. 'I've nine days in which to discover what dark fate Jason has planned for me and you are the only person who can help me in my search. Will you help me, Dotty?'

'I've waited years to slit that bastard's throat,' grinned Dotty, sitting back down on the cold damp stone.

Anne explained to Dotty her plan whilst the birds sang and wind rustled through the trees carrying the sweet sound of freedom.

The Meeting

Jason Kay stood in the floating glass taxi watching his colony of ants below frantically crawl around doing his bidding. The door opened and Diane Moffatt stood, waiting.

'Is everybody assembled?' he grunted, brushing past her towards his desk.

'Yes, Jason,' she replied with that frozen perfect smile reserved just for him.

'It's Mr Kay when we're here and don't ever forget that again.' He sneered, pulling out a single gold key attached to a red key ring from his inside jacket pocket and unlocking the last drawer under his desk containing a silver laptop whilst Diane Moffatt stood at the front of the desk, waiting.

She was now an expert at the game of waiting… Waiting for him to boss her around at work, waiting for him to summon her to his bed at their secret love nest and waiting for him to give her one single sign that she mattered.

Staring at Kay's expensive gold Rolex watch gleaming out from his right wrist, while he sat on his throne reading something on the laptop, Diane reminded herself yet again of why she tolerated the way he stamped all over her with his expensive, Italian-leather, overly pointed shoes like a piece of dog shit.

All she had to do was play the waiting game for just four more years then three hundred thousand pounds would be hers and the words she had spoken to him every day inside her head could finally be said: 'Piss off, you moron.'

'Let's get on with it,' said Kay, closing his laptop and locking it back in the drawer before slipping the key inside his jacket.

Following Kay out of the office and across the hallway to the board room, Diane sensed that the extraordinary urgent meeting called by the board members had rattled him.

Part of her wanted to see his empire crumble, but the other part wanted the three hundred thousand pounds he owed her for selling him her soul.

Standing at the head of the board table, Kay stared down upon the ten shareholders sat in stony silence whilst Diane slipped into the empty chair bedside him to the left, and opened a plain black laptop she'd left earlier in order to record the minutes of the meeting.

Sat to his right was Kay Corporation's chief accountant, Timothy Gibbs, who didn't want the extraordinary meeting but had no choice when all ten board members voted for it.

Timothy Gibbs was a man who wallowed in his elevated status as Jason Kay's right-hand man and confidant at one of the richest companies in the city. In his late forties, with slicked-back, jet-black dyed hair, permanent tan showcasing expensive, pearly white, perfectly even teeth and well-manicured nails, he was a man who took great pride in his appearance. Wearing one of his several identical hand-made black-stripped Saville Row tailored suits, Gibbs looked the part of a man in total control, but underneath the tan he could feel the tiny droplets of fear begin to trickle down his face.

'We want to know what's happened to all the money, Jason,' demanded the elderly man at the far-right end of the table.

Kay stared down the table right at him. 'You don't demand anything. Kay Corporation is *my* company, *not* yours. You bought a small piece of it. I own sixty-five per cent of all the shares, so stop bleating and do what you all do best and collect your pile of unearned dividends every quarter.'

'The other thirty-five percent invested in Kay Corporation is *all* our money, Jason, *not* yours and so we have a right to know what you're doing with it!' interjected the small middle-aged Indian woman on the other side of the table whilst hiding her trembling hands on her lap.

Kay wanted to leap onto the table and kick her right in the mouth, but he needed to win them over until his plan was complete in nine days' time. 'Of course, I realise the importance of every one of my shareholders and fellow board members' investments. That's why I've asked the Chief Accountant Mr Gibbs to attend this meeting and inform the board that the company finances are in good order and reassure you all that your next quarter's dividends will be showing a much larger return.'

All eyes turned towards Gibbs who almost choked on his own fear. He stated, 'Kay Corporation is in an excellent financial position. The reason for the fifty percent shortfall in the last two dividend payments is due to a rather large short-term investment that I can now report will pay substantial returns by the end of the month.'

'What short-term investment? It doesn't show on your last quarterly accounts?' questioned the tubby middle-aged man sat in the middle of the table.

Gibbs looked over at Kay who did what he always did best; lie. 'You are right, ah… Mr Socks,' glancing down at the board members' list of names placed on the table in front of him. 'I made a judgement call; otherwise, Kay Corporation would have missed a once-in-a-lifetime opportunity to make a substantial profit in a very short time, but can personally reassure you all that the next quarter statements will show a full and clear account of everything. As I stated earlier, sixty-five percent of the monies invested in Kay Corporation are mine and I'm not about to risk losing one penny.'

The board members sat in silence… then one-by-one, they got up and shook Kay's hand whilst thanking him for his continued excellent management of their investment before leaving, oblivious to the fact that he knew exactly what they wanted to hear.

Like all gullible fools, the one thing that will win them over is the promise of a golden windfall even when he's been slowly taking *all* of theirs.

'Type up the minutes and distribute them, making sure that you close the door on your way out,' instructed Kay to Diane Moffatt as she left and Gibbs breathed in a sigh of relief.

Kay erupted, 'What the fuck do I pay you all that money for? Your job is to hide what I'm doing, *not* bring it to that pile of idiots' attention.'

'The company books have to show ups and downs; otherwise, the auditors would become suspicious. I've got the real accounts locked away in a safe place, but can't hide the huge sums of money you've been siphoning off the company every month for the past six months to pay the blackmailer... The money is running out faster than anticipated, and therefore, I had no choice but to pay the shareholders less dividends over the last two quarters; otherwise, the pot would be empty before the plan is complete in fourteen days' time.'

'Don't you ever fucking talk back to me like that again because if anything goes wrong, it's *you* who's been defrauding the company and falsifying the books, *not* me? I'm just as innocent as those idiots on the board,' threatened Kay with his hands around Gibbs' throat.

'It's not me that you should be threatening, Jason. I'm doing what you want; it's that snivelling solicitor Simon Dodd that you should be worried about. If he doesn't sign the document, then the entire plan collapses and *you* lose the whole five million pounds!' countered Gibbs.

'You don't need to worry about Dodd. I'll deal with him like I deal with everything. Just make sure that the five million is transferred when all the paperwork is signed and sealed,' said Kay.

They left the room in complete silence, with Kay returning to his silver sports car and Gibbs to his office on the other side of the city, unaware that Diane Moffatt was watching them from her office window. She slipped back into the board room to retrieve the small hand-sized recorder stuck underneath the table in front of Kay's seat.

Pressing the play bottom, her face froze when she realised that Kay's promise of a golden payoff to her of three hundred thousand pounds was as false as him. She threw her head back and laughed until her throat ached, whilst thinking that the six years she had endured his slimy hands all over her body, were all for nothing. 'No fool like a greedy fool,' she said, hating herself more than the man who had corrupted her with a job, city flat and lifestyle unattainable in her world. She smiled at the one Achilles' heel that would be Kay's downfall; that no one, especially a woman, can be smarter or more devious than him.

Returning to her office, Diane pulled out the secret mobile from her designer handbag that Kay had given her to use when he required the other "special unwritten duties" in her contract.

Dialling the number, she knew that once the recipient at the other end answered, there would be no going back…

The Decision

Simon Dodd sat at his desk in his office staring at the huge portrait of his late father on the wall opposite. Every day, he would look at that portrait and despise the man immortalised in it even more. 'How much can a son loath his father?' was the question that had haunted him for sixteen long, dark years.

He could take the portrait down and destroy it, but couldn't because it was his punishment.

For as much as his loathing for his father grew every day, it was nothing compared to the disgust he felt every single minute of the day and long dark nights for himself.

His sentence was to stare at that pompous, cold-hearted, mean, fat and ugly face every day of his life so that he would never forget what he did and what he gave up for the father who promised him freedom then shackled him to chains instead.

James Dodd was a short, fat, blubber of a man with a big bald head, double chin, ugly smoke-stained uneven teeth encased in fat lips that ate and drank too much rich food and expensive wine. Aged sixty-seven, he died suddenly from a heart attack two years after Jason Kay married Anne Price and eighteen months after Reginald Price died of cancer.

Simon often thought how ironic it was that both fathers died before they could see how the contracts they each signed, between themselves and Jason Kay to secure their eternal legacies in the hallway of power by selling their children's future, would fail.

Slowly, he looked down at the file on his desk when the office phone rang. 'It's Dr Pritchard on the line for you, Mr Dodd. He states that it's urgent and can't wait, but won't tell me what it's about.'

Simon's loathing for Pritchard almost outweighed his hatred for Jason Kay, but knew that he would get a call from Kay if he didn't respond. 'Put him through, Miss Smith.'

'What are you playing at, Simon? You need to sign *both* documents now or else all hell will come down on us both from Kay. Remember, he has evidence on what we did. So stop bleating on about the past and secure the future.'

'Secure the fucking future! You forget who you're talking to, Pritchard. I've been there before and look at the glittering future you and my father secured for Anne and me sixteen years ago. How can I trust you to keep your word about the *other* document? It's time to do the right thing before it's too late.'

'It's *Doctor* Pritchard and don't you dare lecture me about the "right thing". You had your chance and blew it sixteen years ago. And remember, I'm the one that's risking everything by getting Kay to sign the *other* document. All the arrangements are in place with the appropriate paperwork signed off by me at my end so get off your moral high horse and complete the last part of the plan as agreed. Then we can both walk away with our conscience clear at last.'

'What about Anne? Don't you have any conscience about what you are doing to her for the *second time* if it all goes wrong?'

'She's stronger than any of us and there's no other way if the plan is to work…'

'You'd better be right, Pritchard,' scowled Simon, slamming the phone down when Miss Smith rushed into the office after the woman. 'I'm sorry, Mr Dodd, but I couldn't stop her…'

'It's OK, Miss Smith. I can deal with this lady. Take an early lunch break.'

'Yes, Mr Dodd,' she said, closing the door and slipping on a slightly worn, old-fashioned black raincoat over her dull office twin-set pleated grey skirt and blouse.

In her early sixties with black/grey peppered shoulder-length hair, plain wrinkled face with a hint of powder and purple lipstick, Ivy Smith had worked for Dodd's solicitor since the age of eighteen.

'What are you doing here, Dotty?' Simon asked, slumping back into the chair.

'So you still remember who I am after all these years?'

'Don't come in here all high and mighty. You deserted her too.'

'Yes. I'm guilty and there isn't a day that goes by that I don't regret abandoning my dearest friend, but you sold her out.'

Staring up at his father's portrait, Simon couldn't deny it any more. 'You're right, but why suddenly sprout a conscience now? What do you want from me?'

'Anne sent me.'

'Anne...?' He could feel his chest crumbling.

'She heard everything through the study door. You need to tell me what that slime bag Kay is up to with Pritchard and what's in that document you refused to sign? Anne has reached out to the both of us for help and this time, we're not going to abandon her to that monster again,' demanded Dotty, staring at the friend she hadn't spoken to for sixteen years and praying that he'd do the right thing by Anne this time.

Simon glanced up at the portrait of his father then smiled. 'It's time to pay what's due,' he said, picking up the file and throwing it down on the desk in front of Dotty.

The Song

Anne pulled out the old silver cassette player containing a single cassette inside from the back of the wardrobe in her bedroom. Dusting it down, she pictured the day twenty-seven years ago when Eric sneaked into the house and gave it to her on her sixteenth birthday. It had been a lifetime ago since she played the cassette, but today was a special day. Dotty had come back to her and Eric was still watching over her like Archangel Gabriele, the guardian angel of lost souls.

Pressing the button on the cassette, her body floated around the room whilst she danced to the song, "The Road to Freedom", remembering the story Eric told her about the great Freedom Fighter

Nelson Mandela, and how in 1990, he was freed from prison after twenty-seven years in solitary confinement.

It became her secret song that she would play over and over again when the house was empty and the dream of a life far away from the prison walls of Treetop Mansion seemed real.

She smiled whilst thinking of the irony that it took Nelson Mandela twenty-seven years to escape and how now in her twenty-seventh year of imprisonment, it was her turn.

Just as the song was almost finished, the hallway phone rang. She froze. No one ever telephoned the house when her husband wasn't there because his instructions were finite. *'Never* personally contact my wife at home under any circumstances.'

All matters pertaining to Hilltop Mansion, including food and house deliveries, were to go through him or via the estate manager.

Any other day, she would ignore the phone and do what all prisoners do; follow their jailer's orders:

(1) Six a.m. Eat breakfast alone in the kitchen

(2) Seven a.m. Prepare breakfast for one

(3) Eight a.m. Clean the kitchen and house

(4) Eleven thirty a.m. Prepare and eat lunch for one in the kitchen

(5) Twelve p.m. Do the washing and ironing

(6) Two thirty p.m. Go to bedroom and wait

(7) Five thirty p.m. The driver pushes the note through the front door

(8) 5.35 p.m. Leave bedroom to read note

(9) 5.40 p.m. Return to bedroom after reading note

(10) Six thirty p.m. Prepare and eat dinner for one in the kitchen then clean up

(11) Seven thirty p.m. Return to bedroom

(12) Twelve a.m. Listen for the footsteps on the stairs and the door slamming shut at the other end of the hallway.

Slipping down the stairs, the constant ringing of the telephone echoed through the house like church bells summoning their congregation.

Placing her hand on the phone, Anne hesitated. What if it were him testing her to see if she broke the rules? He didn't get to finish the punishment at breakfast and her husband always finished what he started.

Hearing the last words of the song "The Road to Freedom" floating out from the bedroom, Anne picked up the phone then whispered, 'Hello?'

The voice at the other end asked, 'Do you know who this is?'

'Yes.'

'I wasn't sure that you would answer.'

''Why telephone the house when you know *his* instructions?

'Because I've uncovered something about *him* that you need to know.'

'Why should I trust you of all people?'

'You're right, but I'm risking everything by contacting you at home.'

'Why would you want to help me?'

'I have my reasons.'

'You're no different than *him*.'

'I'm no saint, but even I have my limits.'

'What's really in it for you?'

'For the right price, we both get our revenge and freedom.'

Anne knew that it might be a trap, but the song was still playing inside her head reminding her that like Nelson Mandela, if she was to be truly free, then she had to be brave like him. 'I'll contact you with details of where and when to meet.'

'I'll be waiting.'

Copying the mobile number from the callers' list on the phone before deleting it, Anne ran back up the stairs to telephone Eric from her secret mobile.

'I need your help!' she said.

He immediately collected the ladder and climbed back up through her bedroom window. The two co-conspirators sat side-by-side on the bed formulating their plan.

8

Detective Sergeant Jack Stone handed the package to the courier. 'Make sure that this is delivered within the hour and tell the recipient to contact me as soon as they have anything.'

Collecting his car keys from the desk, he shouted across to Constable Rita Clark, 'I'm off to the village. Telephone me on my mobile if anything breaks.'

'You got it, Jack,' she answered with a sneaky smirk.

Jack smiled back, knowing that there was no way the plain, plump, admiring Rita would ever end up in his bed because his love of women only went skin-deep.

But looks aside, he liked his female co-worker, Rita. She made him laugh and feel good about himself and there was nothing better than admiration from someone whose life was even less exciting than yours to make you feel on top of the world.

Driving into the picturesque Treetop Village, Jack could feel all eyes upon him when he parked his car in the parking space just outside the newsagent's office, noting that he needed a residents parking permit as he proudly placed his detectives parking waiver badge on the dashboard.

Stepping out of the car, his eyes circled the village. *How the smug rich love to show off their perfect lives!* he mused, recalling the grey concrete street in Stepney where he grew up littered with broken beer bottles in the gutter, thrown by the drunks falling out of the pub at closing time.

Straightening his tie and jacket, Jack walked into the newsagent's office with the air of a man determined to show them all who's in charge. 'I'm Detective Sergeant Stone and I'm investigating the disappearance and possible murder of Jason Kay.' He displayed his detective badge for all to see.

The man behind the counter repeated, 'Murder…?'

'That's correct, Mr…?'

'Ronald Phelps, Sergeant Stone, and the owner of the shop.' He smiled.

'Can you tell me the last time you saw Mr Kay and who you think might want to harm him?' asked Jack, glancing around the tiny, cramped shop filled with an assortment of sweets, cakes, biscuits, chocolate bars, newspapers, magazines and various trinkets for the passing day/weekend visitors to the village.

'It was five days ago when he called in at precisely 7.15 a.m. to collect his newspapers.' He paused before adding, 'Mr Kay was a well-respected resident in the village, Sergeant.'

'That's a very precise time, Mr Phelps?' commented Stone, noting the day and time down in his black notebook.

'Mr Kay was a very precise man in his habits and always collected his newspapers at exactly that time every day.'

'Hmm. And as the local newsagent and centre of the village gossip, I'm sure that there is someone in the village that might not have such kindly thoughts about Mr Kay?'

Mr Phelps looked around the shop, checking that it was empty of prying eyes and ears when he leaned over the counter and whispered, 'I didn't tell you this, Sergeant, but you might want to talk to Councillor Sylvia Platt who lives in the thatched cottage named Strawberry Cottage located on the edge of the village.' He pointed his hand straight out through the open shop door, concluding, 'Just turn to your right when leaving the shop and it's a straight five minutes' walk.'

'Thank you, Mr Phelps, and I may need to speak to again.' Nodded Jack, turning round and walking out.

Ronald Phelps asked, 'How is Mrs Kay doing, Sergeant?'

Jack just smiled whilst carrying on walking adhering to the first rule of being a good detective; namely, never answer a question that might give away your advantage in an investigation.

Strolling through the almost-empty village, Sergeant Jack Stone could feel the invisible eyes peering through the blinds of the neat, terraced, red-bricked cottages and shops. Murder detectives were a common sight where he grew up in Stepney, but not in Treetop Village where all the residents were perfect, law-abiding citizens.

Arriving at the pretty, white, thatched cottage with its little black iron-gated entrance and name sign, Strawberry Cottage, encircled by bright red strawberries, he opened the gate and walked up the thin-shingled drive surrounded on both sides by dozens of coloured potted flowers to the heavy weathered and battered wooden front door that was painted black.

Knocking on the rusty, big, round cast-iron door knob, he gave a little smirk, thinking that fifty odd years ago the cottage would have been rented to the poor workers of the village, but now it's been elevated to a pricey sought-after village property located by the centre of the Green.

'Can I help?' a stone-faced woman asked.

Pushing his detective badge up close into her snobby wrinkled face, Jack asked, 'Mrs Sylvia Platt?'

'It's Councillor Platt and you are?'

'Detective Sergeant Stone and I'm looking into the disappearance and possible murder of Mr Jason Kay.'

'I'm not sure that I can help you with your enquiries, Sergeant,' she said with that air of superiority that he hated more than "honest criminals".

'Your name came up in my investigation as a person who knew Mr Kay well,' he said slyly, stepping past her into the tiny low-beamed hallway.

'Then you had better come in, Sergeant,' she said, irritated by his lack of respect.

Leading the sergeant into a very tiny, almost cramped lounge filled with antique ornaments and furniture, Councillor Platt pointed to a small pink upholstered antique chair for him to sit on whilst she plonked her rather heavy frame into a much larger identical high-backed chair.

'I prefer to stand when conducting my investigation,' he said whilst quietly soaking in every small detail about the suspect.

A spinster in her late fifties with wiry grey hair heavily sprayed with too much hairspray, overly made-up face and thick black eyebrows, large goofy front teeth encased in lips painted dark red and dressed in an expensive French courtier two-piece dark purple straight skirt and jacket, Councillor Platt oozed an air of superiority.

Jack noted, 'You don't seem concerned at the disappearance or possible murder of Mr Kay?'

'Mr Kay was a valued and respected member of the community, Sergeant.'

'It would appear so, but I'm more interested in what kind of man he really was and when and where was the last time you spoke to him?'

'My only dealings with Mr Kay were council-related so I can't give you an insight into his personal life, but can confirm that I last saw him five days ago at precisely 7.15 a.m. at the village newsagent's.'

'Everyone in the village seems to be very precise about the last time they saw Mr Kay, alive,' noted Jack, again.

'That's because Mr Kay always walked to the village for his newspaper every day at the same time. He was a man who lived his life by the very expensive gold Rolex watch on his right wrist that would bleep all the time.'

Noting down the remark about the Rolex watch bleeping in capital letters, Jack continued his questions. 'Can you tell me about the relationship between Mr Kay and his wife?'

Councillor Platt shuffled uneasily in her chair before stating, 'As I said earlier, Sergeant, I'm not privy to the personal details of Mr and Mrs Kay's marriage.'

'May I remind you that this is a murder investigation and if you hold back any information that may be relevant to the case, then you can be charged with obstruction, Councillor Platt.' He enjoyed sticking it to the snobby-nosed old battle-axe.

'All I can tell you, Sergeant, is that Anne Kay used to be a valued member of the village council, but suddenly resigned by letter six months ago without giving a reason and when I enquired how she was the last time I saw Mr Kay at the newsagent, he gave his usual answer of "Everything is as it should be".' She was unable to hide her unease at Jack's prying questions.

'What do you mean by his "usual answer"?'

'All I know, Sergeant, is that when everything was going well, he would always say those words and so I presumed he meant that Anne was fine.'

'Didn't you ever try to contact Mrs Kay yourself?'

"I and the other committee members of the council tried several times, but to no avail.' She gave a nervous cough. 'I'm not sure that it's relevant, but at that same time Anne resigned, Mr Kay also banned all telephone calls and visitors to Hilltop Mansion pertaining to his wife with specific instructions that if anybody needed to contact Anne, then they were to telephone him at his office, Kay Corporation, in the city and leave a message with his personal assistant, a Miss Diane Moffatt. Any deliveries or other such matters regarding the estate were dealt with by the estate manager, Eric Finch, and dropped off at his lodge in the grounds.' She paused suddenly.

Jack asked, 'You were about to say something else, Councillor Platt?' He was intrigued by her sudden collapse in confidence.

She added, 'It's well-known in the village that Mrs Kay suffered from depression over the years since the death of her father, Reginald Price, and that since then her husband oversaw everything with regards to his wife's health and the estate.'

'So let me understand this. Six months ago, Jason Kay cut off all personal phone calls, callers and/or visitors etc. connected to or dealing with his wife at Hilltop Mansion?'

'Yes, but that didn't come from me, Sergeant.'

'Has anybody in the village seen or heard from Mrs Kay in the last six months?'

'No. As far as I am aware, Anne hasn't left the house in all that time.'

'If Mrs Kay is so well-liked, why haven't you or anybody else in the village tried to find out what's going on?'

'I'm not a kind woman, Sergeant, as you may have already gathered. We all have our outer and inner faces. I'm what I am because I need to be relevant rather than the invisible, plain, unloved and unwanted spinster that you, the detective, can clearly see hiding behind my councillor's mask, but Anne never had a choice in who she wanted to be. Her father was a very strict man so when she joined the village council just over a year ago, for a while she came alive and started to believe in herself and that she could make a difference and then it happened again…'

'What happened?'

'*He* did. We may all have two faces that we show the world, but Jason Kay's faces are both that of pure evil. Anne Kay is a woman imprisoned in a life that wasn't of her choosing; first by her father, then by her husband, and whenever some light shone upon her, Kay would take it away.'

'So, if Jason Kay were dead, then she would be free of him?'

'If he is dead, then I won't morn his passing, Sergeant, but I can tell you now that Anne is not capable of murder. She is the gentlest and kindest of creatures that wouldn't hurt a living soul.'

'You seem to know more about Mr Kay and his treatment of his wife than anyone else. Is there something else that you're not telling me?'

Councillor Platt shuffled nervously in her chair again before adding, 'On the rare occasions when Mr Kay called at the council office to collect his wife after a meeting, I noticed that her entire body would shrivel up in fear… and yet he always gave her that loving smile of a husband looking out for his wife, but hiding behind that smile I saw the devil's grin.'

'Are you sure it wasn't your imagination?'

'I've been a councillor for twenty-five years, Sergeant, and in that role, I've supported many charitable organisations, and one in particular was for the women's refuge where I saw that grin on many a supposedly loving husband's face.'

'If you knew that something bad was happening to Mrs Kay, why didn't you do something about it?'

'Because behind my two faces hides a coward, Sergeant. Mr Kay is a very powerful and no doubt vindictive man who would crush me like a handful of crumbling nuts if I or anyone stood up against him,' replied Councillor Platt, adding, 'and if that's all, Sergeant, I have a meeting to attend.'

'For now, Councillor Platt, but I may need to come back to you,' said Jack, leaving Strawberry Cottage with more questions than answers.

Why would a supposedly wealthy woman in her own right allow her husband to effectively imprison her in her own home when she could have paid expensive lawyers to divorce him on the grounds of cruelty?

Returning to his car and starting up the engine, Jack noticed an elderly man attempting to open a window on the ground floor of a large, red-bricked house opposite the other side of the newsagent's. When he stepped back out of the car, Mr Phelps rushed out of the shop, shouting, 'It's all right, Sergeant, that's old Jack Bird trying to talk to his wife, Ethel.'

Jack asked. 'What's going on?'

'It's a sad story, Sergeant. Ted and Ethel are both in their early nineties and have been married for over sixty years. Last year, Ethel tried to stab him with a kitchen knife when he walked into the kitchen holding a pair of garden shears. It turned out that she had been suffering from severe dementia for a long time and Ted told nobody for fear of them being separated. Ethel's mind had reverted back to her childhood when her father used to beat her up and at that moment, she thought that Ted was him and so tried to kill her beloved husband. They've lived in the village for over forty years and were inseparable and did everything together. They had no children and didn't need or want anybody else. Every day, they would walk through the village holding hands. There's is a true love story, Sergeant, and now Ted is alone because Ethel was declared a danger to both herself and him and placed into an isolation ward at Treetop Village Hospital where he's not allowed to see her and so every day, he stands outside her barred window hoping that she will recognise him again.'

Listening to Mr Phelps' sad story as they both watched Ted desperately trying to be reunited with his beloved Ethel, Jack felt an emotion he hadn't experienced in years; empathy.

'It's a cruel world sometimes, Sergeant, as I'm sure you know in your line of work,' said Mr Phelps, walking back into the shop whilst Jack got back into his car and took one last look at Ted crying outside

Ethel's window. He drove out of the village remembering his late parents together when he was growing up. Although poor and rather plain people, their love for each other was just like Ted and Ethel's and how he secretly envied that love.

All his life, Jack had been ashamed of his parents' poor, unremarkable lives when, in reality, they were the rich ones.

Jack Stone became a detective because he thought that it would be full of excitement and intrigue, but the more he investigated people's lives, the more he realised just how messed up their idea of how to attain the perfect life was.

Playing one of his loud punk band tapes to distract him from reality, Jack's thoughts disappeared into a fog until his hands-free mobile rang and the voice at the other end asked, 'Where are you?'

'I'm on my way to question Mrs Kay at Hilltop Mansion after finding out some interesting facts about the Kays' marriage in the village, Boss.'

'Wright and I have just arrived at the house with the warrant, so fill me in.'

Jack read out his notes whilst Steal and Wright listened on the loud speaker. 'Good work, Stone. You head back to Lunsford and check on whether Mrs Kay has ever been hospitalised for depression and if so, find out the name of the doctor who treated her.'

'Yes, Boss,' said Jack, pleased that the inspector actually noted his excellent detective work.

Steal and Wright arrived at Hilltop Mansion. Stepping got out of the car whilst two more police vans drove up, Steal and Wright watched as eight uniformed police officers disembarked the vans dressed in protective white lap clothing and carrying various containers.

Following the officers to the house, Steal rang the front door bell. 'We have a warrant to search the house and grounds, Mrs Kay,' he said, handing it to her and marching straight past as the search team preceded to rampage through the house like a swarm of bees searching for the hidden honey pot.

'You'd better come through to the lounge, Detectives.' She smiled, leading the way. 'I hope that your officers won't make too much of a mess?' she said, sitting down.

'I'm afraid I can't promise that, Mrs Kay,' said Steal, tapping his fingers on the notebook.

'I'm used to broken promises, Inspector.'

'We are now treating the disappearance of your husband as a murder investigation and so I'm afraid every detail of your life and marriage to Jason Kay will now be of interest to us,' stated Steal, watching her face, knowing that when they rang the doorbell three times yesterday, she knew that they would be back. 'Have you anything to add to your statement from yesterday with regards to your husband's disappearance?' he asked.

'No, Inspector,' she replied, knowing that he knew what she was thinking.

'It's been six days now and he hasn't contacted you?'

'That's correct,' she replied.

Steal checked his notebook again. 'It has come to our attention that your marriage to Mr Kay was not a conventional one?'

'Village gossip can be a poisonous mixture, Inspector,' smiled Anne.

Steal was just about to get to the prime question when one of the male uniformed officers entered the room. 'I think you ought to see this, Inspector,' he said.

'Stay here.' Steal nodded to Wright, following the officer upstairs to Anne's bedroom where the police officer pulled back the edge of the beige carpet in front of the bedroom door to reveal a thin wire running across it.

'They're all over the house, Inspector,' he said, showing Steal identical wires across every room, including the front and back kitchen doors.

Stripping the wire out, Steal inspected it closely then smiled. 'It looks like a wire censor,' he said, walking back to the lounge with it whilst instructing the police officer to note where every wire was located and then bag them as evidence.

'Can you explain this wire, Mrs Kay?' he asked, showing it to her before handing it to Wright and returning to his seat.

Anne gave that quiet little smile that both unnerved and intrigued him. 'I'm waiting, Mrs Kay?' he said, irritated that his prime suspect didn't appear fazed by the discovery.

'My husband was a man who liked to control every aspect of his and everyone else's life, Inspector. The wires were there to make sure that I followed the house rules.'

'House Rules?' asked Wright, playing with the wire in her hand whilst trying to fathom whether Anne Kay was either a victim or a cold-hearted murderer.

Anne turned to Steal. 'What did you discover about my unconventional marriage, Inspector?'

'I ask the questions, Mrs Kay,' he said, getting annoyed at her game of cat and mouse when Wright spoke, 'That six months ago, you suddenly resigned from the village council without an explanation and that your husband virtually kept you a prisoner in your own home.'

'That's enough, Sergeant Wright...' instructed Steal, angry that she broke one of the cardinal rules of a murder investigation; never give away your trump card too soon.

But Wright could see what a man couldn't... That *all* women have an invisible code between them. When trust has to be shown in order gain it and by telling their prime suspect what they discovered, she was hoping that Anne would finally open up and let them know the truth about her marriage and life with Jason Kay.

Noting that trust, Anne proceeded to tell her story. 'To explain about the wires and house rules, Detectives, I need to go back to the beginning so that you fully understand how Jason Kay first arrived at Hilltop Mansion and how I ended up marrying a man that I didn't love and loathed with all my being.'

Rooted to their seats, Steal and Wright were shocked by Anne's open confession about her true feelings for her husband and so listened in stunned silence whilst noting down her story in their little black books.

'Jason Kay arrived at Hilltop Mansion thirty years ago, aged sixteen. The estate manager, Eric, discovered him trying to break into the house through the back kitchen door. Dragging him by the scruff of his dirty tee-shirt collar to the estate manager's lodge, Eric tied him to the thick beam in the middle of the lodge before telephoning my father at his office.

'When my father arrived, Eric wanted to hand him over to the local police, but even though Jason was a scruffy, skinny youth with unkempt get black hair and filthy clothes, he could see into my father's inner soul and how much he wanted a son and so manipulated him with his tragic tale about being an orphan and never knowing who his father or mother were and how he survived growing up in one care home after another, until he finally ran away for good on his fifteenth birthday to live hand-by-mouth on the streets and how he was only seeking some food and warmth when Eric discovered him.'

Stopping to take a breath, Anne then continued, 'My father offered him employment under Eric and let him live in an old shed in the grounds where day-by-day, over the years, Jason used my father's need for a son to rise from the ashes of a thief and orphan to become head of Price Corporation and the shining light in my father's eyes whilst I became invisible...'

'Would you like some water, Mrs Kay?' Wright asked, finding herself actually caring about their prime suspect.

'Thank you, Sergeant Wright, but I'm fine. It's just that I haven't told anyone outside Hilltop Mansion the whole story in thirty years. The only person who truly knows the truth is Eric Finch, the estate manager, who could have left sixteen years ago when I married Jason, but stayed to watch over me.'

'Do you think that Eric could have harmed your husband?' asked Steal.

'No. Eric is an honourable man who's like the older brother I never had. To me, he's not just an employee, but my soul mate and beacon of light in a dark world.'

'How did Jason Kay become your husband when your father saw him as a son and could have legally adopted him?' Wright asked, puzzled that Kay would have inherited everything if he became Reginald Price's son instead of son-in-law.

'Ah, good question, Sergeant,' said Anne, continuing, 'my mother died shortly after giving birth to me which destroyed my father in two ways. First, he lost the love of his life and second, he had a daughter instead of a son and heir, but in his grief for the loss of my mother, he promised on her deathbed that he would love and cherish me the same way that he did her and that *no other child* either adopted or born through another marriage would replace their daughter. And so he *couldn't* adopt Jason as his son, but he could make him his son in another way by marrying me and becoming his son-in-law...'

'So Jason Kay marries you and inherits your father's company on his death and changes the name to Kay Corporation?' noted Steal.

'Correct, Inspector.'

'What about the house and estate? Is that in joint names or just your husband's?' he asked.

'My father didn't want to dishonour his promise to look after me on my mother's deathbed and so the estate is in joint names, but should I die before my husband, then it must be sold and *all* the money equally divided between my mother's favourite charities.'

'How much is Hilltop Mansion and Estate worth?' Wright asked.

'As I stated before, Sergeant, my husband dealt with *all* matters concerning the company and estate, but when I was on the council, I did note in some old files pertaining to Hilltop Mansion that he had it valued two years ago by the local estate agents, Bright & Son at four million pounds.'

'So, if your husband died before you, then the estate would become solely yours and you could sell it and pocket nearly five million pounds at today's house prices,' noted Steal.

'I'm afraid not, Inspector. There is another addendum to the clause whereby should my husband die before me, then half the money in the estate goes to my mother's charities and the rest to me. In that way, although my father didn't love me as he would have a son, he did at least keep his promise to my mother in that I would be looked after on his death.'

'Two and a half million pounds is still a lot of money.'

'True, Inspector, but as I stated before, I didn't kill my husband.'

'Why should we believe you?'

'Two reasons, Inspector. First, I believe you need a body to declare my husband legally dead so that half the estate is mine, and second, why would I wait sixteen long, dark years to kill a man who stole my life?'

'We all have our breaking point, Mrs Kay, and perhaps yours took longer to reach?' said Steal.

Anne didn't respond. She knew that without a body, Steal couldn't prove that she killed her husband.

Wright commented, 'But the other side of not finding your husband's body and declaring him legally dead is that you get your freedom back from the man who stole your entire future and father's love.'

'But I'm not *free* as you state, Sergeant. When Jason married me, he insisted that another clause be added, making him my legal guardian in all financial matters, and therefore, I have no access to my *own* money without his agreement and signature. Every month, he would give me an allowance of just fifty pounds to spend in the village. So I'd still be trapped in a house that had become my prison and had grown to hate more than I did *him* and without money to maintain it and the grounds, Hilltop Manson would become a crumbling wreck and I would end up dying in it alone and without hope...'

Steal and Wright glanced at each other, realising that this was *no ordinary murder case!*

If Anne Kay did kill her husband, then she would effectively be worse off without him and yet their gut instincts as detectives told them that she was *guilty*...

Wright felt the wire in her hand and asked, 'You were going to explain about the wires and house rules, Mrs Kay?'

Looking right at the detectives, Anne said, 'I need to go into Jason's study and retrieve the paper from his desk.'

Steal called one of the uniformed officers to accompany her as they walked across the hallway into the once-tidy room now littered with box files and crime scene officers rampaging through every aspect of Jason Kay's life.

Slipping her hand under Kay's desk, Anne pulled out a strip of white paper taped to the underside then walked back into the lounge and handed it to Steal, who read the paper before passing it over to Wright.

House Rules to be followed precisely as listed:
(1) 6.00 a.m. Eat breakfast alone in the kitchen
(2) 7.00 a.m. Prepare breakfast for one
(3) 8.00 a.m. Clean kitchen and the house
(4) 11.30 a.m. Prepare and eat lunch for one in the kitchen
(5) 12.00 p.m. Do the washing and ironing
(6) 2.30 p.m. Go to bedroom and wait
(7) 5.30 p.m. The driver pushes the note through the front door
(8) 5.35 p.m. Leave bedroom and read note
(9) 5.40 p.m. Return to bedroom
(10) 6.30 p.m. Prepare and eat dinner for one in kitchen then clean up
(11) 7.30 p.m. Return to bedroom until 6.00 a.m. next day

Having returned to her seat, Anne continued the story of her "unconventional" marriage to Jason Kay.

'Six months ago, *everything changed*. Jason came home and dismissed all the staff except Eric without explanation. This is a big house to clean and manage, not to mention the grounds, but he sacked the housekeeper, Maggie Frith, who had worked here since I was a child, plus the junior groundsman, Mickey Brown, who helped Eric on the estate. He then told me that I was to write my resignation from the village council with immediate effect and get Eric to drop it off at Councillor Sylvia Platt's cottage. Then he handed me the sheet of paper listing the *new* house rules and informed me that he had cancelled my fifty-pound allowance each month and that I *was not* to leave the house from that day onwards and that all phone calls and visitors to and from the house for me were *banned*. He then went into the kitchen and picked up my mobile from the table and smashed it on the floor.'

Pausing for breath, a slight tear trickled down her face whilst Steal and Wright sat in stunned silence. Anne wiped away the tear with her hand, then continued, 'I protested that even *he* couldn't be that cruel, but he just laughed in my face and did what he *always* did when I disobeyed him or if "everything wasn't as it should be..." The tears flowed again.

Wright handed her a paper tissue from her bag, then asked, 'Do you want to take a break, Mrs Kay?'

'Thank you, Sergeant, but I must finish; otherwise, *he* will always be inside my head, *controlling* me.' She stood up and pulled up her jumper to reveal the bruises.

'Why didn't you tell the police?' Steal asked when Anne sat back down and smiled that quiet smile.

'Because he knew my weakness, Inspector.'

'What was it?' Wright asked.

'Eric... He threatened to have him beaten up by his private army of protection officers who would break his arms and legs and then smash his head so that the man who loved working outdoors since a child and the brother I wished for would end up a mindless cripple in a wheelchair.'

'Does Eric know what you sacrificed for him?' Steal asked.

'After telling me what he would do to Eric if I didn't follow the rules, he went outside to the lodge and informed Eric that if he tried to save me or tell anyone, then his protection officers would break into the house under the pretence of a botched robbery and do to me what he threatened to do to Eric. So, you see, Detectives, *I had no choice.*'

'What about the wires?' Wright asked.

'The jailer's bars...' smiled Anne, adding, 'the next day, a team of workmen arrived and proceeded to place them all over the house so that every second of the day and night, he would know what I was doing and where I was. The moment I stepped past a wire, his bloody gold Rolex watch would bleep and if I wasn't where I should be or doing what I should be doing as per the times listed on the house rules, then...' She stood up and showed them the bruises again. 'So now you know the full story of my marriage to Jason Kay; the man that is admired and respected by everyone in the village, Kay Corporation and the world...'

'Why was the note hidden under the study desk?' Steal asked.

'Oh, I think that a top detective like you has already worked out that my husband wouldn't want the world to know what he was really doing to his wife behind closed doors, Inspector.' Anne smiled.

Steal checked his notebook again. 'It has also come to our attention that you suffered from periods of depression and would ask if you have ever been treated or hospitalised for it and if so, please tell us the name of the doctor who oversaw your treatment?'

'Ah, the village gossip line is always open.' Anne grinned. 'When my father died six months after my marriage, I did go to a very dark place and was treated by the family physician, Dr Stuart Pritchard, who authorised and subsequently admitted me to Treetop Village Hospital for several weeks.'

'Was that because you loved and missed your father?' asked Steal.

Anne paused for a moment then answered, 'The love I felt for my father was double-edged in that it was a complicated, cold and distant love. In my father's mind, I killed his only true love, my mother, when she died giving birth to me and so part of him hated me for that, but the other part tried to love me because I was my mother's daughter, but couldn't and so no matter how much I tried to love my father; he would push me away. When he died, I realised that any hope or dreams I had of him holding me in his arms and telling me that he *did* love me died with him...'

Glancing at Steal who nodded back, Wright asked, 'Was that the only time you were hospitalised? What about when your husband threatened you and Eric six months ago? Did you go to a dark place in your mind then, Mrs Kay?'

'Being locked up in a cold, white, soulless room on my own for twenty-four hours a day without visitors or a kind word is not a place that I ever wished to return to, Sergeant, but whenever I began to form friendships or appear to have a life outside his control, Jason would threaten to get Dr Pritchard to section me again, but no matter how dark I felt inside, I would fight that dark demon. So to answer your question, Sergeant, yes; that was the only time that I've ever been treated or sectioned for depression, but Jason would always explain my sudden withdrawal from life by telling everyone that I had another one of my bouts of deep depression.'

Pausing again in reflective thought, Anne said, 'Although my husband was controlling everything like he always did when I stepped out of line, this time it was different.'

'How?' asked Steal with his detective antenna on high alert.

'There was something about his eyes. Normally when he was in one of his rages, they were dark like the devil inside him, but when I looked into them six months ago, they were *fearful*... It was almost as if it was his *life* that was under threat, not mine and that he was fighting to save it.'

'Did you discover what he was afraid of?'

'No, Inspector. I'm not a detective like you, but I can tell you that for the last six months my husband became increasingly more secretive and would lock himself away in his study when he returned from work until the early hours of the morning.' She stopped suddenly as she remembered Simon's argument with Jason in his study.

Steal asked, 'Is there something else that you need to tell us, Mrs Kay?' He was suspicious that she was still hiding something.

'No, Inspector.' She smiled.

'I don't have to remind you again that this is a murder investigation and no matter how your husband may have treated you, it doesn't detract from the fact that it makes you a suspect in his death,' said Steal, pointing his small finger towards Wright, who nodded back.

It was their secret sign between each other when one of them needed to check that they were both on the same wavelength. In this instance, Steal was perplexed at why Mrs Kay gave up the information about her husband being terrified of something that happened six months ago so easily and yet was clearly hiding what that something was?

Whereas Anne could see that they were suspicious, but to win her freedom she had to play out the game to the end. 'I don't know what my husband was afraid of, Inspector, but all I can tell you is that it involved keeping me a prisoner at Hilltop Mansion for the last six months.'

Closing his notebook, Steal concluded, 'That will be all for now, Mrs Kay.' He stood up and walked into the hallway with Wright when he turned back at the front door and repeated the question, 'Are you remotely interested in whether your husband is dead or alive, Mrs Kay?'

Anne smiled and replied, 'Like I said before, Inspector, I will have to come back to you on that one.'

Watching the last pieces of evidence being carried to the vans from the house, Steal asked the police officer who found the wire, 'Did you locate Kay's missing laptop?'

He answered, 'No, Inspector.'

Wright noted Eric watching them from the lodge and asked Steal, 'Are we going to interview the estate manager, Mr Finch, Boss?'

'Not here. Put him in the car and we'll question him at Lunsford,' he said. He then caught sight of Anne watching Wright escort Eric into the back seat of their police car before driving off and following the evidence vans back to the headquarters.

Wright couldn't resist asking, 'Why did you ask that same question to Mrs Kay again when we left, Boss?'

'Wrong question, Sergeant,' he said with that sly grin that infuriated her when she knew that he knew something that she hadn't detected.

They drove along with silence in the air between the detectives and Eric colder than ice blocks from a freezer.

Steal and Wright quietly contemplated that with every question answered, they uncovered another one unanswered.

But the most searing question that puzzled them the most was; who was the real Jason Kay?

Watching their minds turning over and over from the back seat, Eric had only one thought in his mind: that for the plan to work, he had to outsmart two of the best murder detectives on the force.

9

Six Months and One Week Earlier

Jason Kay stood in his ivory tower looking out into the city, watching the evening skies light up with thousands of shimmering lights whilst darkness descended. His gold Rolex watch bleeped three times as he noted that the time was precisely seven p.m. and the world of work had shut down for another day.

It's his favourite time of the working day; watching all the little ants below fighting to get home while he looked down upon them from his kingdom—Kay Corporation.

'Will you be requiring me tonight?' Diane Moffatt asked as she entered the room from her office.

'No,' he replied with his back to her while she stood behind him, imagining his body crashing through the thick bullet proof glass window and falling down and down into the pit of hell where the burning fires would engulf him in an eternity of misery.

She collected her coat and bag, relieved that he didn't require her "extra services" in his bed tonight.

The more the years rolled on, the more Diane loathed his hands on her body, but what else could she do? Three hundred thousand pounds was the price she agreed for selling ten years of her life to a monster.

Checking his laptop before locking it back in his desk drawer, Kay was unnerved when an email pinged in his private email box. He didn't recognise the address of the sender.

There were *two* people who knew his "secret email" address; Timothy Gibbs and Dr Pritchard.

His gut instinct told him to delete the email and not open it... but his arrogance compelled him to check on who would dare risk hacking into the powerful Jason Kay's private laptop and email account.

Opening the email, his face crumbled when he read, *"Hello Jason, or should I say, Alex...?"*

His body froze in the chair. Kay typed, *"Who the fuck are you and want do you want?"* The seconds ticked louder and louder on the huge office clock hanging on the wall opposite his desk when his email box pinged again.

"Who I am is not important at this time, Alex, but what I want is, and if you value your precious new life, then you must pay the price."

"I'll fucking find out who you are and then I'll rip your throat out with my bare hands!" Jason typed back.

"Your sickening threats might work on your poor wife, Anne, but they are wasted on me, Alex, for I know everything, *and can destroy you and your empire with just* one click *of my smallest finger..."*

"What do you know?"

"Ah, the price for my knowledge and silence is one million pounds..."

"You're fucking out of your league. I've got the best private army and technical team working for me and they will find you!"

"Yeh, yeh... Good luck with that one. Now back to business. For the next six months, starting from tomorrow, you will pay exactly £166,666.66 into an untraceable account, the details of which I will send to your accountant, Timothy Gibbs, after our business is concluded today. When, at the end of each month, I receive the agreed payment of £166,666.66, I will then send you a piece of evidence regarding the secret you don't want the world to know about until on the sixth month, when the one million pounds have been paid in full, you will receive the final bit of evidence and never hear from me again."

"You must be fucking mad if you think that I am going to agree to pay you £166,666.66 every month for six months! First, I don't have that kind of money or access to it; second, how do I know that you won't come back for more or release the so-called evidence to the press anyway and third, why should I trust a fucking blackmailer?"

"Because, Alex, if you don't, then you will lose everything..."

Sitting at his desk, Kay stared at the email not knowing what to do next. For first time in thirty years, he *wasn't in control*!

Part of him wanted to call the blackmailer's bluff, but then his eyes fixed on the name ALEX. He typed, *"I need more proof before I agree."*

The screen went blank and the seconds ticked by like hours. His heart stopped dead when the words appeared: *"Alex Trent, Born 2 March 1970, now aged 50 years old…"*

"If you know so much about me and my company, then you'll know that I don't have the means to pay you £166,666.66 each month from either Kay Corporation or my personal finances." Alex typed furiously and hit "send".

"That's not my problem, Alex, so let's not waste each other's time. We both know that you've been stealing money from Kay Corporation for years to supplement your extravagant lifestyle and that your crooked Accountant, Timothy Gibbs, has been falsifying the books for you," the reply was immediate.

"Then you also know that there's no money *left and that Kay Corporation will be declared bankrupt within the next six months anyway."*

"Ah, the poverty card; I was wondering when you would play that one, Alex, but again, I'm way ahead of you. I know about the five million pounds in the trust fund."

Kay collapsed back into his black leather throne, thinking how the fuck did the blackmailer know about the trust… unless, it was Pritchard?

"No, Alex, it's not *Dr Pritchard,"* typed the blackmailer, reading Kay's thoughts.

"Then you know that I can't access the money; otherwise, I would have sixteen years ago when I married the old man's pathetic daughter."

"Yes, what a shame that you've had to stay shackled to a woman who holds the key to five million pounds and isn't even aware that it's her money *which has been sitting in the trust for sixteen long dark years, growing in interest…"*

"Why not ask for the five million if you know all about it?"

"Because not everyone is like you, Alex; all I require is just enough money to begin a new life, just like you did thirty years ago, but there is one more condition *to our agreement."*

"What the fuck now?"

"The other four million goes to your wife, Anne... After all, it is her money anyway."

Erupting into a blind rage, Kay picked up the laptop and started to throw it across the room... when the light bulb went off inside his head.

Placing the laptop back down on the desk, he typed, *"If you're so smart, you must have worked out how to access the trust when I couldn't."*

"At last, the questions that I knew you were going to ask. The key to unlocking five million is:

(1) Your accountant, Timothy Gibbs

(2) Dr Stuart Pritchard

(3) Secure your wife, Anne, and

(4) Get the agreement of the solicitor, Simon Dodd."

"How?"

"You're the smart one, Alex."

Before Kay could respond, the blackmailer signed off.

Sitting back in his throne, Kay smiled that smug, evil grin when he realised that the whole five million could finally be his... and all he had to do was play for time being.

Kay Corporation was going bankrupt anyway so why not bleed it dry and keep the blackmailer close to him until he could erase the fucker, take back the one million and finally be free of his pathetic wife whilst laughing as he sucked the last bit blood from her father's crumbling empire.

The Accountant

Checking his reflection in the tall mirror hung on the office wall by the door, Timothy Gibbs didn't recognise the man staring back at him. He'd come a long way since landing the prestigious account of Kay Corporation five years ago, enabling him to rise from the ashes of a lowly assistant accountant in the firm Forbes Accountants to purchasing fifty-two per cent of the firm's shares five years ago, making him the senior partner in the newly named Gibbs & Forbes Accountants.

Looking out of his large partners office to the endless rows of open plan desks in the long soulless room leading to the lift at the end, Gibbs pictured himself twenty-five years ago sitting in the back row of one of those desks by the lift and how he used to look up and imagine himself in the partners office one day.

He remembered working from seven a.m. to seven p.m. every day for fifteen long, dark, mindless years just like all the other faceless and nameless nobodies in the room. They grinded away, doing the tedious mundane work without a single word of acknowledgement from the senior partners, who took all the praise and fat bonuses whilst giving their army of pitiless workers poultry pay rises every year. Gibbs' pay didn't even cover the price of the ham sandwich he would buy every day at the sub-way takeaway by the station on his way into work. He would only eat at his desk because the partners didn't approve of the staff taking hour-long lunch breaks away from the office.

At the end of each working day when the building was empty, he would stop and look out of his fancy partners office into that room, wondering if the price he'd paid was worth selling his soul to Jason Kay five years ago when he sought him out and offered him a deal that he couldn't resist.

Gibbs was a good, honest man with a loving wife who thought the world of him even though he earned little money and his career was going nowhere. His life was simple, but uncomplicated and although he would occasionally dream of sitting in the partners office, he was happy and could sleep soundly at night because she was lying there beside him.

Tonight, like every other night for last four years, he would get the train home to an empty house.

He would eat his ready meal cooked in the microwave alone and then read the *Financial Times* newspaper for an hour before checking his *two* laptops at his desk in the dull tiny study until midnight before going to bed and turning over to find her gone... with him left, alone, with only the same torturous nightmare for company through the long, dark, empty night.

He had achieved that dream of sitting in the partners office chair, but the cost of that dream was the loss of his beloved wife, Sandra, when, four years ago, Gibbs arrived home late as usual to find her body floating in the bath...

Every night, he saw her beautiful face looking up at him from the water and remembered the last words she said to him the day before when she told him at the dinner table that her life was empty because the man she loved and married no longer existed and therefore neither did she.

Now every morning in the bedroom, when he put on his hand-made Saville Row stripped suit and combed back his jet-black-dyed hair with gel, he told himself that success comes at a price and that it was Sandra who was the weak one, *not* him. But then, he would turn and look at her picture in the silver frame by the bed and admit that she was the brave one and that he was the spineless coward who fell under the spell of the devil, Jason Kay. He traded the love of his life for the dream of money and position, only to discover that they won't hold him in their arms at night and tell him that they love him.

Closing up his office for the night, Gibbs took the firm's official laptop containing Kay Corporation's accounts with him as usual.

Arriving home at nine thirty p.m., he placed the laptop on his study desk before unlocking the drawer and taking out the *other* laptop when the email box pinged.

Opening it, he noted two incoming emails, but only recognised one. Just then, his mobile rang.

'Gibbs, I've just sent you an email instructing you to pay one million pounds in six monthly instalments of £166,666.66 from Kay Corporation's special account to the account sent to you via the second email that should also have arrived.'

'What the hell is going on, Jason, and who is the other person in the email? Only you and I know about the account.'

'I don't know yet, but they know all about our special agreement and want one million pounds for their silence payable in six monthly instalments.'

'How did they find out? I triple check everything and no one knows what we've been doing for the last five years.'

'So fucking careful that a blackmailer has hacked into the system? I need time to find them before the six months is up and take back *my* money.'

Gibbs couldn't help seeing the irony in a thief and blackmailer stealing from another thief and blackmailer. '*Your* money…?'

'Don't get all high and mighty with me, Gibbs. You wanted the money and position and so happily stole it for the right price. You were bought just like any other greedy little ant and now you're crying because the gravy train is running out and you don't have a ticket to the next one.'

'What about you? Your train is running out too; only I can live with nothing, but you can't…'

'Ah, but my next train will be carrying five million pounds from the trust fund.'

'That's not possible. I've tried everything over the last five years to get the monies released into your name, but Reginald Price made the trust fund conditions iron tight for his daughter only.'

'Just like a blackmailer not being able hack into our system… If they can do that, then we can get to the five million so stop crying and do as I say. We can both walk away with a pot of gold in six months' time.'

'But you know that there isn't enough money in Kay Corporation. You've been skimming from the company profits for the last five years whilst I've been falsifying the accounts, but I can't hide £166,666.66 for one month, let alone six. It's impossible…'

'You've been doing the impossible for the last five years and those idiots on the board of shareholders haven't worked it out yet, and by the time they realise that *all* their money is gone, it'll be too late. So, get your crooked accountant's brain in gear and find a way to pay the first instalment of £166,666.66 and leave the rest to me unless you fancy spending the next twenty years of your pathetic life in prison.'

'If I go down, then you go down with me…'

'Don't fucking threaten me, you little weasel, just fiddle the figures and I'll deal with everything else,' instructed Kay, cutting the line dead.

Sinking back into his chair, Gibbs stared at the laptop when his eyes slowly turned upwards towards the gold-framed portrait hanging in the centre of the wall overlooking his desk. His face lit up at the sight of Sandra and him looking so happy together on their first wedding anniversary. Then the tears flowed onto the desk like forming a pool of shame and guilt.

Clicking onto the other email, he read the blackmailer's one line demand: *"Pay £166,666.66 into account no.666.666.666 Sort Code: 06.06.06 Ref: SAHD by 12 Noon tomorrow."*

Staring at the email, part of him wanted to walk into the bathroom and run the tap until the bath was full and he could climb in when the water would swallow him up and carry him back to his love…

But then, the other part wanted to fix what he had done wrong so that when he was finally re-united with Sandra, she would love him again.

Pouring himself a triple whisky into the glass from the bottle he kept in the lower desk drawer, Gibbs sat back in the chair and grinned.

For the last five years, Jason Kay had slowly eroded any shred of honour from him, but tonight would be last time!

Leaning forward over the laptop, he began his final revenge on the man who stole everything from him.

The Next Day

Standing by the window looking out of his office, Jason Kay checked his gold Rolex watch and noted that the time was ten a.m. precisely.

Returning to his desk, he picked up the phone and rang through to Diane Moffatt. 'I need to leave the office now so cancel all my appointments for the next hour.'

'But you have that important business meeting with the planning officer at the council that you've been trying to get for the last three months in thirty minutes?'

'Don't fucking question my orders, just do it.'

'Do you wish to re-schedule, Mr Kay?'

'You're the overpaid personal assistant so just do your job.' He slammed the phone down.

'Yes, your fucking lordship,' she mocked to a dead line.

Dialling the number on his mobile, Kay was feeling impatient.

The voice answered, 'It's been a while?'

'I need to see you in thirty minutes at the usual place.'

''Anything I should know in advance?'

'Just be there.'

Unlocking the lower drawer, he took out his laptop and placed it in a black leather case before making one last call on his mobile. 'Have you made the transfer?'

'It's arranged for twelve noon.'

'Email me the account details now.'

'Don't you want to know where I got the money from?'

'I don't give a fuck how you found it, Gibbs, just that it's done.'

'The blackmailer will be £166,666.66 richer in two hours' time.'

'Send me the blackmailer's instructions and then crawl back into your hole until I contact you again.'

Opening the laptop on his desk at the office, Gibbs forwarded the blackmailer's email instructions to Kay before calmly sitting back in the chair, content in the knowledge that he'd just set a match to a long line of gun powder that, in six months' time, would explode right back in Kay's face.

The Meeting

Sitting on the bench in the public park not far from Kay Corporation, a tall thin man wearing a long black overcoat, dark almost black sunglasses and matching black-rimmed hat waited in still silence as the world rushed past him in the busy park.

His eyes did not move under the large black glasses, yet he saw and noticed everything. The mother with the two little girls playing on the grass with their tiny white terrier dog and the middle-aged grey-haired, over-weight male jogger running up and down in the same spot for the last ten minutes. Plus, the seven male and six female workers rushing from the station at the back entrance of the park into the long footpath leading to the front entrance of the tall office buildings on the other side of the road.

The man's watch vibrated on his right wrist. He looked down to note that the time was exactly 10.27 a.m. He heard the footsteps of a man walking towards him from behind the bench when he sat down at precisely ten thirty a.m. and his watch bleeped three times.

'Hello Kay. On time as usual,' the man said, almost breaking into a smile.

'I don't pay you to make jokes, Black.'

'The jokes are free but my time isn't so what do you want?'

'I need you to locate the man that sent this to me,' said Kay, opening up his laptop on the bench and showing him the blackmailer's email; the demands and bank account details.

Taking a photo of the emails on his mobile, the man didn't ask why Kay was being blackmailed because right and wrong did not exist in his world, only payment for the job done.

'The email and bank account are both probably encrypted and laundered through many other encrypted bogus accounts so it will require a specialist hacker which will be expensive.'

'Price is no object, just get me the information.'

'It could take a while.'

'Patience isn't one of my virtues, Black.'

'If you want it done right, then you'd better learn some, Kay.'

Kay wanted to rip the smart bastard's teeth out, but even he knew that Black wasn't a man to get on the wrong side of. 'Let me know when you've found him.'

'What do want done with him when we do?'

'I want to be there and watch him suffer *very slowly…*'

The man didn't respond; he just got up, tipped his hat forward and walked down the path whilst Kay watched him disappear into thin air like a ghost.

Replacing his laptop back inside its black leather case, Kay pulled out his mobile and pressed the redial button. 'I need to see you at your office this evening after work.'

'I'm due at my club by eight p.m.,' said Pritchard on his private mobile.

'It's not a request.'

'What's so urgent that it can't wait until tomorrow morning?' asked Pritchard, annoyed at the way Kay *always* talked down to him.

'I need to access the five million in the trust fund ASAP.'

'It can't be done. I've tried and it's water-tight.'

'Nothing's water tight, Pritchard, and this time you *will* find a way, or else they'll be fishing your body out of the Thames,' threatened Kay before signing off.

The Choice

Dr Pritchard sat in his office at the posh private clinic, wondering whether he should just let Kay have the money. For five long years, he'd managed to lie and keep the five million locked up in the trust fund, but now, he feared that his time had run out and if Kay didn't get what he wanted, then…

His mind wandered back in time when he remembered he was a young, newly qualified doctor with high dreams of doing so much good, only to end up a pawn in Jason Kay's evil chess games of greed and corruption.

He would like to plead innocence, but couldn't… because deep down inside, he knew that a good man would have done more to protect the innocent.

Regional Price wasn't a loving or kind father, but he did want to protect his daughter, Anne, before his death and so entrusted that task to the two people he thought would carry out those wishes; James Dodd and Dr Stuart Pritchard.

And so, for the last five years, Pritchard had done everything Kay had asked him to do to keep his wife, Anne, under control, including sectioning her as mentally unstable and locking her away in a mental hospital when her father died instead of treating her for grief.

But even though he couldn't excuse what he had done to Anne over the years, he did at least protect the money knowing that once Kay got his hands on the five million, then he wouldn't need his wife any more. Even a greedy, weak man like him had his limits, but now he had to make a choice between Anne and him.

The Rising of the Dead

While Pritchard searched his conscience, Kay sat at his desk, waiting...

The time was 11.55 a.m. and in five minutes, he would be £166,666.66 poorer.

It was the first time in thirty years that he hadn't been the one stealing the money....

Tapping his fingers on the laptop, he hated the fact that *someone else* was now controlling his life and setting the rules. His watch bleeped three times and an email pinged in his inbox at precisely twelve noon.

Opening it, he read, *"Well done, Alex, I can confirm that the first instalment of £166,666.66 has successfully been received and now, as promised, see the next piece of evidence in the life of the real Jason Kay...*

"Body of nameless and homeless boy, aged between fifteen and eighteen years, found dead *in his bed at Youth Hostel for Homeless Boys in East London at six a.m. on Monday, 5 March 1990. The cause of death registered as unknown. The corpse was buried in an unnamed pauper's grave one week later."*

Reading the email, Kay could feel his body caving inwards. It felt strange to actually feel fear. He'd never experienced it before; in fact, Kay *never* felt any emotion except *rage* when everything wasn't as it should be.

His first instant was to tell the sender to *go fuck himself,* when the blackmailer signed off with one last message: *"It's easy to kill an innocent, invisible nobody, Alex, but even the invisible, leave their mark behind..."*

Staring at the email, Kay did something that he had *never* done before... think about the past and the consequences of his actions, not because he had ever felt any regret or remorse, but pure survival... He read the words, *"It's easy to kill an innocent invisible nobody, Alex, but even the invisible, leave their mark behind..."* over and over again, wondering for the first time in thirty years that if a nameless, faceless, dead vagrant can leave a trace of his past behind, then what about the ones who weren't so invisible?

***

71

The date was Sunday, 4 March 1990 when Alex Trent stood in the long queue outside the locked doors of the Youth Hostel for Homeless Boys aged between twelve and eighteen years, waiting for a bed for the night.

The doors opened at eight a.m. and the curly grey-headed fat man with bad teeth and crumpled black sweatshirt and jeans announced, 'Only the first ten are allowed in for breakfast, lunch, dinner and a bed for the night. Everything is free, but you must produce your ID to prove your age and name to qualify. There will be *no* Exceptions. So if any of you don't fit the criteria, then *leave now*.'

Trent looked up and down the queue, counting thirteen in front of him and too many behind. Two left the front of the line and several the back, making him now number *eleven*…

The youth in front of him grinned as he saw the look on Trent's face. 'Haven't seen you here before and you're *fucked* being number eleven, mate.'

Trent wanted to punch the creep in his cocky filthy mouth, but then if he'd been at the hostel before… 'I need a good meal and bed for the night, so if you tell me how to get in, then I'll give you my lunch and dinner?'

The youth looked up the line and counted that there were now *six* ahead of him in the queue. 'What about breakfast? I can save the eggs, bread and butter to make a cold sandwich with them for the next day?' he asked.

'Deal, now how do I jump up one in the queue and get in without ID?' asked Trent, not giving a fuck about food.

'I knew the moment that I checked you out that you were older than eighteen. I can always fucking tell,' bragged the youth.

'Do you want the food or not? The queue is going down,' pressed Trent.

'See that kid in front of me? I know him. His name is Jason Kay. He's fifteen years old and we've been doing the streets together since we were ten. You need to get his ID and take his place in the queue.'

'How?'

'Easy, just watch and learn,' said the youth, turning back and tapping Jason on the shoulder. 'Hi, mate. It's been a while; how's things?' He embraced him like a true friend whilst slipping his hand inside the youth's filthy, dirty, threadbare jacket and stealing a tatty wallet containing his ID.

'Oh. Same o', same o', Jacky boy,' smiled Jason, unaware that his so-called friend on the street had just stolen his most precious of items.

Turning back, the youth slipped Trent the wallet. The fat man at the door asked the next one in the queue for his ID and Jason pleaded, 'But you know me, Frank. I've been here lots of times in the last three years?' He searched frantically for his wallet and ID.

'No ID. No food or bed for the night,' scowled Frank without a glimmer of pity.

Frank never actually looked at their faces or ID. They were invisible to him. Once the first ten were waved in he would quickly lock the door and rush off for his free fried breakfast. 'But I need the food and bed. Please, you know me. Please, Frank…'

'No ID. No entry. *No exceptions…*'

Turning round to his friend, Jason implored, 'Jacky, you know me. Tell Frank. We were in the orphanage together.'

Jacky boy turned his back on his friend for the price of a bed and three square meals, whilst watching him walk away with his head bowed in despair.

When Frank asked the next youth in the line for his ID, Alex Trent handed him his new identity; *Jason Kay, born 2 March 1970.*

Later that night, when the lights went out at ten p.m. in the long, cold room filled with rows of cheaply made single beds, Alex Trent looked across at Jacky sound asleep beside him. He was thinking he'd fulfilled his part of the agreement and given him a new identity and bed for the night and all for the price of three cheap meals, but if he could betray his best friend on the street for so little so easily, then what would he do should anyone come looking for the now invisible Alex Trent?

Lying in bed, Trent waited until the room was black and everyone was sound asleep in their beds as the large clock on the wall ticked round to two a.m. Slowly, he lifted the pillow from his bed and pushed it down over the face of Jacky whilst smiling that dark, sadistic grin as he listened to the last choking breath of life being extinguished from the fifteen-year-old homeless boy who died for the price of a meal and one stolen ID card belonging to his friend, Jason Kay.

Enjoying his full English fried breakfast, the newly re-born Jason Kay smiled whilst savouring the two large fried eggs that Jacky boy never got to taste…

Leaving the hostel, Trent looked around to check that the alleyway outside was clear before opening the top of a large black rubbish bin by the exit door and throwing the ID card of the late Jacky Jones inside before calmly walking away.

The Last Chance

The time was 7.50 p.m. when Pritchard heard the sound of Kay's car engine turning into the street. He never failed to recognise it. It was the sound of misery… Every time Kay switched that engine off, Pritchard lost another piece of himself.

Since Kay's phone call just after mid-day, Pritchard had sat at his desk frantically trying to think of a way to stop him stealing the final part of Reginald Price's legacy and save Anne. He heard the footsteps on the stairs and watched the seconds tick by to eight p.m. precisely on the wall clock opposite when the door opened…

'Glad to see that you've seen sense, Pritchard.' Kay grinned, strolling in and sitting down on the highly polished brown leather chair whilst noting the file on the desk in front of the doctor. 'My time is valuable so how do we unlock the five million and get rid of my wife?'

Tapping his fingers on the file, Pritchard shoved it across the desk towards Kay who purred and sucked his lips like a wild cat that had just eaten its bloody prey as he read the doctor's plan to steal Anne's trust fund and lock her away in a mental institution for the rest of her life.

'I must admit that you have excelled yourself this time, Pritchard,' laughed Kay, noting the doctor's detailed six-month plan to first, isolate Anne, then, second, declare her mentally unstable before, finally, sectioning her under the Mental Health Act *indefinitely*… thus making her husband administrator and legal guardian of the five million trust fund for as long as she remained *alive*, but incapable of administrating her own affairs.

Placing the file back down on the desk, Kay couldn't help gloating. 'A *living death*... brilliant, Pritchard!'

The doctor sat in stony silence, deploring what he had just sentenced Anne to, but rationalising it by telling himself that Kay had given him *no choice*...

'Oh, stop crying, Prichard,' said Kay, seeing the guilt in his eyes. 'You'll get your cut and then forget all about poor little Anne when sunbathing on your desert island.' He smirked. 'Have you spoken to that sniffling little twerp Dodd about preparing and signing the legal document giving me administrative control over the trust fund yet?' he asked checking that "everything was as it should be" again.

'No. I thought it best to set the plan in motion over the next five and half months to secure yours and my side of the agreement before bringing in Simon Dodd. That way, it'll be *too* late for him to do anything about it and will have no option but to sign the document,' declared Pritchard.

'I like it. Prepare everything and I'll get to work on my pathetic little wife.' Kay laughed while leaving without a single sign of guilt at just sanctioning his wife to *a living death*.

Hearing Kay's engine start up and drive off into the night like the dark angel who had just sentenced the good queen to death, Pritchard picked up the file from his desk and read it again and again. He had made his choice and sold Anne out to save himself... then he spotted his salvation. He quickly dialled the number on his mobile as he knew that this was his *last chance* to finally destroy Kay and save Anne without selling out his soul.

10

Back at Lunsford Headquarters, Eric was detained in the interview room.

'Let him sit and stew for a while,' said Steal to the duty police sergeant whilst watching him through the one-way window separating the suspect from the detectives.

'What about the other warrants, Boss?' asked Wright standing beside him.

'We'll get to them later.' He walked back to the main office where the team were hard at it. He shouted across the room, 'OK, what have you got for me?'

Within seconds, the buzzing room was silent while everyone waited for someone else to answer first.

'Are you deaf and dumb?' said Steal, impatient.

Rita's voice echoed across the room from her desk at the back of the office, 'I checked out Mrs Kay's housekeeper, Maggie Frith, and the junior groundsman Mickey Brown's account of their sacking, Boss, and they both confirmed that Jason Kay did indeed dismiss them without any explanation or warning six months ago and since then they haven't had any contact with either Mrs Kay, Mr Kay or Eric Finch the estate manager. Mrs Frith did, however, state that she had tried on numerous occasions to speak to Mrs Kay at the house for about two weeks after her sacking, but without success. She also said that she knew that Anne was in the house when she called, but felt that she was too afraid to answer the door bell and speak to her. Then she added that a man stating to be employed by Mr Kay knocked on her door just after her last visit to Hilltop Mansion and threatened that if she persisted in trying to speak to Mrs Kay, then both her and her husband Fred would accidentally end up dead in a car crash.'

'Did she describe the man?' Steal asked, finally feeling that they were getting somewhere.

'Only that he was tall, thin, dressed all in black including a large black hat and very menacing, Boss.'

'See what you can find out about him from the employee records at Kay Corporation and check out any private firms or agency dealing in security work,' said Steal, giving a little cough before adding, 'and good job, ah…'

'Rita Clark, Boss,' she said with a sneaky smile at his praise of her work.

Taking a plain piece of white paper, Steal drew a rough outline of a faceless man with a big question mark wearing a hat before pinning it next to Jason Kay on the crime board. He turned round and asked, 'Anything else?'

Jack Stone piped up, 'I've just had confirmation back from Dr Pritchard's secretary that Mrs Kay was admitted to Treetop Village Hospital for severe depression on the death of her father, Reginald Price, six months after her marriage and that she was there for almost two months. On checking the hospital records, it would appear that her husband never visited her once while she was locked away in isolation, but that Dr Pritchard was there every day and sometimes twice a day.'

'Why would the busy, wealthy Dr Pritchard spend so much time visiting just one patient when he could get one of his junior staff to report back to him?' questioned Steal.

'Because he was afraid of something?' concluded Wright

'Precisely,' acknowledged Steal, moving Pritchard's picture on the crime board up beside Jason Kay's and the mysterious faceless man before turning back to Jack.

'Any news on Kay's mobile?'

'Not yet, Boss, but I warned them this morning that if I don't hear back by six p.m. today, then we'll send in the big guns.'

'Keep on it. That mobile can unlock a lot of unknown answers.'

'You got it, Boss,' said Jack, even keener to prove himself now that Steal had finally noticed him.

Staring at the crime board, Steal and Wright were no closer to uncovering who of Jason Kay's inner circle would benefit most from his death? But one thing that they both agreed upon was that Kay didn't have *any* friends.

His entire life was an illusion.

To the world outside, he appeared the perfect husband, businessman and friend, but behind the mask, he lived only for one thing: *himself*!

Looking deeper into the picture of Jason Kay on the crime board, Steal was certain about one thing: if they could find out where Kay came from before he arrived at Hilltop Mansion thirty years ago, then they'll find the answer to who killed him and why?

Turning his head back to the team, he looked around the office until his eyes set upon the one officer in the room he knew wouldn't stop until that quest was completed. He yelled across, 'Constable Clark.'

'Yes, Boss?' She jumped as the whole team turned and looked.

'I want to know every single little detail about Jason Kay's life before he arrived at Hilltop Mansion thirty years ago. There's something not right about his past that we're missing, which came to a head six months ago when his carefully planned life began to unravel.'

'On it, Boss,' said Rita, unable to hide the excitement at Steal giving her the opportunity to prove that she wasn't just a filing clerk, but a *real* detective, until she saw the jealousy on Jack's face and her heart sunk a little.

'Nice one, Boss,' said Wright, happy that a fellow female colleague had been singled out by him in front of the entire team.

'I don't do nice,' said Steal, returning to his office and followed by Wright who secretly knew better.

She asked, 'What about Eric Finch, Boss?'

'Ah, yes. The white knight that watches over his queen,' he said, nodding back at Wright. the two then strolled down the long corridor from his office to the interview room.

The Interrogation

Erich sat in the interview room staring straight ahead at the blank wall whilst the nameless, faceless male police officer, dressed in his blue uniform, stood silently in the corner of the room staring at the same wall.

Eric wasn't afraid. Steal could leave him there, waiting for the next decade and he still wouldn't break.

All his life, he had had only one ambition; to protect the little girl who had nobody except him. Prison wasn't a threat. He'd been in a prison all his life; first with his drunken father, then with Regional Price, who, although treated him well as an employee, never showed him any kindness, and lastly, the cruellest jailer of all: Jason Kay... whom Regional Price showered with gifts and kindness.

No. Prison wasn't a threat, but not saving Anne would crush him into dust.

His eyes didn't move from the wall when the two detectives walked in and sat down opposite him. Steal started the tape recorder on the table beside him, beginning the game of cat and mouse between the three.

'I'll come straight to the point, Mr Finch,' said Steal, opening his notebook whilst Wright sat silently beside him. 'Firstly, this is just an informal interview to gather as much information about your employer, Jason Kay, as possible, and therefore, you are not under arrest and are not obliged to answer any of our questions without your legal representative being present, but it would greatly go in your favour if you did assist us with our enquiries into the disappearance and possible murder of Mr Jason Kay.'

Eric stared straight through both of them without blinking. 'I could have answered your questions at the estate, so why bring me in here and treat me like I'm a criminal?'

'Nobody has accused you of anything, Mr Finch, but our time is valuable and we had collected a lot of evidence at Treetop Mansion and so decided to "kill two birds with one stone", if you pardon the pun, by continuing out questions at Lunsford, but rest assured we will arrange to have you to driven home at the end of our "informal chat".' Steal smiled, flicking through his notebook again before adding, 'Mrs Kay told us all about her husband's threats to have both her and you beaten to a pulp by his henchmen if she didn't follow his new "house rules" six months ago.'

Eric didn't answer when Steal continued, 'How did you feel when he threatened you both?'

'I felt… nothing.'

'Nothing? I find that hard to believe when it's clear from Mrs Kay's statement that she considered you more of a brother than an employee and was willing to imprison herself in her own home rather than see you hurt, Mr Finch,' said Steal, waiting for the sign.

'If you know so much, Inspector, then why don't you tell me what I'm thinking?'

'I don't answer questions Mr Finch, I ask them; so stop playing games and tell me how you killed Jason Kay and if you did it alone.'

'So much for the "informal interview",' smiled Eric. 'Mrs Kay isn't a killer. Her heart and soul are too pure for that, Inspector, but yes, if the opportunity had arisen, then I wouldn't have flinched at killing that cold, ruthless bastard Kay. Unfortunately, someone else beat me to it, and so I never got to experience the pleasure of crushing his head into a pile of bones…'

Steal and Wright looked at each other. Wright asked, 'If it wasn't you, then who do you think it was, Mr Finch, being the estate manager and knowing everyone that either worked for or visited Mr Kay at his home?'

'Hand me a toilet roll, Detective, and I'll write you a list,' mocked Eric.

'Very funny, Mr Finch,' she said.

Steal jumped in, 'OK, the game playing is over. We all know that Jason Kay had many enemies, but who would benefit the most if he were dead besides his wife and yourself?'

'Like I said, Inspector, the list is long, but if I were you, I'd concentrate on the good Dr Pritchard and his solicitor, Simon Dodd; both of whom have their own "secrets" to hide.'

'What secrets? What do you know, Mr Finch?'

'I'm just a simple estate manager, Inspector, but what I can tell you is that Jason Kay couldn't have married Reginald Price's daughter sixteen years ago and taken total control of everything, including imprisoning his wife under "house arrest" and renaming the company Kay Corporation without their help.'

'What makes you so sure that they're implicated?' Steal asked.

'I've had thirty years to study Mr Kay, and yes, he's a devious, manipulative, cold-hearted beast, but like all beasts, he ruled by fear and *not* by being cleverer than his enemies. He was a man that could see his own weaknesses in others and used those weaknesses to drain them of any piece of strength they may have had. That's why everything he did had to have structure and order. Without that, he was just another *nobody* swimming around in the river of life, searching for a way out of the water.'

'Hmm. For a "simple" estate manager, you seem to know a lot about the inner workings of people's minds,' noted Steal, looking straight into Eric's eyes while he sat there in still silence. The Inspector continued, 'Do you know anything about Jason Kay's life before he arrived at Hilltop Mansion when he was discovered breaking in by you?'

Eric looked up and stared right back at Steal. 'I tried to find out where the orphanage was that he claimed to have come from, but when Reginald Price discovered what I was doing, he threatened to dismiss me if I didn't stop.'

'That must have hurt you badly?' said Steal.

'Of course, it did. I'm only human, but I also knew how much Mr Price wanted a son and could see how Jason Kay used that weakness in him. So, I swallowed my hurt pride to protect Mr Price's real flesh and blood; his daughter, Anne'

'Thirty years of simmering hatred can turn a good man into a raging killer,' said Steal.

Eric laughed. 'Who said that I was a good man, Inspector?'

Unable to hid his slight admiration for Eric's consistent loyalty to Mrs Kay, Steal flicked his little finger towards Wright who asked, 'We know about the three-hundred-thousand-pound payoff between Mr Kay and his mistress Diane Moffatt if she stayed with him for ten years, but was wondering if there was anything else that you might know which would benefit her if Jason Kay died earlier?'

'All I know is that Mrs Kay was happy with the arrangement. It meant that she was at least free of him in her bed,' said Eric without a flicker of emotion.

'Are you stating that the Kays' marriage was never consummated?' asked Wright, slightly shocked after hearing how Jason Kay enjoyed demeaning the women in his life.

'I didn't spy on them in their bed at night, Detective,' said Eric, shuffling uneasily in his chair.

Steal and Wright looked at each other, knowing that he was holding something back.

Steal said, 'That'll be all for now, Mr Finch, but be sure of one thing, we will find Jason Kay's body and arrest his killer and accomplices.' Steal turned off the tape and instructed the police officer in the room to arrange transport back to Hilltop Mansion before returning to his office and watching Eric get into the police car from his window, certain that he wouldn't break no matter how hard they tried.

What are you thinking, Boss?' asked Wright, standing beside him, staring out of the same window when she caught a glimpse of Eric looking up at them from the police car back-side window with that same expressionless face that screamed of his guilt and yet in her gut, she felt that he wasn't a stone-cold killer.

Steal answered, 'You can't threaten a martyr, Detective.' He turned round and picked up the next warrant from his desk. 'Let's go and see what the good Dr Pritchard has to say for himself, Wright.'

'Did you say the word "good", Boss?' she joked.

Two Detectives walked out of the building with their army of police officers and cars like warriors on their chariots riding out to destroy the enemy whilst Eric sat in the back of the police car, knowing that Inspector Steal and his trusted sidekick Sergeant Wright wouldn't stop until they had uncovered the truth about Jason Kay's mysterious disappearance.

He knew of Steal's reputation as the detective who always got his man. Eric had never been arrested, but his father, the village drunk, had been thrown into Lunsford Police cells and charged many times over the years for breach of the peace due to being drunk and disorderly.

When released, he would brag in the local village pub and at home with another bottle of beer in his hand about the stories he heard from fellow inmates of the legendry Inspector Steal who would stop at nothing to get his man and how nobody knew his first name because he had *no* friends either in the force or out of it.

Smiling, Eric knew that the name bit was a load of rubbish spouted by his father to gain laughs at the pub, but couldn't deny the fact that Steal's unblemished reputation for always solving the case wasn't.

While the police officer drove the car along the winding country road towards Hilltop Mansion, Eric's mind wondered back to when he climbed through Anne's bedroom window and planned the meeting with the mysterious caller on the hallway telephone.

Fourteen Days Earlier

The woman sat on the small two-seated, white-painted bench hidden in the deepest part of the miniature woodland on the outskirts of Treetop Village.

Listening to the birdsong together with the rustling of squirrels and other creatures of the wood, she breathed in the sweet odour of fresh country air when her heart melted into wistful thoughts and a past that was a world apart from the idyllic woodlands.

The world that she came from was a cold, inhuman place, encased in brick walls that didn't smell of freedom or the sound of happiness and laughter. It was a dark place where nightmares were her constant companion and dreams of a better life only existed in fairy tales.

Looking around the woodland, she never realised how so little could mean so much… Where she grew up, the sight of green grass and tall trees was a fairy tale story in children's picture books that she would flick through in the one place she could escape to every Thursday afternoon when the mobile library stopped in her street and the elderly woman librarian let her look at the books whilst her parents Sid and Elsie were at work.

She was only six years old but was already an old woman. Her only joy was the library, but it was also her torment; because she knew that the joyous colourful pictures in the books were just that, pictures, and that real life wasn't filled with colour and joy, but was grey and miserable.

Born on the poor side of town, her destiny was already decided the moment the midwife handed her tiny little body over to her mother.

Growing up in a cramped, two-up-two-down rented, red-bricked terraced house with her older brother, Tony, in a long grey street filled with the same terraced houses, her future was to become her mother.

At sixteen, she would marry the first man with a job who asked her. Love was only a luxury for the rich. A roof over her head, food on the table and the rent paid every week were a poor girl's only dream of a better life.

Work would be cleaning rich people's houses in-between giving birth by the time she was eighteen and praying that the first born would be a girl so that she could help her at home with the washing, cooking, cleaning and ironing whilst she went out to work doing the same for the rich wives who paid little and expected much.

Growing up, she would ask the same question every day. 'When can I go to school and learn how to be clever so that I can work in an office, Mummy?' only to hear the same answer, 'People like us don't go to school. Poverty breeds more poverty. So stop dreaming, my little girl, and get on with your chores.'

Sat on the bench, she could hardly believe her own story.

After all, it was 2020 and the life she remembered barely thirty years ago didn't exist in the modern fast-paced rich world that she mixed in now, but then rich people only mix with rich people whereas poor people only get to serve the rich.

Looking down at her reflection in the tiny rippling stream, she remembered the kind elderly woman librarian that took a shine to the six-year-old girl and taught her how to read and write when she climbed into her mobile library every week for four wonderful years until, one day, the library bus didn't come any more and she never saw the old lady again.

Until that day, she had never experienced real pain or loss.

She had grown to love that plain kindly librarian in a way that she never loved her mother.

Love comes in many forms, but the best love of all is true selfless love... But when it is taken away without explanation or warning, then it becomes the most brutal of loves.

At the tender age of ten, she learnt her first lesson: never give your love away to anyone ever again unless the price was right.

Twenty plus years later, with a life built in the shadows of rich men paying for her services, she had achieved that little girl's dream of working and living in the world of the rich and powerful, but unlike the happy endings in the rags to riches stories in a book, real-life choices always come with consequences.

She looked up to see a man walking towards her with a gun. 'Miss Diane Moffatt?'

'Who's asking?'

'My name is Eric and Mrs Anne Kay has sent me to collect you.'

'How do I know that you're not one of Jason's henchmen sent to do his dirty work for him?' wondering if this was how her life was to end; her body buried in the woodlands where it would rot away and finally be eaten by the same animals that just a few moments ago made her felt so free and happy.

'You don't, but if I wanted you dead, then I could have shot you in the head with my shotgun.'

'My meeting was with Mrs Kay, not anyone else,' she said.

Just then, Anne stepped out from behind the large oak tree at the edge of the woodlands and sat down on the bench. 'Good to finally meet you, Diane.' She smiled, whilst Eric stood in the background with the shotgun.

'Why scare the fucking shit out of me with this charade?' snapped Diane, breathing a sigh of relief at not being blown to smithereens.

'I had to know that it was you and *not* Jason behind the phone call.'

'Well, now you know, so let's get down to business.'

Anne laughed so Diane asked, 'What's so funny?'

'Oh. Just that I've always wondered what it would be like to meet you face-to-face and now that I have, I find that we are not that unlike. Two women imprisoned by the same jailer for different reasons, but with the same outcome.'

'I'm not Jason's prisoner. I can walk away any time I like.'

'We both know Jason would never allow that. Once his use for you has expired, then you become a loose end that has to be dealt with.'

'What do mean by "dealt with"?' Diane asked, her eyes wandering over towards Eric and the gun.

'I've been married to Jason for sixteen long dark years and in that time, he has had several "personal assistants" that left their overpaid jobs without notice or warning. In fact, Diane, you are the only one that has lasted the longest,' said Anne without a glimmer of spite, but just surprise at why and how she managed to stay so long with a man for whom *no* amount of money could persuade the other mistresses to remain.

'He never mentioned his previous arrangements with his other secretaries, just that he required a woman that would fit into his world without asking any questions and in return would be richly rewarded,' said Diane, now understanding why the other employees at Kay Corporation never discussed Jason's past personal assistants, but always seemed slightly afraid when she asked why there weren't any personnel files about any of them in the human resources office whenever she attempted to dig further.

Anne reached over and put her hand on Diane's. 'We are the same; you and I. Two women trapped in a world that would appear idyllic, but in reality, is a nightmare... I was watching you dreaming whilst sitting on the bench. I know that look so well. It tells the story of a little girl that dreamed of a better life, but ended up chasing the wrong dream.'

'What do mean by the "wrong dream"?'

'I chose this place because it's special, where your thoughts drift into the wonderful world of the woodlands, allowing the real you to finally emerge. I have such a place like this with a stream and well where I would meet my best friend and we'd dream of a future that got lost, just like yours. You lost yours because you followed the wrong dream. I lost mine because I put my father's dream before my own.'

Diane looked at Anne and for the first time felt empathy for another woman. They were always an adversary to overcome. Someone who had what she wanted and was therefore her enemy. 'I always imagined you a weak, pitiful, rich woman who married the wrong man, but now I see that you are the stronger one. To have sacrificed your dream for a father who "sold you out" in the name of love and then survive all those years living under the same roof with that monster he sold you to without breaking… I'm not sure that I would have been as brave, Anne?'

'Enough of this sisterhood bonding,' interrupted Eric, checking his watch. 'Time is running out and we need to get back to Hilltop before *him.*'

The two women couldn't help giving a little chuckle at their grumpy guardian angel. Diane reached inside her expensive designer bag and pulled out the USB drive, 'This is a copy of a secret recording I took at the last shareholders' board meeting with Jason and his chief accountant, Timothy Gibbs, concerning the dwindling profits of Kay Corporation. The interesting part is what Jason and Gibbs argued about when the shareholders left. It seems that Jason has been stealing money from the shareholders for the last six months whilst Gibbs falsified the books for him. But what is more intriguing is that Jason is being blackmailed.'

'Blackmailed?' said Eric, his ears pricking up.

'Oh, for God's sake, stop interrupting, Eric, otherwise we'll never get home,' joked Anne, giving a grumpy cough whilst checking the perimeter.

Diane continued, 'There's more. It appears that Jason is attempting to steal five million pounds from the company, but I can't trace any record of that kind of money anywhere in Kay Corporation.'

'That's because it's *my* money and not the company's,' said Anne. 'My father set up a trust fund in my name so that Jason would never get his hands on it. He told me about the trust on his deathbed just before he died, saying that he regretted taking Jason in and letting him marry me and that he *did* love me…' She wiped away the tears. 'He said that he wanted to protect me from him and honour his promise to my mother that I would always be looked after. He also made me promise never to reveal to anyone except Eric that I knew about the five million, including Dr Pritchard and James Dodd, but he died just before he could tell me where the money was.'

'Well, Jason has found a way to access the money and is using Gibbs and James Dodd's son, Simon, to unlock it,' said Diane, handing Anne the evidence.

'Simon…' said Anne, physically shaking.

Diane reached out and held her hand, recognising the look of pain and hurt in her face

'What do you want in return?' Anne asked, clutching the evidence in her hand like a poisonous dagger through her heart,

Diane sat quietly for a moment whilst looking around the woodlands then back at Anne and Eric, the grumpy guardian angel. 'Nothing... I came with the intention of selling you something I thought was so valuable that I could ask any price for it, but now realise that I wouldn't be taking the money from Jason, but you,' she said.

Anne stood up and embraced her new friend. 'Thank you. I will remember this day and what you did for me.'

'If you need anything else, and I mean, anything... then you have my number,' said Diane, disappearing into the magical woods, feeling free for the first time since she left home at sixteen and never went back.

Tiptoeing through the woodlands and back to the four-by-four estate hidden just inside the entrance behind several large oak trees, Anne and Eric drove back to Hilltop Mansion in stunned silence.

Parking the car outside the lodge, Eric placed the ladder back underneath Anne's bedroom. She climbed up and heard him ask the question that she never expected to hear; 'What are you going to do about Simon?'

11

Steal and Wright arrived at the private home of Dr Prichard with their army of police officers and forensic team. The inspector rang the doorbell on the highly polished black front door of the two and a half millions' worth white-painted, three-storied terraced town house with basement located in the highly sought-after Knightsbridge postcode.

'It seems that misery pays very well,' sneered Wright, looking down the long road filled with dozens of overpriced white-painted terraced houses that would be a fraction of the price on the wrong side of town.

'People don't pay good money to hear that they're *happy*, Sergeant,' smirked Steal.

The door opened and a tall, thin, frozen-faced woman in her mid-fifties with short-cropped, red-dyed hair wearing a black uniformed shirt and skirt with flat black shoes asked, 'Yes, what do you want?'

Shoving the warrant in her hand, Steal and Wright marched into the house followed by their army.

'Dr Pritchard isn't here and he never mentioned this…' She groaned, dialling his office number on the dark wooden hallway telephone stand. 'Let Dr Pritchard know *immediately* that the police are at his home rampaging through everything like wild horses…'

'There are dozens of them here too,' said his secretary, Olive Bence, watching the wild horses trample through her carefully kept files with tears in her eyes. Keeping Dr Pritchard's office in order was her one purpose in life.

Watching it being callously ripped apart in just a few furious minutes by wild animals dressed in blue uniforms and white protective clothing was soul-destroying.

Pritchard marched straight past her and out of the office to his car as if she were invisible.

Disconnecting the housekeeper, Olive sat at her desk, staring at the empty filling cabinets and bits of paper strewn all over the floor and desk as the wild animals departed, leaving her wondering what it had all been for?

Pritchard rushed from his car into the house to discover his housekeeper spitting blood from the kitchen whilst watching the search team wreck her immaculate home. He spotted Steal and Wright going through the desk drawers in his office.

'What the hell is going on?' he demanded, marching into the room whilst quickly glancing up at the painting on the wall behind the desk. Steal spotted the panic in his eyes and turned round to see a portrait of the young, newly qualified Dr Pritchard.

'An interesting portrait, Doctor,' he said, leaning over and lifting it off the wall.

'Careful with that, Inspector,' blurted Pritchard, grabbing the gold-framed portrait from him and running his hands along the back before placing it back up on the wall.

'It must hold some precious memories of another time?' said Steal, flicking his little finger towards Wright who nodded back, signalling that she had seen it too.

'It was painted by my late uncle who loved doing portraits of happy family events and so reminds me of a very special day when my parents held an extended family gathering to celebrate their eldest son becoming a newly qualified GP,' said Pritchard with a sad smile on his face when he looked at it again.

'I wonder how proud they would be of you now, Doctor?' said Steal, glancing at the portrait whilst noting the shame in Pritchard's eyes when he looked at the painting.

'Life isn't a simple journey, Inspector, as I'm sure you know well,' said Pritchard, turning his back to the wall.

'Speaking of your work, Dr Pritchard, I would be grateful if you could clear up some questions that have been puzzling my colleague and I with regards to Mrs Kay's state of mind and her marriage to Jason Kay?'

'You didn't need to wreck my office and house to question me, Inspector,' retorted Pritchard, slumping down on the cosy, slightly worn brown leather two-seater sofa in the corner of the office.

'I apologise for any inconvenience, Doctor, but I have a job to do and it isn't always a pleasant one,' said Steal, strolling around the desk whilst running his eyes over the portrait again He continued, 'I understand that you committed Mrs Kay to a mental hospital under strict isolation for several weeks using the Mental Health Act when her father died of cancer six months after she married Jason Kay?'

'That's correct. She was in a very unstable state of mind and needed twenty-four-hour care under a safe environment.'

'Surely grief for a dead father doesn't require being locked away in a mental institution without any visitors for weeks on end when some carefully prescribed medication at home for mild depression from her doctor would have been more beneficial and kinder?'

'I think that I'm more qualified than you, Inspector, to make that medical judgement, but will add that Mrs Kay was extremely unstable and could have harmed herself; therefore, it was imperative that she be kept isolated and away from anything that she might be able to use against herself.'

'So are you stating for the record that she had "suicidal thoughts"?'

'I don't understand why you are asking questions about Mrs Kay's state of mind sixteen years ago when it clearly has no relevance to the disappearance of Jason Kay seven days ago, Inspector,' countered Pritchard shifting nervously on the sofa.

'I'll be the judge of what is relevant in my investigation, Dr Pritchard,' said Steal, flicking his litter finger out.

Wright checked her notebook and asked, 'Can you tell us about the five million trust fund set up by Anne Kay's father in her name only before he died and why he excluded her husband from having any access to the monies?'

Wiping the tiny pellets of perspiration forming on his forehead with his fingertips, Pritchard coughed and shuffled about on the sofa. 'How did you find out about that. Anne knows nothing about it.'

She recalled the text she received from Rita Clark in the car just before they arrived at the house, with an attached copy of the original bank details of the trust set up in Anne Kay's maiden name on the Channel Islands sixteen years ago when searching through the archive records of Reginald Price's old and debunked bank accounts.

Wright smiled when she said, 'Just answer the question, Dr Pritchard.'

'I'm not a solicitor so cannot comment on any legal or financial matters, but can state that Reginald Price was a complicated man in many ways and often did and said things that appeared irrational to the outside world, but made perfect sense to him.'

'But with your medical background and knowledge, you would know all about the inner fears and thoughts of people's minds, Doctor?' said Wright, noting his highly anxious state in her little black book.

'I only treated Mr Price's daughter so cannot give you any reasons as to his state of mind when he set up the trust fund in her maiden name only.'

'So you *do know* about the five million pounds, Dr Pritchard?' interjected Steal.

'I know that it exists, but that is all I know, Inspector. Like I stated earlier, I was and still am Mrs Kay's doctor and only deal in her health and nothing else.'

'But if she were diagnosed as, say, "not fit in mind and body" to look after her own affairs such as the five million trust fund, then I presume that you, as her doctor and expert in mental health issues, could recommend that another person such as her husband and even *yourself* become the official administrator of the fund?'

'If you are suggesting that I would do anything to harm Mrs Kay or even kill her husband, then you're even madder than the patients that I treat, Inspector,' countered Pritchard.

'People kill for a lot less than a share of five million, Dr Pritchard.'

'Well, you're wrong, Inspector. If I wanted to get rid of Anne and steal her money, then I would have done it a long, long time ago and not have waited until I'm an old man and too decrepit to enjoy it.'

'Being old doesn't mean that you're not a killer, Doctor,' said Steal, staring right through him.

A police officer entered the room. 'We've finished our search, Inspector, and are ready to leave when you are.'

'We'll return everything to you when we're done, Doctor,' said Steal, leaving with Wright and the team whilst Pritchard watched them drive away from the study window before checking the back of the portrait again.

'It's not there,' he said, when the housekeeper, Martha, entered the room holding a large brown envelope in her hand. 'But how did you know?' he asked, taking the envelope and pulling out *two* documents from inside.

'I've been your housekeeper for twenty-seven years, Doctor, and dust and clean everything in the house including *all* the pictures hanging on the walls. So when I saw the police arrive through the lounge window, I knew that you wouldn't want them to find the envelope and quickly stuffed it under the cooking tray in the oven.'

'Did you look inside, Martha?'

'No, Doctor. I'm not interested in what you do, just that you pay me well and let me run the house the way I like to, and therefore, want to keep my job and home for as long as possible.'

'But how did you know that I didn't want the police to find it?'

'I didn't, but people only hide things that they don't want found, Doctor.'

'I don't understand, Martha? I could be a criminal and yet you protect me from the police when I've hardly spoken half a dozen kind or personal words to you while you've lived and worked in this house all these years?'

'It's not rocket science, Doctor. I'm a woman who lives within her own space. I don't like or court affection or friendship, but do require order and structure in my life. Being your housekeeper provides me with exactly that. You pay me to keep your house and life in order and in return, I get to live in a very nice home without having to put up with a nagging husband and children. I'm not a kind woman, Doctor, but I will miss working for you when the time comes for us both to move on.'

Dr Pritchard looked at Martha and smiled. 'I've never asked you about your family.'

'I don't have any, Doctor. I was born alone, grew up alone and will die alone. That is the story of my life and I accept it without tears or regrets.'

Staring up at his portrait on the wall whilst holding the evidence in his hand, Pritchard gave a little smirk then said, 'I'm going to retire to the Caribbean in the near future and would very much like it if you would continue to be my housekeeper in my new home, Martha.'

'That would suit very well, Doctor,' she said with a hint of a smile as she walked back into the kitchen to prepare dinner.

Pritchard dialled the number on his mobile. 'The police have just searched my home and office and will be calling on you next, so hide the documents *now* and tell them nothing except what we've agreed…'

Seated in the car, checking the other warrants in the file, Wright asked, 'Where to now, Boss?'

'I think we will give the solicitor, Mr Dodd, a visit,' he said informing the police officer of their next suspect on the list before driving off and checking his rear car window to spot Pritchard sheepishly spying on them from the study window.

'There was something stuck to the back of that portrait,' said Wright, noticing Steal watching Pritchard.

'Whatever it was, he was afraid that we'd find it and yet looked terrified when it wasn't there? Dr Pritchard is up to his neck in the disappearance of Jason Kay and knows a lot more about the trust fund than he's letting on,' said Steal, irritated that he couldn't work out who was conspiring with who to cover up the disappearance and murder of Jason Kay.

'Do you think that Mrs Kay knew about the five million trust fund in her name only, Boss, and if so, why didn't she just take the money and leave her husband years ago?'

'Good question, Sergeant, but what puzzles me more is why did her father hide the money away on the Channel Islands so that Jason Kay couldn't access it, considering he loved him like a son and literally gave him everything else including his own daughter?'

'Everywhere we look, we keep coming back to who was Jason Kay before he arrived at Hilltop Mansion,' noted Wright.

'Find the mysterious blackmailer and we find out whom and why Jason Kay was murdered…' said Steal.

Five Months Earlier

A month had already passed and Kay was no closer to finding out who was stealing *his* money as he sat at his desk in the study, staring at the laptop, waiting… His mobile rang.

'What have you got for me, Black?'

'The man's a ghost. My team have drawn a blank.'

'What the fuck am I paying for? You're the so-called "Covert Operator" who knows everything and everyone so why can't you dig up one sniffling little blackmailer?' demanded Kay, stumping around the study like an angry spoilt child when his Rolex watch pinged three times. 'It's five minutes to midnight and that fucker will be demanding another payment.'

'Then you have two choices. Pay what you owe me and I'll leave you to him or pay him the next instalment and buy more time so that I can dig deeper, but to do that, my fee will be *double…*'

'Who's the fucking blackmailer now…?' yelled Kay.

'Don't threaten me. I'm your only hope so either pay up or shut the hell up.'

Checking his watch, Kay saw he had two minutes left. 'Don't fucking let me down again, Black.'

'I want this *ghost* more than you. No one gets the better of me,' said Black, dialling another number on the mobile. 'It's done,' he said with a sneaky grin whilst adjusting his large black hat in the car front mirror before starting up the engine then driving out of Treetop Village. The music stopped on the radio and the DJ announced the midnight hour.

The Next Payment

"Hello, Alex, and here we are again. How quickly time flies in-between emails, but I digress. The second advance on my one million is due by twelve noon tomorrow and to refresh your memory, the details are; Pay

£166,666.66 into account no.666.666.666 Sort Code: 06.06.06 Ref: SAHD. Once I have received the monies, then I will send you the next instalment in your fascinating life story…"

Reading the email, Kay smashed his fist on the desk, denting the highly polished green/brown leather top in the centre when he heard a noise coming from the hallway and opened the door… to find the house eerily empty. Creeping up the stairs, he opened the door to Anne's bedroom where she was fast asleep.

Returning to the study, he emailed Gibbs to confirm the second instalment… before finally falling asleep in the chair three hours later. When his watch pinged three times, he woke up to discover he had lost twelve hours and another £166,666.66. Just then, the inbox pinged on his laptop and he read the email.

"Freddy, the eldest son of local police constable, John Wilding, missing for three days with no clues. He was last seen walking to work at the local garage three miles away on Friday morning at seven thirty a.m."

Leaning over and throwing up into the waste paper bin by the desk, Kay couldn't believe what he'd just read. 'How the fuck does that bastard know about him? It's been thirty years, and his body was never found… Who are you and how the fuck do you know all about me?'

Dialling the mobile, Kay erupted, 'I don't care what it costs. Find that ghost and deliver his head to me!'

'No problem,' replied Black, smelling the gourmet steak lunch the waiter had just placed on his table at the posh city hotel where he was staying on Kay's tab. He waved to the wine waiter standing in the corner of the room. 'Another bottle of this delicious red, please, and add it to my bill.' He smiled, tucking into the blood-red rear steak whilst still wearing the black hat.

Having slept through the night, Kay missed his usual walk to the village when he telephoned Diane Moffatt and instructed to clear his diary for the rest of day before ordering his wife to prepare her usual lunch for one, then stomped up the stairs to take a shower whilst Anne carried on as normal.

She didn't question why he missed his daily walk or work for the first time in thirty years. It would be a dangerous thing to do… and so continued with the house rules as if *he* wasn't there whilst secretly smiling to herself, knowing that he didn't know that she had heard *everything* from the top of the stairs last night at midnight… and quietly revelled in the thought that the great Jason Kay was actually *afraid*!

Stepping out of the shower, Kay quickly covered his face in shaving cream before running the sharp blade down the left side of his jaw line when he felt a stabbing pain from the razor as it drew blood… and he saw the past come back to haunt him in the bathroom mirror…

Thirty Years Earlier

It was a bright sunny Thursday afternoon when Alex Trent drove into the local garage to leave his fifteen-year-old open-topped, slightly tatty, two-seater silver sports car for its yearly MOT and check-up.

Stepping out of the car, Trent spotted three garage mechanics sniggering in the corner. 'What's so funny?'

'Nothing, Alex. We just love working on hopeless cases,' joked the tall, lanky youth with his face, gloves and overalls covered in oil.

'Mr Trent to you, goby mouth, and at least I own my own car whereas you just get to service other people's.'

'Here we go again. The-great-I-am lecture. Well, you're wasting your breath on us, *Mr Trent*. We all went to the same school and you're no better than the rest of us. At least we have a proper job and future. You just do the donkey work for your old man. So piss off and we'll let you know when or if your old pile of junk passes the test this year.'

Watching the three mechanics laughing at him, Trent clenched his fists and stormed out… when a light bulb went off inside his head and the perfect solution to his problem materialised right before his eyes.

One Week and One Day Later

'See you later, alligator,' smiled Freddy, biting into a half-eaten fried egg sandwich whilst opening the front door.

The woman shouted, 'One day, you'll get up early enough to eat breakfast at the table with the rest of the family.'

'Love you too, Mum.' He laughed, slamming the front door and sashaying through the newly built housing estate filled with three- and four-bedroom houses like the cockerel who'd just laid the hen.

'Are you up for the big game at the Fox and Hound tonight, Freddy?' shouted the short stubby youth from his car parked outside the last house at the edge of the estate.

'You bet, Bloggsy. See you down there at eight p.m. sharp and have my usual ready.'

'Maybe one day you'll get the first drink in?' laughed Bloggsy, driving off with the car radio blazing out punk music to the entire world.

Finishing the last morsel of his sandwich, Freddy skipped along the desolate road leading to the garage at the edge of town when he heard a familiar sound and turned round.

'What do you want?' he asked, looking down the road to see if there were any other vehicles, to discover none… except for the fifteen-year-old open-topped, slightly tatty, two-seater silver sports car parked inches away from him.

The tall, lean youth got out and smiled. 'Thought you might want a lift now that I have my wheels back.'

'I'm good, thanks,' said Freddy, turning back and walking off down the road when he felt a large pain in the back of his head and everything went blank.

'What the fuck… What's happening…' he mumbled, opening his eyes to see total darkness. He felt an icy cold air cut into his bones as he tried to speak, only to find his mouth taped shut and his arms and legs bound.

When the darkness lifted, he heard the voice, 'Hello again, Freddy.' Trent stared down at him with that same cold, detached grin that both the students and teachers at school hated.

Pulling the tape off his mouth, Freddy yelled, 'Where am I and what the hell are you doing, Alex?'

'You're inside an old freezer stored in the family barn that hasn't been used in years so *no one* will be coming to save you, Freddy, not even your stupid policeman father.'

'Why? What have I ever done to you to deserve this?'

'Nothing, you're a nobody, but a mouthy nobody who showed me no respect and so won't be missed and your body will be put to good use.'

'What do you mean by my body…?'

'I'll explain everything to you slowly so that your little brain can absorb it all,' said Trent, putting on a pair of large black plastic gloves before bending down and picking out a giant set of tweezers from the toolkit box on the floor, then leaning over the freezer. 'First, I need to extract *all* your teeth…' He began pulling them out one-by-one whilst laughing at Freddy's screams of agony going unheard to the outside world.

Soaking up each drop of blood pouring out from his captive's mouth, Trent carefully placed each tooth in a large plastic bag until Freddy was toothless.

'That's a job well done even if I do say so myself,' he said, enjoying listening to the cries of despair pouring out from the freezer. He bent down and picked up a large bottle of acid. 'And now, for final piece of the plan, the fingertips…'

Taking the acid, Trent slowly poured the bottle over each one of Freddy's fingers while he yelled out in torturous agony until they had *all* disintegrated into bone.

Packing the toolbox, the plastic bag of teeth and empty bottle of acid into a large black plastic rubbish bag, Trent stood over the freezer looking down upon Freddy's bloody, mutilated body.

'They say that it takes several hours for the human body to shut down completely in a freezer if the temperature is set just above freezing… And I must say, it's been real fun bonding together like true mates.'

He taped Freddy's mouth back up before closing the freezer lid and covering it with hay at the back of the barn. Picking up the black plastic bag, Trent carried it outside before locking the barn door and placing the bag in the boot of his car. He drove off, laughing.

12

Steal and Wright drove into the long, curved crumbling tarmac drive leading to Simon Dodd's house.

'What a wreck,' said Wright, checking out the large Victorian double-fronted detached house surrounded by overgrown oak trees, hedges and grass.

'A spacious double-fronted detached property with character in a prime location requiring some "updating",' said Steal with a sly grin as he parked the car right in front of the house, followed by the rest of the army.

Simon Dodd opened the door. 'I've been expecting you, Inspector,' he said, standing in the middle of the porch, watching the detectives walk towards him with the warrant.

'News travels fast in this neck of woods,' said Steal, handing him the warrant whilst continuing into the house with the team.

'Dr Pritchard telephoned me when you left his home and I've just received a call from my secretary informing me that your other officers have just arrived at my office,' said Simon, following them in and closing the door.

'Then we can dispense with the unnecessary chit chat and get down to business, Mr Dodd,' said Steal, glancing around the large wide hallway with a huge winding, dark-varnished oak staircase in the centre, surrounded by matching wooden panels on every wall and doors, leading to several rooms on two floors. Everything about the Victorian house spoke of a past rich in money and grandeur when all Steal and Wright could see was a house full of neglect and sadness.

'Let's talk in the lounge, Detectives,' said Simon, leading them into a large, dark, oak-panelled room cramped full of tatty Victorian furniture and ornaments that would once have adorned the room with pride and status, but now screamed of despair.

Shifting a pile of paperwork from the threadbare dark-velvet, three-seated, high-backed chair onto the floor, Steal and Wright sat down, disturbing inches of dust that floated in the air before finally settling back down on their suits.

Simon asked, 'Can I get you anything to drink?'

'No, thank you,' said Wright, coughing while attempting to wipe the dust off her trousers, only to end up swallowing more.

Steal went straight for the jugular. 'It's now been seven days since Jason Kay vanished and yet no one, especially his wife, appears that concerned, Mr Dodd?'

'Jason Kay wasn't a good man, Inspector, as no doubt you have discovered during your investigation and it's no secret that I couldn't abide him. In truth, I hated the man... but he was a client who paid well, and therefore, my feelings towards him were irrelevant. Business is business, Inspector,' said Simon, standing nervously by the large coloured-glass double doors looking out onto a wilderness that was once a well-kept Victorian garden.

'It would appear from the last financial accounts of your company that Jason Kay was, in fact, your *only* client since the death of your father, James Dodd, fourteen and half years ago,' said Steal, glancing around the crumbling house, noting that Simon continued to look out into the garden and not at them.

'That's because I inherited Kay's business on my father's death, together with the firm and house,' said Simon; his eyes fixed on the wilderness outside.

'How can you "inherit" a client you clearly don't want?' asked Wright, coughing out dust.

'My father stipulated it in his final will and testament. Effectively, I can't sell the family business or dismiss Jason Kay as a client unless Kay personally dispenses with my services as his solicitor.'

'Why did your father do that to you?' asked Wright, finding herself feeling sorry for him.

'Because I never wanted to be a solicitor and my father knew that I would sell the business when he died and so made sure that I couldn't by doing a deal with Jason Kay to secure his continued legacy through me in the firm...'

'What was the deal?' interjected Steal.

'I think you've already worked that one out from your search etc. at Dr Pritchard's offices and house, Inspector,' said Simon.

'Reginald Price instructed your father to set up the five million trust fund in his daughter's name only with Dr Pritchard as her personal physician. He entrusted this sacred task to his oldest friends, hoping that they would protect his daughter both legally and mentally from Jason Kay who would try anything to get his greedy hands on the five million should he find out. But your father broke that sacred promise to his old friend and client by telling Jason Kay about the secret account, but held back how he could access the money, then blackmailed him into being his *only client* and paying an exurbanite annual fee knowing that Kay wouldn't sack you until he got his hands on the five million.'

'I can see how you gained your reputation, Inspector Steal,' smiled Simon, looking straight into his eyes. He confessed, 'Jason Kay had been trying to get his hands on the five million for the last sixteen years without success.'

'But if *you* had found a way to release the monies with Dr Pritchard's help, then you would be finally free of Kay and your father's legacy,' noted Wright.

Simon turned his head back and stared out into the wilderness again. 'I could never do that, Sergeant. You see, as much as I hated both my father and Kay, I cared for Anne more and knew that once Kay got his hands on the money, then he wouldn't need her any more...'

'Did Anne Kay know about the trust fund and were you secret lovers?' Steal asked.

'No on both accounts, Inspector. Reginald Price knew that Kay would find a way to *extract* the information from Anne so protected his daughter by not telling her, but in doing that he bound both my father and then myself to a secret that has both haunted and chained me to a *living death* for the last sixteen years...'

'But if Jason Kay was dead, then both you and Mrs Kay would be free and rich?' said Wright, writing down every last detail in her notebook.

'If it were that simple, then I would have killed Kay sixteen years ago and besides, if I did indeed murder him as you suspect, then why hide the body when I would need it to break free of the chains?' said Simon, oblivious to the officers and forensic team turning his home upside down whilst continuing to stare into the wilderness.

A police officer entered the room and informed Steal that they were done.

'Is there anything else that you wish to add to your statement, Mr Dodd?' asked Steal, standing up.

'No, Inspector,' he said with his eyes fixed on the wild garden.

Wright couldn't help but ask the question that intrigued her the most, 'What did you want to be if not a solicitor, Mr Dodd?'

Simon turned his head back and their eyes locked together to become one, and he gave a wistful smile then answered, 'A farmer.'

'Why?'

'Freedom, Sergeant, freedom...'

'Then why not just sell the house and buy the farm whilst your staff continued to run the business, leaving you free to be a farmer?' she asked, puzzled.

'Because my father loved his legacy more than his son... and so locked the sale of the house together with the business insuring that I couldn't sell one without the other, imprisoning me in the two places I hated more than him.'

'It would appear that you and Mrs Kay both had fathers who valued their own legacies more than their children's happiness,' said Wright.

Simon looked into her eyes and for a brief second glimpsed the same pain.

Steal touched her on the arm. 'I believe we're finished for now, Sergeant,' he said, walking to the front door with Wright clearly affected by Simon's statement. 'We'll let you know when you can have your files etc. back, Mr Dodd,' continued Steal, making his way to the car and driving off whilst Simon watched them disappear before closing the door.

Driving back to Lunsford, Steal waited for Wright's usual list of questions, only to find deadly silence and wanted to ask her what was wrong, but knew that she wouldn't answer. Everyone has their secrets, including him, but now wasn't the time to unleash them.

He said, 'Simon Dodd was well-prepared for our visit. Dr Pritchard had primed him. He told us just enough to appear the victim in all this when in reality, both he and Pritchard are up to their necks in the disappearance and murder of Jason Kay.'

Awakening from her thoughts, Wright came back to life. 'I agree, Boss, but every time we come back to the same question; who would gain the most from Jason Kay's death and why hide the body if everything depended upon him being found dead?'

'We'll solve it, Sergeant. After all, I have a reputation to uphold and you are Detective Liz Wright because you're *always right*,' he joked, noting a slight smile creep across her lips as he drove along the winding country road, wondering why this case, of all the cases they had worked on together in the last six months, appeared to affect her the most?

But what intrigued him even more was why she was so determined to become a murder detective at the age of only ten years old when little girls played with dolls and dreamed of becoming beauty queens?

'They've just left and I told them exactly what we agreed.'

'Good. We're almost there, Simon, so don't lose your nerve now. In seven days' time, we can both finally expunge Jason Kay from our lives and start living again.'

'You'd better be right, Pritchard, or the one who'll lose the most will be Anne and I can't let that happen to her again,' said Simon, dropping the mobile on the dusty chair and closing his eyes, picturing the last time he saw the only true love of his life.

Thirteen Days Earlier

The clock on the wall struck twelve noon-time while Anne sat in the kitchen, staring at nothing...

A day had passed since her meeting in the woods with Diane and knew what she had to do next, but was afraid to ask the question. Just then, her secret mobile rang. 'Hi, Dotty, it's so good to hear your voice.'

'You too, but you sound sad?'

'I found out something about Simon yesterday that both angered and crushed me.' She watched the tear drops fall on the kitchen table and wiped her face.

'Is it about the five million trust fund in your name only?'

'How did you know about that when my father made me promise never to tell anyone except Eric?'

'I did what we planned at our secret place and went to Simon's office yesterday. He showed me the file and told me everything…'

'I'm sorry I couldn't tell you about the trust fund, Dotty, but I couldn't break a deathbed promise, even if it was to my father.'

'Don't apologise for being a good daughter, my dearest Anne.'

'So, you know that Simon has betrayed me again…' She was unable to stop the tears drowning the kitchen table in a pool of grief.

'He didn't and hasn't betrayed you. He is trying to save you, but will need your help. Trust in what you once had and you can both have it again.'

'What have you discovered, Dotty?' asked Anne, suddenly coming back life again.

'I think that Simon should tell you himself. He wants to meet you and is waiting for your call.'

'It's too risky. What if Jason finds out?'

'Freedom requires courage, my dearest Anne, and I don't know of anyone more brave or courageous than you.'

'But I can't come to his office and he can't come to the house. Jason would know…'

'Use our secret place. After all, it's where wishes can be made and come true.'

'But it's our place, Dotty.'

'It always will be, but the well needs two lovers bound together as one to make their wish come true.'

'I love you, Dotty.'

'Ditto. Now stop crying and make that call. I'll text you his mobile number.'

Within seconds, her phone pinged. Her hands trembled when she dialled the number and heard his voice. 'Is it really you, my love?' he said.

'It's been so long since I heard you call me your love.' She cried.

'I say them, every day and night inside my head before I go to bed and wake up.'

'Me too,' she said, wiping the torrent of tears from her wet face with the tea towel she took out from the cupboard drawer by the sink.

'I need to tell you everything, my love,' said Simon, unable to hide the pure joy at finally hearing her soft voice again.

'Dotty and I have a secret place where we used to meet as children. It's hidden in the meadow at the back of Hilltop Mansion. There's a tiny road leading to it just before you get to Hilltop Road. Park the car there and follow the stream to the well.'

'What about Jason?'

'He won't be home until late.'

'I'm leaving home now. I'll be there in three hours.'

'I'll be waiting.'

Looking up at the clock on the wall, Anne noted that it was 12.13 p.m. and she had just enough time to complete the washing and ironing before returning to her bedroom by two thirty p.m. where she would wait for Jason's driver to put the note through the door, telling her that he won't be home for dinner. The note was always the same, but it was Jason's way of keeping her locked into the house rules by making sure that she was there every day at precisely five thirty p.m. to collect it.

But today, she won't be sitting alone in her bedroom. At three p.m., she will dance through the meadow to meet her love... but first, she must tell Eric.

'He betrayed you once. He could do it again...' he said, pacing the lodge floor with his mobile.

'I trust Dotty and she said he wants to help us. I must see him, Eric. I need to know the truth about what really happened sixteen years ago,' she said, holding back the tears.

'Then I'm coming with you.'

'You need to be here in case the driver or Jason comes home early. I need you to do this for me, Eric.'

'I don't like it. He will know about the secret place and if he tells Jason…'

'I must take the chance. I have no choice.'

'Then leave your mobile on and if I hear anything… I'll track him down and blow his fucking head off with the shotgun.'

'I love you too, my dear Eric,' she said, checking the clock again and noting that the time was now 12.22 p.m.

Driving along the road, Simon spotted the sign for Treetop Village then checked the route planner in the car when his heart started to race.

In less than twenty minutes, he would see Anne again; only this time, there will be no hallway to cross or Jason to fight.

Spotting the almost invisible road behind the back of the meadow, he drove down it and heard the sound of running water when the opening appeared and he parked the car.

Holding the file in his hand, he followed the stream whilst listening to the sound of freedom when his heart stopped at the vision of Anne standing by the well.

Within seconds, their bodies were locked together as one.

They floated around the well, like teenage lovers stealing their first embrace. The minutes ticked by like seconds while they clung on to each other, afraid to let go. Finally, reality returned.

'I've imagined this moment thousands of times in my dreams over the years, but never thought that it would ever become real,' said Anne, her body collapsing down upon the stone seat.

Simon slipped in beside her. 'Is this real, my love, or am I dreaming too?' he said, clasping his hand tight around hers.

Closing their eyes, they sat by the well for what seemed like hours when Anne finally opened her eyes and asked, 'Why did you let me go, Simon?'

Releasing her hand, he stood up and confessed his guilt with tears of shame in his eyes. 'I've never let you go in my heart, my love, but I did fail to protect you.'

Looking up at the bright sky above and then back down at Anne, he told her the whole story of how his father betrayed them both and that for the last sixteen years, he had been imprisoned in a job and home he hated, but couldn't leave because if he did, then Jason would find a way to steal the five million and kill her.

Listening to him and seeing the same pain in his eyes that she saw in hers every day when she looked in the mirror, she asked, 'Why didn't you tell me? I would have run away with you with nothing to my name. We could have had another life if only you asked me to go with you…'

'Jason would never have allowed us to leave. I know that he killed our parents once he got what he wanted from them, but I can't prove it…'

'But my father died of cancer and yours of a heart attack?'

'Pritchard falsified the medical records, but my father was smarter than that. Jason had planned for and blackmailed him into paying his firm hundreds of thousands of pounds that he stole from your father's company over the last sixteen years in the hope of unlocking the five million.'

'Did Dr Pritchard murder my father and then yours…?' she asked, her body almost collapsing with a mixture of rage and guilt as she pictured her father fighting for his last breath of life on his deathbed whilst the doctor he trusted as a friend stood over him, watching, yet still did nothing.

'I don't know that for sure and Pritchard has never confessed his part in their deaths, but if he didn't do it himself, he helped Jason cover the murders up by falsifying the death certificates.'

'Then he's as guilty as Jason, only more… because our fathers trusted him with their lives and he betrayed them both for thirty pieces of silver,' said Anne, turning towards Simon and pounding her hands on his chest, crying. 'You should have told me… you should have told me…'

'I couldn't. Jason would have killed us both. I was trying to protect you, my love, but I was wrong… I'm weak and don't deserve your love or forgiveness, but I can at least try and make amends now if you'll let me.'

Pulling her body away, Anne leaned back on the stone seat and looked up at Simon's pitiful face filled with shame and guilt. When the anger melted away, she realised that she was just as *guilty* as him.

'I forgive you,' she said, wiping away the tears. 'For sixteen years, Jason Kay has spun his dark spider's web of lies, blackmail, corruption and murder to take everything away from us... well, *no more*! It's time to cut the web and kill the spider.'

Opening the file, Simon confessed and showed her everything.

He told her of Pritchard's plan to free them *all* and finally have their revenge upon Kay.

Listening to Simon's and Pritchard's plan, Anne's heart lifted. For the first time in sixteen long dark years, she could see the light shining towards her. Yet so much depended upon so many.

She asked Simon, 'Can you trust Pritchard after everything he has done?'

'He's a sick old man whose clock is running out and has already risked everything by betraying Jason. So, do I trust him? No, but do we need him for the plan to work, yes...' said Simon.

'Then we'll use him like he's used our fathers' trust and friendship' said Anne, hesitating for a moment. 'What about the accountant, Timothy Gibbs? He stole my father's money for that snake and now he's conspiring with him to steal my five million to pay a blackmailer one million who's threatening to expose Jason's past before he came to Hilltop.'

'How do you know all this?' asked Simon, seeing a new stronger woman emerging before him.

'Jason's personal assistant and mistress Diane Moffatt gave me this as proof and will help us if I ask her,' she said, handing him the USB drive.

'What does she want in return?'

'Nothing, except the same as we do; her freedom,' she said, trusting in that her new friend would keep the promise she made in the woods to be there should she need her.

'Don't worry about Gibbs. With this new evidence provided by Diane Moffatt, he will have *no choice* but to help us, but what about Eric?' Simon asked, knowing how protective he was of Anne and how much he despised him for being so weak when she needed him the most.

'I trust Eric with my life,' she said, giving a little grin, knowing that he was listening to everything on her mobile.

'I take it Dotty will be on board with the plan?' said Simon.

'Need you ask such a silly question?' laughed Anne. Then she dropped the bombshell. 'My father told me on his deathbed that he had a "secret file" on Jason.'

'What file?' said Simon, shocked that Anne had kept so many secrets from him, but then so had he and all because Jason Kay slowly sucked their courage and love from them.

'He died just before he was going tell me where it was and what was in it, but I now realise that Jason must have uncovered what my father was doing and it cost him his life.'

'If we could find that file, then we can finally destroy Jason,' said Simon, pulling Anne up towards him and kissing her.

She pulled away and turned round to the well. 'I've waited sixteen years to feel your love again,' she said.

Simon took out a 50p silver coin from his pocket and threw it down the well. They watched it float to the bottom where it disappeared into the mud, sealing their future and love together forever.

13
Lunsford Headquarters

With the seventh day almost over, Steal and Wright stared at the crime board, attempting to piece together the evidence.

'Everyone on this chess game of murder wanted Jason Kay dead,' said Steal, pacing the floor like a lion sizing up its next meal. 'Any news on Kay's missing laptop?' he asked, turning towards the team, only to hear silence. 'Keep looking. We need that laptop.'

'What about the five million, Boss?' said Wright, pointing to the pictures of Simon Dodd and Anne Kay. 'I think the solicitor and Mrs Kay are lovers and he told her about the secret trust fund in her name, but her husband found out about them and so they had no choice but to kill him and dispose of the body while they work out a way to release the monies and disappear. With five million, they could easily vanish with new identities.'

'A good theory, Sergeant, but there's still something not right that we're missing. Plus, we keep coming back to Kay's laptop. If they killed him, why bury the laptop with the corpse?' said Steal, then shouted across to Rita Clark, 'Did you find anything out about Jason Kay's past before he arrived at Hilltop?'

Clutching her notes, Rita leapt to her feet. 'I found a birth certificate in the name of Jason Kay born at an East End nuns' orphanage in the year 1974, where his mother, Bridget Kay, aged fifteen years old, died while giving birth. According the orphanage records, her parents were very religious and so left the baby at the orphanage where the nuns named him Jason Kay. It seems that he remained there until he was ten years old, then he ran away with another orphan boy named Jacky Jones. After that, the records of the two friends becomes patchy, but it would appear that they became what was known as "street kids" e.g., living amongst the tramps and vagrants on the streets of the East End. They got separated, but would occasionally meet up for the night in homeless hostels where things suddenly turn a bit strange.'

'What do you mean by "strange"?' interrupted Steal, intrigued.

'I found an old newspaper article reporting the death of an unnamed homeless youth aged between fifteen and eighteen years of age who was found dead in his bed after apparently suffocating in his sleep at a homeless hostel in East London at approximately six a.m. on Monday, 5 March 1990. His corpse was buried in unnamed pauper's grave one week later. But the strange thing, Boss, is that the day before his death, the records show both a Jacky Jones and Jason Kay signing in *together*, yet the next day, the same records show that only Jason Kay signed out with no record of his friend leaving except for the strange death of the unnamed youth whose corpse appeared to be of similar age to Jacky Jones and who vanished into thin air after the date of 5 March 1990?'

'Good work, Constable Clark,' said Steal, staring at the picture of Jason Kay on the board whilst scratching his head. 'Why would Kay kill his best and apparently only friend from the orphanage and then destroy his identity?'

'Because something happened between them after they signed in that frightened Jason Kay so much, he had to silence his friend for good,' surmised Wright.

'But what was it that Jacky Jones knew about Jason Kay that cost him his life and identity?' said Steal, when the "light bulb" lit up inside his head. 'Jones knew that Kay was a fake... and that somehow, he'd stolen his friend's identity, which means that the thief who broke into Reginald Price's home thirty years ago claiming to be the orphan Jason Kay wasn't just a fake and a liar, but a stone-cold killer.'

'There's something else,' said Jack, stepping forward and holding up Kay's mobile in front of the team, 'The technical wizards at the telephone company managed to retrieve this...'

Staring at the mobile, the team saw a picture of a tall thin man dressed in a long black overcoat and hat, throwing what looked like a large brown file into a lake. 'This was taken at twelve thirty p.m. on the day that Kay disappeared seven days ago,' said Jack

Where's the lake?' Steal asked, checking the picture on the mobile again.

'The last mapping reference recorded on the phone before it was wiped clean showed the park where it was found by the old woman,' replied Jack.

'Get the forensic and diving team out to that park *now* before it gets dark and instruct them to search every inch of that lake for the file then see what information you can dig up about the man in black?' instructed Steal.

'You got it, Boss,' said Jack, picking up the phone on his desk whilst Steal stared at the shadowy outline he'd drawn of the mysterious, faceless man with the large black hat on the board.

Wright asked, 'Do think that he's our killer, Boss?'

'I'm not sure. The man in black is the same man who threatened Mrs Kay's housekeeper, Maggie Frith, and so was probably destroying the file for Jason Kay, but why would Kay take a picture of a file he didn't want anyone to know about then leave it on his mobile for all to see?'

'Because he *didn't* take the picture?' surmised Wright.

'Precisely,' acknowledged Steal. 'We've been led around like puppets on a string. We were meant to find the mobile and picture, but nothing else. Whoever wiped Kay's phone clean knew exactly what they were doing. For the last seven days, *everyone* on that board has been leading us a merry dance. Feeding us snippets of information to send our investigation off on another wild goose chase while they sit back and watch us play their game,' said Steal, furious at being taken for a fool. He called out to Rita again. 'What have you dug up from the personnel files at Kay Corporation re private security and/or covert organisations employed by Jason Kay?'

Flicking through the reams of paperwork on her desk, she answered, 'Nothing, Boss. I've gone back sixteen years when Jason Kay took over the business from Reginald Price and there's no record of any private security and/or covert organisations employed in the company. I've also gone through all of Mr Kay's bank and financial records and again drawn a blank. It would appear that the people he employed to do his "dirty" work, including the man in black, work

113

under the radar and must get payment via cash or another bank account that isn't recorded at Kay Corporation or anywhere in this country.'

'What about the Channel Islands where Reginald Price set up the trust fund for his daughter or any other off-shore banks in other countries who hold secret accounts for shady businesses or criminals to launder their money?' added Steal.

'I'm trawling through them at the moment, Boss, but so far have come up with nothing. Whatever covert organisation or bank Jason Kay used, he kept them well-hidden,' said Rita.

'Keep on it, Clark. No organisation, criminal or otherwise, is that *invisible*… Somewhere, someone has left a trace,' said Steal, adding, 'I bet my next month's pay packet that what we're looking for is on that missing laptop.'

'Will do, Boss,' she said.

Jack leaned across his desk and whispered, 'Impressive work, Rita.'

'You too, Jack.' She smiled whilst secretly bursting inside with excitement at him finally acknowledging her existence.

'That's it for today, team. Finish up what you've got left to do then go home and relax,' instructed Steal, nodding to Wright to do the same. 'We'll begin again early tomorrow morning.' He walked back to his office when he stopped and turned round, staring at the crime board. He said, 'No one on *my* team is anyone's puppet!'

The Lake

The sunset had almost disappeared from the evening sky when the diver emerged from underneath the water, clutching a file which he handed to the police officer waiting in the car.

Back at Lunsford, the office was empty except for Steal, who sat at his desk staring through the glass window at the crime board when the police officer walked in holding the file. 'We recovered this from the lake, Inspector,' he said, placing the file wrapped inside a transparent waterproof bag down on the desk before leaving.

Wiping the waterproof bag with his hanky, Steal opened the file to find a single piece of plain white A4 paper inside with words typed in red ink. *"If you've found the file, then you know that Jason Kay didn't take the picture. Justice isn't always fair, Inspector. And so, sometimes, REVENGE is the only option!"*

Throwing the note back down on the desk, Steal took out a sharp paper knife from his drawer and walked out into the main office where he stood in front of the crime board and cut the shape of a cross with the knife through the blank face of the man with the black hat, swearing, 'No one fucks with me!'

14

Four Months Earlier

'You've had *another* thirty fucking days and nights to bring me that bastard's head,' yelled Kay, pacing the study floor whilst the residents of Hilltop Road slept soundly in their beds as the midnight hour approached.

'The man's a ghost... even the dark web uncovered nothing about him.'

'You've been using that same excuse every bloody day since the first day... I'm beginning to think that you're the ghost.'

'If I wanted to extract one million from you, Jason, I wouldn't wait three months, let alone six. I'd just fucking point a gun to your head and threaten to blow it off,' countered Black, sipping a mouthful of twenty-five-year-old malted whisky at the hotel bar.

'I'm bleeding money and if you don't find him soon, Black, I'm fucked!'

'Every time you pay him, he gives you another clue. If you want me to unmask the blackmailer, then I need to know what he knows about you.'

'I don't pay you to investigate me,' scowled Kay.

'I don't give a monkey's uncle what you've done or who you've killed, but whatever the blackmailer has on you took a lot of digging and favours to unearth, which means that he will have left a trace of himself along the way somewhere,' said Black, signalling to the bartender to replenish his empty glass whilst Kay paced the study floor like a rat caught in a trap between *two* hunters.

'How do I know that you won't take the information and use it like *him*?'

Taking another sip of whisky, Black tipped his hat and smiled. 'I'd be out of business if word got round that my "clients" couldn't trust me or my contacts. I'm not interested in the rights or wrongs of the people who hire me, just that they require my very special services without any comebacks to them.'

'What guarantees do I have that if I forward you the blackmailer's emails, no one else will see them?' asked Kay. His gold Rolex watch pinged three times.

'None, except my word, which has been good enough for you in the past when you've used my services without any leaks.'

'Text me the address, but this is your last chance, Black. Fail again and you'll see what I do to those who double-cross me,' warned Kay.'

'Don't forget who your threatening,' countered Black, cutting him off before savouring the final drops of whisky whilst staring at his reflection in the mirror behind the bar.

The bartender asked, 'Do you ever take that hat off, Mr Black?' She was curious as he'd always worn the same long black coat and hat when drinking at the bar and/or eating breakfast, lunch and dinner whilst all the staff in the hotel stared at him and yet, if asked, couldn't describe one single feature about his face or anything else about the man in black named Black.

Tipping his hat, he gave a sly grin whilst leaving a very large tip on the counter before walking to the lift and pressing the button. The door opened and he stepped inside, lifting his head as he turned round, sending a cold chill all the way down the bartender's spine as the lift doors slowly closed and he disappeared.

The Next Day

The small minute hand clicked around to 11.57 a.m. on the large clock on top of the medieval church tower hovering beneath the tall glass skyscrapers whilst Kay sat in his office, watching his fingers tremble as they hovered over the incoming email box on his laptop.

They weren't the trembling fingers of a man with a guilty conscience, but the shaking hands of a man who had buried too many dark secrets that had now been unearthed by someone who had uncovered every single one of them.

Pressing his finger down upon the keyboard, he shook with a mixture of rage and fear when he read the blackmailer's email.

"Hello again, Alex, and I'm pleased to inform you that as per our agreement and your instructions to your faithful accountant, Mr Timothy Gibbs, the sum of £166,666.66 was deposited into account no.666.666.666 Sort Code: 06.06.06 Ref: SAHD at twelve noon today, making a total payment so far of £499,999.98. Now that wasn't too painful... but I hope that you will take comfort in the fact that we are halfway through our agreement with no casualties so far. I say this because I know that you are trying to find me, Alex, but warn you that if you break our agreement in any way, then it will be you that will suffer the consequences of your actions this time..."

Smashing his fingers down upon the keyboard, Kay typed, *"Did you think that I was just going to sit back and let you steal one million from me without doing anything?"*

"Of course not, Alex, but I'm not the one that's afraid..."

"Don't call me Alex. My name is Jason Kay and I make the rules, not you!"

"You can cancel our agreement today, but then I won't be honour-bound to complete my end of the deal and will walk away with £499,999.98, without sending you the next instalment in the true-life story of Alex Trent alias Jason Kay... and a firm promise that the price you'll pay for not continuing will be much higher..."

Leaping up from the desk, Kay banged his head against the bullet proof glass window whilst staring down upon the thousands of trapped ants rushing about beneath the skyscrapers then laughed out loud at the irony of suddenly feeling like one of them.

Returning to the desk, he calmly typed, *"It seems that I've met my match and so congratulate you, but why work against each other when we could be an unstoppable force together?"*

"Nice try, Alex, but I value my independence and somehow don't think that you are a man who likes to share power."

"Enough of this bullshit game of pretend niceties. I want what I've paid for so send me your worst and I'll decide who's afraid of whom!"

"Until next month, Alex. I leave you with this farewell gift..." The blackmailer signed off leaving Kay staring at an empty screen.

'What the fuck!' he yelled, pacing the floor.

Diane Moffatt rushed in. 'Are you OK, Jason?' she asked, concerned after hearing him swearing and cursing from the open door in her office.

'How many times have I told you not to fucking call me by my first name in the office?' he said, dismissing her like a piece of rubbish.

'Yes, *Mr Kay*,' she said, turning round to walk back to her office, mumbling under her breath, 'Ignorant bastard.'

A courier arrived with a package. 'Special delivery for a Mr Alex Trent?' he said.

Kay grabbed it from him. 'I'll take that,' he said, signing the name Jason Kay.

'Who's Alex Trent?' asked Diane, curious that she had never come across the name or man at Kay Corporation before.

'No one that concerns you, now get on with the job I pay you for, which includes cancelling and re-scheduling all my appointments for the rest of day and should anyone ask where I am, you don't know,' he ordered, locking his laptop back in the drawer before leaving the office with the package.

Diane returned to her office, spitting fire whilst watching him leave the building from the window and enter the park opposite, holding the package.

Returning to her desk and typing the name Alex Trent into the search engine on her computer, she discovered that there were over one hundred men with the same name, but none that appeared to work in the city.

Kay sat on the bench in the park, staring out at the lake while holding the package. He ripped it open to find a large brown envelope inside.

Tearing the seal on the envelope, he pulled out a thick manila file with the name Alex Trent printed on the front in large black bold letters.

'It can't be the same file... I shredded everything in it myself...' He was about to open it when the mobile pinged inside his jacket pocket and he read the text. *"By now, you will have received the file, Alex. What a shame you went to so much trouble to destroy it only to discover that the man who commissioned it outsmarted you even on his deathbed."*

Reading the file, Kay saw his entire life unfold without a glimmer of emotion or regret.

It had been nearly sixteen years since he first set eyes upon the file and nothing had changed. To justify his abominable actions, he reasoned that everyone he had ever destroyed or killed deserved their fate.

To be the man he imagined himself to be required a coldness that few human beings possessed, but as he stared at the name of the man on the tombstone in the last picture added to the list of bodies since he destroyed the original file, Kay couldn't avoid feeling a moment of regret for the father that he always wanted, but never felt he had, until that day when he broke into Hilltop Mansion thirty years ago and Reginald Price took him in and gave him everything, including his daughter, and ultimately his life...

Sixteen Years Earlier

Regional Price sat by the fire in the lodge, staring into the flames whilst the cold autumn wind howled outside. Eric walked in wearing muddy boots and thick waterproof clothing.

'I didn't know that you would be visiting today, Mr Price?' he said, worried.

Reginald Price never visited the lodge without notifying Eric first since he moved out and Jason Kay moved in six months ago after marrying his daughter; but today, he felt the need to sit with the man whom he had known since boyhood and yet never really appreciated until it was too late.

'I'm sorry to call on you out of the blue, Eric, but I just wanted to sit with you for a few minutes before...'

Discarding his boots and outer clothes, Eric laid a few more logs on the fire before sitting down beside the man he loved more than his own father and yet could never find the courage to tell him.

'Before what, Mr Price?' he asked, suddenly feeling afraid for the old man he always thought was fearless.

Pulling his eyes away from the flames, Regional Price turned towards Eric and stared deep inside his eyes. 'I've not done well by you

120

over the years, Eric, and for that, I am truly sorry. I gave my love to the wrong son… and now I must correct that wrong,' he said, wiping the tears from his eyes.

'I don't understand, Mr Price,' said Eric, feeling his body melting inside like the logs on the fire.

'You don't need to, Eric; just know that one day, I will make things right for both you and Anne. I have done a great wrong and before I leave this mortal place, I need to destroy the evil that has wormed its darkness into my heart and then took everything I hold dear from me.'

'What can I do to help you?'

'Be there for my Anne when she needs you and always remain faithful to who you are, my faithful Eric,' he said, placing one more log on the fire before standing up and encasing his hands around Eric's face. 'Always remember this moment, Eric, as will I,' he said, kissing him on the forehead like a father would to his son before walking back out into the howling wind.

'This steak is overdone,' moaned Kay, ringing the tiny gold bell beside his dinner plate on the dining room table.

The housekeeper and cook, Maggie Frith, rushed in from the kitchen.

'How many times have I told you that I like my steak cooked blood rare.'

'I'm sorry, Mr Kay. I can cook you another one in a few minutes,' she said, shaking.

His wife sat at the other end of the long, highly polished mahogany table, too afraid to speak up for the woman who had been more like a mother to her than a housekeeper.

Anne had been married to Jason Kay for just under six months, but already he controlled her life with a cruelness that even she could never have imagined.

She had tried to tell her father so many times, but he only saw the son that Kay knew he wanted and so believed in the lies when he told him that Anne was mentally unstable instead of his own daughter's cries for help.

'Don't bother. I've lost my appetite.' He groaned, pushing the dinner plate across the table when the front door opened and Reginald Price stormed into the dining room, holding a large brown envelope.

'I need to speak to you right now, Jason,' he said in a tone that shocked both Anne and Maggie.

'What's wrong, Reginald?' Kay asked, furious that he had raised his voice at him in front of his wife and the housekeeper.

'This was *my* house long before you married my daughter and moved in, so I'll see you in the study in five minutes,' ordered Price, marching back out to the hallway to the study with the file.

Smashing his fists down on the table, Kay stood up and yelled at Maggie, 'Escort my wife to her bedroom then leave. You can clean everything up tomorrow.'

'Yes, Mr Kay,' she said, shocked; he never liked anything left undone.

The two women watched him storm out of the room into the study, slamming the door behind him.

'I've never seen your father so angry,' whispered Maggie, holding Anne's hand as they crept up the stairs to her bedroom.

'Maybe Father believes me now and things will change,' said Anne, kissing her on the cheek before closing the door.

Maggie rushed back down the stairs to collect her coat from the kitchen and leaving via the back entrance.

'I know everything about you, Alex Trent,' said Price, throwing the file down upon the desk whilst watching Kay's face turn to ash at hearing his real name.

Picking up the file, Kay flicked through the pages and pictures, more shocked at how Reginald Price had uncovered so much more about him than the despicable acts he'd committed to achieve his ambitions.

'I see that you've left no stone unturned, Reginald,' he said, furious that his loving father-in-law had been secretly investigating him behind his back without him knowing.

'I believed in you when you broke into my home all those years ago and wormed your way into my heart, but no more... Anne will start divorce proceedings tomorrow on the grounds of cruelty and you will resign from the company and relinquish all shares in it before leaving this house never to return again; otherwise, I will give this file to the police and you can spend the rest of your life behind bars.'

'How did you come by this information and how do I know that this is the only copy?' Kay asked, not bothering to waste his breath denying its contents.

'You don't ask the questions any more, *Alex*, but for the sake of my daughter's reputation I will let you walk away with the same things that you arrived with... the clothes on your back.'

'I deserve more than that after all the years that I've had to put up with your pitiful need for a son and marrying a woman not worthy of my love.'

'You're incapable of loving anyone except yourself. But what angers me the most is that I didn't see who you really are until it was too late... when I let you marry my precious daughter and then dismiss her cries for help as you slowly tried to break her spirit. But I am a man of my word, not like you, and so will let you walk away a free man in exchange for the file and my daughter's life back.'

'What's stopping me from just taking the file now and silencing you for good?' threatened Kay.

'The two men standing outside the house with guns,' said Price.

Kay opened the front door to see two six-foot-plus muscle-bound bodyguards, dressed all in black and brandishing high-powered revolvers, stood by Price's chauffeur-driven Rolls Royce.

'It would appear that you leave me with no choice, Reginald,' said Kay, steaming with rage.

'My solicitor has already prepared all the paperwork and Dr Pritchard will counter sign everything as a witness. Be at my old office at ten a.m. sharp tomorrow morning to sign everything and don't try to double-cross me, Alex, because you won't win this time,' warned Price, picking up the file and leaving.

The Next Day

Kay stood upright at the top of the long, winding staircase. Stretching out his left hand upon the dark, highly polished banister, a long, lingering grin ran across his face whilst he surveyed the large Victorian hallway below.

Slowly, he walked down the stairs running his hand along the banister until he stood in the middle of the hallway. Turning his body towards the large mirror on the wall, the grin grew bigger as he checked his reflection.

Everything was as it should be.

His tall, well-toned body donned an expensive grey suit, crisp white shirt and red silk tie. The face was smooth and chiselled with perfect white teeth and dark, deep-set brown eyes. The hair was cut short at the temples with a hint of grey, but thick and dark on the top.

Turning round, he stared into the large Victorian kitchen where Maggie was preparing breakfast while he ran his eyes over the contents on the table.

There was one china plate with two boiled egg cups perfectly placed in the centre with the silver spoon positioned beside the cups. Two slices of thickly buttered white bread cut into eight pieces lay on another plate to the left and a large, circular china mug and saucer aligned to the right. Salt and pepper at the centre of the table with the empty china teapot and milk jug. On the cooker was a saucepan filled halfway with cold water, three extra-large raw eggs and glass timer placed exactly at the centre.

Everything was as it should be…

'I'll be back in thirty minutes,' he said, noting the time on the large iron clock hanging on the wall above the arguer was precisely seven am.

'Yes, Mr Kay,' said Maggie, relieved that she hadn't made any mistakes.

Opening the front door, Kay stepped outside onto the large, crazy-paved entrance porch then set the timer on his gold Rolex watch for exactly thirty minutes before doing his usual daily walk to the village for the newspapers.

Returning home, Kay's watch bleeped three times. He opened the front door and proceeded into the kitchen where he ate breakfast alone as usual whilst reading the newspapers at precisely seven thirty a.m.

Thirty minutes later, Anne heard the front door slam shut from her bedroom, followed by the sound of his latest Sliver Sports car engine

124

revving up. She watched him drive off from the window, smiling at the thought of a few hours of freedom. She remembered her father's outburst at the dinner table the night before, and feared what her husband might do to him for daring to challenge his authority.

The Final Meeting

Regional Price stared out of window into the city from the office where he used to reign as the king of his empire Price Corporation until it was re-branded Kay Corporation three months after Jason Kay married his daughter and stole his life's work.

Turning round, he stared at the pile of paperwork strewn across the desk then smiled as he checked his watch. In exactly sixty minutes' time, at ten a.m., he will have regained his throne and banished the black knight for good. He picked up the telephone on the desk and dialled a number.

'He will be here in less than one hour and then you will receive the other half of the payment when all the papers are signed.'

'Don't trust a word that comes of his mouth and drink nothing, not even a glass of water. He will try to seduce you into feeling that you've won, but that's when he's at his most dangerous. Just get him to sign the papers and leave. Under no circumstances must you allow him inside your head. Let him in again and you're a dead man.'

'Don't worry. The file you compiled will always haunt me... I've built a company from nothing and have made millions and yet I let a monster fool me for years...'

'But he didn't. When I contacted you two months ago, something inside you chose to believe my story when others didn't. I've been waiting for years to make Alex Trent finally pay for the monstrous crimes he committed upon everyone in that file. The money isn't payment for the file, Mr Price; it will be used for a better cause.'

'What will you do with the one million?'

'It's better that you don't know. Just take comfort in the knowledge that Alex Trent's victims will finally receive the *justice* they deserve.'

'I haven't told him about you or how I received the file and that you possess the original, but I did give him my word that this was the only copy and that I wouldn't hand it over to the police if he signed the papers and left.'

'You are an honourable man, Mr Price, so keep the file and your word, but know this, Alex Trent isn't honourable, and so doesn't deserve an honourable fate.'

'I have two bodyguards standing outside my office and my good friend the solicitor, James Dodd, who prepared the legal documents is arriving at nine thirty a.m. with my other dear friend, Dr Stuart Prichard, who will witness and countersign everything.'

'Good, but just in case I suggest that you make another copy of the file *now*, then hide it in a safe place and don't tell anyone where, including your friends'

'But what about my word and that I trust my friends?'

'If all goes well, then you can destroy the copy, but should it not… then make sure that it's *never* found by Trent or your friends.'

Reginald Price hesitated for a moment then confessed, 'When I read the file you sent me two months ago and I learnt the truth about the real Jason Kay, I had my solicitor draw up legal documents in the form of a trust fund for five million in my daughter's maiden name, Anne Price, so that should anything happen to me then she would have enough money to leave him and be free. The money is hidden in a secret bank account on the Channel Islands.'

'Does the solicitor know where the bank account is?'

'No. I only set up the account yesterday and was going to tell James today when he gets here at nine thirty a.m.'

'Don't. If you love your daughter, then trust *no one*… Five million will corrupt even a good friend.'

'I will let you know when it's all done,' said Price, disconnecting the line whilst noting the time on his watch was 9.20 a.m. He picked up a gold pen from the ink stand on his desk and scribbled a quick note on the writing pad beside it, before handing the file and note to the tall, dark, shaven-headed muscular bodyguard in his late twenties standing guard outside the door.

'Take these to the main office and instruct one of the secretaries to photocopy everything inside the file except the note… then get her to put the copies inside another file with the note before sealing it in a large envelope and posting it to this address. Then come back here before ten a.m. with the original file and should anyone ask, you know nothing about the other file or note.'

'Yes, sir,' said the bodyguard, leaving seconds before James Dodd and Dr Pritchard arrived.

'I see you are well-prepared,' said Dodd, checking the documents on the desk noting: The divorce papers, two letters typed in the name of Jason Kay resigning from the board and Kay Corporation plus transfer papers returning all shares back to Regional Price, including the company name back to Price Corporation.

Circling the desk again, Dodd gave a nervous twitch before he looked up at his friend and asked, 'I don't see the file on Kay anywhere, Reginald?'

'That's because it's in a secure place until all the documents on the desk are signed and witnessed by the appropriate parties,' said Price, noting how uneasy his old friend suddenly appeared in his presence.

'It's 9.58 a.m. and Kay will be here in two minutes so would it not be prudent to have the file on the table just in case?' suggested Pritchard, giving a nervous cough as Price stared into his old friends' eyes and felt the knife of betrayal cutting into his heart...

The clock on the wall ticked round to ten a.m. and the bodyguard standing outside the door escorted Kay into the office before walking back to his post.

The other bodyguard returned with the file. 'You wanted this by ten a.m., Mr Price,' he said, handing it to him minus the note before re-joining his colleague outside.

'Shall we get on with the business at hand?' said Price, slipping the file on a small side table under the window before walking over to the desk and signing *each document* with the gold pen before turning round and handing the pen to Kay. 'Your turn and then their's,' he said, glancing over at his friends who lowered their eyes.

'I prefer to use my own,' said Kay, pulling out a silver-tipped ink pen from his inside jacket pocket and separating it into two, before leaning down over the desk ready to sign when he turned his head up towards Price and said, '*No one* takes what is mine!' He stabbed the tip of the pen into Regional Price's hand. He smiled when he added, 'How ironic to be killed by the very same pen that should have been used to sign both yours and your daughter's freedom.'

Feeling the ink penetrate through his hand into his veins, Reginald Price looked over at his friends' betraying eyes and asked, 'Why?' only to hear silence. He turned back to face his killer and promised, 'This is not the end.'

'Oh, I think so, Reginald...' Kay grinned and moved closer, whispering, 'Right now, a slow-dissolving non-traceable poison is running through your veins. In twelve hours' time, your body will begin to shut down and then in another twelve hours, you will be dead. Your good friend Dr Pritchard will sign your death certificate stating cancer... while your other loyal and trusted friend, Mr James Dodd, will shred *all* your carefully prepared documents, including your beloved daughter's divorce papers, but excluding her trust fund for five million, which you will sign over to me, *today*, plus the details of the bank account where you've hidden the money. Otherwise, Dr Pritchard will sign another death certificate stating your daughter's *suicide* due her depressed mental state after your sad demise.'

'You must be mad if you think that I'm just going to hand over the five million to you. Once you've got the money, then my daughter is as dead as I am.'

'If you don't, then I'll make sure that *every second* of her life will be like a living death... until I find the money. Then I'll finally release her from the hell that *you* put her in by *not* giving me what I want.'

Regional Price turned to his friends again and pleaded, 'We've been best friends since university and I know that you don't want to do this... that this evil monster is threatening you both, but if we *three* stand together *now*, then we can destroy him!'

They turned their cowardly eyes away, leaving their friend standing alone. Dodd and Pritchard's continued silence twisted the dagger further into Reginald Price's heart as he watched Kay stroll across the room to pick up the file from the table by the window then walk over to the shredder beside the office door where he slowly destroyed every single piece of evidence inside, leaving just the empty file cover which he ripped apart with his bare hands whilst laughing.

He turned towards Price and said, 'Time to pay for your betrayal.'

'I will tell you where the money is hidden after I speak to my daughter alone at Hilltop,' said Price.

'Don't try to outsmart me, Reginald, by telling her where the money is hidden in the hope that she can escape because you know from reading the file that I will take great pleasure in extracting the information from her personally,' threatened Kay.

'I just want to let my daughter know that I love her before I die,' said Price, feeling the poison rushing through his body. He stumbled against the desk and the bodyguards rushed in, brandishing their guns.

'Are you all right, Mr Price?' asked the bodyguard who copied the file as he helped him sit down whilst the other one lined up Kay, Dodd and Pritchard against the wall with his gun... leaving Kay no choice but to nod his head in agreement at Price's request to see his daughter alone.

'Yes, thank you...?' replied Price.

The bodyguard stared into his eyes and said, 'David, sir, my name is David and you are safe with me.'

'I know, David, and thank you, but everything is OK now and would like you to drive me home to Hilltop Mansion.'

'Yes, sir,' said David, escorting him out of the office into the lift and down to the underground car park whilst the other bodyguard watched over the three captives until David sent the order through on his mobile to release them and return to the car park where they drove off in the Rolls Royce with Reginald Price struggling for breath in the back seat.

David asked, 'Should we go to the hospital, sir?'

'No. It's too late for me, David, but not for my daughter. Take me back to Hilltop. I want to die in my own bed with Anne by my side holding my hand,' he said before dialling the number on his mobile. 'You were right. He was far more dangerous and devious than I imagined and now I have less than twenty-four hours left.'

'It's not your fault, Mr Price. Alex Trent has been getting away with murder for years...'

'He's destroyed everything, including the file,' said Price, coughing up blood into his hanky.

'Did you make the copy?'

'Yes, and I've hidden it in a place that he will *never* find.'

'Are you sure?'

'My daughter's life depends upon it so *yes*, I am sure, but he will try to find out how I got the file and when he does, he'll come after you,' warned Price.

'You're right, but I've been tracking Alex Trent since his *first kill*... and can hide within the shadows, waiting, until I finally get *justice* for *all* his victims, including you.'

'I'm going to tell Anne where the file and trust fund are hidden so that she can give the file to the police and then live her life free of him.'

'To protect your daughter, you *can't* tell her anything. Trent will know that you've told her and she'll never get the chance to spend the money or hand the file over to the police.'

'But then I've left my daughter with that monster and failed her again.'

'I promise you, Mr Price, that no matter how long it takes, I will *free* your daughter and exact revenge for your murder and will always regret seeking you out and sending you the file instead of destroying Alex Trent myself.'

'I'll hold you to that promise and you have five hundred thousand pounds of my money to help you keep it,' said Price, ending the call before sending another text.

Closing his eyes and resting his head against the soft brown leather seat, he pictured Anne's face smiling down at him whilst holding his hand as the two bodyguards drove him back to Hilltop, leaving the three conspirators behind, panicking.

'What the hell went wrong, Jason?' exploded Dodd, terrified at what Price would do to the friend that betrayed him.

Kay wrapped his blue stripped silk tie around Dodd's throat until he could hardly breathe. 'Don't ever fucking talk back to me again,' he threatened, releasing him, whilst Pritchard watched in sheepish silence.

'When I contacted you last night after Price's visit to *my* house, you guaranteed that you would have the bank account details for the five million before I arrived at ten a.m.'

'Reginald was going to tell me when I arrived at nine thirty a.m., but he became suspicious and so I didn't want to risk alerting him any further by asking the one question that would confirm his distrust even more,' grovelled Dodd.

'And what about you, Pritchard, why didn't you extract the information from him or are you just as useless as your pathetic friend?' taunted Kay.

'Reginald Price didn't build a multi-million-pound corporation from nothing by being stupid. He out-played all of us and now that you've *murdered* him before he could tell James about the bank account details, the five million will die with him,' countered Pritchard, secretly relieved that Kay didn't get his hands on the money, but quivering with fear at what he was going do next.

'I still hold the trump card; his beloved daughter Anne will do anything I tell her to do now that I've broken her spirit.'

'What are you planning to do?' asked Pritchard, ashamed at betraying his oldest and dearest friend for fear of losing his own pathetic reputation when Kay's mobile rang.

'Keep a watch on the house until I get there,' he said, staring right through Dodd and Pritchard with those cold, black eyes, adding, 'If you both value what's dear to you, shred everything on the table and then follow me to Hilltop.' He watched them destroy *all* the documents before leaving. The two betrayers stood alone together, like sheep waiting to be slaughtered.

Pritchard asked Dodd, 'What did he use to get you to betray our best friend?'

'He phoned last night and threatened to have my son *killed* if I didn't tell him everything,' said Dodd, ashamed at his own cowardness and yet still too afraid to fight back. He turned towards Pritchard and asked, 'And you?'

'One of his henchmen arrived at my house late last night with an envelope. Inside was a copy of a statement from a doctor that I worked with when I was a Junior GP in a large hospital. He claimed that I had caused the death of a patient by giving him the wrong medication and then covered it up by falsifying the medical records.'

'Was is true?'

Hesitating, Pritchard answered, 'Yes... I was young and foolish, but there isn't a day that goes by when I don't regret what I did. That's why I left general practice and hand out happy pills to the rich. I can never hold another human being's life in my hands again.'

'What about the doctor who made the statement? Why has he made it now after all these years of silence?'

'Because Kay probably had something on him. That's what he does, seeks out your deepest secrets and weaknesses then uses them to crush you,' said Pritchard, picturing the young child lying in the hospital bed, dying, because he was in a hurry to leave and meet his friends at the bar and so didn't take enough care or time over the tiny life he held in his hands.

Unable to live with what they had done to their oldest and dearest friend, Dodd and Pritchard pledged to redeem their treachery and honour Regional Price's courage by devising a plan to protect Anne and make sure that Kay never got his murderous hands on the five million.

The Final Hours

The Rolls Royce drove into Hilltop Mansion when David rang the doorbell and Maggie opened the door.

'I have brought Mr Price home. He's a sick man and wants to sleep in his old bed tonight, but needs to see his daughter before her husband arrives.'

'I will let Mrs Kay know then prepare his room while you help him in and his daughter will show you where to go,' said Maggie, glancing at Reginald Price sitting in the back seat of the Rolls Royce before rushing into the lounge and alerting Anne sat on the sofa.

Anne rushed out into the hallway to find her father struggling for breath. She and David helped him up the stairs to the bedroom at the far end of the hallway whilst the other bodyguard waited and watched for Kay in the car.

While Maggie quickly made the bed with fresh sheets, Anne and David helped her father undress and into an old spare pair of pyjamas he stored in the top drawer of the tall dark mahogany chestier drawers by the wardrobe.

Safely tucked up in his king-sized four-poster bed, Regional Price looked up at the three sad faces staring down at him and smiled. 'Could you please get me a glass of cold water, Maggie?' He coughed up blood.

'Yes, Mr Price,' she said, holding back the tears whilst wiping the blood off the pristine white sheets with her hanky before rushing out of the bedroom to the kitchen.

Price's eyes locked into Anne's. 'I would love a single shot of my favourite thirty-year-old malt whisky from the dining room, my dear.'

'Right away, Father,' she said, dashing out of the room, crying.

Price then beckoned David closer with his finger. 'You and your friend need to leave the house *now* before *he* arrives... or else you will both pay for helping me.'

'But what about you, sir? It's my job to protect you and I failed...' said David, scanning the room with his hand on the gun holster, just in case.

'No one could have done a better job, David, and you've proven your loyalty to me through your silence about the copy of the file. You must *never* disclose it to anyone, even my daughter; otherwise, Kay will stop at nothing to get his hands on it.'

'What file?' smiled David.

Price asked him to fetch his mobile from the inside pocket of his blue suit hanging in the wardrobe. 'Put this number in your phone. A man called Jeremy Caine will answer your call and arrange payment of fifty thousand pounds directly to you with another sum of twenty thousand pounds to your associate.'

'But you've already paid me well for my services.'

'You will both need to disappear for a while,' warned Price.

Copying the number into his mobile, David was reluctant to leave the old man and two women alone in the house.

When Maggie and Anne returned, Price ordered, 'You must go now, David. My daughter and Maggie will care for me.'

'I won't forget this day, Mr Price,' he said, taking one last look at the three helpless beings he had just been ordered to leave behind when every fibre in his body told him to stay. His mobile rang.

'I think we're being watched,' said the other bodyguard from the driver's seat of the Rolls.

'Start the engine, I'm on my way,' said David, rushing out of the house and getting into the front passenger seat. The other bodyguard drove out of the drive into Hilltop Road when a man dressed in a black suit got out of a black car parked on the opposite side of the road and shot the driver in the head with a silencer. David grabbed the steering wheel whilst pressing his foot down on the accelerator, leaving the man standing in the middle of the road watching his target disappear out of sight before he could fire off another bullet.

'I got one, but the other one got away,' he said, informing the boss on his mobile.

'Forget him. He's just a hired nobody. I'm on my way and will be there in thirty minutes. Keep watch till then,' ordered Kay, checking that Dodd and Pritchard were following close behind him from the car's side-view mirror.

'Yes, sir,' said the man coldly, walking back to the car and joking with the other hired gun at how much blood spurted out of the bodyguard's brain when he shot him in the head.

Anne and Maggie tended her father in the bedroom, unaware that her husband was just minutes away.

'I need to speak to my daughter alone for a few minutes, please, Maggie,' said Reginald Price, smiling at the faithful housekeeper who had loved and cared for Anne more than her own father.

'Yes, Mr Price,' she said, wiping his forehead with a damp towel before squeezing Anne's hand. 'I'll get a fresh bowl of water and towel.' She smiled, leaving them alone and returning to the kitchen to cry alone.

Staring up at his daughter's tearful face, Reginald Price felt his body drowning in a river of mixed emotions; anger, betrayal, fear, hatred, loss, love and finally, regret.

Anger at himself for not being the father he should have been and hatred for the man who stole all his love, leaving none for Anne.

But what he regretted the most was the terrible loss of time that he could never get back with Anne and the fear that she would *never* forgive him for not seeing how precious and wonderful a daughter she was and how he betrayed his promise to her dying mother to love their daughter as he did her.

Struggling for breath, he confessed, 'I'm sorry that I failed you both as a father and protector and don't expect you to ever forgive me for all the years of cruel coldness that I showed towards you. When your mother died giving birth, I blamed you, an innocent baby, when I should have rejoiced in your birth.'

'Sitting down on the chair beside the bed, Anne held her father's hand and said, 'I love you, Father, and always will, but now I understand that you only had enough love in your heart for one woman, my mother, and when she died, a part of you died with her.'

Squeezing Anne's hand tight in his, Regional Price confessed, 'There's a deadly cancer rushing through my body and so I have little time left to undo all the wrongs that I have done against you, my precious child, so I have set up a secret trust fund in your maiden name, Miss Anne Price, containing five million in order that you can leave the monster I forced you to marry to preserve a crumbling empire that meant more to me than your own happiness...' Price coughed up some more blood.

Maggie rushed back into the room and blurted out, 'Mr Kay and two other men in another car have just driven in.'

Struggling for breath, Price beckoned Anne closer and whispered, 'I have a *secret file* on Kay's real identity and the crimes he committed before he arrived at Hilltop. Use it to destroy him before he finds the five million... and tell no one about the file or money, except Eric, including my solicitor and Dr Pritchard. Trust *no one*...'

'Where is the file and money hidden?' Anne asked, hearing the footsteps at the top of the stairs as her father attempted to speak, but had no words. Then, he closed his eyes.

She heard *his* voice as he walked into the room, with Dodd and Pritchard behind, to see her holding his hand. 'What did your father tell you?'

'Nothing, except that he loved me and wished that he had been a better father,' she said.

Kay grabbed her by the arm and pulled her away while she and the others watched in silent horror as Kay shook her father's dead body, raging, 'He's fucking died too quick. He should have had another twelve hours.'

'What do you mean by another twelve hours?' Anne asked, shocked that no one in the room except Maggie and herself seemed surprised about her father's sudden death. Then she remembered his final words of warning, and saw the look of guilt and betrayal on James Dodd and Dr Pritchard's faces.

Kay demanded, 'What else did your father say to you before he died apart from the pathetic lie that he loved you?'

Turning her head back towards her husband, Anne held her breath and answered, 'Nothing except that he was dying of some *deadly* cancer.'

Studying her face, Kay looked for the lie behind the lie.

Maggie interjected, 'I think that I should take Mrs Kay back to her bedroom. Her father has just died suddenly and it's clear that she is in shock.'

'Fine, I'll speak to her later when I've dealt with matters here,' said Kay, dismissing his grieving wife with an icy coldness that shocked even Maggie as she helped Anne back to her bedroom.

Lying down on top of the bed, the two women held hands for a moment. Maggie then quietly slipped out of the room, leaving Anne alone with memories of a father who, while alive, showed her nothing but a cold detachment... but in death, confessed that he *did* love her. She heard *his* voice in the hallway and a terrible darkness crawled inside her head as she pictured what he would do to her if he ever found out that her father had told her about the file and five million.

Whilst Reginald Price's body laid barely cold in his bed and Anne sheltered under the bedsheets, hiding from the world like a small child, Maggie sat alone in the kitchen wondering what the future would be without Mr Price.

Kay paced the study floor demanding answers. 'You told me that it would take twenty-four hours for the poison to go through his body and kill him.'

'That's if he was a younger man and in good health, but he was getting old and clearly not as healthy as he pretended to be,' countered

Pritchard, remembering the last medical mistake he made that cost a child's life.

Clenching his fists, Kay turned his rage towards James Dodd. 'Tell me that you found out where the five million was hidden before the old man snuffed it?'

'I told you at the office that Reginald suspected something and so I have *nothing* to go on…'

'Then what fucking further use do I have for either of you now that the golden goose is dead and I inherit everything?' threatened Kay.

'Nothing, except that as Reginald Price's solicitor, I drew up his last will and testament which has *several clauses* in it; which mean that you *don't* get everything and Anne is well-protected should you try to do anything to her. So, if you want my help, then it comes with conditions…'

'And what about you, Dr Pritchard, do you have "conditions" too?' taunted Kay, imagining blowing both their miserable heads off with a shorn-off shotgun.

'If you want my help with your wife whilst James searches for the five million and sorts out the other legal matters regarding Reginald's Estate etc. then, yes, I too have conditions,' said Pritchard, crossing his fingers behind his back in the hope that Kay won't see through his and Dodd's plan to protect Anne and redeem their cowardly betrayal of their friend.

Realising that he still needed them until he didn't, Kay agreed to their conditions, unaware that he had signed a contract that would run and run… until sixteen years later, it would finally run out.

The Lonely Grave

Parking the car in the local woods by Treetop Village, David dug a deep hole in the earth before placing the corpse of his colleague inside and filling it back up. Hiding the grave with dead leaves and broken tree branches, he stood over it for a moment to say a few words of farewell to a man he hardly knew and yet felt great sorrow at his pointless death.

Returning to the car, he dialled the number he had stored on his mobile. Jeremy Caine answered.

'I was expecting your call,' he said, recognising the number from the text that Price had sent him earlier.

'Mr Price is dead and so is my colleague,' said David.

'I'm sorry to hear that, but not surprised. Jason Kay is not a man to cross.'

'Mr Price said that you would arrange payment of certain monies?' said David.

'I will text you an address for a PO box where you will find an envelope with your name on it containing a key to a locker at Heathrow Airport. Inside the locker, there will be another envelope containing fifty thousand pounds in cash.'

'What about the twenty thousand for my dead colleague?

'I will arrange for the money to be delivered to his next of kin.'

'Is Caine your real name and how do you know Mr Price?' asked David, curious.

'I'm the Money Man, that's all you need know, David. Just collect your money and disappear and don't ring this number again because it won't exist after this call.'

Starting the engine, David took one last look at the lonely invisible grave of the nameless dead bodyguard before driving off...

The Voice

Closing the file, Kay sat on the bench in the park, watching the swans glide effortlessly through the water, producing a tidal wave of ripples that cut through every obstacle in their way until there was none left. They finally stopped at the other end of the lake and claimed possession of whatever they deemed was theirs.

It had been a long time since he had thought about his "other self" and the life he would have lived if he hadn't been like the swans in the lake who appeared graceful and calm whilst floating majestically through the water, at the same time, underneath their feet, were ruthlessly destroying anything that stopped them from reaching their destination.

Tapping his fingers on the file, he contemplated his next move. He could destroy the file again, but that would be pointless when the blackmailer will magically produce another copy to taunt him with. He could give the file to Black so that he could track down the blackmailer.

Or, he could just fucking take what money was left in Kay Corporation, and disappear again… after all, he was growing tired of being *Jason Kay*.

The *voice* of his "other self" crept inside his head and told him what to do.

15

Anne sat at the kitchen table, enjoying eating her breakfast alone. She would like Maggie to be in the house with her, but for the final piece of the plan to work, her faithful housekeeper must stay away.

It seemed a lifetime ago when Inspector Steal and Sergeant Wright knocked on her door to investigate why her husband had been missing for five days... She smiled at the thought that it was just *three days* ago and yet they had been the longest three days of her life.

Sipping another mouthful of tea, she couldn't help but give a little laugh at the irony of life. For years, she had watched her husband spin his web of lies until the truth no longer existed and hated every single lying word that came out of his mouth, but what she hated even more was that he made her like him.

Every lie told required another lie to make it appear the truth. So when he lied, she had to lie too; otherwise, his lie would be uncovered. And so her whole life became one big fat lie... until the truth no longer existed and she became invisible.

Deep down inside, her invisible self prayed for the truth so that the lies would stop and the real Anne could finally be seen.

But for the real Anne to emerge, she must spin a web of lies so entwined that just one broken silk thread would destroy the entire web... and everyone inside it.

She had lived in fear for sixteen years and yet never felt more terrified for her life and those that she loved than now.

Finishing the last mouthful of cornflakes, she feared that the two bulldog detectives had locked their jaws into her life and all those she loved and wouldn't let go until they had uncovered the real truth behind the disappearance of her husband.

Clearing the breakfast table and wiping it down with a damp cloth, Anne deliberately left a tiny little tea stain on the surface. The house was still clean and tidy and "everything was as it should be", except for the tea stain, which, although it annoyed her, and part of her was tempted to wash it away, the other part, the real Anne, rejoiced in leaving it there, just because she could! Her mobile rang and the next thread in the web of lies was spun...

'The file with the note has been sent to the inspector,' said the voice.

'The inspector is no fool and won't take kindly to receiving an empty file with a cryptic note, which I fear will only make him and Sergeant Wright even more determined to uncover the real truth,' she said.

'You're right and I don't like using good detectives in this way either, but we have no choice if final justice is to be done for all the innocent victims that your husband destroyed and/or killed, including your father and you, Anne.'

'For years, I dreamt of a faceless stranger miraculously appearing from out of the darkness to destroy *him* and save me from a marriage worse than hell, but I could never have imagined that sixteen years later, that dream would come true. Only the faceless stranger isn't just one man, but two ghosts from the past come back to haunt their tormenter... and do to *him* what *he* did to them.'

'Your dream is the dream of *all victims*, Anne. The dream of *hope*... Don't give up now. We're so close to finally putting *all* those ghosts to rest, including *him*.'

'I know, and I thank you both from the bottom of my heart for never giving up on your dreams of justice.'

'Stick to the plan and all will be well.'

'I will,' she said, checking the tea stain on the table again and smiling before leaving it there and nipping out to see Eric at the lodge to update him whilst thinking how wonderful life was now that *he* was no longer there.'

Mr Black

Black sat on the bed in his hotel suite surrounded by piles of paperwork whilst drinking a large mug of black coffee. Tipping his hat downwards over his face, he quickly nipped off the bed to check that the corridor outside was empty before locking the door and pressing the redial button on his mobile.

'I've just confirmed the delivery of the empty file to Anne. We must be extra vigilant now as Inspector Steal will be even more determined to dig further.'

'We expected that, but without a body or any evidence of where it might be, Steal is unable charge Anne or any of her accomplices with murder. He may join some of the dots together and even be smart enough to uncover who we are, but he will still need a body to make anything stick.'

'I hope you're right, because I've had to dig into the darkest corners of myself to achieve justice and don't like what I have become in the process.'

'When you reach into the fires of Hell, you will get burnt, but think of all the other innocent people in the future that *he* would have gone on to harm if we hadn't done what was necessary.'

'There's no going back now and so we must wait for Steal's next move,' said Black, disconnecting the call and tidying up all the paperwork in the correct order before putting everything back inside the file.

Holding the file, he walked over to the built-in cupboard under the large mirror in the middle of the room where he unlocked the hotel safe stored inside. Placing the file inside the safe, he stopped for a moment to look at the picture of a young man taped to the inside of the safe door before gently running his fingers over his face and smiling as he closed the safe and tapped in the code 08.07.1970.

Standing up, he checked his reflection in the mirror and for a moment couldn't remember the man hidden beneath the black hat. He took it off and stared into the face of a ghost from the past.

Thirty Years Earlier

The time was five a.m. on a crisp chilly Friday morning when Police Constable John Wilding sat alone in the kitchen drinking his usual large mug of black coffee, together with two thick slices of buttered white toasted bread spread evenly with thick chunky marmalade.

At five fifteen a.m., he quickly ran the hot water tap over the mug and plate before leaving them to dry on the draining board and doing the usual check in the hallway mirror.

'Yep, I still got it,' he joked, smiling at the tall, lean, toned, good-looking man in his early forties with strong, white, even teeth, a firm jaw line and thick close-cropped dirty blond hair with flecks of grey at the temples.

Straightening his police uniform before checking that the walkie-talkie was in working order and covering his head with the police cap, he proceeded upstairs to make sure that everyone was safely tucked asleep in their beds.

Opening the door to the main bedroom, he quietly sneaked in and gently kissed his wife on the cheek, whispering, 'Love you.'

She whispered back, 'Ditto,' before turning over and falling back into a deep sleep.

Two more to go as he opened the bedroom door and checked that his teenage daughter was sleeping safe and sound before opening the last door and smiling at the sight of his twenty-year-old son snoring loudly whilst spread-eagled all over the bed.

Happy that his beautiful family were safely asleep in their beds, Wilding got into the car and drove off for work at the local police station as normal at five thirty a.m., unaware that he would never see his untidy, snoring, yet much-loved and treasured son Freddy ever again.

Days and then months went by without one single lead as to what happened to Freddy Wilding after he left for work at eight a.m., his usual time, on the same Friday morning to do his usual fifteen-minute walk to the local garage, only to never arrive.

Constable Wilding left no stone unturned as the entire town searched for his son, and the police checked every inch of the road he walked along every day to work. He interviewed all his old school friends, including Bloggsy, and work colleagues at the garage to find nothing… except when one of them mentioned Freddy poking fun at Alex Trent the week before he went missing when Trent came in to have his annual car service.

But when Constable Wilding called at the farm with two other police officers to question Alex Trent about Freddy, he just laughed and said, 'Why would I bother wasting my time thinking about what a mouthy garage mechanic jealous of my silver sports car said to me a week ago?'

'So you have nothing else to add to your statement?' Wilding asked, feeling his twenty-five-year policeman's gut instincts shouting *guilty*.

'Your son is of no interest to me, Constable Wilding, dead or alive,' he said, walking away into the farm house.

Without any further proof, Wilding's superior officers wouldn't issue a search warrant for Trent Farm.

Just four days later, a terrible tragedy struck the farm and the mystery of his missing son Freddy slowly disappeared into the slush pile of police files marked "Unsolved Cases".

And so the long search for justice for his son Freddy began. Fourteen years later, having taken early retirement from the force, Wilding found Alex Trent and sent the file he had been collecting on him to Regional Price, only for Trent to outsmart him again. He would have to wait another sixteen long dark years and commit a crime that would haunt him to the grave in order to catch the killer of his beloved son, Freddy.

One Year Earlier

Parking the car in the underground car park of Kay Corporation, Wilding stared at the photo of his family on the car dashboard. It was a happy photo of a time when life was good and the future bright, but that was a lifetime ago when his wife still loved him and his children were young sprogs finding their feet.

Now he was a haggard seventy-two-year-old divorced man, estranged from his grown-up daughter and grandchild, because he couldn't be a father or grandfather when he wouldn't let go of the pain of the past.

But if he stopped now, then it would have all been for nothing and so it went on as he took one last look at the haggard face in the car

144

mirror before meeting the man that would finally help him close the file on Alex Trent for good.

Stepping out of the car, he walked towards a tall thin man in his mid-fifties with a thin face, shaven, silver-grey hair dressed in a black suit, tie and shirt, leaning against a black car by the lifts.

'Mr Black?' he said, shaking his hand.

'A pleasure to meet you at last, Mr Wilding,' said Black, checking around the car park before the two men slipped inside the car.

'I won't waste your time with small talk, Mr Black. You know what I want and I'm prepared to pay you well for your services.'

'Your offer of five hundred thousand pounds is very generous and tempting, but I'm afraid I must decline. You see, I can earn the same amount of money by informing Jason Kay all about you and gain a very well-paying future long-term new client in the process.'

'But when I contacted you two weeks ago and sent you the file on the real Jason Kay, you agreed to arrange a meeting with him today at ten a.m. so that you could discuss offering him your unique services whilst secretly gathering information for me to finally bring him to justice.'

'In my "unique", as you put it, line of business, Mr Wilding, I don't care what kind of men or women my clients are or what they have done, just that they pay very well and aren't interested in how I get the job done; whereas you are an ex-man-of-the-law on a mission of justice, which, frankly, I don't give a fuck about except that you wouldn't be a long-term high-paying client with connections to other long-term high-paying clients.'

'What kind of a man are you, Black?' retorted Wilding.

'A practical man, Mr Wilding,' he said, pulling out a gun from inside his jacket pocket, stating, 'I'm afraid that this meeting is now over and you had better find a good place to hide because my *new* client will probably want to deal with you in a more "permanent" way once I've received the due payment of five hundred thousand pounds for giving him your file and no doubt another five hundred thousand for cleaning up any loose ends.'

'You treacherous bastard!' said Wilding, grabbing the gun. The two men wrestled in the car when the gun went off and Black slumped back into the car seat.

Stepping out of the car and checking that the car park was empty of witnesses, Wilding glanced around for the security cameras, noting that there were two on either side of the lift pointing outward into the car park, meaning that Black had parked in a "blind spot".

Satisfied that he was safe for the moment, Wilding got back in the car and checked that Black was dead before searching the car for the file which was inside a black briefcase on the back seat along with a long black coat and large black hat. He had an epiphany!

Staring at Black's dead body, he could be him except for the twenty-year age gap, but then who would see his face under the large black hat… and he knew all about Black from the file he had collected on him.

Dragging the body out of the car and into the boot, Wilding checked his watch, noting that the time was 9.50 a.m. He grabbed the coat and hat from the back seat before locking the car and pressing the button on the lift whilst putting on the coat and hat to cover his face before stepping into the lift for Mr Black's meeting with Jason Kay at ten a.m. which went well as Wilding listed all Black's covert operations for his secret clients, having memorised them from the file he had compiled on him.

Leaving the office, Wilding drove Black's car to a nearby scrapyard where he paid the owner in cash to crush the car into a metal box, sealing Black's fate forever in the land of discarded trash before hiring a cab back to the car park where he collected his car and drove off, still wearing the black hat and coat.

Staring at the face of the ghost from the past, Wilding could only see Black's face. To gain Kay's trust, he had had to play the game of being Mr Black and for the first six months, when Kay called upon his unique services to deal with a problem that required other methods to solve it, he would have to find a way to please Kay and yet not harm another innocent victim; which he managed to do until six months ago when the first stage of the plan was instigated and he was sent to threaten Anne's housekeeper Maggie Frith at her home if she didn't stop trying to contact her at Hilltop after she was sacked.

Seeing the terror on her face when he threatened her and her husband, Fred, still haunted him to this day. For the last year, he had become the man he killed in order to destroy the man who killed his son.

16
Lunsford Headquarters

Steal arrived early in the morning before Wright and the others. He took photocopies of the empty file with the note: *"If you've found the file then you know that Jason Kay didn't take the picture. Justice isn't always fair, Inspector. And so, sometimes, REVENGE is the only option."* Plus, copies of his other file notes on Kay down into the basement of Lunsford where the cold cases were buried deep within the endless rows of dust-covered files.

Staring down the long dark aisle leading to the centre of the basement, Steal could see an old black man with grey hair seated amongst hundreds of files piled high on either side of a tatty black plastic table.

Walking down the narrow aisle, Steal smiled as the old man took off his thick-rimmed gold glasses and looked up. Their eyes locked.

'Well, as I live and breathe; it's the man of Steal come back from the dead.'

'You can talk, old man,' laughed Steal, stretching out his arms to embrace his old friend and mentor Chief Inspector Tom Millard, who retired over twenty years ago after being shot and left for dead.

Steal looked around at the thousands of dead file cases that the top brass upstairs at Lunsford no longer cared about, except Tom who spent his retirement searching through the files, hoping to find justice for the forgotten victims because true detective work cost money, resources and time that the new police force could no longer afford to pay for.

'How long has it been since you walked amongst the dusty dead, Steal?' Tom asked, clearing some files off a chair on the other side of the table.

The Inspector sat down and looked at his old friend again. 'Too long, you haggard old codger,' he joked, noting that Tom had grown old in the last five years.

With no front teeth, a slight limp to his left leg, creaky bones, dark rings under his tired grey-black eyes from reading too many old files and more wrinkles on his craggy face than a spider's web, the retired chief inspector looked older than his seventy-six years.

'I'd offer you a drink, but I only have enough coffee in my flask for one,' said Tom, who was always generous with his knowledge and time, but never shared his coffee with anyone, even Steal.

'I see that some things never change,' smiled Steal, happy to see an old ghost from the past who reminded him that he too had a heart, somewhere.

'Enough of the small talk, Steal, what's brought you down here after all these years, because it's not for my sparkling personality and good looks?'

'I miss your grumpy old logic, Tom, but you're right as usual. I need your help to solve a puzzle that has more pieces in it than the puzzle should have.'

'Now that's a puzzle that I'd love to solve,' said Tom.

Steal showed him the empty file with the cryptic note plus his file notes to-date on Jason Kay and all the suspects involved in his murder, including the picture of the mysterious Mr Black.

Flicking through the files, Tom asked, 'What pieces of the puzzle do you want me to find?'

'Who was Jason Kay before he arrived at Hilltop Mansion thirty years ago, because my gut tells me that wasn't his real name, and why would he kill his only friend Jacky Jones at the homeless hostel and then destroy his ID card unless he could identify who the real Jason Kay was and whether he was still alive? And what connection has the man in black got to do with Jason Kay's past?' said Steal.

'I'm sure your team of keen officers upstairs, are already on this, so why ask me to do what they are already doing?'

'Because they're not you, Tom, and because you search where no one else does and somewhere amongst the thousands of files in this hell hole of lost cases that you spend your life flicking through is the answer to the extra pieces of the puzzle that will help me solve the real reason behind the disappearance and murder of Jason Kay?'

'Well, what else is an old man with a limp and no one at home left to love or care for going to do with his time but solve a "killer of a puzzle"?' joked Tom.

Steal smiled at the man who was once more a father to him than his own. Tom added, 'Don't morph into me, Steal. You still have time to let love back into your heart and not end up on the scrap heap of tired old detectives who spent their lives solving other people's problems, leaving nothing over for those waiting at home.'

'Now I know why I only ever come down here every five years, old man. I forgot how annoying you can be when you're trying to deliver a sermon on life,' said Steal with a lump in his throat.

The two men stared at each other with a sadness in their eyes for a friendship and past that neither of them would ever experience again.

Steal walked back down the narrow aisle, leaving his old friend alone with a pile of dusty old files for company.

'Where have you been, Boss?' asked Wright, leaping out of the chair when he returned to his office with the original file from the lake and his file notes.

'Nowhere you'd like to be, unless you wished to get that multi-coloured silk waistcoat of yours covered in cobwebs and dust,' said Steal, smiling at her quirky sense of style.

The note slipped out of the file sent by Black. Steal picked it up before walking out into the main office and pinning it on the crime board next to the crossed-out blank face of the man in the black hat. 'This note was delivered inside the empty file late last night after the search team pulled it out of the lake in the park opposite Kay Corporation.'

'Was that the file Kay pictured being thrown into the lake on his mobile, Boss?' asked Rita, slipping out from behind her desk for a closer look.

'Yes, but as we discussed yesterday, I don't believe that Kay took the picture and think that it was this man' — he pointed his finger at the faceless man in black — 'he's the key to unlocking Jason Kay's past so dig deep and wide, team. We need to find him,' ordered Steal, returning to his office with Wright, who asked, 'What next, Boss?'

'We go back to the one who controls the flow of money and dig deeper,' said Steal, picking up the warrant to search the office and home of the accountant, Timothy Gibbs.

17

Four Months Earlier

Kay walked back through the park to the office, holding the file, with just one thought running through his mind. His mobile rang. 'Did you hear from the blackmailer?'

'Yes.'

'What did he send you?'

'A file,' replied Kay, stepping into the lift at Kay Corporation and pressing the button to the top floor.

'What was in the file?'

'Nothing that you need to know about,' said Kay, sitting down at his desk with the file in front of him.

'But I thought we agreed that you wanted me to use whatever he sent you to find him?'

'I've changed my mind and won't be requiring your services any further on this matter, Black.'

'Why?'

'Because I don't pay for failure and you've failed once too often, which can only mean one thing.'

'I wondered how long it would take for you to connect the dots, Alex…' said Black.

'My name is Jason Kay and don't think that we're done, Black. Remember, I know all about you from the file I compiled after our first meeting so you'd better run and run because I want *my money* back and your head with it,' threatened Kay, feeling good at finally outing the blackmailer when he heard the laugh followed by the sting.

'You're not the only person who can change identities, Alex. Did you think that I was just going to walk into your life as *me*? The file you have on Mr Black is worthless. He's as dead as all the other innocent victims in that file you have on your desk. So, good luck searching for a ghost.'

'Who the fuck are you?' demanded Kay, standing up and looking out of window to see who was spying on him from one of the hundreds of tower blocks overlooking the city.

'I'm not the blackmailer, but I know him well and you won't find him or me until we want you too.'

'This was never about money, was it?'

'The dead don't need money, Alex, but to rest easy in their graves they do need *revenge*,' said Black, hanging up and leaving Kay staring down at the file, wondering which ghosts had come back from the dead to haunt him.

John Wilding stood at his hotel window on the penthouse floor, watching Kay pacing his office through the high-definition binoculars.

He had a perfect view of Kay's office from his grand penthouse suite, plus the park beneath where Kay sat on the bench with the file, and so knew the exact moment when to ring him on his mobile.

Placing the binoculars on the sideboard by the bed, Wilding called the other ghost from the past. 'He knows about us.'

'Good. We knew that he wouldn't pay the whole one million once he had worked out that we wanted more than just the money and he had no other option but to cut and run, taking the remaining five hundred thousand pounds that Gibbs was stealing for him.'

'He'll be desperate for the five million now that he's afraid of being exposed.'

'Then it's time that we progress to the final stages of the plan and tempt the greedy spider into the web.'

'Let me know when you start contacting the others.'

'I will, but first we must wait for him to contact me with the offer that he thinks I can't refuse and will save him.'

'Be careful; he'll be even more dangerous, now that he realises he could lose everything.'

'That's what I'm counting on…'

Kay sat in his office, staring at the file when he pressed the redial button on his mobile and Timothy Gibbs answered.

'Jason. What can I do for you?'

'I'm not paying the blackmailer any more money. So if he contacts you, don't respond. I will deal with him myself.'

'Have you found out who he is and what about the five hundred thousand I've already sent him?'

'Not yet, but I will and retrieve the money.'

'So, I don't need to take any more money from the company?'

'I didn't say that. You'll continue to take the £166,666.66 for next three months as planned, only you'll transfer the payments totalling five hundred thousand pounds into my personal bank account instead.'

'But you don't need the money now.'

'Don't tell me what I need, Gibbs, just do it.'

'But I'm taking all the risks here.'

'You're getting paid well to do it and don't forget I'm not a man to double-cross,' threatened Kay, ending the call.

Staring at the file on the desk, Kay smiled as he recalled sitting on the bench in the park, watching the swans glide effortlessly from one side of the lake to the other before disappearing…

With five million from his wife's trust fund secured through the help of Gibbs, Pritchard and Dodd, plus the one million stolen from the company retrieved back from the blackmailer when he would trick him into revealing himself would buy him a very comfortable new life and name far away from a life and world that he once coveted, but now no longer required or needed.

But first, he must gain time to set his plan of escape into motion and so needed to keep the blackmailer and his sidekick Mr Black on the hook until he could work out how to secure the release of the trust fund into his name without actually killing his wife and losing it for good.

Once he's done that, he could safely disappear with six million to kick-start his *third* new life.

Unlocking the desk drawer, Kay pulled out his silver laptop to compose the email that would secure his future and destroy his enemies.

"I'm sure that Mr Black or whatever his name is has already informed you that I'm not playing your game any more and that the threat of you exposing me for whatever crimes you think that I have committed is now defunct, but rest assured, I won't be sitting waiting for you to strike.

Yet, I do admire a good adversary and so make you both a one-time offer of two options that I hope will intrigue your sense of fair play.

After all, you're the blackmailer preaching a higher moral code in defence of your criminal actions and so should accept my offer in the spirit of fair play, unless you're just another greedy crook seeking easy money."

Pressing the send button, Kay flicked through the file on his desk again, curious at why the blackmailer had sent him a file containing pictures and details of what he had already paid for when he was expecting a new revelation for his last instalment of £166, 666, 66...?

Wondering if he had overplayed his hand with the blackmailer and Mr Black, Kay suddenly felt afraid... when his inbox pinged.

"Hello again, Alex. I must confess that I am intrigued by your email and wording of 'fair play' from a man devoid of any moral code whatsoever, but am prepared to listen to your two offers before making my decision on your final future."

Reading the reply, Kay wanted to reach inside the laptop and rip the blackmailer's throat out, but the bait was set and hook thrown into the water and now all he had to do was wait for the enemy to bite.

"I'm glad that you appear to be a crook with honour and so here are the two options offered to you:

(A) Pay back the five hundred thousand pounds you've already stolen from me and walk away still alive, or

(B) Call a truce for the remaining three months while I wind up Kay Corporation and settle my affairs at home, including making arrangements to divorce my wife. Once I've done that, then we can arrange a meeting with both you and your co-conspirator Mr Black out in the open with other people in sight e.g. the park opposite the office so that I can see my enemies face-to-face before the truce is off and the best man wins."

Pressing the send button, Kay didn't have to wait long for the reply.

"Hi, Alex, I must confess that I was a little surprised at option (A). I mean, really, threatening to kill a ghost... But option (B) does appeal. After all, I've waited a long time to see the face of the man who turned me into a ghost and so, yes, we have an agreement, but only if I set the date and time for the meeting in the park? After all, a person can't be

too careful and I wouldn't want you to hold all the cards in the game, but in the spirit of good will and if you were to accept my slight, but obvious, amendment to option (B), then I will forward you the next chapter in your real life-story that was omitted from the file on your desk."

Reading the blackmailer's reply, Kay typed, *"Why send me an incomplete file if you know everything about me and why not include what I've already paid for and then claim that it's free of charge?"*

"Because I enjoy playing games with you, Alex; just like you revelled in playing games with all your victims before you discarded them without mercy. Did you think that I was going to play fair when you never have...?"

"Then how can I trust you to abide by our new agreement if you're just another crook without honour?" replied Kay, furious at being taken for a fool.

The blackmailer replied, *"Because I'm willing to trust a crook and killer without honour and so that makes the game an even playing field."*

Reading the reply, Kay realised that the blackmailer and Mr Black were far more devious and smarter than he had originally anticipated and that agreeing to leave the time and date of the meeting to the opponents threatened his plan to eliminate both of them in one shot. But his ego at always winning was bigger than his fear, plus the desire to know what the last payment of £166,666.66 had bought him and how much the blackmailer really knew about the real Alex Trent was too tempting to resist.

Typing the word *"Agreed"*, Kay pressed the send button, knowing that there was no turning back now.

The inbox pinged and the *latest chapter* in the life of Alex Trent alias Jason Kay unfolded in black and white.

The Funeral

The black clouds opened up, releasing a torrent of rain down upon the mourners while the local vicar, Reverend Smyth, said his usual last words of how loved, well-respected and liked the deceased lying cold in the coffin was when alive.

Glancing around Treetop Village's local church graveyard, filled with hundreds of graves marked with an assortment of tombstones engraved with loving words for the deceased, Simon Dodd wondered how many of those words edged in the tombstones were true.

Watching the rain crashing down upon his father's coffin, Simon couldn't help thinking that even in death, James Dodd managed to escape the storm, leaving him behind in the middle of it. The rain suddenly stopped and the vicar ended his sermon with the words "may he rest in peace".

Stepping forward and throwing down a handful of earth upon the coffin surrounded in a pool of water, Simon glanced across his father's grave to see Anne standing nervously beside her husband. The skies opened up again and the rain poured down. The mourners quickly abandoned the floating grave of James Dodd for the warmth and safety of the local church hall and the grand free farewell luncheon.

While the food and drink flowed in abundance, Simon had to endure listening to the endless platitudes about how his father was more than just the local solicitor and how they hoped that his son would carry on the huge mantle James Dodd had left behind when Jason Kay raised his wine glass towards Simon and smiled.

Two Weeks Earlier

Pacing the floor in the study at James Dodd's home, Kay yelled, 'You've had two years to find out where Reginald Price hid the money and all I hear from you is nothing…'

'I'm doing my best, Jason, but wherever Reginald hid the money it's not in a place that was connected to any of his business dealings or any other companies or financial institutes that I've come across in the past as his solicitor,' pleaded Dodd, cowering in the chair behind his desk.

'You keep saying the same old rubbish whilst I'm paying you a fortune for work that any idiot solicitor could do.'

'But that was the agreement. It's costing me a lot of time and money searching for the missing five million and I've lost many long-established good-paying clients because I haven't got the time to deal with their complicated affairs properly.'

'What about your pathetic son, Simon; can't he deal with your "other clients"?'

'Leave Simon out of this, he's my son not yours, and I'll decide what's best for him and his future, not you,' countered Dodd, angry at the way Kay always belittled everything Simon did.

'You dare to fucking tell me what I can or can't do or say,' stormed Kay, grabbing the whisky bottle from the drinks cabinet in the corner and downing two shots straight from the bottle. 'I'm the one that gives the orders and you've got one week to find the money or else, your son will pay the price for your failure!'

'Don't you dare touch Simon!' shouted Dodd, standing up and slamming his fists down upon the desk when he felt a sudden dagger-like pain piercing into his heart before collapsing over the desk, clutching his chest. He pleaded, 'Help me, Jason, help me…'

Pouring a triple shot of whisky from the bottle into a large glass from the cabinet, Kay slowly drank the whisky whilst savouring every single plea for help… He'd reached the last drop by the time James Dodd begged no more…

Wiping his prints off the half-empty bottle and glass, Kay placed them back inside the cabinet before coldly walking out of the house and driving home, thinking, *Time for the useless son to start earning his keep.*

Reading the email, Kay couldn't fathom how the blackmailer knew that he was with James Dodd the night he died.

There were no cameras installed inside James Dodd's house and grounds all those years ago. The old man was too mean to pay for them and it was only when Simon moved into the house six months later after inheriting it and the business that the security was updated.

Tapping his fingers on the laptop keyboard, Kay couldn't resist asking the question when he typed, *"How did you know about that night and the funeral two weeks later?"*

Pacing the floor whilst waiting for the blackmailer's answer, Kay began to wonder if he really was a ghost from the past come back from the dead to punish him. The inbox pinged.

"Hi, Alex, and the answer to your question is ghosts see and hear everything, so be warned; you can't kill a ghost twice. But a ghost can kill you..."

Closing the laptop and smashing his fists down on top of it, causing a dent, Kay could feel the rage burning inside him like a volcano about to erupt when the answer suddenly became clear and he opened the laptop again.

"You're no fucking ghost, but I did make one mistake that night. I forgot about the bloody tape-recorder Dodd hid in the bottom drawer of his desk at the office to record any conversations that he had with clients that he thought might lead to legal problems later. He must have taken the tape home with him that night for our meeting, knowing that he might need it to use against me. But how did you get hold of it after all these years, because it couldn't have been from that moron of a son Simon; otherwise, he would have used the tape years ago to get out of my clutches and it still doesn't explain how you knew all about the funeral and luncheon later?"

"What a pity that you didn't think about the tape all those years ago as you watched James Dodd slowly die in cold blood when you could have saved him, but to answer your question, I didn't get the tape from Simon and I'm afraid you will have to wait a little longer before I tell you how I know everything about your past, present and future, Alex.'

Fuming at the blackmailer's constant game of riddles, Kay typed, *"I didn't kill the old bastard; he'd just outlived his usefulness and as for you deciding what I should and shouldn't know, enjoy the moment while you still can."*

"I will and I look forward to watching you beg for the mercy that you didn't give to Freddy Wilding, Jacky Jones, Reginald Price, James Dodd and... when they all begged you for their lives."

18
The Blackmailer

The blackmailer sat at the computer in the dimly lit room with his face hidden beneath a black hooded sweatshirt. Signing off the email with the last words *"When they all begged you for their lives..."* he sank back into the high-backed black leather chair and pressed the redial button on his mobile. 'He knows about James Dodd's tape recorder, John, but not the funeral.'

'Then the plan is moving towards its end,' said John, pleased to receive the call that he was waiting for.

'Now we move onto the next stage.'

'Who will you contact on the list first?'

'The back-up man and once he's in the loop, then we move onto the others and I will let you know who to call upon next.'

'Good, until then, be careful.'

'You too, my friend, and have a drink for me.'

'I will,' said John, signalling the barman at the hotel bar to refill his empty whisky glass.

Leaning forward onto the steel-legged black plastic-topped table, the man called up the email address on his computer then typed, *"Hello, Timothy, I write to confirm that my agreement with your employer Jason Kay has now changed and that he will no longer pay me the last three instalments of £166,666.66, which he has stated you have been informed about, but it's now the time to choose sides, Timothy...*

When you sent me the message that you understood what it was like to be his victim and offered to help bring him down immediately after making the first instalment of £166,666.66, I was suspicious that he had put you up to it in order to trap me, but now I see that you were and still are a good man searching for a way to repent your criminal actions on behalf of a man that drew you into his dark world of greed and corruption, unaware that for every penny you stole from the company at his instruction created another victim of loss at the other end... You were always going to be an integral part of my plan, Timothy, even before your offer of help, but now I'm giving you the chance to choose to do what's right and not be his victim any more, but be warned; once you've chosen your side, there's no turning back."

Reading the email, the blackmailer's fingers trembled before he pressed the send button. He didn't want to force Timothy Gibbs to help him, which was the original plan, before he offered his services; but sometimes, to do a good thing, first you have to do a bad thing.

The inbox pinged with the reply, *"I'm in all the way to end, no matter what the price..."*

"Welcome aboard the team, Timothy, and I will be in contact soon with further instructions. Until then, please be extra vigilant and watch your back because he will be watching it too."

Swinging the chair around, the blackmailer surveyed the single-spaced room that had become both his prison and seat of power for the last year.

With its claustrophobic steel grey soundproof walls, no windows, low-hanging lights, tiny single-mattress bed with stained bedsheets in the corner, two cloth rails filled with identical outfits with a mirror hanging off the rails and a makeshift single bowl sink underneath, free-standing fridge-freezer, microwave, radio, and six floor-to-ceiling storage shelves loaded with box files and computer equipment, the grey single-sized garage metal storage unit hidden amongst hundreds of other grey storage units was the perfect place to be invisible... but also the loneliest.

The only people that ever came to the isolated piece of land filled with hundreds of steel containers located on the outskirts of the city were the security guards doing their regular rounds every hour on the half-hour day and night, plus the ad-hock flow of short and long-term hirers.

The guards had become used to seeing unusual hirers come and go over the years, but had never seen one that chose to make one of the soulless steel units packed together in the place they nicknamed "No Man's Land" their home.

When he paid triple the amount of the fee up front in cash for a two-year hire of the single unit, plus the same again for another unit next door, the manager asked no questions and so the guards asked no questions even when every morning at precisely eight a.m., he walked into the steel erected office and placed a hundred pounds in cash on the table before pulling up the security footage of the previous twenty-four hours and wiping it clean.

None of the guards could describe the nameless man that lived in Unit 82 and kept his car next door at number 83.

Dressed in a black hooded sweatshirt, joggers, trainers, gloves and wearing large dark sunglasses no matter what the weather, they didn't give a fuck who he was or where he came from, just that each day, the four guards took it in turns to pick up the hundred pounds in cash left on the table.

Walking over to sink, the blackmailer picked up a bucket of cold water by the side and poured half into the sink. Pulling back the hood from his head, he submerged his face into the ice-cold water, bringing his tired eyes back to life again.

Lifting his face up from the water, he wiped it dry with the tatty towel hanging on the hook stuck on the side of the sink. Straightening his back, he stared into the mirror, wondering who he would have become if Alex Trent hadn't stolen his name and life thirty years earlier.

The man in the mirror was a ghost come back from the dead… only this ghost never died, but the man whose name he took in order to live, did.

The forty-five-year-old face in the mirror could be almost handsome if it wasn't for the dark rings and wrinkles around the lifeless grey/black eyes that matched his shaven peppered-grey hair and pale grey face. When you spend your life living in the shadows, you become that shadow.

Opening the fridge door, he pulled out an ice-cold bottle of lager before leaning back into the high-backed black leather and closing his eyes. The ghosts of the past visited him again…

Thirty Years Earlier

Waking up under the railway bridge, the hungry, cold and desperate fifteen-year-old teenager looked around at the other faceless, nameless tramps sheltering from the cruel world outside and wondered if this was going to be the rest of his life.

With no home, parents, family and name, he had no future, unless he went back to claim it.

Crawling out from under the bridge, he began the ten-mile walk back to the last place he had a name, when, just as he turned into the alleyway, he recognised the face of the youth walking out of the hostel clutching an ID card in his hand.

Hiding in the shadows of the alleyway, he watched the youth throw the card into the rubbish bin. He slipped back into the street and hid inside the doorway of the pawn shop opposite the alleyway, where he waited until the youth disappeared into the crowded shopping street before returning to the alleyway and climbing into the bin to retrieve his name and future, only to discover that the name on the ID card wasn't his.

Taking the ID card, he returned to the only place he knew; the railway line, where he stayed for the next five days and nights, eating whatever crumbs the other homeless tramps threw him until the sixth morning when he woke to see a tall, thin man in his early fifties with a bald head, pale thin face, withered blue eyes set deep in a circle of dark wrinkles and wearing a long grey raincoat standing over him.

'I've been watching you for the last five days and nights and wondered if you were interested in a proposition?' the man asked.

'I'm not for sale, so go away and leave me to die in peace.'

'I'm not here for your body, but would ask you another question before you turn down my proposal.'

'What question?'

'Do you want to *live dying* or *die living*?' the man asked, glancing around at the half-dead tramps huddled together under the bridge.

The boy replied, 'Die living.'

'Then come with me and I will teach you things that you'll never learn here and give you a future that you never dreamed possible. A home with food on the table every day and more money than you ever could have imagined earning, but be warned, the price for your new future will be a lonely life filled with lies and more lies in order to protect the innocent and punish the guilty. A life lived within the Shadows.'

Looking around at the *living dead,* the boy reached inside his coat pocket and held out the ID card retrieved from the bin when the man bent down and pulled him up off the ground and smiled. He said, 'Welcome to the World of Shadows, *Jacky Jones.'*

The tall man in the raincoat died five years ago after working in the Shadows for forty-five years, but his legacy lived on through the forgotten homeless boy he rescued from under the railway bridge. He left him everything in his estate, including a large three-bedroom detached house, £750,000 in savings and a letter giving him complete control of the invisible covert organisation hidden deep within the Shadows of the police force, known only to a trusted few as, "The Department".

Set-up from the money the man had stolen from his own wealthy criminal father before he died from a bullet to the head by an unknown assassin, The Department didn't exist in the normal world of law and order, and therefore, the rules of justice used within it didn't either.

Mr A (short for Alexander Forbes) taught Jacky everything about the world of living and working within the Shadows before he died. The Shadows is a lonely and often dark place of deception and lies... It's a place where the few that work within it spy upon the lives of both the innocent and the guilty in order to bring justice to the criminals that hide within the "Shadows of the Law".

If you have a secret, The Department will find it out. If you prey upon the lonely and afraid, The Department will punish you. If you escaped justice by corrupting the law, The Department will correct that and if you killed another innocent human being for your own evil gain, then The Department will avenge that death.

Opening his eyes and taking another mouthful of lager, the real *Jason Kay* could hear the ghost of *Jacky Jones* inside his head, begging him for forgiveness at betraying their friendship by stealing his name and future and giving it away to a stranger.

Part of him had already forgiven Jacky because his death afforded him the chance of a new identity and life that would never have been possible had he remained Jason Kay.

But the other part couldn't until Alex Trent had been brought to justice for killing Jacky just because he was a "loose end" and tainting the name of *Jason Kay* with the blood of so many innocent victims.

Jacky never told Mr A about the man he saw in the alleyway thirty years ago, because he was ashamed to admit that he'd stolen his friend's identity and used it to start the new life Mr A offered him, but when his friend and mentor told him that he had only months left to live and was leaving him everything in his estate because he'd grown to love him like the son he never had, Jacky couldn't lie any more; otherwise, he was no better than the criminals they sought to bring to justice.

After hearing Jacky's confession, Mr A smiled and said, 'You're a better man than Jacky Jones would have been if he lived and kept his name, just as I have tried to be a better man than my father was by keeping his name and using it to right his wrongs.' Hesitatingly, he confessed, 'I've known about who you really are, Jason, for a long time, but chose to keep it from you for selfish reasons, which I now realise was wrong and I hope that you can forgive me one day. But I did it because I didn't want to risk losing you once you reclaimed your name and identity back.'

Collecting a file from the safe hidden in the wall inside the wardrobe located in the bedroom at his house, Mr A handed it to Jacky and said, 'If you wish to find this man, then I will do everything in my power to help you before I die and whatever you decide to do with him will be your choice. You have lived in my house since the day I found you under the railway bridge and worked with me every day since that day in the basement where I set up and ran The Department. You are the son I would have had if I'd married and lived a normal life, but I can no longer hold you to a life that I selfishly locked you into because it made a lonely old man happy to have someone to love and share his life with.'

Stood in the middle of the basement, Mr A stared at Jacky for a what seemed a lifetime, then confessed his darkest secret, 'I shot my father in cold blood with one bullet to the head while he begged on his knees for mercy. But what mercy had he shown to all the innocent people he had ordered his men to kill, including my partner and best friend Sergeant Mick Dooley, because he couldn't be bought. After that day, I resigned from the force that I loved and made a vow to never let the rules of law and order be used to fail the innocent and let the guilty go free.'

Walking up the stairs to the house, Mr A turned round at the top of the basement and smiled down at Jacky when he said, 'Now you know who I really am and what I've done and what you choose to do with that information is now up to you, my son.'

Finishing the lager, Jacky pulled out the file Mr A gave him five years ago from underneath the laptop on his desk and read the note inside. *"If you have received this file, then I am already dead. My name is Reginald Price and inside is the story of the man that stole your name and life. Read it and if you want justice, then ring this number…"*

After Mr A's confessions, Jacky went away for a short while with the file.

Reading about Alex Trent over and over again, then picturing Mr A's tortured face when he confessed killing his father and using his tainted money to set up The Department, Jacky suddenly realised that he didn't choose his name or life, but that life had chosen it for him… just like Mr A didn't choose to have a father who valued money more than people's lives.

No new life chooses to be born into the world. They don't choose who their parents are and they don't choose the name that their parents give them, but like Mr A, when life forces them to make a choice, then that's when they discover who they really are.

Returning home, Jacky put the file away until the day came when he held Mr A's hand before he died in his own bed at home six months later.

Standing alone over Mr A's grave with a copy of the file three weeks later, Jacky knew that God had forgiven him for his sins because he had already served a life sentence for killing his father by living in the shadows of the law for forty-five years.

Remembering the old man's final words to him on his deathbed, when he made the orphan boy he took in, promise not to waste his life living in the Shadows like him, Jacky buried the file deep in the freshly dug earth above the grave. He swore to bring Alex Trent to justice before fulfilling his promise to the old man he loved like a father to pass the mantle of The Department onto another before moving out of the Shadows into the light and whatever new chapter life had decided for him.

Throwing the empty lager bottle into the trash bin with all the other bottles, Jacky looked around the steel cage he had lived in for the past year again, then smiled at the thought that in just over three months' time, he will lock it up for the very last time and hand the keys back.

It had been five years since he dialled the number Reginald Price wrote on the note in the file when John William answered and the two men began their final journey together to bring Alex Trent to justice.

Three names, three ghosts; one dead, two alive.

Jacky Jones, Alex Trent, Jason Kay.

Soon, Alex Trent would be face-to-face with his other self, Jason Kay, and all the ghosts from the past both alive and dead will finally be put to rest.

Three names, three ghosts; two dead, one alive.

Pressing the redial button on his mobile, Jacky set the final phase of the plan in motion when the man he secretly hoped would be his replacement asked, 'Is it time?'

'It is. The meeting will be in the park opposite the office. I will let you know the time and date soon. He will be prepared, but this time, he won't win.'

'Is Mr Black sure that he will be using the same man?'

'He's been watching Alex Trent's every move and has sent me a picture of the man Trent uses for his "other" jobs,' said Jacky, forwarding it to him from his mobile.

The man confirmed, 'It's him.'

'Once this is over, I have another proposition for you, but be warned, it will require you living and working in the shadows of the law.'

'What other type of work would a man like me do?'

'I look forward to showing you your new venture when this job is done.'

'I won't fail you.'

'I know,' said Jacky, disconnecting the call. He felt a strange sensation pass through him… Hope!

Hopefully, it's not too late to fall in love and have a family of his own and maybe that family will love the real him, whoever that may be. But in the meantime, he had one last job to finish.

For the last thirty years, The Department had spread its net far and wide from the tiny basement of Mr A's house.

The dark web is a cold, calculating place where criminals hide and prey upon their victims without mercy… but if you know how to infiltrate that web and use their own technology to bring them down, then that is what the gods call karma.

The Department may have been born in the tiny basement of Mr A's house, but its tentacles have spread across the world, including the very core of the police force and Lunsford.

Jason Kay hadn't disappeared yet, but when he would, Jacky had already calculated that Inspector Steal would be allocated the case.

When the wealthy owner of Kay Corporation suddenly went missing, Lunsford Headquarters would have no option but to allocate his case to their best detective on the force, Inspector Steal.

Steal was well-known for leaving no stone unturned in his determination to solve every case that he took on and it was that determination Jacky and John Wilding were gambling everything upon.

Through his contact at Lunsford, John Wilding knew everything about Inspector Steal and how he worked a case.

Just like a game of chess, if you can anticipate your opponent's every move before they play it, then you control how the game ends.

Every move that Inspector Steal and his partner Sergeant Wright would make in the investigation of the disappearance and possible murder of Jason Kay had already been carefully calculated and planned.

A good detective follows the evidence and clues they unearth in their investigation, but if the trail of evidence and clues has already been laid out, then there can be only one conclusion.

Jacky didn't feel good about using Steal and Wright as pawns in his game of chess to bring Alex Trent to justice, but if he was to save Anne and everyone else who had helped him and John in their quest for final justice, then so it must be…

Pressing the redial button on the mobile, Jacky called his friend and co-conspirator. 'I've just spoken to the "back-up" who has confirmed that the picture you sent is the same man.'

'Good. Then we will be ready.'

'I will come back to you shortly with details of the meetings.'

'Excellent. It will be good to finally be free of this bloody hat,' said John, staring at his reflection in the bar mirror, praying that if all went to plan, then he can finally discard Mr Black from his life for good and return home as John Wilding.

Flicking through his list of contacts, Jacky moved onto the next stage of the plan when he typed a text message to his source at Lunsford. *"The trap has been set and the bait taken. Are you still in?"*

Pressing the send button, Jacky waited for the reply with a nervous uncertainty.

Over the years, The Department had bought many a source in the police force for the right price… but when John William approached the one that would be a key player in their game of chess with Inspector Steal, it wasn't money that bought their services, but closure.

Tapping his fingers on the mobile, Jacky waited… and waited… until, finally, the source answered, *"I am."*

Relieved, Jacky replied, *"I will let you know when the game has begun."*

Having secured the source, Jacky must now secure the "money trap" if he was to lure Alex Trent into the spider's web before swallowing him up.

Flicking through the file again, Jacky gave a little smile.

When he first read the file about Alex Trent, it was like reading the devil's book containing all his darkest crimes and secrets, but now the file had become his Bible; for what better way to destroy the devil than by using his own book of secrets against him!

Using the dark web, Jacky emailed the money man. *"Hello, Mr Caine, it's been a while since our last communication, but now I write to inform you that the time has come for you to finally have the opportunity to fulfil your contract to your deceased client, Reginald Price, and release the five million, plus interest, to his daughter, Anne. But I must also warn you that the plan John Wilding and I have instigated to achieve this aim will involve using the money to snare Mr Price's killer and Ann's husband, Jason Kay... I realise that you are under no obligation to assist us in this endeavour, but would point out that you have been guarding Anne's money for the last sixteen years and that this could be the last opportunity for you to honour your obligation to her father before it's too late."*

Sending the email, Jacky knew that without Mr Caine's collaboration, the entire plan would collapse. Five million is a lot money and can corrupt even the most honourable of men, but to the money man, five million was small change in a business where his clients dealt in *billions*.

Waiting for the reply, Jacky pressed the play button on the radio by the computer and listened to the song "Sleepy Waters".

Closing his eyes, he imagined sitting on a bench at the seaside, watching the clear blue water gently flowing in the sea while the sun set slowly down upon it. The inbox pinged and he opened his eyes to the darkness again. He read:

"You are correct in your assumption, Jacky, that I have no obligation to assist you in your quest for justice. My client was Regional Price, not you, but I always try to do at least one good deed a year before I meet my maker. It so transpires that you are in luck because you are this year's good deed, but my services don't come free. My fee for assisting you and Mr Wilding would be the sixteen years' interest on the five million. Agree to my terms, then we have a deal."

Reading the email, Jacky couldn't help laughing. After all, that's what money men do; they take your money, then charge you a bloody fortune when you ask for it back.

Sixteen years' daily interest on five million for doing absolutely nothing... Hell, who wouldn't want to be the money man?

Typing, *"I accept your terms and will be in contact with details soon,"* Jacky then sent another email to the accountant, Anthony Gibbs, confirming that he had secured an avenue to Anne's five million trust fund and will be in contact with further instructions as to his part in the plan.

Pressing the send button, Jacky gave a huge sigh of relief at having secured the collaboration of the first *four* names listed in John Wilding and his plan to destroy Jason Kay/Alex Trent.

The back-up man

Police source

Money man

The accountant

Ticking their names off the list, he counted *seven* more to go. But to secure the next one on the list would require a personal visit from Mr Black.

Pressing the redial button on his mobile, Jacky confirmed, 'It's time to bring in the doctor.'

'I take it that the bait is set in stone,' said John, flicking through the lunch menu at the hotel whilst scratching his head underneath the hat. He'd love to take the damn thing off whilst eating lunch, but Jason Kay had spies everywhere.

'It is and when you call upon Dr Pritchard, remind him of his promise to his late friends Regional Price and James Dodd to protect Anne and the trust fund until her husband is no longer a threat. Then he will be free to use his position as her doctor to trap Kay into the net. Once he's done that, then he can bring the solicitor, Simon Dodd, into the loop, leaving the last five on the list when it will be time...' said Jacky, adding, 'Then you can eat your lunch without scratching your head.' He laughed at the sound of John's noisy finger nails digging into his hair.

'Says the man who lives in a steel shed,' joked John, flicking his fingers at the wine waiter, while Jacky pulled up his hood and locked up the shed before walking two miles to the burger café by the petrol station on the main road to celebrate the *beginning-of-the-end* by ordering one king-sized burger, large fries, coffee and apple pie for dessert.

19

Steal and Wright arrived at the home of Anthony Gibbs with their usual army of officers to find him waiting at the door.

'I see news travels fast in the world of high finance,' said Steal, handing him the warrant.

'When my office in the city is invaded by dozens of your men ripping it apart, then obviously my secretary wastes no time informing me,' said Gibbs, showing the detectives through to the study as the search party went through his house like a tornado.

Sitting at his desk, Gibbs stared at the detectives with a still calmness that unnerved Steal.

He asked, 'Can you explain why you have been systematically stealing large amounts of money from Kay Corporation for years including five hundred thousand in the last six months, Mr Gibbs?'

'Yes, Inspector,' replied Gibbs, not bothering to deny Steal's accusations.

'You realise that by admitting your fraudulent activities, your firm Gibbs & Forbes, of which you're are a senior partner, will be closed down and a full investigation and audit of all yours and the company's financial dealings instigated, culminating in you being disbarred from your profession as an accountant and ultimately being charged and sentenced to a substantial prison sentence once convicted,' said Steal, waiting for Gibbs to show some sign of emotion.

Looking up at the picture of his wife Sandra on the wall, Gibbs calmly stood up and handed Steal a file from on top of his desk. 'I think you will find everything you need to know in here, Inspector,' he said, sitting down and staring back up at his wife.

Wright noted, 'She has a lovely smile.'

'Yes, she did,' said Gibbs, holding back the tears.

Wright said, 'What would she think of you now, Mr Gibbs?'

'I will have to wait until I see her again, Sergeant, before I could answer your question,' said Gibbs with a dark sadness in his eyes that Wright had only ever seen once before.

Flicking through the file, Steal noted that it contained the *real accounts* for Kay Corporation before passing it over to Wright.

He asked, 'Why are you giving us the evidence to convict you now, Mr Gibbs?'

'Because I'm tired of all the lies and secrets, Inspector, and because I no longer have to any more,' said Gibbs.

'Did you kill your client Jason Kay because he discovered what you were doing or because he was going to disappear with all the money and leave you to take the blame?' asked Steal.

'I'm a thief and a coward, Inspector, but I'm not a murderer. Once Kay went missing, I knew that it was only a matter of time before the truth about the money would come out. Jason Kay persuaded me to embezzle the money from the company and shareholders for him. He was a man who liked to live like a king, and didn't care how he treated his subjects in order to be that king, but I took his thirty pieces of silver thinking that it would give me what I thought was missing from my life. All it did was destroy my life... and so now, I have nothing left to lose, Inspector.'

Reading the file, Wright asked, 'I note from the accounts that the sum of £166,666.66 was paid every month for three months into an untraceable account and not Mr Kay's. Where did the five hundred thousand pounds you stole go, Mr Gibbs, if not to you?'

'I'm afraid I don't know, Sergeant. Mr Kay instructed me to pay the money to the account each month and so that's what I did. He never said what the money was for or who it went to and I never asked because he wasn't the kind of man you questioned.'

'So you're telling us that you stole all that money for Mr Kay and never wondered what he was doing with it or even attempt to find out who the account he supposedly instructed you to transfer the money into belonged to?' interjected Steal.

'Yes, Inspector, I am, and I don't expect you to believe me, but you can turn my whole life inside-out and won't find a penny of all that money that Jason Kay stole from the company he persuaded Reginald

Price to give him. Kay was a very bad man, Detectives, who took whatever he wanted and if you didn't do what he asked, then he had ways of persuading you,' said Gibbs.

'But he paid you for your services?' interjected Wright.

'You're correct, Sergeant, but there comes a point when the thirty pieces of silver become worthless.'

'Is that when you killed him, Mr Gibbs?' asked Steal, again.

'I'm a weak and cowardly man, but I'm not an evil man like Kay was and I couldn't kill another human being, not even a man like him, Inspector.'

'And you expect us to believe that you didn't kill the man that you have just confessed ruined your life?' said Steal, still trying to figure out why Gibbs was effectively handing him the evidence to arrest him when he could have just destroyed the file and blame Kay for everything because a dead man couldn't deny it.

'I don't expect anything, Inspector, except to be punished for the crime of betraying the trust my clients placed in me when I stole their money for Kay,' said Gibbs without a flicker of fear at the prospect of losing both his reputation and freedom.

'Do you fear the death sentence, Mr Gibbs, because your confession here today together with the evidence you've so calmly volunteered to give us make you our prime suspect in the murder of your client Jason Kay?' said Steal, not believing for one second that Gibbs was capable of killing Kay, but a hundred per cent certain that he knew who did.

'I died a long time ago, Inspector,' said Gibbs, looking at the picture of Sandra again.

Wright added, 'Just because you've confessed your sins and aren't afraid to die, Mr Gibbs, doesn't mean that she will welcome you back.'

'I know, Sergeant, but I've nothing left except the *hope* that she might...' said Gibbs, with that same dark sadness in his eyes that Wright and *now* Steal recognised.

The Inspector cautioned the suspect before signalling to one of the officers to arrest and handcuff him on charges of embezzlement and fraud and the suspected murder of Jason Kay.

Watching Anthony Gibbs being handcuffed and taken out to the police van, Steal and Wright felt an uneasy sense of victory about his confession.

'Do you believe him when he says that he didn't kill Jason Kay, Boss?' asked Wright, still trying to get the picture of Gibbs' eyes out of her head.

'Yes, Sergeant, but there's something missing here that I just can't see. It's almost as if I'm watching myself playing me and yet I'm not me because I don't feel in control,' said Steal.

Wright jumped in, 'I know, Boss, I feel the same. It's like we're playing the parts of ourselves in a film about a crime we've solved and yet the script that we've been given reads the same, but doesn't make sense because the clues we followed to solve the crime aren't right.'

'That's it! You've hit it on the nail, Sergeant,' said Steal, walking over to Anthony Gibbs sat in the back of the police van with Wright behind.

'I know what your game is, Mr Gibbs, but it won't work because, somewhere, either you or one of your co-conspirators have made a mistake and when I uncover that mistake, then I'll find Jason Kay's body and the real killer.'

'I have no idea what you are talking about, Inspector,' said Gibbs, turning his face away and staring into nothing. The police van drove off back to Lunsford.

'What do mean by the "mistake", Boss?' asked Wright, even more confused than before.

'This case was never about the police finding Jason Kay, but about uncovering who he really was and letting the world know, but in order to do that there has to be an arrest; otherwise, the case can't be officially closed without a body or a reason. Anthony Gibbs is a tortured man who wants to be punished, even if it's for a murder he didn't commit. Therefore, he's the perfect *martyr* in a crime that was never meant to be solved. But with a signed confession by Gibbs, it will be filed under "case closed, body never found",' said Steal.

'But why doesn't Gibbs just confess to killing Kay and tell us where the body is hidden whilst revealing his double life? Why hide the body at all?' asked Wright, still confused.

'Because without a body, we can't prove who actually killed him and his wife becomes the grieving widow once her husband's reputation has been destroyed, plus she is free of the man who kept her a prisoner in her own home for sixteen years, and without an actual dead body, her missing husband can't be legally declared dead, which means that she technically gets control of everything, including all the money her husband had been stealing from the company for years,' surmised Steal.

'But there is *no* money! We've checked all Jason Kay's bank accounts and now Gibbs' and there's no trace of where it went and I don't believe that Anne Kay was aware of what her husband was doing all those years and so wouldn't know where he hid the money,' said Wright.

'That's what Gibbs wants us to believe and with his "conveniently timed confession" and no trace of Jason Kay's money trail to tell us where it all went, then the powers to be upstairs will be more than happy to stamp the case *solved*. They have an arrest and confession, plus Kay's reputation as an "upright citizen" in tatters, so nobody will give a fuck about where his body or the money is and Gibbs will no doubt have a good lawyer who'll get the jury's sympathy on his side, and so will get the punishment he's been seeking for being a cowardly thief, and be out of prison in just a few years because the man he killed was a monster and he was just another one of his victims. So, everybody wins. The wife gets her freedom and money and the accountant gets a "get-out-of-jail-early card" for confessing to a murder he never committed and the Big Boss upstairs gets an easy conviction and the press off his back,' said Steal, spitting fire. He added, 'But in every game, there's always the losers, *us*... The detectives who solved the case in a film about their case that was *all one big fat lie!*'

'What are *we* going to do about it, Boss?' Wright asked, furious at how the killers of Jason Kay were using the law and them to effectively "get away with murder".

'Break Anthony Gibbs' story and get to the truth,' said Steal, driving back to Lunsford.

The Confession

Anthony Gibbs stood up against the wall as the camera clicked when the station custody sergeant took his picture.

How far he had fallen in such a short time!

He had lost a loving wife, a career he once felt proud of. And a family that he never got to have because he chose thirty pieces of silver instead of love. Now, all he had left was an empty shell of a body.

Pressing his fingers on the ink, he looked at the black stains in the squares on the paper and felt an emptiness that only a drowning man without a lifeboat could understand.

Wearing the plain cell clothes of a prisoner, the custody sergeant led him to his temporary single cell located at Lunsford Headquarters and just eight minutes' walk along the long thin corridor to the interview room not far from Inspector Steal's office.

Sat on the wooden seat inside the cell, he waited in silence. The custody sergeant pulled back the hatch on the cell door before unlocking it and escorting him to the interview room, where he sat in silence again, staring at the wall, oblivious to the presence of the police constable standing with his arms crossed in the corner. The door opened and Inspector Steal and Sergeant Wright entered.

Placing the file and other paperwork on the table, Steal checked the tape recorder. Wright sat down next to him, neatly placing her notebook, pen and interview file on the table in front of her.

Four bodies in the room:

One stood in the corner like a stone statue.

Two sat side-by-side, determined to extract the truth

One sat alone, seeking redemption.

Pressing the tape recorder, Steal cautioned the prisoner about his rights. The door opened just then and the lawyer entered the room. 'I didn't request any legal representation,' said Gibbs, staring right through the plump, bald-headed, middle-aged man in a rumpled grey suit.

'I'm your court-appointed lawyer who's been allocated to you because you've declined to give details of your own lawyer and would strongly advice you not to say another word until I have spoken to you in private first, Mr Gibbs,' said the man, coughing nervously into a dirty hanky before putting it back in his pocket.

'I thank you for your advice, but I am happy to answer any questions put to me and so would ask that you kindly leave,' said Gibbs, not even bothering to look at the man who had offered to possibly save him from a charge of first-degree murder.

'But...' said the man, but Gibbs refused his counsel again, including waiving all rights regarding giving his confession. The court-appointed, clearly relieved lawyer, left...

Playing the tape back, Steal listened to Gibbs' refusal of legal counsel again before making a point of instructing Wright to note it down in the interview file for clarity.

Calmly sitting back in the chair, Steal began the interview.

'When you confessed to stealing money from Kay Corporation for your client Mr Jason Kay, you stated that you were paid by him to do it, but have no idea where the money went or what he did with it, Mr Gibbs?'

'That's correct, Inspector,' replied Gibbs, staring right through him.

'You also stated that you didn't kill your client, Mr Jason Kay, but weren't surprised that someone hadn't done it sooner?'

'I did, Inspector,' said Gibbs.

'So for the tape, you are confessing to being a thief and a liar, but not a murderer, Mr Gibbs,' said Steal.

'I confess that I stole money from Kay Corporation for Jason Kay, but that is all I did. I didn't kill Mr Kay and I don't know who did or where his body is. Is that clear enough for your tape, Inspector?' replied Gibbs, turning his head towards the tape recorder.

Sending the single to Wright with his little finger, Steal began a different form of questioning. He asked, 'Are you a good liar, Mr Gibbs?'

Startled, Gibbs replied, 'I don't quite understand your question, Inspector.'

'It's simple enough, Mr Gibbs; for the last five years, you've been stealing money for your client Mr Kay and covering it up with one lie after the other to the shareholders and board members of Kay Corporation; your partners and fellow work colleagues at Gibbs &

Forbes; Mr Kay's wife and now widow, Anne Kay; her Doctor, Dr Pritchard and solicitor, Simon Dodd, and your wife, Sandra Gibbs, who I understand committed suicide in her bath at home where you found her.'

'My wife's suicide has nothing to do with Jason Kay or my confession here today,' said Gibbs, his face collapsing into a guilty mess.

'Are you absolutely sure about that, Mr Gibbs?'

'I loved my wife more than anything else in this world and miss her beautiful presence in my life every single second of each day since her death, so don't dare tarnish her memory with your cruel and stupid questions, Inspector,' countered Gibbs physically shaking in the chair.

'I apologise for upsetting you with regards to you wife's suicide, but to get back to the point of my original question, "Are you a good liar?" What I meant was that once you tell one lie, then you have to tell another to hide the first lie, and then another and another until every word spoken is just another lie...'

'And you'd be an expert in the art of lying, Inspector?' mocked Gibbs.

'I've interviewed, studied and arrested hundreds and hundreds of liars over the years, Mr Gibbs; some of whom have committed the most heinous of crimes and lied to cover them up, and many have even gotten away with murder, until they say that one lie too many, causing all the other lies told before it to collapse down upon them. Then, the truth finally emerges,' said Steal, pausing for a moment before adding, 'you are *not* a good liar, Mr Gibbs. You could lie to the shareholders and board members of Kay Corporation, Mrs Kay, her doctor and solicitor and even your partners at Gibbs & Forbes because you could reason to yourself that they were detached from your life and therefore unaffected by any lies you told them, but you couldn't lie to the one person that was your *whole life*; your wife. She could see through every lie that you told her about how you'd risen from the ashes of a lowly accountant to the senior partner in the firm that didn't even know you existed before Jason Kay by hard work and determination. Every time you told a lie to your wife, a little piece her love for you died inside her, until, eventually, there was none left and so she left.'

'You can't know that!' shouted Gibbs, banging his fists on the table whilst picturing Sandra's empty face staring right through him at the dinner table the night before her suicide when she told him that her life was empty because the man she loved and married no longer existed, and therefore, neither did she.

'You said in your statement that you were "tired of lying", Mr Gibbs, so why not stop lying now and tells us the whole truth about the *real* identity hidden behind the shell of Jason Kay and who killed him and why?'

Gibbs stared across the room with a blankness in his eyes that scared even Steal. Wright stretched her hand across the table and rested it upon his. 'I know that you are a good man, Mr Gibbs, who lost his way, but it's not too late to find your way back to the man that your wife fell in love with and married.'

Looking up at Wright, Gibbs smiled when he asked, 'Can you bring my wife back from the dead, Sergeant?'

Stumbling on her words, she replied, 'No, I can't.'

'Then I repeat my statement. I did *not* kill Jason Kay and have no idea who did or where his body is hidden. I am a thief and a *bad* liar, according to the expert opinion of Inspector Steal, plus a miserable failure as both a husband and man… and for those crimes, I duly accept whatever punishment both the law and whatever god there may be on the other side deems fit to sentence me to.'

Steal's gut instincts told him that Gibbs was holding back the whole truth, but now knew that it would be useless to push him any further because you can't threaten a *martyr*.

Smiling, he couldn't help wondering what was so special about Jason Kay's wife, Anne, that seemingly insignificant men would rather choose to go to prison for the suspected murder of her husband than give her up for committing the crime that he was certain she had committed.

First the estate manager, Eric Finch, wouldn't break down under interview and now the company accountant, Anthony Gibbs; both were lying their heads off for a woman he reasoned they had nothing to gain from by protecting. He could understand the lovelorn lost lover and solicitor, Simon Dodd, lying for her, but not two men who appeared to have no romantic or monetary interest in her whatsoever, except that they both hated her husband Jason Kay for their own reasons and therefore were compliant in his death?

Staring across the table at Gibbs, the inspector instructed Wright to hand the prisoner his written statement whereby he duly signed and dated it. The door opened and Constable Rita Clark entered the room.

Walking over to Steal, she whispered a bit too loudly, 'There is an old man called Tom Millard in your office with a file he said was imperative that you had to see with regards to the disappearance of Jason Kay, Boss.'

Standing up, Steal noted for tape recorder that he and Wright were leaving the room before switching it off and instructing the police constable in the corner to escort the prisoner back to the custody sergeant and his cell.

Leaving the room, Steal turned round for one last look at Gibbs sat at the table as the two men locked eyes. That's when the inspector knew…

Following Rita, Steal and Wright walked back to the main office where everyone was busy trying to look busy. Rita returned to her desk and Steal his office to find his old friend and mentor Tom stood waiting for him with a file in his hand.

Entering the office, Steal instructed Wright to update the team on the current situation and confession of Anthony Gibbs before closing the door and sitting down.

Staring up at Tom, he waited to hear what his old friend had uncovered hidden deep within the dusty files of Lunsford basement that was so important he left the safe sanctuary of the dead for first time in over twenty-five years to visit the very room that he once ruled from as the first black chief inspector of police at Lunsford. The place he promised to never to return again after his partner was killed and him left for dead in broad daylight in the car park opposite Lunsford Headquarters, and where there was a perfect view of the crime scene from his office window every day to remind him of the *secret* that he could not tell anyone, not even Steal, because if he did, then his whole reputation as the first black chief inspector of police at Lunsford would be put under microscope and dissected.

Glancing over at the window, Tom didn't move from the spot where he stood. He literally threw the file across the room onto Steal's desk, then said, 'I've discovered the missing pieces of the puzzle regarding who the real Jason Kay was and why his friend Jacky Jones died at the homeless hostel thirty years ago.'

Opening the file, Steal read Tom's carefully written hand notes accompanied by assorted evidence and statements going back thirty years, beginning with:

1. The mysterious disappearance of Freddy Wilding who had a run-in with an old school associate and client, Alex Trent, one week earlier at the garage where he worked.

2. Followed by Constable John Wilding accusing Alex Trent of being implicit in his son's disappearance one week later at Trent Farm only to come to a dead end when his superior officers wouldn't issue a search warrant for Trent Farm.

3. A mysterious fire broke out at the farm four days later after Constable John Wilding's visit when the entire Trent family, including Alex Trent, his mother and father, younger sister and older brother were burnt to ash in the barn with only tiny fragments of their chard clothes on the bodies left to identity them.

4. Just twenty-four hours later and a few miles away, another unnamed youth was suddenly found dead with no ID card to prove who he was and yet he matched the description of a homeless teenager named **Jacky Jones** who signed in the night before with his friend, **Jason Kay**, who left the hostel just minutes before the body was found, only to turn up a few days later being caught red-handed breaking into Hilltop Mansion by the owner **Reginald Price**.

Closing the file, Steal stared at his old friend and noted, 'So you think that *Jason Kay* was really this *Alex Trent* who, according to the file, had murdered *six* innocent people in cold blood, *four* of which were his own *parents, older brother* and *younger sister*…?'

Trying to hide his trembling hands, Tom answered, 'Not just *six* innocent people, Steal, but *eight*... I think he also killed Reginald Price because he discovered the truth and then Simon Dodd's father, James Dodd, because he no longer wanted to be Trent's victim.'

'How did you uncover all this information when my entire team couldn't?' asked Steal, watching his old friend's hands and suspecting that he was lying, because he too was a *bad* liar, especially to him. The one man who trusted him the most, and yet here Tom was spinning a lie within a truth to cover up what the real truth was.

Just when Tom was about to the answer, the telephone rang on Steal's desk. He picked it up and yelled, 'What is it. I'm busy conducting an investigation.'

'This is your boss, Chief Superintendent Phelps, Steal,' said the man at the other end of the line.

The Inspector spluttered out a half-attempted apology.

'Enough of your futile attempts at being apologetic, Steal; I'm ringing to inform you that I know about the recent arrest and confession of your prime suspect, Anthony Gibbs, with regard to the disappearance and murder of the prominent businessman Jason Kay, including the recently uncovered new evidence that he was really a serial killer named *Alex Trent.*'

'But I haven't had a chance to complete my investigation yet and have only literally just discovered about Jason Kay's connection to Alex Trent this very second, which begs the question: how did you find out about it, sir?' asked Steal, furious at being played like a puppet on a string.

'I have retired Police Constable John Wilding in my office who has apprised me of his thirty-year investigation into the disappearance and he believes in the murder of his son Freddy Wilding by Alex Trent. He has given me a copy file of his investigation to-date, including his conclusion that Alex Trent had also killed Jacky Jones' friend of Jason Kay when he stole his ID card. Mr Wilding was contacted by your retired boss, Chief Inspector Tom Millard, after you requested his assistance in this case and who I believe is in your office at this very moment,' said the superintendent.

Steal looked up at Tom and it all became clear.

Just when Steal was about to explode, Wright rushed into the office. 'There's been an "incident" in Anthony Gibbs' cell, Boss.'

'What "incident"?'

'He's dead, Boss.'

'I'm afraid I will have to get back to you, sir,' said Steal, slamming the phone down and rushing out of the office with Wright and Tom Millard close behind.

Entering the cell, Steal saw Gibbs' body sitting motionless on the wooden seat with his eyes wide open, almost as if he was staring right at him. Wright and Tom entered the cell with the custody sergeant.

'How did he die?' Wright asked.

The Custody Sergeant replied, 'I don't know. I was doing my usual half-hour-on-the-hour check-up when I pulled back the hatch and noticed that he seemed to be struggling for breath. I opened the cell door and he literally died before my eyes... and yet, he hadn't eaten or drunk anything since he returned to the cell and there was no sign of any cuts or marks on his body, plus I did the usual search for any hidden sharp blades etc. before I left him, which leads me to believe that he may have had a heart attack?'

'Has forensics been informed?' asked Wright, more intrigued at the look on Steal's face as he stared at the body.

'Yes,' the sergeant replied.

Steal moved towards the body and Wright asked, 'What is it, Boss?'

Taking an ink pen out from his jacket pocket, Steal slowly opened Gibbs' lips to find tiny fragments of a white pill inside. Carefully pulling his mouth open, he noticed something dark tucked at the back of the tongue. When the forensic team arrived, 'I think you'll find what you need in here,' he said, watching them pull out a broken piece of filling from the back of Gibb's throat.

Bagging the evidence, the forensic officer said, 'I can't confirm it yet until I've checked the body and filling back at the lab, but initially, it looks like the deceased hid a cyanide pill inside a lose filling which he probably pulled out and swallowed. His death would have been fairly quick and painless.'

Just as Steal turned his attention towards Tom, Sergeant Jack Stone entered the cell.

'Chief Superintendent Phelps and another man called John Wilding have just arrived in your office, Boss,' he said, staring at the body of Gibbs.

'Then we'd better not keep them waiting,' growled Steal, heading back to his office, followed by Wright, Stone and Millard.

Wright suddenly stopped at the cell door and looked back at the lonely figure of Anthony Gibbs' corpse, wondering whether their harsh line of questions about his wife's suicide had finally pushed him over the edge.

Walking back into his office, Steal saw the middle-aged, red-faced, bloated body of Chief Superintendent Phelps sitting in his chair. With overly whitened, slightly crooked teeth and jet-black dyed hair and a fondness for too much red wine at police functions, Chief Superintendent Phelps wasn't on the inspector's favourite people's list. Standing beside him, holding a file, was a tall, thin man wearing a black coat and hat…

'Fuck me, he looks like…' said Jack when Steal cut short the sergeant before closing the door on both Wright and him, stating, 'There is to be *no* interruption unless the bloody building is on fire.'

Returning to their desks, Wright, Jack and the whole team pretended to get on with their jobs whilst slyly watching the fireworks explode through the clear glass bullet-proof window of Steal's office.

'I've just been informed that your prime suspect Mr Anthony Gibbs has committed suicide in one of our cells shortly after being questioned by both you and Sergeant Wright, Inspector,' said the chief superintendent, running his tongue over his teeth; an annoying habit that made Steal cringe every time he opened his fat mouth.

'It would appear that Gibbs was going to kill himself no matter who questioned him, Chief,' countered Steal sharply before continuing, 'he had hidden a cyanide pill inside a filling at the back of his mouth. The forensic officer will confirm this once he's completed his full examination, but needless to say, Anthony Gibbs had no intention of either going to trial or prison, but had every intention of signing a false statement before killing himself so that it can't be retracted or denied.'

He stared straight at the chief before calmly moving his eyes over to John Wilding and then Tom Millard.

Standing up, Chief Superintendent Phelps gave that pompous satisfied smile that annoyed Steal more than his constant rolling-tongue-over-tooth habit. He said, 'Well, that is good news, indeed, Inspector; especially for you and Sergeant Wright, because I wouldn't have wanted to investigate the interview methods used by two of my best detectives. But now, I can give a formal press release stating that our prime suspect planned to commit suicide once he confessed to the crimes of theft, fraud and the subsequent abduction and murder of his client Jason Kay, which I will now also be able to confirm was the serial killer, Alex Trent, thus solving and clearing up at least *eight* unsolved murders, which will go down very well with the powers that be at the government with regards to our public image with the press and the rising crime rate.'

'Not to mention, a possible promotion for certain parties,' scoffed Steal.

'Don't over-estimate your position here, Inspector,' threatened Phelps.

'But what about uncovering the truth or doesn't that matter any more in today's cash-strapped, public-imaged-obsessed police force…Chief Superintendent,' countered Steal, feeling his blood boiling inside.

'You have the signed statement from a troubled man with a guilty conscience; otherwise, why kill himself, plus thirty years of dedicated investigative detective work from two of the most respective retired police officers on the force. So *you will* inform your team that the case of Jason Kay has been solved and is now officially closed,' ordered Phelps.

'But we haven't got the body or…'

'That's enough, Inspector,' interrupted Phelps, suddenly seeing all the faces staring at them, arguing through the window from the office outside. 'Once forensics confirm Anthony Gibbs' pre-meditated suicide, write up and sign your final report as per the evidence provided in the copy file Mr Wilding will hand over to you today, but without your "personal opinions" in the report, and have it on my desk within the next forty-eight hours. I will then issue a press release by close of business at five thirty on that day,' ordered Phelps, before turning his attention towards Tom Millard. 'I wasn't at Lunsford at the time the assassination on both you and your partner took place. I was just a newly qualified young officer out of the Police Academy, but have always had a high regard for both you and your work and it's been an honour to have met you at last, Chief Inspector,' he said, shaking Tom's hand, unaware of the real truth behind that tragic day before turning back and nodding his thanks to John Wilding. He walked straight past Steal and out of the office as the team frantically pretended to be working.

Slamming the door shut, Steal turned to face his old friend but could barely speak the words when he asked, 'Why, Tom, why...?'

'You asked for my help, Steal. I didn't come to you,' he answered with a guilty sadness hidden in his words.

'You were waiting for me...' said Steal, unable to hide the hurt in his voice.

John Wilding interjected, 'It's not what you think, Steal. Tom didn't betray your friendship. We came to him...'

'Who's *we* and don't even bother to lie, because you've got what you wanted; the case is "effectively solved and closed" according to Chief Superintendent Phelps, but it will be *my name and signature* on that fucking final report and I'll be dammed if I will sign it unless you can prove to me that it was worth the lifelong friendship of two good detectives,' yelled Steal.

Wright opened the door and asked, 'Are you OK, Boss?'

'What bit of "no interruptions unless the bloody building is on fire" didn't you understand, Wright?' snapped Steal.

'The bit where everyone can hear you losing control, Boss,' said Wright.

Steal looked out into the office to see his entire team staring at him in shocked silence. 'Point taken, Wright,' he said, nodding his head at her in a half-attempted apology. She closed the door and he pulled down the blinds inside the office before sitting down in the chair.

Tom looked at him and confessed, 'You're right. I was waiting for you, but I would never, ever, betray you; please believe that even if you don't believe anything else that you've heard here today, my old friend.'

'I'm listening,' said Steal, praying that Tom was right.

John Wilding placed the file he was holding on the desk. 'Everything you need to know is in here. It's the *real* file, Steal, and not the one that I gave to Chief Superintendent Phelps when I requested to see him in his office earlier today, or the blank one with the note inside that your divers found in the lake. All I ask is that when you read it, you do so with not just a detective's mind, but with the victims' too... then you'll be ready to return to the beginning; nine days ago, when you and Sergeant Wright first knocked on Anne Kay's door. Only this time when you knock, we'll *all* be there waiting for you. Anne will tell you about the *trial* four days earlier and the day her husband went missing. Then, if you still want to change your final report before handing it in to the chief superintendent, we won't stop you, but if you are the man that Tom told me about and I can see now that you are, then as a fellow officer of the law who once believed in the justice system like you, I hope and pray that you will see that there was no other way to get final justice for *all* the victims and ghosts you will meet inside the file.'

Straightening his hat, John Wilding opened the door and walked out with Tom behind him, leaving Steal with the file.

Holding the door handle, Tom took one last look at his old friend opening the file before shutting the door to see the entire team staring at the two old, forgotten, retired detectives. John Wilding took off his hat and nodded at them before disappearing.

'Wasn't that Steal's old boss, Chief Inspector Tom Millard, who literally died and came back from the dead in Lunsford car park a million years ago?' noted Rita, leaning over Jack's shoulder.

'Yeh... and legend has it that he's the only one on the force who used to call Steal by his first name and knows the *real reason* why the boss stopped using it,' said Jack.

Wright interjected, 'Haven't you two got any work to get on with?'

'Yes, Sergeant, but you've got to admit it's surreal. First Steal's old boss comes back from the dead, literally, and Mr Black turns out to be another old, practically dead, detective, John Wilding, who's also one of our prime suspects on the board...' said Jack, itching to know what was in the file Wilding had in his hand when he entered Steal's office, but didn't when he left?

'Whatever is going on, you can bet that the boss will get to the truth and then inform us when he's good and ready. Until then, we've still got our jobs to do,' said Wright, desperate to open the door and ask Steal what the hell was going on, but knowing that now wasn't the time to test their partnership.

20
The File

Whilst the team outside his office shuffled papers around and whispered in corners, Steal hid behind the blinds staring at the *file*. Eventually, he opened it... to see the true story of *Alex Trent*, written chapter-by-chapter like a biography, outlining his life before and after he became *Jason Kay*, and up to when he disappeared nine days ago after leaving for his meeting in the park.

Chapter 1
The Sacrificial Lamb

Anthony Gibbs waited while the custody sergeant unlocked the door to his cell. Stepping inside, he heard the turning of the key in the lock before seeing the sergeant's bulging dark blue eyes staring back at him from behind the hatch. It clicked shut, and he was alone again in the soulless grey box with just his thoughts for company.

Sitting on the wooden seat, he smiled; not the smile of a happy, contented man, but the smile of a lonely, sad man waiting for the light to return back into his life.

Glancing around the grey box, Gibbs thought that it was a fitting place for him to make his peace with everyone that he had betrayed both in life and death.

Leaning his head against the cell wall, he thought back to the moment just over six months ago when the consultant at the hospital informed him that his annual medical check-up and blood tests had come back with the results that he had lymph cancer which had spread throughout his body and was terminal, leaving him with only a few months left of life.

To any other patient sitting in the consultant's room, the diagnosis would be devastating, but to Gibbs, it was almost as if God had given him a *second chance*.

A dying man can't be bought any more.

A dying man can't be threatened any more.

A dying man has no fear any more.

And dying man has nothing left to lose any more.

But a dying man is free to choose how he takes his last breath...

That was just two days before Jason Kay instructed him to make the first payment to the blackmailer, and the day he decided to get his revenge on the man that stole his life and wife from him.

And so, the alliance with the blackmailer, Jacky Jones, and all the other victims was forged... but to close the case of the murder of Jason Kay without uncovering his missing corpse, there had to be a prime suspect and a signed confession, and who better to sign that confession than a man who had already been given a death sentence, but was free to choose how he breathed his last breath on earth.

It was easy for Anthony Gibbs to sign the confession.

He was thief and a liar...

But not a killer.

But who would believe that he didn't murder Jason Kay, when the autopsy of his body by the police forensic officer, uncovers that he was already a dead man, and therefore, had nothing to lose by killing the man that ruined his life.

Slipping his fingers inside the back of his mouth, he pulled out the filling containing the white pill.

Placing it on his tongue, Gibbs heard the beautiful sound of Eva Cassidy's voice singing "Sandra" and his favourite song, "Fields of Gold" as he pictured the two of them holding hands whilst strolling through the golden hayfields on a bright sunny morning before disappearing into the light together.

Chapter 2
The Bait

In order to snare a beast, you must first prepare the bait... that will tempt it into the trap. And what better bait for a greedy beast than the very food that it loves the most and can never resist?

The back-up man, the police source and money man were all in place and so Mr Black called upon Dr Pritchard to remind him of the promise he made to his late friends, Regional Price and James Dodd, to protect Anne and the trust fund.

Pritchard already knew that he had the perfect bait to trap Kay. Ever since Jason Kay married Anne Price, the doctor had been hiding that bait until the time was right... but now that Black had told him that the real Jason Kay/Jacky Jones had secured access to Anne's five million trust fund, he could set the bait with the documents and so contacted the beast.

Sitting in Dr Prichard's office, Kay listened as the doctor lied about how he had finally uncovered where the five million was hidden and how Kay could release it by signing *two* simple documents.

Document One: Anne Kay must be declared mentally unstable and a danger to herself, her husband and the community, leaving Dr Pritchard no option but to prepare the necessary medical paperwork and legal documentation to have her incarcerated in a secure hospital facility for an indefinite period of time. But in order for the doctor to do that, Kay would have to sign the legal document, giving his consent.

Document Two: In order to get access to the trust fund and his wife's financial affairs, Kay required a legal Power of Attorney prepared and signed by the family solicitor, Simon Dodd.

Once he had both those documents, then he had *total control* over Anne's life and money.

Leaving Pritchard's office, Kay was on a high.

Once all the paperwork was in place and signed, then everything would be his... and he'd finally be rid of the pathetic wife he had to endure for sixteen years, leaving him free at last to rule the world without restrictions.

But while Kay was licking his lips in delicious anticipation of the tasty bait that was awaiting him, the doctor contacted Simon Dodd and brought him into the plan.

With the bait set and ready, Jacky Jones and Mr Black could now prepare the trap. But to secure the perfect trap, you must first have all the pieces fitted together in the right place.

The back-up man

The police source

The money man

The accountant

The doctor

The solicitor

Now all they needed was the other *five* pieces:

The wife

The friend

The estate manager

The mistress

The housekeeper

And so, the solicitor told the friend when she charged into his office, then the friend told the wife, who told the estate manager. The two met the solicitor and the mistress, while the housekeeper waited in silent ignorance for the sign that she could finally return to Hilltop Mansion and Anne again...

Chapter 3
The First Bite

'Simon Dodd has just telephoned me to confirm that he has finally signed the Power of Attorney and will be contacting your secretary shortly. All that is required now is for you to come into my office today and countersign one last piece of paperwork before I can arrange the date and time for Anne's admission to the hospital,' informed Pritchard on the phone to Kay.

'What paperwork?' questioned Kay on his mobile, while staring across at Anne in the kitchen from the hallway as he prepared for his usual walk into the village.

'I forgot that you needed to sign the hospital's Interment Form before they will accept Anne as a patient,' lied Pritchard, holding his breath and praying that Kay doesn't hear the tremble in his voice.

'I can be there in two hours,' said Kay, checking his watch and noting that the time was almost seven a.m. before adding, 'What about the money transfer?'

'Once you've signed off on the hospital Interment Form and I've delivered it, then legally you have all the right paperwork in place to get the accountant to liaise with the banker holding the trust fund and arrange the transfer of the five million into your account,' said Pritchard, relieved that Kay had taken the *first bite* of the bait.

'Excellent,' said Kay, placing the mobile in his jacket pocket before adjusting his tie in the hallway mirror with that cold, smug grin that he always had when "everything was as it should be".

Turning and giving one last look at Anne preparing his usual breakfast, he walked out the door and down to the village like a god floating on air.

Chapter 4
The Second Bite

Kay felt a sudden chill run down the back of his spine when Pritchard's secretary Olive Bence showed him into the doctor's office.

'Thank you, Miss Bence,' said Pritchard, as she smiled wistfully at him before closing the door behind her.

'Where's the "Interment Form" that you forgot all about?' asked Kay, feeling that cold chill down his spine, again.

'Right here,' said Pritchard, picking up four sheets of paper from his desk and handing them to Kay who began reading every single word on each page. When he turned to the last page, his mobile rang inside his pocket.

Placing the papers down on the desk, Kay pulled out the phone. 'What is it?'

'I've just noticed that you have a double booking in the diary at the office for tomorrow morning at ten a.m. and need to know which one you would like me to change, Mr Kay?' asked Diane Moffatt, adding, 'Oh, and your solicitor, Simon Dodd, telephoned to confirm that he has signed the "Power of Attorney" form you requested.'

'What the fuck do I pay you for? Sort out the mistake *you* made and don't bother me again with stupid questions,' yelled Kay, cutting her off before turning back to Pritchard. 'Fucking women, they're all just good for one thing.'

'Tell me about it,' joked Pritchard, quickly flicking the Internment Form over to the last page. 'As you've noted, Jason, it's all in order and ready to sign on the dotted line.' He handed him his gold ink pen.

'I prefer to use my own,' sneered Kay, taking out the silver-tipped ink pen that he used to kill Reginald Price with and was now using to lock up his daughter in a mental hospital before throwing away the key.

Signing on the dotted line, Kay couldn't help smiling at the irony of "killing two trapped birds with one strike of the same pen".

Opening the door, Kay turned round and gave that cold, smug grin when he said, 'The stupid bitch did confirm that Dodd has signed the Power of Attorney, so all that needs to be done now is for you to let me know when the hospital has received the Interment Form, then I can arrange for the transfer of the money with the appropriate parties.'

'No problem,' replied Pritchard, picking up the form and carefully placing it in a file marked "Urgent". Kay closed the door behind him and left.

Looking out the window, Pritchard waited until he saw Kay drive off in his fancy silver sports car before sitting back down at his desk and opening the file. A sneaky grin of relief crept across his face as he remembered pressing the silent button on the desk phone when Kay got to the last page of the Interment Form, and Olive Bence saw the red light flash on her phone in the outer office. She telephoned Diane Moffatt with the words, 'It's a go' and Diane dialled Kay's mobile. Pritchard had slyly slipped another page under the last page of the Interment Form while Kay was shouting down the phone at her.

Pulling out the original last page of the Interment Form, Pritchard tore it up into tiny pieces before throwing it in the bin and replacing it with another page hidden inside the desk drawer.

Taking the signed fifth page from the file, Pritchard took out another file from the drawer and placed the page inside it.

Picking up the desk phone, he dialled the number. Mr Black answered and the doctor said, 'He has bitten the *second bite.*'

Chapter 5
The Deadly Bite

Staring down at the minions rushing about beneath him from the glass lift while he ascended upwards to his penthouse office, Kay breathed in the air of power, thinking that everything was finally as *he* had planned it should be.

Stepping out of the lift, Kay strolled over to the desk and sat down on his throne with an arrogance that only an untouchable ancient mythical god could feel.

Diane Moffatt glided into the office; a picture of calm tranquil beauty that even took *his* breath away.

'You're looking particularly good today,' he noted, running his eyes over her slim, perfectly shaped body whilst thinking tonight would be a good time to celebrate his victory.

'I've changed the appointment that I doubled-booked, Mr Kay, and was wondering if it would be all right if I took an extended lunch break today as I am meeting an old girlfriend for lunch and catch-up and she's only in the city today for a job interview.'

Feeling generous, Kay replied, 'Take as long as you like, but keep your evening free and put on something extra special to go with the champagne that I will be bringing with me.' He placed his mobile on the desk, ready...

'Are you celebrating something, Mr Kay?' she asked, giving that sweet "I'm at your complete disposal" smile whilst thinking, *Not if you take the* last bite, *shit head.*

'Just be ready and don't ask questions that are above your pay grade,' he mocked. His mobile pinged on top of the desk and he read the text from Pritchard. *"Interment Form delivered and the banker has contacted our accountant who's waiting for your further instructions."*

Feeling untouchable, Kay couldn't help playing God when he looked up at his secretary and smiled smugly. 'Get me the accountant,

Anthony Gibbs, on the telephone before you go to lunch. You can collect the champagne for tonight.'

'But the wine shop is at the other end of town, which means I won't have time to meet my friend for lunch.'

'She doesn't pay your wages, so stop crying and do as I instruct.' He watched her scurry back to her office like a whipped dog running back to its cage.

Sliding back into his leather chair, Kay imagined what he could do with five million pounds in the bank when the telephone rang on his desk.

'I have Mr Gibbs on the line for you,' said Diane in that cold tone that she reserved for him when upset.

'Put him through,' he instructed, enjoying hearing the annoyance at him hidden inside her voice for ruining her lunch date with an old friend.

'The banker is waiting for your instructions of where you want the five million to be transferred, Jason?' said Gibbs.

'Have him put it into my "special account", plus the other five hundred thousand you've been taking from the company over the last three months. Then text me when it's done so that I can check that it's *all* there before I make arrangements to dispose of the two other irritating problems and reclaim the five hundred thousand, they stole from me.'

'As you wish,' acknowledged Gibbs, hanging up.

Unlocking the drawer with the key from his coat pocket, Kay pulled out the silver laptop and opened it up. The mobile pinged on the desk and he smiled whilst reading Gibbs' text, *'The transfer is complete."*

Logging into his secret personal bank account in Switzerland, Kay leapt into the air and yelled, 'What do you think of your useless son now, *Father?*'

Calmly sitting back down, he stared at the laptop for ages and ages whilst repeating the words *£5.5 million and all mine… £5.5 million and all mine…* over and over again whilst laughing at the memory of his father's last words to him before he died, "You'll reap this day…"

Diane Moffatt walked back into the office and enquired, 'Did you want vintage champagne or sparkling white?'

'I don't give a fuck what it is so long as it's expensive,' said Kay, irritated at her interrupting his moment of "triumphant self-gloating".

She looked up at the sky through the window behind him and asked, 'What's that floating in the air?' moving over to the window.

He stood up and turned round to see, nothing... 'Your brain, you stupid bitch.' He laughed as she ran out of the office in tears. He coldly sat down and typed, *"I've sorted out my affairs regarding my wife etc. and am ready to meet in the park when you are."*

Pressing the send button on the email to the blackmailer, Kay coolly sat at his desk, waiting... whilst staring at the bank transfer on the laptop with that cold, smug grin of satisfaction plastered across his face.

Barely twenty minutes later, the email inbox pinged. *"Hi, Alex, I'm so glad that you've finally decided to do the right thing by your wife and can now confirm that Mr Black and I will meet you in the park opposite your office at precisely twelve noon tomorrow. You can see your enemies face-to-face at last before the truce is off and the best man wins."*

Replying, *"Can't wait..."*, Kay pressed the send button before picking up his mobile and typing the text message, *"The meet is on for twelve noon tomorrow in the park."*

Within seconds, the phone pinged with the reply, *"I'll be ready..."*

Closing up the laptop, he placed it back in the drawer before locking it up and slipping the key inside his jacket pocket.

Strolling into Diane's office, a cruel grin crept across his face when he saw her sitting at her desk, crying.

'Oh, for god's sake, pull yourself together and stop whining, woman. Go to your bloody lunch. You'd be no good in bed tonight anyway. I'll celebrate tomorrow night when I've tidied up the loose ends of my business deal tomorrow at twelve noon.'

'Oh, thank you, Mr Kay.' She smiled, wiping away the tears with the paper hanky from the tiny flowered tissue box on her desk before adding, 'Is there anything else you require before I take my lunch break?'

'Yes. You can reserve their best table for one at the Royal Hotel in the city at twelve noon today, and don't bother telephoning me with stupid questions while I'm eating my lunch,' he said, leaving the office for an extended celebration of his triumphant day before driving home to Hilltop Mansion and the last breakfast his wife will prepare for him to eat the next morning at precisely seven thirty a.m. when Dr Pritchard will call with a copy of the signed hospital Interment Form.

Watching the beast step into the lift and subsequently disappear out of the building from the office window, Diane couldn't help gloating when she said, 'Enjoy your expensive wine with your lunch just like I will enjoy drinking your expensive champagne tomorrow night, alone...'

Slipping back into Kay's office, she slid her hand underneath the desk and carefully pulled out a small piece of plaster indented on the outer side with the imprint of a key.

Returning to her office, she smiled whilst remembering slipping the key out of the lock in the drawer and pressing it into the plaster before returning it back into the lock and sticking the plaster smooth-side-up under the desk as Kay stood staring at nothing through the office window whilst calling her a brain-dead stupid bitch.

Carefully placing the plaster inside an empty silver pill box before sliding the box into her red Gucci bag, Diane couldn't help smile at the sleight of hand trick the bouncer at the nightclub where she worked many years ago as a "waitress" taught her and how it would one day be part of Kay's final undoing.

With the plaster secure in the pill box, Diane pressed the redial button on her mobile. 'The meeting is on for twelve noon tomorrow in the park and he will no doubt have his back-up man ready.'

'Then so shall we, Diane,' said Anne, sitting at the kitchen table waiting for her call.

'I've taken an imprint of the key and will get it cut today when I buy the champagne that he won't get to drink.'

'Be careful, Diane, he's still very dangerous,' warned Anne.

'You too, he'll be even crueller tonight now that he thinks he's won.'

'Don't worry, I'm used to cruel.'

'I'll sort the laptop and his mobile tomorrow as planned.'

'Good. Until then, be safe and be smart.'

'Ditto,' said Diane, slipping on her coat and strolling out of the office to get the key cut before buying the most expensive champaign for tomorrow night at the wine bar whilst ordering lunch for one on Kay's expense account.

'Cutting an extra-large piece of dark chocolate cake she made from Maggie's special home-cooked recipe, Anne scoffed a huge mouthful covered in melted chocolate whilst savouring every delicious moment, knowing that she was eating *his* favourite cake that no one else was allowed to touch.

Licking the dripping chocolate off her lips, she pressed the redial button on her mobile.

'You'll get fat,' teased Dotty, almost smelling the chocolate down the phone.

'Oh damn, too late now,' laughed Anne, swallowing the cake in one go. She confirmed, 'The trap is set for twelve noon tomorrow in the park. Say your prayers tonight, Dotty.'

'I will, my dearest Anne, and can't wait to see you at the trial.'

'Me too,' said Anne, signing off and dialling the next contact.

Maggie answered, 'Ah, you're eating my special chocolate cake so that must mean good news?'

'How come everyone knows what I'm eating when they can't see me?' asked Anne, stuffing another spoonful of cake in her mouth before repeating, 'The trap is set for twelve noon tomorrow in the park. Say your prayers tonight, Maggie.'

'Don't I always, my girl.'

'I'll see you at the trial,' said Anne.

Eric opened the kitchen door just then and helped himself to an even bigger slice of cake before sitting down and eating it from his hand. 'Did I hear that right?' he asked, having overheard Anne's conversation with Maggie while coming through the door.

'Yes, you did and stop eating *all* my cake,' she joked, then her face went still. 'I know that you don't pray, my dear friend, but maybe tonight you might make an exception?'

202

'Maybe…' grinned Eric. He pinched another piece of cake and downed it in one mouthful whilst staring at her from the across the table. His eyes took on a scared look; he was not sure if he could protect her this time.

Anne smiled at him whilst she tapped her fingers on the mobile. Eric knew that Anne didn't want him there when she made the last call.

'I'll be off then and will you see at the trial,' he said, opening the kitchen door and strolling back to the lodge to pray for the first time since he was that small boy praying to an unacknowledging god for his alcoholic father to stop drinking.

Dialling the number, Anne waited and waited… He answered.

'I know, my sweet love. Gibbs and Pritchard have already been in touch. Soon, we can be together forever and nothing will stop us from our dream this time,' said Simon.

'I can't believe that the dream is finally becoming real,' she said, suddenly afraid that *this was the dream*, and she'd wake up to discover that *he* was still there.

'Just another few hours until the trial, when everyone *he* ever hurt will have their wish, my sweet Anne. Until then, dream of our new home and life together.'

'I will, my love, I will…'

Reading Anne's and Simon's last words in the file, Steal began to understand what it was like to be inside the victim's mind.

Being a detective can be a soulless job. You can't choose who *not* to arrest. Your job is to solve the crime and arrest whoever committed it.

But sometimes, the *bad* guy is actually the *good* guy, except in the eyes of the law where there are *no* sides; just the crime and then the punishment.

Resting his eyes for a moment, he leaned down and pulled out the whisky bottle from the bottom drawer and poured himself a *very* large shot into the coffee-stained mug on the desk before downing it in one shot.

Checking his watch, he saw that it was getting late. He opened the office door to see the team still working. 'That's enough for tonight, everyone. Go home and see your families.'

'What about you, Boss?' asked Wright, worried for her partner and friend.

'I've still got some paperwork to do.'

'I'll see you tomorrow then, Boss?'

'You will, Wright,' he said, closing the door and returning to the file whilst everyone packed up and left, relieved to finally go home and forget about being an officer of the law for a few hours.

Pouring out another *large* whisky into the mug, Steal flicked over the page to read the next chapter.

Chapter 6
The Trap

Kay stood upright at the top of the long, winding staircase, surveying the large, Victorian hallway below as usual before slowly walking down the stairs into middle of the hall when he turned to admire his reflection in the mirror.

Every morning was the same; except this morning. He wouldn't be walking to the village to collect his newspapers as usual at precisely seven a.m.

Staring at the perfectly prepared breakfast table and then over at Anne placing three extra-large precisely timed cooked eggs on the breakfast plate, Kay couldn't help but feel a minute bit of pity for his wife's last moments of freedom. The doorbell rang, and she turned round to see him standing in the middle of the hallway, smiling back at her with that dark, smug grin that only meant one thing. The doorbell rang again and she pulled her head upright and her eyes met his. He felt a sudden icy cold chill run down the back of his spine. When the doorbell rang for the third time, he turned away and opened it... to see Dr Pritchard and two large muscle-bound bulging men with shaved heads dressed in white hospital uniforms standing on either side of him.

Without uttering a single word, Kay opened the door wide and stepped aside. The three men walked straight past him into the kitchen.

Pulling out an envelope from his inside coat pocket, Pritchard placed it down on the centre of the kitchen table, then stated, 'Mrs Anne Kay, I have come at the instructions of your husband, Jason Kay, to place you under my care until further notice. Please do not be afraid as this is for your own protection and wellbeing.'

'But I know nothing about this, Doctor...' she protested. The two male nurses escorted her out of the kitchen into the hallway and past Kay, then out onto the front porch. She turned round and pleaded,

'Please, not that place again, Jason, please, I beg you… Have I not been a good wife and done everything that you have asked of me? Please, Jason, please, I beg you…'

Standing at the door, he watched his wife being locked up in the hospital's van like a criminal whilst crying out, 'Please, Jason, help me, help me…' The van drove off and her cries for help disappeared into the early morning wind.

Closing the door, Kay calmly walked back into the kitchen and ate his breakfast before getting into his silver sports car and driving off to the city to prepare for his meeting in the park at precisely twelve noon whilst thinking that everything was coming together just as he had planned it should be.

The First Step

Kay arrived at the main entrance of Kay Corporation with a lightness in his step and brightness in his manner that shocked the guard standing at the entrance door.

'Good morning, ah…?'

'Ken, Mr Kay, my name is Ken,' the guard replied, amazed that he had finally spoken to him for the first time in the fifteen years he had stood guard at the front entrance.

'Indeed,' acknowledged Kay, not really giving a toss as he walked straight past the guard into the lift.

Stepping out of the lift into his office, he saw Diane Moffatt standing at the front of his desk and holding a white envelope in her hand. 'This was delivered about thirty minutes ago marked "for your attention only" by a man in a black suit who wouldn't leave his name,' she said, handing him the envelope before returning to her office.

Opening the envelope as he sat down at his desk, Kay grinned when he read, 'I'm set up and ready in the agreed spot. See plan attached. I will await your signal of the *two nods* and both your problems will be resolved."

Checking his gold Rolex watch, he noted that the time was 10.23 a.m. 'Only another ninety-seven minutes to go.' He smirked, checking the plan again before putting it back in the envelope and slipping it inside his inner jacket pocket.

Unlocking the desk drawer, Kay opened the laptop and signed into his Swiss bank account to see that the £5.5 million was still sitting there waiting for him.

Smiling that satisfied smug grin, he rang through to Diane Moffatt. 'Just checking that my diary is clear for today and that you have the champagne ready on ice for tonight at the flat?'

'Everything is as you instructed, Mr Kay,' she said in her smooth "I'm at your complete disposal" tone.

'Excellent,' he said, leaning back and staring at the £5.5 million again whilst pressing the call button on the mobile. Pritchard answered.

'Just checking that the *patient* has been delivered to her new accommodation and that everything is in order?'

'The *patient* is settled and sedated and as comfortable as she can be,' replied Pritchard in his detached doctor—client—patient tone.

'Excellent,' said Kay, adding, 'keep me updated; after all, I wouldn't want her to suffer unnecessarily.' He leaned back and checked his watch again, noting that only twelve minutes had elapsed.

Feeling a sudden surge of doom creep over him, Kay paced the office floor like a lion pacing up and down inside his circus cage, growling at the faces of the public peering at him through the bars whilst mocking the great jungle king's new throne of power. The office phone rang on his desk.

'Yes, what is it?' he asked, sitting back down and staring at the laptop again to see that the money was still all there.

'I have your estate manager, Mr Eric Finch, on line for you, Mr Kay. I did inform him that you were not to be disturbed today, but he seemed very concerned about your wife.'

Smiling, he said, 'Put him through.'

'Sorry to contact you at the office, Mr Kay, but I fear that something has happened to your wife because she doesn't appear to be at home and no one has seen her in the village, including Maggie her old housekeeper. I was out fixing a fence at the far end of the estate this morning and so didn't see her leave the house from the lodge.'

'Mrs Kay is in hospital being treated for the reoccurrence of her "mental condition" and so won't be at the mansion for some time, and therefore, you have no need to bother me again with your "concerns", Mr Finch. I would strongly advise you to do the job that I pay you for and not stick your nose into my wife's personal affairs,' said Kay, feeling the surge of doom lifting from him as he belittled and bullied Eric just for caring about his wife.

'As you wish, sir,' said Eric, hanging up.

Kay checked his watch again and noted that the time was now 11.26 a.m.

Feeling *all powerful* once again, Kay closed the laptop and locked it back in the drawer before placing the key in his jacket pocket and dialling through to Diane Moffatt. 'I've decided to leave the office early for my meeting.'

'Yes, Mr Kay, and I look forward to celebrating with you tonight,' she said, smiling that secret smile that she did when "karma" was about to come round and visit those who think that they had escaped it.

Picking up his mobile from the desk, Kay strolled into the glass lift and out of the building, nodding to the guard, Ken, at the entrance, again, before crossing over the road and entering the park where he went and sat on the bench by the lake to watch the swans gliding effortlessly through the water whilst secretly trampling on anything that got in their way underneath with their huge webbed feet.

Kay watched the swans ruthlessly destroying anything that got in their way and congratulated himself on doing the same to those he deemed dispensable, including his own father and siblings. Diane Moffatt sat in her office reading over the copies she made of the note and plan the man in the black suit delivered to Kay.

Smiling to herself, she thought how easy it was to open the letter with the heat from the boiling kettle and re-seal it with the special glue stick she hid at the back of her drawer.

Over the years, she had steamed open many letters that Kay had received by "special delivery", but none had proved to be the one that she was seeking to use as leverage against him for money and a way out of the life that seemed so attractive. He interviewed her for the *two* jobs he required, only to discover that once he had bought her, she could never leave him until he no longer required her.

But today, she steamed opened the letter that would finally set her free on her terms, and not his.

Scanning the note and the plan through on her computer, she emailed it to Jacky Jones who forwarded it to their back-up man, David Fox, who had his own score to settle with the man that shot his partner and fellow bodyguard point blank in the head with one bullet at the instructions of Kay after killing Reginald Price with his silver-tipped ink pen.

Having completed her first task, Diane then slipped into Kay's office and unlocked his drawer with the duplicate key she had cut. Lifting out the laptop, she wiped it clean of *all data* before slipping it into a black plastic bag and taking the lift down into the basement car park where she smashed it into tiny pieces inside the bag with a large stone hammer she had hidden behind the four huge rubbish bins that were due to be emptied the next day.

Without Kay's laptop, there were no clues to follow... And with no clues to follow, there was no trail to track... And with no trail to track, there was no evidence to find... And without evidence, there was no suspect to arrest and convict.

Unless a new set of clues were placed on the trail of evidence leading to a suspect for Inspector Steal and his partner, Sergeant Wright, to interview, arrest and convict.

Having destroyed the laptop, Diane returned to the office and checked her watch, noting that the time was touching 11.55 a.m.

Placing her mobile on the desk beside the computer, she carried on doing her job until it was time to take a lunch-break in the park.

The Lock

Kay's gold Rolex watch pinged three times when he looked down to note that it was precisely twelve noon.

Standing up, he straightened his jacket before turning round and walking over to the green in the centre of the park to see it alive with people sitting on the grass and surrounding benches, eating their lunch whilst watching the swans swimming in the distant lake.

The sound of laughter and carefree relief from their mundane office jobs and desks for a heavenly hour echoed through the air. Kay glimpsed two men strolling casually towards him through the lunch-time picnickers on the grass.

Within a blink of an eye, they were stood barely two metres in front of him, when, just for a moment, he felt that same icy cold shiver run down the back of his spine. 'We meet at last,' he said, recognising Mr Black. He then asked, 'Well who the hell are you really then?'

Taking off his hat, Black answered, 'I am the father of the son you killed and the man that has spent the last thirty years seeking justice for the son that I never got to grow old with.'

Looking closely, Kay suddenly recognised the likeness in the eyes and the mouth. He said, 'So you're Freddy Wilding's father. I remember you now. You're that idiot police constable who tried to get me arrested for his disappearance and murder at the farm, only to be sent away with your tail between your legs.' He laughed in his face.

'My name is John Wilding and this time, I won't be walking away with my tail between my legs, Alex Trent.'

Tempted to nod his head, Kay held back. He turned towards Jacky and mocked, 'And who the fuck are you and what crime did I commit against you that merited blackmailing me for five hundred thousand pounds of *my* money?'

Lifting his head up, Jacky looked right into Kay's eyes and grinned when he answered, 'I am you…'

'What the fuck do mean, by you're *me*?' asked Kay, staring right at him, but seeing nothing.

'I'm *Jason Kay,* the boy whose name and identity you stole thirty years ago at the hostel.'

'All I did to you was "borrow" your ID card to claim a bed and meal for the night,' said Kay, standing face-to-face with the other half of himself.

'But it wasn't your name or identity to use, Alex, it was mine... and now I've come to claim it back.'

Suddenly feeling the dark shadow of doom creep over him, Kay stepped backwards and nodded his head *twice*... He felt a sharp stabbing pain in the back of his neck and turned round to discover David Fox standing behind him, holding a silver-tipped ink pen in his hand.

Rubbing the tiny prick on his neck, Kay felt his body collapsing inward when Jacky moved closer and whispered in his right ear, 'Time to reap what you sowed, Alex.'

Lifting him up, Jacky and David strolled back through the park with Kay sandwiched in the middle. He saw Diane Moffatt walking towards them.

Strolling past, she slipped her hand inside Kay's jacket pocket and smiled into his face whilst pulling out his mobile before carrying on walking towards the lake, where John Wilding was waiting for her with the empty file and note sealed inside the clear waterproof plastic bag.

Deleting all the data on Kay's mobile, Diane then took a picture of the man in black, throwing the file into the lake.

Watching the file sinking down into the bottom of the lake, John turned round and smiled at Diane, then tipped his hat towards her before walking on. She turned round to see the distant outline of four men disappearing out of the park into the crowd together.

Breathing in the fresh air, Diane sat on the bench and took out a plastic lunch box and small sealed coffee flask from her rather large overfilled bright pink Gucci bag.

Sitting back, she ate her lunch whilst watching the swans in the lake fighting each other over the bread crumbs thrown into the water from the passers-by before strolling back through park. She wiped her prints off the mobile and hid it in the bushes at the entrance.

Skipping across the road to Kay Corporation, Diane beamed a heavenly smile at the guard standing at the entrance. She said, 'Have a lovely day, Ken.'

'You too, Miss Moffatt,' he said, tipping his head towards her whilst thinking, *First the mean boss and now his sad secretary...*

Maybe my luck is changing and I'll get that massive pay rise and bonus I've been dreaming about for the last fifteen sodden years?

Turning to the last page, Inspector Steal read...

The *final chapter* in the double-life of *Alex Trent* shouldn't be written in words...

To understand being inside a victim's tormented mind, you need to hear their darkest fears and pain spoken from within that tortured soul's voice.

To hear those Voices, Inspector Steal, knock on Anne Kay's door tomorrow morning at 10.00 am when they will *All* be there waiting to speak not only for themselves, but for the Ghosts whose Voices have long been forgotten...

Then if you still want to change your Final Report before handing it into Chief Superintendent Phelps, the Victims and the all the Ghosts that you have met inside The File won't not stop you...

Finishing the last drop of whisky from the bottle before leaving the office with the file, Steal switched on the car radio as he drove home to hear Chris Rea singing the song "The Road to Hell", then stopped the car and turned round to drive in the opposite direction. He arrived at Sergeant Wright's apartment.

Taking the file with him, Steal walked up the stairs to the first floor and knocked on the door. Wright opened it in her cosy spotted fluffy teddy bear pyjamas.

He said, 'Read this tonight and then if you decide *not* to come with me to Anne Kay's house tomorrow morning at ten a.m., I will understand. But whatever decision you make, it will be *my* name and signature on the final report to Chief Superintendent Phelps and *my* career on line, not yours, Wright.'

'Yes, Boss,' she said, taking the file.

Steal smiled and said, 'Nice pyjamas,' before walking back down the stairs and driving off.

The Ninth Day

Steal's alarm went off at six a.m. He turned over and stared at the bright yellow light beaming back at him from the radio clock on the chest of drawers beside the bed as the DJ on the early morning breakfast show played his usual jingle. 'Wakey, Wakey, sleepy heads, it's time to rise and shine with your favourite DJ, Sunny Jim Logan.'

'Piss off,' groaned Steal, leaning over and switching radio channels only to hear another overly bright cheery-voiced DJ playing funky 1980s rock music.

Switching channels again to yet another bright and breezy DJ, Steal slowly dragged his body out of bed when the mobile by the radio pinged and he read the text, *"Every Holmes needs a Watson to watch his back. We are **Steal & Wright** and where you go, Boss, so do I!"*

"I'll pick you up at 9.15 a.m. sharp and remember, I like my coffee on the go and black with no sugar," replied Steal, smiling.

The reply came back, *"Don't forget, Boss, I'm Sergeant Liz Wright, the Detective who's always RIGHT; especially when it comes to your coffee."*

Switching radio channels for the fourth and final time, only to hear irritating Sunny Jim Logan once again, Steal gave up and went to take his usual cold shower whilst thinking that it felt good to have another Watson beside him to watch his back and make his coffee the way he liked it again.

21
The Three Rings

The woman scrubbed inside the large circular mug with the scorer until every tea stain was removed before wiping it dry and carefully placing it back on the mug stand, when the doorbell rang.

Looking up, she stared out of the kitchen window with a quiet stillness that engulfed the room in a calm serenity before continuing to wipe down the sink and worktop then turning round to survey the room with her soft blue eyes, noting that everything was as it should be. The doorbell rang again… and she waited.

She was in no hurry. She wanted to enjoy the quite moment. To savour the feeling of complete emptiness, when the doorbell rang for the third time, and she smiled.

Slowly, she walked into the large Victorian hallway to see the shadowy outline of a man and woman through the coloured-glass front door, where she caught sight of her reflection in the large hallway mirror opposite.

It had been nine days since she last looked into the mirror and didn't like what she saw, but today, the reflection of the forty-three-year-old woman staring back at her was different.

Sliding her hand over her newly coloured thick, luscious, long and dark silky hair, she smiled at the pale, lined almost girlish face looking back her whilst thinking that they were no longer the lines of pain and torment, but of freedom and hope…

Walking to the front door, she smiled again whilst thinking that no matter what judgement and sentence the man and woman standing inside the porch declared about her crimes today, she would accept that sentence even if it were behind prison bars… where she would still be free.

Opening the front door, Inspector Steal said, 'I believe you are expecting us, Mrs Kay?'

'Please, come in, Detectives,' she said, opening the door wide before leading them into the large, dual-aspect sitting room opposite the kitchen.

The Final Chapter
Jury of Victims

Standing in the doorway, Steal and Wright's eyes slowly surveyed the room, counting *nine* people sitting in a circle on wooden chairs with five more empty chairs, three in the outer circle, forming a *jury of twelve*... plus two more dead centre in the middle of the circle.

Walking over to the circle of people sitting in silence, Anne pulled back one empty chair. 'Please, if you wouldn't mind stepping inside and sitting on the chairs in the centre, Detectives?' she said.

Steal and Wright slipped through the space and sat down.

Sealing the circle with the empty chair, Anne placed a file on the floor in front of the detectives. 'Welcome to the jury of victims, Inspector Steal and Sergeant Wright. On the floor is the *last* and *final file* detailing the trial of Alex Trent, which will be yours to take and do with as you wish once you have heard all the evidence here today. This *court room* is not full of *innocent people*, Detectives, but even the *guilty* require a defence before final judgement and sentence is passed. Do you agree to listen to the voices of the jury of victims who passed their final judgement and sentence in the trial of Alex Trent before passing *your* final judgement and sentence upon them, Detectives?'

Steal looked over at Wright, who nodded her head.

'We are listening,' he said, when Anne proceeded to identify each of the jury of victims by name before telling the detectives about the trial and *final chapter* in the double-life of Alex Trent/Jason Kay.

1. The father — John Wilding
2. The blackmailer — Jacky Jones
3. The solicitor — Simon Dodd
4. The estate manager — Eric Finch
5. The doctor — Dr Pritchard
6. The mistress — Diane Moffatt

7. The bodyguard — David Fox

8. The friend — Dotty Short

9. The housekeeper — Maggie Frith

10. The first empty chair — Anne Kay

11. The second empty chair — Anthony Gibbs

12. The last empty chair — Alex Trent…

22
The Trial

Kay gradually opened his eyes to see a sea of bodies seated in a circle of chairs with him sat in the middle of the circle, alone.

Feeling his head swimming around inside his body, he tried to stand up from the chair, but had no legs or arms.

Shaking his head, he tried to stand again… and then again… when, suddenly, he realised that his body was encased inside a *straightjacket*.

Frantically trying to free his arms and legs, shouting, 'Get me the fuck out of this contraption,' he collapsed back into the chair, exhausted.

The mist cleared from his eyes and he looked up to see his wife, Anne, standing over him, holding a file. 'But this can't be…? You're locked away! I saw them take you…'

'And now you see me again. Only this time, you're the one locked in a straightjacket.'

'What the fuck is going on?' he demanded, still trying to release his trapped body from the straightjacket.

Anne bent down and looked right inside his bewildered eyes, then smiled when she said, 'Welcome to *your trial*, husband.'

Looking up at his wife, it suddenly dawned on Kay that he was *now* the prisoner and she the jailer.

Staring down at his body again, Kay noted that the straightjacket's legs and arms were strapped around the chair, trapping him inside the chair.

Moving his head upwards to the circle of faces on the chairs, a terrible premonition of darkness suddenly crept over him when he saw the ghosts of the past come back from the dead to judge him.

Believing that this was all just a stupid dream, he attempted to stand up again when the chair toppled over and he fell on the floor, helpless. Two men lifted him up off the floor and he looked up at their faces.

'But you're both supposed to be dead…?' he said.

John Wilding replied, 'It's not that easy to kill a Ghost, Alex.'

Realising that there was no way out, until he could think of a way out, Kay relaxed back into the straightjacket before pulling his head upright and staring straight at the jury of victims, demanding, 'Well, let's get on with the fucking trial before I die of boredom sitting here staring at a bunch of nobodies…' He spat in their faces whilst inside, frantically, trying to think of a plan to escape.

Anne requested the first *victim/juror* to step forward and Kay asked, 'Who the fuck are you and what did I ever do to you?'

'I was the bodyguard of Reginald Price, the man you killed with this pen,' said David Fox, showing him the silver-tipped ink pen that he took from Kay's inside jacket pocket just after he stabbed him in the back of the neck with his own identical silver-tipped pen filled with tranquilising drops.

Staring closer, Kay laughed out loud. 'So you're the idiot bodyguard who went on the run because you couldn't protect one little old man that you're still crying about sixteen years later.'

'You're right, I didn't protect Reginald Price and there isn't a day that goes by that I don't replay the moment he died in his bed, *not* blaming me for failing him, but I didn't protect another friend that day which you also killed…'

'I didn't kill anybody else that day,' said Kay, racking his brains.

'You didn't point the gun into the face of my friend and partner, but you pulled the trigger when you ordered your man to kill both him and me in cold blood,' accused David.

'Your fellow partner and so-called friend was a paid bodyguard just like you were, and just like you he wasn't very good at his job; otherwise, he would be alive and my man would have been dead in the street with a bullet in his head instead,' defended Kay.

'My friend and partner, wasn't just in the wrong place at the wrong time. He had a wife and family who loved him and he saved my life that day and so I owe him; a-life-for-a-life… just like I owe Reginald Price a-life-for-a-life.'

'Well, you got the pen so go ahead and stab me again; after all, I'm trussed up like a turkey ready for the slaughter, but then that would make you just like me; a cold-blooded killer pulling the trigger on its defenceless victim,' mocked Kay.

Stepping closer, David said, 'I enjoyed shooting your back-up man in the head with his own bullet. And I don't feel any remorse. He was a hired killer waiting to pull the trigger on two more innocent victims on *your* instructions, just like the day he shot my friend and partner in the head at point-blank-range sixteen years ago.' Bending down, he whispered, 'He was the idiot hired killer who was too busy watching his targets to hear me coming up behind him when I stabbed him in the neck with this silver-tipped ink pen before taking his gun and shooting him in head at point-blank range.'

'And so now, you're going to take out that fucking pen again?' said Kay, swallowing his own spineless spit.

Stepping back, David smiled. 'I'm not here to kill you, Alex Trent, I'm here to *judge* you for the cold-blooded murder of Reginald Price and Alan D. Mitchell, the bodyguard whose name you didn't even know or care to know.'

Sitting in the chair, Kay waited.

Anne stepped forward and asked, 'Alex Trent, how do you plead to the crimes put forward to you by David Fox; guilty or not guilty?'

'Spitting at Anne, Kay countered, 'I don't recognise this fucking trial or the so-called jury of victims, and I answer to *nobody* in this room. My name is Jason Kay and this is *my house* and I make the rules in it. I don't answer to the name of Alex Trent. He died in a fire thirty years ago and I'm not that man.'

Wiping the spit off her shoe, Anne turned towards David and asked, 'David Fox, how do you find against the defendant, Alex Trent, on behalf of the jury of victims, guilty or not guilty?'

Staring straight at the defendant, David raised his right arm, forming the shape of a gun with his fingers. Then said, 'Guilty.' Stepping closer, he pointed the gun again and repeated the words, 'Guilty…' He moved forward for a third time and pressed the gun into the defendant's forehead, stating, 'Guilty.'

Releasing his fingers from Kay's forehead, David returned to his seat in the circle of jurors.

Kay shouted, 'I repeat. I don't recognise this court of fucking nobodies…'

Noting David Fox's verdict of guilty in the file with her silver-tipped ink pen, Anne turned to ask the second victim/juror to step forward.

Diane Moffatt stood up and walked into the centre of the circle.

'You must be fucking joking,' laughed Kay, continuing, 'You're no bloody *victim*. I took you from hell and placed you in heaven, so how can you claim the right to judge me when I gave you a life that a tart like you would never have had?'

'My name is Diane Moffatt and I'm not a tart. I'm a human being with feelings. I have a heart and a soul; two things that you don't possess, Alex Trent, or whatever name you choose to call yourself because no name can hide the darkness that exists inside that shell of body you take such pride in showing off to the world,' countered Diane.

Hissing at her face like a poisonous snake ready to pounce on its prey, Kay spat out, 'I took you from a seedy nightclub hostess and made you into what you are today. I gave you a posh flat to live in, nice clothes to wear, an expense account for champagne and wine plus an overpaid job as a secretary that was way above your pay grade and abilities. I didn't require your services in bed on an hourly treadmill like your clients in the nightclub and didn't beat you when you had a "headache". And for all those riches and luxuries that I lavished upon you, all I asked from you in return was ten years of compliance to my rules when you would have walked away with a golden handshake of three hundred thousand pounds. So I ask you again, Miss Moffatt, how can you claim to be a victim when I saved you from being a victim?'

Glancing around the circle, Diane spread her arms open wide and confessed, 'You're right, I was a victim when you met me in the nightclub, but I was a victim with a dream and a purpose of my own. I was saving to go to college to qualify as a librarian and help other poor girls growing up on the poor side of town so that they too could become more than just a child bride, mother and lowly paid cleaner/housewife at the mercy of a drunken husband who only ever noticed he had a wife and a partner on a Friday and Saturday night when the pubs were closed and he required her to spread her legs before passing out.'

'So what are you crying about then? I didn't stop you from going to college or night school and you could have walked away anytime you liked, but didn't,' accused Kay, enjoying picking apart her accusations.

Breathing in, Diane stood up straight and argued, 'For six long years, you slowly stripped away my identity piece-by-piece, just like peeling an onion, until there was nothing left inside of me except a rotten core and I lost the girl with a dream. I lost my humanity. I lost my ability to feel compassion for others. I lost the will to laugh and even cry, because if you don't feel anything inside, then you can't shed any tears, I let you corrupt me with *your* darkness until I'm ashamed to say that I forgot who I was before I met you. And yes, I did try to walk away many times, but where would I have walked to? I had no dream any more... I had no purpose or hope any more except clinging onto the fantasy that three hundred thousand pounds would save me. But deep down inside my rotten core, I knew that no amount of money could save me from what I had become, an empty shell of *you*...'

Catching her breath, Diane turned round and smiled at Anne. 'Then I met a woman in a magical wood who gave me back my heart and soul. A woman who was once a girl with a dream like me, only this woman never gave up on her dream. This woman never lost her humanity or compassion for others. This woman made me laugh again and even cry at my own selfishness. This woman is your wife, who had endured your cruelty and suffered your brutality far beyond what I ever did. She made me ashamed of what I had become, of what you had moulded me into. This woman gave me back myself before I met you. And so, yes, I was a victim when I met you, but I was my *own* victim, and free to walk away to a life that I would choose whenever I was ready. But *nobody* is free to walk away from you, the great and powerful Jason Kay, until you throw them away like trash,' said Diane, stepping back.

Anne touched her arm and the two women melted into one.

'Oh please, save me from this sisterhood crap,' mocked Kay, secretly seething inside at the sight of both his wife and mistress turning against him, together...

Anne stepped forward and asked, 'Alex Trent, how do you plead to the crimes put forward to you by Diane Moffatt, guilty or not guilty?'

'I don't answer to my fucking wife or mistress,' said Kay, attempting to stand up and shove his body at them, but unable to move out of the straightjacket and chair.

Anne turned towards Diane and asked, 'Diane Moffatt, how do you find against the defendant, Alex Trent, on behalf of the jury of victims, guilty or not guilty?'

Stepping into the centre of the circle, Diane turned towards the defendant and pointed her finger straight at him, then said, 'Guilty... Guilty... Guilty...' before returning to her seat in the circle of jurors.

Kay yelled, 'Fucking betraying bitch!'

Noting Diane Moffatt's verdict of guilty in the file, Anne turned to ask the third victim/juror to step forward when Maggie Frith stood up and walked into the centre of the circle.

'Oh, here we go again, another crying female bleating on about how mean her boss has been to her,' laughed Kay, furious at having to sit tied to a chair and be accused by a lowly housekeeper.

'Do you see me crying, Mr Kay, or should I say, Mr Trent,' said Maggie, suddenly finding her voice after years of contrite obedience.

'Precisely, what have you got to cry about? You're a bloody housekeeper and not a very smart one either. I paid you to do a simple job and this is how you repay me? I should have fired you sixteen years ago when I married your pathetic pretend-daughter, but I let you stay and play mother. So how can you claim to be a victim when all I've done is show you pity and pay you a wage for a doing a job that you would have gladly done for nothing just to be a surrogate mother to a daughter that's not even your blood,' mocked Kay, sneering over at Anne, knowing that he was still able to hurt her with just a few well-chosen cruel words towards those she loved.

Fixing her eyes right in the defendant's, Maggie let rip. 'Just because you can't see my tears, it doesn't mean that I'm not crying inside, but that's what you do, isn't it, Mr empty-shell-of-a-man? Find your victim's weakness and then slowly pick away at it until there's nothing left inside that victim but a hollow hole for you to fill up with your poisonous cruelty. You knew how much I loved Anne and how much she loved me and so that's why you kept me on as the housekeeper when you married her sixteen years ago. Every time you were cruel to her, I saw you look at me and give that snake-like grin. You knew that I was crying inside, but that's what you enjoyed, two victims for the price of one. You knew that Anne was afraid for me if I challenged you or went outside Hilltop Mansion for help and so preyed upon her need to protect me just like you used my fear of what revenge you would exact upon her if I told the world outside about the horrors you committed against her inside the prison you kept my sweet girl locked up in,' accused Maggie. A stream of tears flowed out of her eyes and Anne stepped forward to comfort her. 'Please, I must finish this on my own, my sweet girl, otherwise I will always remain his victim,' she said, smiling lovingly at her whilst holding her hand up to stop her.

Kay interjected, 'Oh for Christ's sake, first you can't cry and now you can't stop fucking crying! No wonder women are the weaker sex and men rule the universe! Do you see me crying even though I'm trussed up like a turkey ready for the slaughter? No, you bloody well don't, because whatever you do or say to me in this charade of a court room, I will never be anyone's victim. So how can you claim to be a bloody victim when you were free to come and go as you pleased and could have saved your precious "daughter" if you really did love her and had the balls of a man to do something about it?' He lapped up Maggie's tears like nectar to a stinging wasp.

Standing her ground like a warrior mother protecting her family, Maggie countered, 'You can't cry because you have no soul or heart. You don't feel love or pity for anyone else other than yourself, because your body is just an icy shell of cold ambition. You don't understand sacrifice for others because that would require compassion, which a cold-blooded selfish taker like you doesn't possess. You're just a hollow hole filled with poisonous venom, who, even now as you're tied to that chair, still think that you can beat me down with cruel words and vicious taunts. You knew that every time I left Anne alone in this house with you, I cried and cried torrents of tears for her alone in my bedroom at night. You had made me, a strong, independent, vibrant and happy woman who feared nothing and no one, into another helpless, voiceless victim for you to taunt and play with at your pleasure, and when you were done playing your cruel games with me, you fired me… because I was no longer of any use to you as a victim when you'd already arranged other plans for your wife.'

Wiping the tears from her eyes, Anne stepped forward and asked, 'Alex Trent, how do you plead to the crimes put forward to you by Maggie Frith, guilty or not guilty?'

Kay turned his body to face Maggie and Anne, then held his head upright and spat three times in the air before slithering back into the chair, silent.

Turning her head back towards Maggie, Anne asked, 'Maggie Frith, how do you find against the defendant, Alex Trent, on behalf of the jury of victims, guilty or not guilty?'

Stepping defiantly into the centre of the circle, Maggie turned to face the defendant. Raising her hand, she moved closer then pressed one finger dead centre in the middle of his forehead whilst staring right inside his cold eyes when, without a single second of hesitation, she declared, 'Guilty… Guilty… Guilty…'

As she turned her back, Kay hissed and spat at Maggie whilst cursing her under his breath. She calmly returned to her seat in the circle of jurors.

Noting Maggie Frith's verdict of guilty in the file, Anne turned to ask the fourth victim/juror to step forward. Eric Finch stood up and walked into the centre of the circle.

'I need to do a bloody piss and shit *now*; otherwise, it'll be all over the chair and nice clean beige carpet,' demanded Kay, wriggling about inside the straightjacket. Anne turned round and pulled out a piss-pot from behind the sofa and passed it over to Eric who couldn't help the wide grin spreading across his face when he stepped three paces forward and said, 'You can bloody piss and shit into this, *sir*.' He placed the piss-pot directly under the centre of the chair.

Bending down to see the pot beneath his legs, Kay erupted, 'I can't relieve myself in this. My pants will be covered in piss and shit.'

'There's a hole in the chair and straightjacket, and besides, what's a little piss and shit to a man whose entire body is one big fat pile of excrement,' said Eric, unable to hide the sheer delight on his face at finally seeing the great Jason Kay reduced to pissing through his pants into a pot.

Frantically trying to release his body from the straightjacket, Kay couldn't hold back any more when the *shit-hit-the-fan* and everything just poured out from underneath his legs into the pot.

Humiliated and ashamed, Kay sat upright in the chair and cursed his accusers, 'Do you feel brave now sitting on your clean arses whilst watching me fill up mine with my own excrement?'

'But that's what you did to your wife with a simple swipe of your fancy silver-tipped ink pen when you had her body strapped into a straightjacket and locked away in a single soulless ten-by-seven square metre white-washed wall cell containing a hard wooden boarded bed and one piss-pot,' accused Eric, wanting to punch him right between the eyes when he saw the pain on Anne's face as she remembered being locked in the hospital's isolation cell when her father died and Kay had her sectioned while he took control of her fiancés and life.

Squirming around in his soiled pants, Kay argued, 'She was mentally unstable and needed treatment. I'm *not*... And what the fuck has it to do with you what I decide for *my* wife. How does that make *you* a "victim" when you're just an overpaid hired lackey who spends his time hiding in a wooden lodge dreaming about saving the princess in the castle, when you spend your pathetic life digging around in the dirt?'

'You're the mentally unstable one. You cold-bloodedly killed the man that took you in when he caught you stealing from him and loved you like a son. He gave you a loving home, life and future and then his beloved daughter, but that wasn't enough for you. No, you had to *take everything*! You broke Reginald Price's heart. He cried in that wood lodge when he begged for *my* forgiveness for giving all his love to *you* and leaving none left over for his own daughter and the boy that was always there for him, but never saw until it was too late,' said Eric, barely able to control his rage.

'So now we have the real reason you're here in this mock trial. You're no bloody victim. You're just a jealous little nobody who dreamt of Reginald Price adopting you as his son instead of me and having everything that I have, including marrying his daughter, but didn't have the balls or brains to take it all for yourself.' Laughed Kay, knowing that Eric couldn't deny his accusations.

Looking over at Anne and then back at the jurors of victims, Eric opened up and confessed, 'I loved Reginald Price more than I loved my own father, but not as son loves a father. I loved working for him and being with him, and yes, I would have done anything for that old man who never showed me anything other than respect and kindness. He valued who I was and what I did. He took time to share his thoughts with me and to listen to mine. He never ever belittled my work and valued my opinion as his employee. He was everything my father wasn't... and yes, everything I wished my father was... but how many people in this room can truly say that they had never wished for that perfect father or mother when their own parents let them down?' Spreading his arms around the circle, Eric stopped at each juror/victim, including Anne. He hesitated for a moment before coming back to the defendant.

'Reginald Price was a wonderful employer, mentor and friend to me, and for that, I loved him with all my being, but he wasn't a wonderful father. He didn't treat his daughter, Anne, well. He was, as all parents are and will continue to be, an imperfect human being, but he didn't deserve to be murdered in cold blood by the man he thought loved him like a father, only to discover that *you* loved his money and possessions more. I'm not jealous of you because you are everything I despise in a man. You take and never give. You destroy and never build. You are the jealous one, not me, but I am your victim, and therefore, have a right to be on the jury of victims. Yes, I could have struck you down at any time with my bare hands. I'm bigger and stronger than you both physically and mentally; whereas, you are weak and cowardly, but you possess a darkness in you that reaches out and destroys even the most powerful of enemies. You knew that as long as you controlled your wife's life, you controlled mine too.

'I didn't desire or want to marry Anne Price, I loved her like the sister I never had and she loved me back as that sister, and so we protected each other like loving brothers and sisters do. You used that love to control both of our lives just like you do with everyone that possess something you want, including your own family. You destroy goodness and spread darkness. Everything and everyone that you touch becomes your victim, even a strong man like me,' accused Eric, feeling ashamed at admitting to being beaten down by a small, insignificant, cowardly man not worthy of the spit in his mouth.

Gently smiling over at Eric, Anne stepped closer into the circle until she was face-to face with the defendant. She asked, 'Alex Trent, how do you plead to the crimes put forward to you by Eric Finch, guilty or not guilty?'

Still squirming inside his soiled pants, Kay protested, 'My name is Jason Kay, your fucking husband, and this man is *no* victim. He's always hated me ever since your father brushed him aside thirty years ago and so has *no* right to be here judging me. I didn't put a gun to old man Price's head; he chose me because I was the better son he never had, not that moron. So stick that in your stupid file and shove it up your treacherous backside, you fucking bitch.'

'Well, you would know all about *treachery*, husband,' said Anne. She glanced down at the stained carpet under the chair and smiled when she added, 'What a mess you've made of the clean carpet and as you no longer have a housekeeper or wife at your beck and call, you'll have to clean it up yourself; otherwise, *everything won't be as it should be* when the trial is over and sentence is passed.'

Turning her head swiftly towards Eric, she asked, 'Eric Finch, how do you find against the defendant, Alex Trent, on behalf of the jury of victims, guilty or not guilty?'

Stepping forward, Eric wrapped his powerful hands around the straps on the straightjacket, then lifted the chair and Kay's body up into his face, locking their eyes together before pronouncing, 'Guilty... Guilty... Guilty...'

Releasing the defendant, the chair fell back onto the carpet as Eric re-joined the circle of jurors.

Noting Eric Finch's verdict of guilty in the file, Anne turned to ask the fifth victim/juror to step forward. Dr Stuart Pritchard stood up and walked into the centre of the circle and Kay spat right into his eyes.

He asked, 'And what did my treacherous wife offer you to betray *me*, the man who was going to make you rich enough to retire in style to your dream location in the sun?'

'Nothing,' replied Pritchard, breathing in the air of freedom at last.

'You bloody liar. You're an old man with failing health and a secret dodgy medical history you've tried to hide. If it wasn't for me keeping you on as my wife's physician, you'd be languishing in a prison cell for killing one of your own patients with the wrong medication years ago. You're *no* victim. I saved your miserable career and reputation,' accused Kay, shell-shocked that Pritchard had chosen his pathetic wife's future over his.

'I may be an old man, but I'm not dead yet. But soon, I will be called to judgement by a higher court than this one here today,' said Pritchard, lifting his arms upwards towards the ceiling. 'My trial will be swift because I won't need to defend my crimes when I have only one plea to enter; guilty as charged.'

'So what the hell are you doing here bleating on about being a victim when you've just admitted being guilty of whatever crap you're about to claim that I forced you to do... because you were *afraid* of me,' mocked Kay.

Relaxing his arms, Pritchard looked over at Anne and confessed, 'Everything I did against you on behalf of that creature on trial over there, I now beg your forgiveness in front of him and my fellow victims/jurors. I locked you away in that soulless cell when your father died believing that I was protecting you and the money your father bequeathed to you under the trust fund when in truth, I was weak and afraid for myself. I told myself that because I was your doctor, I could control the situation when another doctor wouldn't have cared what he did to you on behalf of your so-called husband. I convinced myself that I was avenging your father's murder by that miserable excuse for a human being when in reality, I needed to extinguish *my* own guilt at not saving my oldest friend when he asked for my help and I turned my back on him.'

Turning round to face Kay, Pritchard proclaimed, 'I have no defence against what I did on behalf of this man on trial here today except to say that I too am also his victim.'

'What utter rubbish,' attacked Kay, desperate to escape the straightjacket and stuff Pritchard's betraying words down his throat. 'You got well-paid for being my wife's physician and the only reason you've turned traitor now is because you're still trying to save your own miserable skin.'

'If I wanted to *save my own miserable skin* as you put it, then I wouldn't be here confessing *all* my crimes which are being noted down together with yours in that file... that Inspector Steal and Sergeant Wright will read when this trial is over and use as evidence against each and every one of us in this court room.'

'Then you're *all* stupid! If you hand that file to the police, they will know what you did to me here today and over the months when you plotted together behind my back to exact your pathetic revenge when all you had to do was go and tell them what crimes you think I was guilty of instead of playing the victim,' countered Kay, staring at the file in Anne's hand, desperate to know what *final ending* she had planned for him, but too afraid to ask.

'No one on the jury of victims believes that they will get due justice for the terrible crimes you committed against them and their loved ones. You've managed to escape punishment for the last thirty years and would no doubt escape it again if we just handed you over to the police. No, the file isn't about evidence, but how the justice system failed *all* the victims in it, leaving them with no other option except to exact their own justice,' said Pritchard, turning to face his fellow jurors/victims and stating, 'I'm guilty of many things, but it is because of that shame and guilt that I am also a victim of the defendant. He took my guilt and shame at failing my patient when I was a young doctor and blackmailed me to be his unwilling conspirator. Yes, I should have done the right thing and confessed my mistake to the medical board, but once this man injects his poison into you, there is *no* escape except when he is done with you and administers the lethal dose.'

Once again, Anne asked, 'Alex Trent, how do you plead to the crimes put forward to you by Dr Stuart Pritchard, guilty or not guilty?'

Kay replied, 'What's the fucking point when you've already decided that I'm guilty?'

'So to clarify for the file you are now stating that you are guilty of *all* the crimes put to you by the victims in this court room?' she noted.

'Don't you try and trick me, you bitch. I'm guilty of nothing except being smarter and more successful than everyone who thought they were better than me.'

Noting the defendant's comments in the file, Anne turned and asked, 'Dr Stuart Pritchard, how do you find against the defendant, Alex Trent, on behalf of the jury of victims, guilty or not guilty?'

Smiling at Anne, Pritchard turned and faced the defendant before stating loudly to the court, 'Guilty… Guilty… Guilty…' then quietly returned to his seat in the circle of jurors, still remembering the patient and his old friend Reginald Price whom he failed.

Noting Dr Pritchard's verdict of guilty in the file, Anne asked the sixth victim/juror to step forward. Simon Dodd stood up and walked into the centre of the circle. Kay ignored him and looked straight over at Anne.

Feeling weak and tired from being strapped inside the straightjacket and chair for what seemed like days instead hours, he said, 'Before I have to listen to another bleeding-heart-story, I need some food and water; otherwise, I'll be dead long before you and your soppy lover over there get the chance to stick the knife in yourselves.'

'The only killer in this room is *you*, and yet you ask for kindness from your victims when you showed them none? You beg for food and water when you starved me of both when I didn't follow your "house rules" to your satisfaction. You call me names and say I'm an adulteress when you have had countless mistresses and know that I have been a faithful wife because if I weren't, I'd be standing over my lover's grave,' said Anne, glancing over at Simon.

Kay saw the love glowing out of them towards each other. 'I'm not interested in another bloody character assassination from two useless cry-baby cheats playing tough now that you think you have the upper hand. Just get me some food and water before I pass out and your farcical trial crashes to an early end.'

Unable to hold back the laughter at the irony of Kay's demands, Anne replied, 'Your request is denied and if you pass out, then we'll throw a bucket of cold water over you and shove a hard-boiled egg in your mouth, minus the two slices of buttered bread and pot of tea.'

'You—'

'That's enough, Kay,' interjected Simon, stepping closer. 'You're not going to bloody faint or die on us. You're too fucking arrogant and self-possessed for that. Even now, your brain is ticking away thinking of the terrible punishments you're going to inflict on everyone here when you "miraculously" escape that straightjacket and stroll out of this room victorious over all the odds yet again.'

'My, my, the soppy little son who hated his father and yet never had the balls to tell him or make his own way in life is giving me a lecture on *my* life. At least I made a life of my own choosing and not the one that my old man would have chosen for me,' countered Kay, still raging with hatred inside for a father who burnt alive in a barn thirty years ago and for whom he never shed a single tear.

Stepping back, Simon slowly circled the chair, running his eyes up and down Kay's body before returning to the same spot where he stood in silence.

Kay demanded, 'What the fuck are you staring at?' He suddenly felt nervous.

'I'm staring at the man who killed my father without an ounce of remorse and wondering what kind of man is really lurking beneath that smooth exterior you display for the world outside these walls. You let me believe that my father didn't love me when in truth, he did in his own way. You let me believe that my father didn't want me to have another career and life other than carrying on the family business when in truth, he was trying to protect me from you. You let me believe that I was worthless and therefore I became worthless. You stole sixteen years of my life which I spent hating a father that died to protect me when I could have mourned at his grave and told him that I did love him. You imprisoned the only woman that I ever loved in a marriage of untold misery and made her believe that I didn't care, knowing that without her love I was a broken shell of a man.'

'You can't plead the "I'm the innocent victim card" to me. You prepared and countersigned the legal Power of Attorney, giving me total control over my wife's life and finances in collusion with that

231

other lying hypocrite Pritchard sitting over there in judgement over me when he prepared and countersigned the Interment Form declaring my wife mentally unstable and giving me, her husband, the power to incarcerate her in a secure hospital facility for an indefinite period of time. You are as guilty as me; otherwise, you wouldn't have "betrayed the love of your life" by doing what I wanted. You chose to protect your own pathetic life instead of hers when your spineless back was up against the wall,' accused Kay, glancing over at Anne with that dark, snake-like grin he gave having beaten her down again with just a few well-chosen cruel words.

Simon calmly countered, 'Like you, Jason Kay or should I say Alex Trent, not everything that both I and Dr Pritchard prepared and you signed was as they appeared to be.'

'No. No. No...that's not right...' panicked Kay, noting the sly, satisfied smiles on not only Simon and Anne's faces, but every single face sitting in the jury of victims. 'I read both those documents line-by-line and page-by-page before signing them and they both clearly stated the name of my wife, Mrs Anne Kay, as the unstable marriage partner with me, her husband, Mr Jason Kay, as having control of everything. And it's *my* signature on those forms, *not* hers, so that means that I, Jason Kay, still *control* everything and I won't sign anything in this room today or any other day, handing control of *my* empire over to that woman.' Feeling the power surging back through his body, he concluded, 'And a dead man can't sign anything so go ahead and fucking kill me, because I still win... even from the grave!'

Sitting upright inside the straightjacket, Kay waited for Simon to crumble just like he always did. Anne opened the file and pulled out *two* white sheets of A4 paper before handing one to Simon, when they both held them up in front of him and he read the name Jason Kay and *not* Anne Kay typed in the appropriate sections followed by his *wife's* signature instead of *his* written in ink on the bottom lines of the legal Power of Attorney and hospital Interment Forms.

Bending down, Anne waved Kay's silver-tipped pen in front of him and smiled... before slipping both legally signed forms back inside the file.

Returning to her usual spot, Anne nodded over to Simon who smiled back.

Kay exploded, 'This isn't happening! You can't do this to me! It's fraud! You slipped those pages into the documents and got me to sign them illegally. They won't hold up in a court of law and I'll have you all arrested for it. You won't get away with it, I won't let you! Do you hear me? I *won't* let you!'

'My, my... the *great* Jason Kay won't let *us* get away with it...,' mocked Simon, stepping closure and whispering in his ear, 'But we already have.'

Straightening his body, Simon asked, 'How does it feel to have signed *all* your power, possessions and life away with the same *silver-tipped ink pen* that you used to *kill* Reginald Price with and lock his daughter and your wife away in a hospital cell for the rest of her life? How does it feel to be completely and utterly at the mercy of the person or persons controlling every aspect of your life? How does it feel to feel less than worthless? And how does it feel to be the "victim" of your *own* scam? Mr Jason Kay/Alex Trent/victim?'

Tearing away at his body inside the straightjacket, the defendant protested, 'I'm *no* victim. I'm Jason Kay and I will destroy *all* of you. I'm *no* victim... I'm *no* victim...'

Noting the defendant's threats down in the file, Anne stepped forward and asked, 'Alex Trent, how do you plead to the crimes put forward to you by Simon Dodd, guilty or not guilty?'

Staring straight ahead, Kay ignored his accuser and repeated, 'I'm Jason Kay and I will destroy *all* of you...'

Noting Kay's no plea, and repeated threats to the jury of victims in the file, Anne turned towards Simon and asked, 'Simon Dodd, how do you find against the defendant, Alex Trent, on behalf of the jury of victims, guilty or not guilty?'

Standing firm, Simon pointed his finger dead ahead at the defendant, then pronounced three times, 'Guilty... Guilty... Guilty...' before returning to his seat in the circle of jurors and finally finding peace within himself for the father he thought never loved him, but died proving that he did.

Noting Simon Dodd's verdict of guilty in the file with Kay's silver-tipped ink pen, Anne waited for Kay's usual last words of protest only to hear, silence... She turned to ask the seventh victim/juror to step forward and Dotty Short stood up and walked into the centre of the circle.

Running his eyes up and down the pretty petite five-foot woman in her early forties with bright blue eyes and a slinky strawberry-blonde bobbed hair.

Kay mocked, 'Not another night-club whoring bitch that I fucked for money and who's now claiming to be another one of my victims? I don't even remember you let alone fucking you, so go ahead, spin your web of lies, I could do with a good laugh.'

Skipping forward three steps, Dotty coolly said, 'What an arrogant bastard you really are! You don't remember me because even if you were the last man standing on earth and I the last woman, I wouldn't let you "fuck me" as you so poetically put it because I wouldn't want to populate the future human race with your genes.'

'Huh, you may look like a painted doll but you've got a mouth on you like a gutter tart,' countered Kay, leaning forward and spitting out, 'If you're not an ex-mistress or secretary of mine, then who the hell are you and what have I ever done to you that gives you the right to sit in judgement of me?'

'You stole two eight-year-old little girls' future...'

'I've never had anything to do with kids and especially silly little girls. I hate them. They're an irritating annoyance that I'd rather stamp out with my foot, so stop talking in riddles and tell me who the fuck you are?'

'For a man who claims to be so smart, you really are dumb. I'm Anne's best friend, Dotty Short, whom you stopped her from seeing years ago. We grew up together, played together, laughed together, cried together, had dreams together and made wishes in a well together with an old coin when we were just eight years old. We had a future planned together. We had a life-long bond together that you broke. You ripped apart the beautiful, bright, shiny light which glowed inside that little girl, my friend, and replaced it with fear and terror. You stole my best friend and soul-mate from me and imprisoned her in your dark world of control and possession,' accused Dotty, losing the sparkle in her eyes as she wiped away the tears.

'I didn't steal anything from you. What the fuck has two silly little girls making a stupid wish down some bloody old well got to do with you claiming to be a victim? Your "best friend" over there was a grown woman when I married her and if she chose not to see you any more, then it was *her* choice and nothing to do with me. I didn't even know you existed and that she had any "best friends". I mean, look at her... she's drab, plain, boring and can't even boil an egg right. What half decent good-looking woman would want to hang around with her? Beautiful, bright, shiny light, what storybook did you pick that out of? It's about as far-fetched as your crappy name, Dotty,' laughed Kay.

'That's right, pick on the little woman. You weren't so cavalier with my fellow juror, Simon. No, it's much easier to feel brave when your victim can't hit back. Enjoy punching women with your fist? Just like you used to punch your wife! She stopped seeing me because you destroyed anyone or anything that she loved and cared for... She was afraid not only for herself, but for me. She never stopped being my best friend and I never stopped being hers, but we lost sixteen years of companionship, joyous laughter, dreams and precious time together that can never, ever be replaced. You switched the light of hope out of my dearest Anne and left her to crawl around in your isolated prison, helpless and afraid. You took away her *voice* and without that, no one could hear her despair... and when you did that to her, you also did it to me! How could I save my dearest Anne when she was too afraid to save herself?'

Smiling over at Dotty, Anne stepped forward and asked, 'Alex Trent, how do you plead to the crimes put forward to you by Dotty Short, guilty or not guilty?'

'This is a stitch-up. You're so-called "best-friend" that I never knew about suddenly appears as a juror/victim in this mock trial... How much did you pay her to pretend to be your "friend", because no bitch that looks like her would hang around with mousy little you!' laughed Kay.

'Says the man who had to steal another man's name to hide behind because if people knew what a pathetic bully the *real* Alex Trent was, they'd run a mile...' interjected Dotty, unable to stop the words tumbling out as Anne noted the defendant's no plea and usual taunts to the victim in the file before turning towards Dotty. She asked, 'Dotty Short, how do you find against the defendant, Alex Trent, on behalf of the jury of victims, guilty or not guilty?'

Sliding elegantly into the centre of the circle, Dotty turned towards the defendant and pointed two fingers straight up in the air forming a *v* sign before loudly stating, 'Guilty... Guilty... Guilty...' She resumed her seat on the circle of jurors.

Kay shouted, 'Fucking lying bitch!'

Noting Dotty Short's verdict of guilty in the file with the ink pen, Anne turned to ask the eighth victim/juror to step forward.

Anthony Gibbs stood up and walked into the centre of the circle.

'That's right, crawl in behind the back of a woman for protection, Gibbs, because you're definitely no sodden victim. If it wasn't for me, you'd still be a faceless accounts clerk sitting in line with all the other faceless clerks, earning a pittance that I saved you from and elevated you into a partner for the very accountant firm which wouldn't even allow you a lunch break. And this is the gratitude I get from the faceless nobody who wasn't even a man until I made him into one?' taunted Kay.

Eyeing the defendant up and down, Gibbs breathed in the air of freedom. And boy did it feel good! 'Your cruel taunts used to break me, but not any more. Now I'm a *free* man and can at last be the man that I should have been and not the man you proclaim to have created. So go ahead, spill out that poisonous bile that you so cleverly target towards your chosen victims behind closed doors, but never get heard outside those doors.'

'I made you fucking rich and you took the money. We had a "business arrangement" which served us both well, so don't bloody stand there and bleat on about being another one of my victims behind closed doors crap. You stole money from the shareholders and fiddled books whilst taking your cut, but miraculously sprout a conscience now the chips are down? You're just trying to save your own skin like all cowards do. Do you see me apologising for being smarter and better than my opponents? No, you fucking don't. A real man *owns* his victories and never apologises for doing what's necessary to beat down his enemies and win,' attacked Kay, sticking the knife in deeper. 'Even though I'm trussed up in this fucking straightjacket, I can still see you cowering in front me like the little pathetic weasel you really are. No wonder your wife killed herself...'

'My wife died because I forgot who I was and let you corrupt me with your false promises of a golden future! You seek out the weakness in those you need to use and then either break them, or corrupt them. Either way, they become another one of your victims. You tie them up in an *invisible* straightjacket and then, slowly, bit-by-bit pull in the straps until they suffocate inside that jacket! Yes, I took your money. Yes, I stole from innocent people, and yes, my beautiful innocent wife, Sandra, would be alive today if I hadn't met you and believed in your false words. But I'm not standing here today in front of my fellow jurors and victims to deny *my* part in my wife's suicide.'

'Then what are you doing here because the police will eventually investigate my disappearance and uncover all the money that *you* stole from *my* company and arrest you and throw you in jail. You don't have the balls to hack being locked up inside a prison cell for years and years with hardened criminals that'll slit your throat for the price of a packet of fags, Mr Anthony sniffling Gibbs...?' taunted Kay, looking for the sign that he had broken his opponent down yet again, only to see a peaceful calmness emanating from Gibbs that sent a shiver of fear through him that he'd *never* experienced before.

Anthony slipped his hand inside his jacket pocket and pulled out a photograph of Sandra. Kissing her beautiful face, he whispered, 'Soon, we'll be together again, my love...' before turning the photograph around and showing it to the defendant. 'Look at this innocent face and remember it, because you'll never see it where you're going.'

Leaning his head back, Kay laughed, 'Oh, I get it, now you're going to take the coward's way out before the police arrest you for fraud and embezzlement and swallow a bottle of sleeping pills just like your sad wife did! And here I was thinking that you had finally grown a pair of balls when all the time you had none...' Kay was feeling top dog again when Gibbs pulled out an *invisible knife* then stuck it in deep.

237

'The police will arrest me and I will confess to fraud and embezzlement. I will swallow a cyanide pill and commit suicide inside that prison cell you took such pleasure in describing, but before I swallow that lethal pill, I will *sign* one more confession.'

'Oh yeah… what's that?'

'Your murder…' smiled Gibbs.

'What the fuck?' said Kay.

Gibbs twisted the knife in again. 'I'm a dying man. I've just a few weeks left to live so why not confess to killing a man that ruined my life? Why should any other victim in this court room suffer any more at your hands when I'm already a dead man standing?' he said, carefully replacing the photograph of Sandra back inside his jacket pocket before adding, 'How does it feel to be beaten down and crushed by a faceless nobody?'

While the defendant took the time to comprehend Gibbs' final words, Anne stepped into the centre of the circle and asked, 'Alex Trent, how do you plead to the crimes put forward to you by Anthony Gibbs, guilty or not guilty?'

Pulling himself together, he answered, 'Now that I know a dying man is going to kill me, why should I bother even fucking answering your stupid question when you've already pronounced sentence before the trial is even over?'

'Because you're the great Jason Kay/Alex Trent and don't believe in losing, so why not play the game out to the end and see if you can *win* this time,' said Anne, noting the defendant's no plea yet again in the file before turning towards Anthony. She asked, 'Anthony Gibbs, how do you find against the defendant, Alex Trent, on behalf of the jury of victims, guilty or not guilty?'

Touching the photo of Sandra safely tucked away inside his jacket pocket, Anthony looked dead ahead at the defendant, then said without hesitation, 'Guilty… Guilty… Guilty…' before returning to his seat in the circle of jurors when they all stood up and nodded their eternal gratitude and friendship in synchronised silence for the man who would go to his grave protecting his friends.

Noting Anthony Gibbs' verdict of guilty in the file, Anne turned to ask the ninth victim/juror to step forward. Jacky Jones stood up and walked into the centre of the circle.

'Ah, the sneaky little blackmailer who thinks that he has a right to be *me* and take everything that I've made and created, including the five hundred thousand pounds that Gibbs stole from Kay Corporation just because I borrowed your ID card thirty years ago at the hostel for a free meal and bed for one night. I may have borrowed your name, but you're no saint. You watched me throw an ID card in a bin whilst hiding in the alleyway and then snuck it out from the bin after I left instead of facing me man-to-man and demanding your ID card back... so don't stand there and preach to me about morality when you stole your so called "best-friend" Jacky Jones' name and used it to become a dirty little blackmailer,' accused Kay, unable to hide his uneasiness at standing face-to-face with a ghost resurrected from the dead to reclaim his birth name.

'First, I'm *no* blackmailer, and haven't stolen five hundred thousand from you. Whatever money was transferred will be given back with interest to the innocent shareholders that you've been systemically stealing from for years to finance your lavish lifestyle and the rest will be returned to its rightful place. Second, I'm *no* thief... but did need to attract your attention and what better way to do that than by threatening to take away everything that *you* stole from your victims?'

'Why not just take the money in one shot and return it to its rightful place instead of sending blackmailing emails over six months listing my "so-called crimes"?' countered Kay.

'But what fun would there be in that, Alex? I wanted you to experience what it was like to be the victim. You've enjoyed thirty years of blackmailing and threatening hundreds of victims just because they had what you deemed to be your God-given right to take. Even when you were being blackmailed, you still carried on blackmailing others.' He paused for a moment as Jacky remembered his first meeting with Mr A under the railway bridge. 'There was a moment thirty years ago when I was just fifteen years old and hiding under a railway bridge with dozens of other lost and forgotten souls when I nearly become your *ninth* ghost in the ground. Then a tall stranger came along and asked me a question, "Do you want to *live dying* or *die living*?" As I glanced around at the half-dead tramps huddled together under the bridge and replied, *"Die Living"*, he took my hand and I was re-born as Jacky Jones. That tall, kind man's name was Alexander Forbes who set up and ran an invisible covert organisation hidden deep within the shadows of the police force, known only to a trusted few as "The Department". Mr A, short for Alexander, showed me that just because bad things happen to you it doesn't mean that you can't take those bad things and turn them into good. He taught me everything he knew about running the department and in return, I didn't use Jacky Jones name to blackmail, threaten and *kill* more victims, but to get justice and finally, closure, when the law failed them. Jacky Jones betrayed me for the price of a meal and a bed for the night, but he didn't deserve to *die* for being hungry and tired, and so instead of hating him, I forgave him because he didn't have an Alexander Forbes to come along and save him like I did thirty years ago when you killed my best-friend just because he was a lose end.'

'How big of you to forgive your betraying friend when in truth, I did you a favour by killing him. When he died, you were free to become a "better version of him" according to you. And as for nearly being my *ninth* corpse, I'm flattered that you've been keeping count of all the dead bodies that I've supposedly buried over the years. But are you sure you've got the number right? I mean, just eight over thirty years? A poor record for a *serial killer*... wouldn't you agree? And if you've known about my *true identity* for the last thirty years, why didn't you do anything about it instead of nothing... and prevented more deaths?' taunted Kay.

Jacky looked over at Anne who nodded her head. John Wilding stood up from the jury of victims and walked into the circle, carrying another file which he handed to Jacky.

Standing side-by-side, the two men bowed their heads in remembrance. Jacky then stepped forward and placed the file on the defendant's knee... and Kay read the note pinned on top. *"If you have received this file, then I am already dead. My name is Reginald Price and inside is the story of the man that stole your name and life. Read it and if you want justice, then ring this number..."*

Stepping back, Jacky stated, 'Alexander Forbes gave me that file five years ago, shortly before he died. After reading it, I dialled the number on the note and John Wilding answered. We joined forces together. I've only known about your existence for the last five years when you killed your wife's father Reginald Price in cold blood. But it has taken my friend John Wilding thirty years to get justice for the murder of his son, Freddy, by your hands. And not because of anything that he had done wrong, but because the justice system and the law that he once loved and pledged his life to failed him when he went to them and they turned their back him, leaving him and all the other victims in that file with only *one* choice.'

'You bloody lying pack of hypocrites…' laughed Kay, pretending to not care whether he lived or died whilst inside, he was literally shitting his pants, again. 'Using the law to excuse blackmailing, kidnapping and imprisoning me in my *own* house in a straightjacket whilst you play out your fucking *mock trial* to justify your pre-ordained outcome of guilty so that you can cold-bloodedly *kill* me without a conscience? 'You're *no* better than me. You're worse! At least, I don't pretend to be righteous and good. It's dog-eat-dog in this world. And I have no intention of being my opponent's bloody meal when I can make them mine first.'

'I'm not going to stand here and pretend that I'm not enjoying seeing you squirm like the little rat you are, strapped inside the very same straightjacket that you instructed Dr Pritchard to prepare for your wife. I'm not going to pretend that I didn't enjoy blackmailing you for money that was never yours in the first place. And I'm not going to pretend that I wouldn't like to take a sharp knife from your kitchen drawer and cut your heart out with it and feed it to the stray dogs that hide in the woods at the back of Hilltop Mansion… except that your heart is so full of poisonous envy and hatred that it would probably kill them. And even stray dogs deserve a better meal than your ruthless, cold heart,' said Jacky, stepping forward and retrieving the file before handing it back to John Wilding.

'Very poetic words for a blackmailer who's also probably a liar, because five hundred thousand pounds is a lot of money and when push comes to shove, how do I know that you'll return all that money when I won't be alive to see it?' challenged Kay, still trying to work out a plan of escape inside his head whilst panicking at the thought that he was fast running out of options for the first time in thirty years of being *top-dog* in the pack.

'There are many ways to die… Some are fast and painless. Others are slow and agonising. So, I repeat the same question that Mr A asked me thirty years ago when I saw the black-dog-of-death coming for me. "Do you want to *live dying* or *Die Living*, Mr Alex Trent?" smiled Jacky.

'I don't answer fucking riddles and I don't recognise the name of Alex Trent, because he doesn't exist any more; the same as *you* don't. I've earned to right to be Jason Kay whereas you didn't have the balls to claim it back when you had the chance thirty years ago?' growled Kay, still picturing himself as top-dog when he no longer had any arms or legs to fight with.

'I offered you my hand in friendship and gave you the chance to answer the "riddle" in the hope that you would take the opportunity to learn to be a better man, but in order to know the answer you would need to realise how *precious* life is even when you think you no longer care whether you *live* or *die*…' said Jacky, pausing before ending his case with, 'When I joined forces with John Wilding and my fellow jury of victims, I began with just one quest:

'"Three names, three ghosts: one dead, two alive…
Jacky Jones, Alex Trent, Jason Kay…"

'And now that I've finally come face-to-face with my *other self*, who has haunted and shadowed me for thirty years, and see that you are just *an empty shadow*, I can now leave you behind in the shadows.

'"Three names, three ghosts; two dead, but only one *still alive…"*

'I don't need to claim my name back any more, Alex Trent, I know who I am, but the question I now put to you is, do you? Because there's a *third* name that befits the *real* you hiding behind the other two.'

'I fucking know who I am,' protested Kay.

Anne stepped into the inner circle and asked, 'Alex Trent, how do you plead to the crimes put forward to you by Jacky Jones, guilty or not guilty?'

'What fucking crimes? I borrowed his name and he did to the same to his betraying friend, so we're even, and as for smothering his so-called best friend in his bed, well, it turns out I did the new *Jacky Jones* a favour. So how I can be *guilty* when the only ghost in the ground is a worthless, betraying, lying scumbag?'

Noting the defendant's not guilty plea in the file, Anne turned towards Jacky and asked, 'Jacky Jones, how do you find against the defendant, Alex Trent, on behalf of the jury of victims; guilty or not guilty?'

Facing the defendant, Jacky answered, 'An innocent man doesn't kill another human being simply because he considers them worthless... And so, I find you Guilty... Guilty... Guilty...'

Having pleaded his case, Jacky nodded his head towards his fellow victims John Wilding and Anne Kay before returning to his seat in the circle of jurors.

Kay shouted, 'What's my sodden name then?' Anne noted Jacky Jones' verdict of guilty in the file before turning to ask the tenth victim/juror to step forward.

John Wilding turned his head to face the defendant and Kay growled, 'I'm still waiting for your blackmailing best buddy Jacky boy hiding amongst the women over there to answer my question; "What's the *third* bloody name he's decided to Christen me with?"' He was half-amused, but the other half more afraid than curious.

John Wilding smiled and answered, 'Jacky didn't choose your *third* and last name; your wife did...'

Fuming, Kay turned his head towards Anne and demanded, 'What fucking right do you have to choose another name for me and then brag about it being my last... when you were a useless wife with the brain and intelligence of a gnat?'

Without a flicker of emotion in her voice, Anne answered, 'Sixteen years of being married and living with that foul mouth of yours gives me *every* right to choose the name that I secretly called you inside my head every single second of the day that I had to endure being your wife.'

'You wouldn't dare answer me back like that if I wasn't tied up in this fucking straightjacket!'

'You'll get your turn to challenge me and discover your *third* name when I get called upon to plead my case against you from the jury of victims; until then, you are answerable to John Wilding,' said Anne, noting the defendant's threatening comments in the file.

Still fuming at not being able to "teach the bitch her usual lesson", Kay turned his fury onto John Wilding. 'So now, it's the turn of the cry-baby police constable who couldn't get me arrested thirty years ago and has failed every year since then. Some policeman you are? No wonder it was so easy to kill your mouthy son, Freddy. Like father, like son, as the saying goes.' He laughed, waiting for John to take the bait.

Raising his head slightly, John locked his eyes into Kay's. 'I've pictured this moment every single day of my life since you murdered my Freddy thirty years ago and laughed in my face when I questioned you about it at your father's farm. I saw the darkness in your eyes then just as I see it now, but what I never understood that day was why kill an innocent apprentice car mechanic in cold blood just because he poked fun at you in the garage where you had your car serviced a week earlier. Unless, his corpse was more valuable to you than your own; because you're supposed to be a pile of charred bones and ashes alongside your father, mother, brother and sister, who all burnt to death in a fire inside the barn at Trent Farm just four days after I questioned you about my missing son. And yet, here you are, very much alive, *Mr Alex Trent...*' accused John, wanting to light a match to the straightjacket and watch him *burn alive* whilst screaming in agony; just like he must have heard Freddy's cries of terror inside the burning barn.

'Are you sure that you *really* want to know how your mouthy little Freddy died, ex-Police Constable Wilding, because it's not a happy tale?' Kay asked, eager to oblige, but unable to resist taunting his accuser first.

'We both know that you can't wait to tell me so go ahead, spill your bile because my Freddy is listening to you as well. Only a ghost can't be murdered twice, but it can reach out from the grave and leave its eternal mark on his killer.'

'Nice try, Constable Wilding, but I'll take my chances; after all, I'm a "monstrous serial killer" according to your blackmailer friend, so bring on the ghosts. I'll survive them *all*, just as I have for the last thirty years,' challenged Kay.

'Just tell me how and why my son Freddy died and why did you murder your entire family, because you had it all... A family that loved you, plus an easy job and money earned working on your father's farm and a ready-made business to inherit together with your brother and sister. You had a future that many twenty-year-old boys never get the chance to have and can only dream about, so why destroy it all to end up queuing in a line of homeless youths a day later for a meal and bed for the night?' asked John, waiting for the answer to the question that had puzzled him the most—why murder *five* innocent people to end up losing it all?

Smiling, Kay said, 'You had better sit down, Constable Wilding, because it's a long, harrowing tale...' He took a deep breath whilst still smiling as he began his story.

'I killed your Freddy because he irritated me and I didn't like him, but he also was, as you put, "the perfect corpse". He was the same age, height and weight as me and so that made him my first ghost... but I have to admit that the idea of killing him didn't enter my head until that day at the garage when I took my silver sports car in for a service and he mouthed off to me in front of the other mechanics. I was contemplating killing my family for a while, but didn't have a "full-proof plan" in mind; until I saw Freddy, and it *all* fell into place. I hated my parents; especially my father, who told me every single day since I was four years old that there was something *wrong* inside me. I loathed my mother because she never stood up for me, but always agreed with him. I hated my older brother and younger sister because they always thought that they were "better" than me when they were just spoilt brats who knew how to suck up to my parents. But when my father told me a few days before I had my sliver sports car serviced at the garage that he had disinherited me from his will and was leaving everything split fifty-fifty to my useless brother and sister because the family were afraid of me and wanted me to leave *my* home and rightful inheritance by the end of the month, then that's when I decided to *kill* them all. But how could I get away with murdering my entire family without being arrested and charged when the police would read my father's final will and see that I had both the motive and opportunity? But as you kindly reminded earlier, you can't kill a ghost twice but you can escape justice if you're already a ghost. And so all I needed was Freddy's corpse, but if the police were to believe that it was my charred body in the barn alongside my family, then I had to *erase* any trace of Freddy Wilding.' Pausing for a moment, Kay said, 'Now it gets to the *fun* bit, which I can skip if you don't want to hear exactly how your son died because I've already told you the "why" that you so desperately wanted to hear from me for the last thirty years.'

Still standing, John replied, 'If I'm to pass judgement today, then I must hear everything.'

Giving that dark, cold grin, Kay continued, 'I needed a few days to prepare my plan and kill my parents and so the large old freezer stored behind the hay stack at the back of the barn that used to be stocked with sheep and pig carcases came in very handy to store Freddy's body in once I had knocked him out and placed him in the boot of my car, that day he disappeared walking to work.'

Laughing out loud, Kay continued, 'Oh what fun I had that day when he come round and found himself trussed up inside that freezer, half-frozen to death and scared shitless. But you should have seen the sheer terror in your son's eyes when I explained in specific detail what I was going to do to him and why... First, I outlined precisely why I needed to extract *all* his teeth... then began pulling them out one-by-one whilst listening to his screams of agony that went unheard from inside the isolated barn as the family were out in the fields cutting hay. Then after soaking up every drop of blood pouring out from his toothless mouth, I carefully placed each tooth in a large plastic bag before sealing it and disposing of the evidence later. Second, I needed to get rid of *all* his fingerprints. So, I slowly poured a large bottle of acid over each one of his fingers until all that was left was disintegrated bone. You should have heard your Freddy's howls of pain when the acid burnt into his skin. It was a glorious sound, Constable Wilding,' howled Kay like a wild beast before continuing, 'Lastly, I needed to keep Freddy's body in the freezer for four days while I organised killing the family. But what fun would there be in just killing Freddy there and then once I'd mutilated his body when I could lower the temperature of the freezer just enough for him to die very slowly, freezing to death, with his mouthed taped shut so that nobody could hear his cries for help.'

'You evil sadistic bastard!' yelled John, grabbing him by the throat.

Anne stepped forward and reached her hand out to him, then said, 'That's what he does, John... That's who he is... Don't let him soak up your pain. Freddy is in a safe place now and watching everything. Don't let him inside your head.'

Releasing his throat, John stepped back.

Kay coughed and spluttered before continuing, 'I enjoyed killing my family. It was easy. I spiked their tea with just enough sleeping pills to make them feel drowsy then I told them that I needed to show them something in the barn as they followed me out and saw Freddy's body lying on the haystack. My father turned round and looked at me with those accusing eyes...'

Stopping for moment, Kay hesitated then said, 'I can still hear his final words *"You'll reap this day..."* crying out from inside the barn before collapsing onto the hay when I threw the lighted match onto his body before locking the door and leaving them ALL inside to burn in their own nightmare...' He leaned forward and stared right inside John's heart when he told him, 'But the sweetest thing of all is that while you were questioning me at the farm about your precious Freddy four days earlier, his frozen body was still inside the freezer in the barn just a few feet away and right under your stupid nose all the time you were playing the great detective.'

Sliding back into the chair, Kay gave that dark, cold grin when he concluded, 'I do have one regret about that day in that I had to leave my precious silver sports car behind; otherwise, the police would have found it suspicious. It was my very first silver sports car and will always hold special memories for me; especially how neatly Freddy's body fitted into the boot when I stopped to give him a lift the last day he walked to work only to end up in an old freezer with the remains of some sheep and pig carcasses for company.'

The silence in the court room was overwhelmingly suffocating. Not even the stray cat sitting on the ledge outside the window stirred.

When the trial began, the jury of victims were prepared to hear the worst of Alex Trent's crimes, but not to hear the *sheer pleasure* in his voice as he admitted to committing them.

Looking around the silent court room, Kay's impatience for a reaction got the better of him when he asked, 'Now that you finally know the how and why I killed your precious Freddy, Constable John Wilding, do you feel any better for it? And has it brought you the *closure* that so many victims claim they need when searching for the truth?'

Gathering his thoughts and composure, John answered, 'There's more than one ghost sitting in judgement of you today, Alex Trent, but there will be *one* that shall be touching you on the shoulder soon to remind you of its final words *"You'll reap this day..."* as you threw that lighted match into the barn.'

'You can't mess with my head. Those words were spoken thirty years ago and that day has long passed and I'm still here, whereas that old fucker is just a pile of ash blown away in the wind,' mocked Kay.

Smiling, John concluded his case against the defendant with a final warning, 'There was *no time limit* on those words... just as a ghost doesn't need a body in order to touch you on the shoulder.'

Breathing in, Anne asked, 'Alex Trent, how do you plead to the crimes put forward to you by John Wilding, guilty or not guilty?'

Taking a moment to think, the defendant replied, 'Well, I can hardly deny this one now, can I, since I've already confessed to killing my entire family and one mouthy little car mechanic? But you can't say that they all didn't have it coming to them? I mean my own father disinheriting me and throwing me out just because he didn't like my character and so decided to leave everything to my inferior brother and sister? And if Freddy Wilding had kept his goby mouth shut that day when I took my silver sports car in for a service, then I wouldn't have given him a second thought or glance. It *all* fell into place. So I plead *half-guilty*, with mitigating circumstances. Namely that if my father didn't want me as his son, then I don't recognise the name Alex Trent. I'm the successful businessman Jason Kay and the largest shareholder in Kay Corporation.'

Noting the defendant's comments in the file with a slightly amused smile as she wrote the words "successful businessman", Anne turned towards John and asked, 'John Wilding, how do you find against the defendant, Alex Trent, on behalf of the jury of victims, guilty or not guilty?'

Moving three paces forward, John took out his old retired police constable's badge from inside his wallet then pressed it into the centre of the defendant's forehead and said, 'This is for your father, mother, brother and sister. Guilty... Guilty... Guilty... Guilty...' Stepping back three paces, John pounded his police badge against his chest *three times*, stating, 'This is for my son, Freddy Wilding. Rest in peace now, my precious boy. Guilty... Guilty... Guilty...' As he placed the badge carefully back inside the wallet, Anne noted John's "several" verdicts of guilty in the file before handing it and the silver-tipped in pen over to him.

John asked the eleventh victim/juror to step forward and Anne Kay turned to face the defendant whilst John stood in her place with the pen and file.

Staring down at her husband, Anne couldn't help savouring the moment. She asked, 'How does it feel to be *me*?'

Feeling the straightjacket getting tighter and tighter as he wriggled around inside, causing his body to overheat with sweat and rage, Kay hissed and spat like a poisonous snake swallowing its own venom.

'Take this fucking thing off and then dare repeat those words to me again, you bitch!'

'But what fun would there be in that?' she said, smiling that same dark, cold grin that he took such pleasure in taunting her with every single day during their sixteen years of marriage.

Unable to comprehend being belittled and mocked in front of others by his wife, Kay countered, 'Just like you to sneak in last behind the other sniffing bitches; I've had to endure the Dotty friend, the old hag housekeeper and the scorned mistress. At least the men had some meaty stories to accuse me of, whilst all you've got is being a poor down-trodden little housewife who was nothing when I married you and is still nothing now.'

'I'm *not* playing your nasty little word and mind games any more. I'm done with that just as I'm done with *you*! I'm no longer your victim or your wife. I'm divorcing you on the grounds of mental and physical cruelty and will take back everything that you took from my father and me.'

'You can't do that! Your father signed his entire estate, including Hilltop Mansion, its extensive grounds, his company and all the shares in it over to me, *legally*, when I married you and renamed the company Kay Corporation. And you have no proof of any so-called "physical or mental cruelty" to produce against me that will stand up in court because no one outside our marriage saw or heard anything. And the only witnesses you have are an old housekeeper and estate manager who have their own axe to grind against me when I became master of Hilltop and them,' he threatened, feeling tiny droplets of perspiration dripping down from his forehead onto his lips as he attempted to swallow them into his mouth.

Anne nodded over to John who stepped forward with the file and pulled out the legal Power of Attorney and the hospital's Interment Form duly signed by the appropriate parties, including the signature of one Mr Jason Kay on the legal Power of Attorney handing control over every aspect of his life and fiancés to his wife.

'You're *not* accusing me of anything. You're perverting the law. You've already decided that I'm guilty; otherwise, why not present your so-called case against me like all the other victims have done before you so that I can present my defence? And why the hell bother divorcing me when you've already decided to kill me anyway when this fucking farce is over?' protested Kay.

'I'm not going to stand here and present any case against you. I've already endured your sick games of mental and physical cruelty for the last *five thousand, eight hundred and forty-seven days* as your wife and prisoner. I already know that no matter what I accuse you of here today, you will both deny and dismiss my claims as "irrelevant" because you don't consider me "relevant" as a woman, person or wife. I'm divorcing you regardless of the outcome of this trial because I don't want the name Mrs Anne Kay to define who I am or my future any more. I don't want hatred and revenge to poison everything and everyone in my life.

But I do want the world to know that the man who kept me prisoner inside Hilltop for those five thousand, eight hundred and forty-seven days wasn't the man that walked amongst them when he stepped outside this house and morphed from a sadistic, brutal wife-beater and controlling beast into the charming devoted husband, successful businessman and all-round good-guy named Jason Kay...' admitted Anne, pausing for a moment and looking around the room at all her fellow jurors and victims. She confessed, 'No one in this room is totally innocent. Yes, we have all been your victims, but in turn have created other victims because of that. So despite what I said earlier that no matter what I accuse of you here today, you will both deny and dismiss my claims as "irrelevant" because you don't consider me "relevant" as a woman, person, or wife, I want to believe that somewhere inside that shell of a body you occupy there's a *real* human being fighting to get out. Because, even now, after everything you have done to me, including murdering my own father, I need to *forgive* you. For without forgiveness, there can be no peace. And I'm tired of being tired of life, so I'm going to give you what you *never* gave to any one of your victims; *compassion!*'

Walking over to John, she took the file and pen in her hand then turned to face the rest of the jurors/victims and asked, 'I know this is *not* what we agreed, but if we don't give the defendant the chance to repent for his crimes and ask for our *forgiveness*, then we are *no better* than him.'

One-by-one, they *all* nodded their agreement as John returned to his seat on the circle of jurors and Anne turned to face the defendant. She asked the *twelve* victim, Mr Alex Trent/Jason Kay to plead his case for leniency to the jury of victims...

Taking Anne's plea for compassion to the jury of victims as a sign of "weakness" on hers and their part, Kay seized the opportunity to become top dog in the pack again. 'Before I plead my case, I have two requests to make,' he said with that same smooth disarming smile that Anne sneakily watched him practice in front of the hallway mirror from the kitchen every day before he took his daily walk down Hilltop Road into Treetop Village with that perfectly rehearsed smile to everyone he met.

'What are they?' she asked.

'First, if you truly mean what you said about being compassionate, then release me from this straightjacket, and second, I deserve the right to know what my third name is that you've written down in that file?' he said, careful to be *polite* in his request when inside his head, the words he was really saying were, 'Release me from this fucking straightjacket and I'll rip that file out of your hand and stuff it and your *third* name down your treacherous throat, bitch.'

Noting the defendant's two requests in the file, Anne replied, 'With regards to your first request, you have to earn the right to be released from that straightjacket by convincing this court room that you *too* are capable of compassion towards others. Secondly, your *third* name will be revealed to you once you've presented your defence to the jury of victims when final judgment and sentence is passed.'

Tapping her fingers on the file with Kay's silver-tipped ink pen, Anne waited to see who would emerge next, the beast or the charmer. She knew *both* well, but had never personally experienced the *charmer* before until now.

Realising that he couldn't fool the one person who could see and hear the lies behind the lies, Kay decided to tell the *truth* for the first time in his life. And how he was going to relish telling his audience who the REAL Alex Trent/Jason Kay was!

Tilting his head upwards towards Anne, he said, 'I think it would be best if you were seated before I begin my defence.' He realigned his body inside the straightjacket until he was seated face-to-face with his accusers, including his wife who had returned to the empty chair on the circle of jurors. He cleared his throat. 'Freddy Wilding wasn't my first kill. No, that was much earlier... when I was just four years old. And there have been many, many more bodies over the years and definitely a lot more than just the eight that Jacky Jones recalled when he kindly informed me that he nearly became my ninth, which doesn't count in my calculations because killing himself isn't the same as actually being killed by me, personally. If the truth be told, I don't know how many actual *bodies* have been buried in the ground over the years. I only recall the ones that are *relevant*... '

'What do mean by *relevant*?' interrupted John Wilding, unable hide his disdain at the "casual" way the defendant talked about killing innocent people.

'The ones that I took pleasure in killing myself such as your son, Freddy,' replied Kay, smiling as he continued, 'To kill well, you need to practice and what better place than on a farm where there was an abundance of different animals. I killed our sheep dog, Rex, when I was just four years old because my father treated him with more respect than me, his own son. I dipped his favourite sweet treats in rat poison and then watched him choke to death in the yard, where my father found me standing over his corpse with the sweats still in my hand and hit me across the face. But it didn't hurt much compared to the pain I saw in my father's eyes at losing his beloved Rex. After that, I got the taste for watching animals die so I regularly killed stray cats, dogs, foxes, birds and any creature that crossed my path in a variety of ways, but the most enjoyable kills were when I stamped on them with my feet until they crushed to death underneath whilst screeching in pain. Then, at the age of seven, I killed my first *human life*... our neighbour's daughter, Kitty, who was one year older than me and a real annoying little cow.'

Stopping for a moment to catch his breath, Kay continued, 'I was out in the back garden of the house playing on the swings whilst my brother and sister sat on the grass eating red jelly when Kitty rushed out of the house and challenged me.

'"I bet that I can swing higher than you?" she boasted, jumping on the other swing and laughing louder and louder as she swung higher and higher.

'I shifted my body and swing over to hers and she flew off into the air, landing in the large oak tree at the edge of the garden, smashing her head against the trunk before falling to the ground. My parents and her mother came running out of the house to see her body lying, broken and dead on the grass.'

Smiling as he pictured the exact moment in his head, Kay said, 'My father looked at me and knew what I had done, but said nothing... just like my cowardly brother and sister said nothing as they watched me shove Kitty off the swing. My mother also knew, but how could she tell her friend and neighbour that her *own* son had killed her only daughter? After that day, my parents *never* left me alone again with my brother, sister or any other children or visitors to the farm. And as I grew older, they grew colder and colder towards me and yet still kept my secret for fear of blackening the family name, *Trent.*'

Watching Anne frantically writing his story down in the file whilst holding back tears, Kay could feel the power surging inside him when he continued his defence, 'My next *relevant* kill was when I was eleven and half years old and just started secondary school where I met Freddy Wilding and all the other kids that didn't want to play with me at break time or sit beside me in the classroom because I was better than them and they didn't like that. But there was one little brat named Danny Sanderson, who constantly challenged me in front of his so-called friends by calling me names such as weirdo, thicko and retarded whilst laughing in my face. So one day when he was alone in the toilets, I took my revenge. I locked the main door and waited until he had pulled the chain then when he opened the toilet door, I pushed him back in and shoved his head down the toilet pan, until he was half-dead. Then I unzipped my trousers and relieved myself all over his mouthy face whilst listening to him choking to death on my excrement. Then I sat him back up on the toilet seat and left him there with piss all over his face. Oh, how I enjoyed that one. The teachers in the school wrote it down as a "tragic accident", but suspected that it was me after talking to the other kids and yet did nothing about it because they were more concerned about the school's reputation than one cocky-mouthed student who got what he deserved.'

Easing back into the chair, Kay could see the disbelief and horror on the jurors' faces, which just empowered him more as he took delight in telling them about his growing list of *relevant kills*.

'After that kill, I had to wait eight long boring years until Freddy Wilding. All the kids in school stayed away from me and likewise in the town and on the farm where the casual workers would snigger behind my back, but never to my face. In fact, everybody I came across avoided me so I had to make do with killing animals again, but it wasn't the same. Then Freddy forgot his place at the garage and got mouthy with me in front of his friends and it *all* fell into place.' Smiling,

Kay added, 'You could say that I owe Freddy a debt of gratitude because killing him freed me from my restrictive life as *Alex Trent* and opened the door into my new life as *Jason Kay* where killing became easier and easier.'

Tilting his head slightly upwards and to the side, he laughed. 'I could name each one of my kills since Reginald Price took me in thirty years ago, but this trial would go on forever and ever. So I'll quickly skip over the *three* secretaries I had before Diane Moffatt whom I poisoned with their *last* fancy champagne meal when they thought that I was going to give them their "final bonus" after completing their five-year contract each as my mistress. Silly bitches! Why would I give them a fat payoff for doing what they did for a pittance before I elevated them to my personal whores?'

Glancing over at Diane, he grinned. 'You should be grateful, Miss Moffatt, that you lasted twice as long as the others and didn't get to have the final champagne meal I'd planned for you before you betrayed me with my wife.'

Feeling the hatred rising inside of him for the two women that "got away", he recalled another easy kill to make him feel better. 'Then there was the village tramp who sat on the bench by the green every day in Treetop Village who spoiled the picturesque view of the village and ruined my daily walk, *making everything not as it should be...* So one day a couple of years ago, I stopped and gave him a slice of Maggie Frith's delicious chocolate cake laced with rat poison.'

Giving that that dark, cold grin, he added, 'I can still see the smile on his face now as he stuffed that cake into his mouth and lapped it up whilst thanking me for my kindness. Yet, nobody in the village cared enough to find out his name or where he had come from and the local coroner didn't even want to waste tax payers' money doing an autopsy on the nameless, homeless, irrelevant tramp so just buried his corpse in a pauper's grave in the scruffiest part of the village cemetery with no name or cross to remember him by. That's how precious his life was.'

Breathing in, he noted, 'I could go on and on listing both *relevant* and *irrelevant kills* that I have done over the years, but what would be the point? When you're dead, you're dead and nobody gives a shit. My father dug a hole in the fields and buried Rex without a single tear for his beloved "best friend", then went out the next day and bought another sheep dog and named him Rex. And the distraught mother of Kitty had another little cow eighteen months later and then another two years after that. One gone; two replacements. That's how "valued" her life was.'

Contemplating, he continued, 'Just look at all the unattended gravestones in the cemeteries all over the world that nobody visits except the weeds. Sooner or later, *everybody* dies. And all that really counts is *how you live*!'

Giving a smug, dark grin, Kay stared right into the heart of the jury of victims, then said, 'I can see the anger in your eyes and the shock on your faces as you sit there listening to my confession whilst struggling to hold onto that "compassion" my wife promised on behalf of you all. You expect me to repent for my crimes and beg for your forgiveness, but how can I do that when I don't? When I was *Alex Trent*, nobody wanted to be my friend. In fact, everyone was afraid of me, including my own parents. Yet, I couldn't help being him because I was born that way. But when I became *Jason Kay,* everyone wanted to be my friend and no one was afraid of me. They admired and respected me. And some even wanted to be me. Yet, inside, I was still *Alex Trent*, the boy and man that nobody wanted to emulate, but they couldn't see that because I had created the perfect son, husband, friend, neighbour and successful businessman in my alter ego Jason Kay.' Laughing out loud, he confessed, 'It's such fun being *two* different faces on the same coin. Inside Hilltop Mansion, I'm free to be what I was born to be without *any* restrictions, whilst outside, I become what the world wants me to be. That way, I get *everything* I desire without giving up *anything*.'

Staring over at Anne, Kay coldly added, 'Ever since I shoved that bragging cow Kitty off the swing for thinking that she was "better than me", I've never let another little cow forget her place. You may have married Jason Kay, but you lived with Alex Trent.'

Studying her face closely, he couldn't help notice that she was different somehow... when it suddenly struck him. 'You look prettier and almost beautiful and yet you're the same. Your hair's the same, your teeth are the same and your face is the same...?'

Smiling, Anne answered his puzzling dilemma with a conundrum, 'A doctor once told me that it takes forty-three muscles to frown but only seventeen to smile.'

'Your point being...?'

'I never smiled *once* in the five thousand, eight hundred and forty-seven days that I lived with Alex Trent. That's why miserable, sad people look old and tired no matter how young they are.'

Laughing out loud, he said, 'I didn't know that you had a "sense of humour" inside that empty head of yours.'

She replied, 'I do now...'

Replacing the mocking laughter with that dark grin that Anne knew so well, Kay concluded his defence, 'Now that you know *everything* about the man that you were married to for the last *five thousand, eight hundred and forty-seven days* in which you *never* smiled once, do you still feel compassion for me? Do you still feel the need to *forgive* me? Or do you just want revenge? Because if I were sitting in your chair, I know what I would choose.'

Standing up, Anne turned to face the jury of victims, then said, 'If you find for the defendant, Alex Trent, then stay seated, but if you find against the defendant, Alex Trent, then stand up and speak your verdict of "guilty", clearly for him to hear.'

One by one, the jury of victims stood up and pronounced their verdict:

1. The father — John Wilding — Guilty
2. The blackmailer — Jacky Jones — Guilty
3. The solicitor — Simon Dodd — Guilty
4. The estate manager — Eric Finch — Guilty
5. The doctor — Dr Pritchard — Guilty
6. The mistress — Diane Moffatt — Guilty
7. The bodyguard — David Fox — Guilty
8. The friend — Dotty Short — Guilty
9. The housekeeper — Maggie Frith — Guilty
10. The accountant — Anthony Gibbs — Guilty

Noting each one of the *ten* jury of victims' verdicts of "guilty" in the file, Anne stayed standing. She turned to face the defendant before stating the eleventh and final verdict of "guilty" as his wife, Mrs Anne Kay.

Having recorded *all* the verdicts from the jury of victims in the file for the last time, Anne asked the defendant, Alex Trent, one final question that had been slowly nagging away inside her head like a little worm that wouldn't go way until it was answered, 'Have you ever *loved* anyone, human or animal, in your entire life? Or indeed, do you even know *how to love* anyone, human or animal?'

Glancing down at his wrist to see that it wasn't there, he answered, 'I loved my gold Rolex watch…'

Half-amused and half-horrified, Anne asked, 'Why the watch?'

'Because it does exactly what I want I it to do when I require it to do it. And because I can rely on it to make *everything as it should be* when the timer pings three times.'

'Then you can keep the gold Rolex watch,' she said, nodding to the other jurors who smiled their agreement.

'Why?' he asked, curious.

'Compassion…' she replied.

'And what about forgiveness?' he asked

Smiling, she answered, 'It's easier to forgive when all that I feel for your now is *pity*.'

'How dare you pity me when I've achieved far more with my life than you ever have?' he yelled, consumed with rage at how the stupid little cow had not only managed to outsmart him, but also had the audacity to feel *pity* for the man who had made her life a *living hell* for the last sixteen years of their marriage.

'I dare because you've lost *everything* you desired simply because you wouldn't give up *anything*. And for that, I pity you because you have never known and will never know now what it is like to *love* and *be loved.*'

Defiant to the end, he countered, 'I don't need love because emotions are unpredictable; whereas, my gold Rolex watch never required twenty-four-hour constant attention and didn't let me down once when I set my requirements into its precise mechanism.'

'But even a gold Rolex watch needs a battery to live; otherwise, it dies. When it won't ping three times to confirm that *everything is as it should be,*' said Anne, holding the watch up for him to see before taking out the battery and throwing it in the bin.

Staring down at the tiny round metal battery inside the bin, Kay laughed then said, 'I taught you well, didn't I?'

When two muscle-bound shaven-headed male nurses that took Anne away entered the room, and the realisation of the jury of victims' final quest for justice suddenly hit him.

Lifting his head up to face his accusers, he asked, 'What is the *third* name that you will write on my gravestone?'

Handing the gold Rolex watch to one of the male nurses, Anne replied, 'No one on the jury of victims is a cold-blooded killer like you, but *revenge* we can live with.'

'You can't keep me locked up in a hospital cell forever. I'm the successful businessman and prominent land owner Jason Kay and the police will be searching for me.' He started feeling the dark shadow of fear creeping over him.

'But don't you remember? Anthony Gibbs killed you before signing a confession and then would kill himself without telling the police where he disposed of your body. So *nobody* will be looking for a dead man when the case has already been solved and filed away with all the other "dead files" in the basement of Lunsford Police Headquarters by retired Chief Inspector Tom Millard,' said Anne.

The two male nurses lifted Kay's body out of the chair as Anne stepped forward.

Opening the file, she took out a single white sheet of A4 paper and held it up in front of him. 'Both Alex Trent and Jason Kay must pay for their crimes, together, but as both are officially dead in the eyes of the law, which is *never* wrong, I give you your *third* and last name, Mr A J Adnegveill, whose last thirty years of life will *not* be *everything that you planned it should be...*'

'What kind of fucking name is that?' shouted Kay as the two male nurses locked his body in-between theirs and carried him out of the room into the hallway.

Anne replied with a huge grin, 'It's an anagram of the two different faces on the same coin of Alex Trent and Jason Kay, that you had "such fun" being, but will now have *no* escape from when one face battles with other for supremacy inside a soundproof ten-by-seven square metre cell whilst trapped inside the straightjacket.'

'You can't do this to me. I won't let you. I won't let you!' protested Kay as the male nurses dragged him, yelling and screaming, from the house.

Anne and the rest of the jury of victims watched him being bundled into the white hospital van from the entrance of the porch. The van drove off and Anne closed the door on *The Adnegveill* for the last time.

Closing the file, Anne handed it to Inspector Steal. 'Now you know *everything*. My husband isn't dead, but will wish *every day* that he lives that he were. That is *our* justice, Inspector. I hope and pray that it will be yours and Sergeant Wright's too, but if it isn't, then you know where to find us.'

Taking the file, Steal and Wright slowly walked past the jury of victims and out the front door.

Anne said, 'Do you remember when you asked me whether I was remotely interested in whether my husband was dead or alive, Inspector?'

'I believe you answered that you would have to get back to me on that question,' he said with a hint of intrigue in his eyes.

'Well, I can definitely confirm "alive", Inspector.'

Smiling, she slowly closed the door whilst watching the two detectives drive off with the file and future lives of the *eleven* victims of the serial killer, Alex Trent/Jason Kay in their hands.

23
The Two Sides of Law

It was six a.m. in the morning and Steal hadn't been to bed.

Slumped in an old cracked brown leather chair by the fireplace in the dingy study/third bedroom of his late parents' 1930s semi-detached house with the curtains drawn, allowing just a thin shaft of light through into the centre of the room, he stared down at the file that had been sitting on his lap all night long.

Today, he must decide what side of the *law* to choose.

Pulling out his inspector's badge from inside his rumpled dark grey jacket pocket whilst picturing Constable John Wilding pressing his old police badge against the defendant's forehead, he glanced up at the dusty gold framed picture of his parents' wedding day on the mantelpiece above the fireplace when the complicated relationships between Anne Price and Simon Dodd's respective fathers flashed through his mind and he laughed out loud at the irony of life repeating itself over and over again.

Drawing back the curtains, the full glare of the early morning sunlight shone through his body into the room while he breathed in its warm energy, knowing exactly which side of the *law* he was going choose.

Taking his usual cold shower, Steal skipped breakfast and picked up Wright en route to Lunsford.

Sitting quietly whilst listening to the car radio, Steal and Wright wondered who would ask the question first. The soulful voice of Duffy echoed through the car, begging for mercy and to be released.

'Do you ever wonder what the world would be like if nobody had any secrets and life was just one long happy journey from inception to the grave?' Steal asked as he drove into the car park at Lunsford and Duffy's plea for mercy drifted away into the radio when he turned the engine off.

'A wise old lady once told me that a secret is only a secret if it's never told. So what would be the point in wondering about something that you're never going to be sure isn't there because a secret is only a secret if it's never told,' said Wright.

Steal confessed, 'Today, I'm going to choose mercy over the letter of the law and let a serial killer remain dead so that his victims may live... but to explain why I've made that choice, I would have to tell you a secret and I'm not able to do that.'

'I know that you know that I have a secret too... so that makes us even partners in the secret world of secrets, Boss. And besides, where Holmes goes so does Watson, so let's go and close the case on the kidnap and murder of Jason Kay, partner.' She smiled when the two detectives walked side-by-side into Lunsford Headquarters and Steal updated the team as per Chief Superintendent Phelps had instructed, but as they listened in silence to the words coming out of their boss' mouth each one of them knew that they were false... and yet accepted without question why he had chosen to close the case of the disappearance and murder of Jason Kay when he knew that Anthony Gibbs wasn't the killer.

Thanking his team for their excellent work in solving the case, Steal left for his meeting with Chief Superintendent Phelps in his office before the press release when Sergeant Jack Stone and Constable Rita Clark carried on doing their jobs in silence because like Steal and Wright, each of them had their own secret to hide of why they joined the police force.

The Press Release

Standing in front of the cameras outside Lunsford Police Headquarters with Wright to the left and Steal to right of him, Chief Superintendent Phelps championed the brilliant detective work of *his* team at uncovering the serial killer Alex Trent alias Jason Kay and the *nine* unsolved murders he had committed.

Holding the copy file up in the air, he stated, 'Inside this file is the last statement and confession of Anthony Gibbs, the man who kidnapped and killed Jason Kay before taking his own life. It is with regret that Anthony Gibbs died whilst in police custody, but after a full autopsy on the body the coroner has concluded that no police officer at Lunsford could have known about the secret cyanide pill he hid in a filling inside his tooth.'

Stepping forward into the cameras, Phelps concluded, 'My heartfelt sympathy goes out to Jason Kay's wife, Mrs Anne Kay, who was totally unaware of her husband's real identity as Alex Trent the Serial Killer and the man who killed her own father. So I would ask that you all now allow her the privacy and space to mourn the murder of her father and the terrible deception of her husband's double-life in peace.'

Turning round, Phelps handed the file back to Steal then whispered, 'I'm pleased that you saw sense, Inspector; now bury the file with all the other solved cases in the basement and move onto the next.' He waved to the cameras again whilst smiling broadly before waltzing off the stage like the cat who had just lapped up the biggest bowl of cream in the world.

Standing alone on the stage when everyone had left and the cameras stopped flashing, Steal and Wright looked at each and gave that little smile that said, "Fuck you, Phelps, and fuck your kind of *law*".

Steal's mobile pinged and he read the text, *"Thank you from The Eleven..."*

Showing the text to Wright, the two detectives walked back into Lunsford side-by-side. The team stood up and clapped as Steal returned to his office and Wright her desk, knowing that some secrets must never be told.

24
Closure

Steal looked at the copy file sitting on his desk, again…

It had been two weeks since the press release and he still hadn't plucked up the courage to take the file down into the basement as per Phelps' instructions. He could give it to Rita Clark to do, but knew that he must face Tom himself before the silence between them became permanent.

Taking a quick swig of whisky from the bottle that was always in his bottom drawer and half empty, he picked up the file and headed for the basement where Tom was sat in his usual spot at the "empty" table. He looked up to see Steal standing in the shadows.

'I've been waiting for you and the *last* File,' he said, standing up and holding out his arms, praying that they won't be rejected.

They fill up and the tears roll down the two friends' faces as Tom told Steal the secret that must be told if old and new wounds are to be permanently healed.

Sitting at the table, Tom retold the story of Alexander Forbes who shot his own father, Shaun Forbes, in cold blood with one bullet to the head while he begged on his knees for mercy because he killed his partner and best friend, Sergeant Mick Dooley, for being an "honest" cop.

Stopping to take a drink of coffee, he continued, 'But what I didn't tell anyone was that the day before Alexander shot his father, we argued about the *law*. He was young and eager, but also reckless and slightly arrogant and I got annoyed at him preaching to me about the rules of law when his father was the ruthless gangster Shaun Forbes and so shoved his father's crimes in his face.

'He shouted back, "I'll show you that I'm *not* my father's son…" The next day, Alexander followed his father to an old desolate warehouse where he met Mick Dooley and the two men argued about money. Dooley wanted more but his father laughed in his face.

"'No one threatens me," he said, then shot him in the mouth. When he saw Alexander coming towards him with a gun, he laughed. "You can't shoot me, I'm your father!"

'Pulling the trigger on the gun, Alexander cursed his father's bloody corpse as he stood over it and pledged "I'm *not* my father's son!" It turned out that Dooley wasn't as honest as Alexander thought, but he had a wife and three kids and a police pension that she would have lost if the truth about him came out so Alexander came to me and confessed to killing his father. I agreed to keep his secret and rewrote the story of Dooley's death by stating that he was working undercover for me when the operation went badly wrong and one of Shaun Forbes' henchmen shot Dooley then fled before I arrived to find the bodies...'

Feeling the words wither inside his mouth, Tom gulped down the rest of his coffee then confessed, 'I did a bad thing, Steal... I told Alexander that I would only help him if he resigned as an officer of the law because I couldn't trust him *not* to kill another criminal or low-life if he lost control of his inner rage again in the future. And so he agreed, and we never had any contact again. But in truth, I was ashamed for myself. I knew that he wasn't responsible for his father's sins and that even though he bore the same surname, he joined the police force to use that name as a force for good and not evil and so redeem his father's legacy.'

Pounding his fist on the table, Tom said, 'I was responsible for Alexander killing his father, *not* him... If I hadn't lost my temper and goaded him about the sins of the father being re-born in the son, he wouldn't have tried to prove me wrong and end up killing his own father and losing the career that in my heart I knew he loved and just wanted to be the best he could be in order to serve and protect all the innocent victims that couldn't speak for themselves, of which he was one.'

Lowering his head in shame, Tom further confessed, 'I turned my back on a good man for selfish reasons so when Jacky Jones contacted me through John Wilding and told me the story of Mr A and his secret organisation called The Department that he'd set up with his gangster father's money to get justice for all the innocent victims that the law failed and let the guilty go free, I knew that this was *my* chance at redemption. I couldn't go back and undo what I had done to Alexander, but this time, I wouldn't turn my back on his adopted son, Jacky, who knew about me from a letter Alexander left him after he died. In the letter, Alexander didn't blame me; instead, he said that if ever Jacky sought me out, to say that I wasn't to blame and that sometimes a bad thing can turn out to be a good thing. So I agreed to help them. I never wanted to betray you, Steal, but I'm an old man of seventy-six hurtling towards his grave and I don't want to go there with a secret that had been slowly eating away at my soul for all those lonely dark years that I sat at this table, day-after-day, and year-after-year with the dead, hoping to feel alive again...'

Looking down at the solitary file on the table in front of Steal, he said, 'This is the file that I've been searching for and the one that will finally give me closure on my past and set me free from this place.'

But deep down inside his soul, Tom knew that even though he was now free from the dead in the basement, he wasn't free from the dead in Lunsford Car Park until he confessed his other, even darker secret to someone before the Grim Reaper came to collect.

Staring into his old friend's eyes, Steal placed his hand on the file and pushed it across the table until it was sitting right under Tom's tired old face.

'Then you had better file it *now*, you haggard old codger, so that we can go and get fucking pissed drunk together.' He could sense that Tom hadn't confessed everything, but knew that this wasn't the time or place to drag up another old ghost from the past.

Picking up the file, Tom smiled tears of laughter when he said, 'Only if you're fucking paying.'

'Don't I always, you stingy old goat?' grinned Steal, as the two friends disappeared through the long dark aisle like old shadows drifting into one. Tom slipped the file into an empty space in the long endless rows of the dead and forgotten.

25
The Final Goodbyes

The mourners stood around the recently dug grave, holding a single red rose in each of their hands.

Staring down at the newly chiselled gravestone, they smiled whilst reading the words, "Here lie the bodies of Anthony Gibbs and his beloved wife, Sandra, whose enduring love for each other in life lives on forever in eternity together."

Kissing the single red rose before bending down and placing it in the first hole of the silver flower pot sitting under the centre of the gravestone, Anne whispered, 'Rest in peace, dear Anthony and Sandra, for God has a big heart and forgives those who can't forgive themselves for the sins of others.'

Stepping back, Anne watched as one-by-one, each of the jury of victims placed their red rose in the next hole whilst whispering their final words of gratitude to the man that gave his life in order that they may all live theirs.

With *all* the holes filled with a single red rose, the jury of victims circled the grave, forming a halo around Anthony and Sandra before bowing their heads in two minutes' silence.

The bells in Treetop Village church tower rang out for midday prayer. Anne held her head up high into the bright blue sky and said, 'When the bells stop ringing on the twelve chime, all the ghosts of those passed can finally rest in peace when our old lives end… and the new ones begin.'

'I didn't realise that you were so poetic,' joked Simon, slipping his hand into hers.

'It's amazing how just a month ago, I would never have thought that either, yet here we all are; free spirits with a whole wide world out there to explore,' she said, catching Jacky Jones smiling broadly while he glanced around the cemetery. She asked, 'What are you looking for?'

'The tramp's grave,' he said, turning round. 'I was thinking that it could have been me in that unmarked pauper's grave all those years ago under the bridge if Mr A hadn't come along and saved me. So, I was wondering if I could move him to a better place and give him a name on a proper gravestone like Anthony, but I'm not sure where and what name?'

Pointing her hand across the cemetery, Anne noted, 'There's a lovely bench just over there under the shade and protection of the oldest oak tree in the village, with just enough earth behind it for a single grave. Visitors sit on the bench and look out into the entire cemetery and think that would be a good place for Ben R T Champ to rest in peace.'

Nodding his head, Jacky smiled and said, 'I agree, but tell me why that name?'

'It's an anagram of the words "tramp" and "bench",' she grinned.

'But of course, it is,' laughed Jacky, adding, 'Where do I go and who do I pay for Ben R T Champ's new grave?'

'The Church Warden will be here when we leave.' She felt a tap on her shoulder. Anne turned round to see Diane Moffatt. She asked, 'And where will your new life begin, Diane?'

'Where it started, back home, but first I'm going to enrol in college to become a librarian. I will take all my books in my library bus to the streets that no one cares about and all the other forgotten children who deserve the right to read and dream about a better life.'

'Then you had better take this with you,' said Anne, turning to Simon who handed her a single white envelope from his leather briefcase. Diane opened the envelope to discover a single cheque made out to Miss Diane Moffatt for three hundred thousand pounds'

Wiping the tears from her eyes, Diane was speechless with gratitude and love. The two women embraced. She said, 'This is a lot of money that you could use for your new life with Simon,' giving them both a cheeky grin.

'Jeremy Caine sent me my father's trust money of five million pounds, plus I will have £2.5 million when I complete the sale of

Hilltop Mansion to my neighbour, Mr Henry George, who's mega rich and has always wanted to own the biggest and oldest house in Hilltop Road.'

'And what future will you buy with £7.5 million in the bank?' asked Diane, still staring at the cheque but still not quite believing it was real.

Pulling out a *new* gold-tipped ink pen from her bag, Anne leaned over and wrote an address on the back of the envelope. 'Send me a picture of your library bus when you start your new life. I'll send you back the same,' she said.

'That's a promise,' said Diane, folding the envelope and cheque safely inside her black Gucci bag before leaving all her new friends behind that she'll never, ever forget.

Whilst the dwindling jury of victims watched Diane disappear amongst the gravestones, David Fox sidled up to Jacky and asked, 'Do you fancy some company on the way back to the hotel after you've spoken to the church warden. We can discuss that project you mentioned?'

'That would be good, David,' said Jacky, strolling over to the church.

David turned and asked Anne, 'Would it be OK for me to say goodbye to your father?'

'I think he would like that.' She smiled, pointing to a large black granite gravestone with gold lettering in the centre of the cemetery by the huge circular flower beds. He nodded his gratitude before walking through the centre of the cemetery via the tarmac footpath, pausing at Reginald Price's grave for a few quiet minutes before carrying on out into the car park where Jacky Jones was waiting, standing beside his car. The two men drove off out of the village.

Looking around at the smaller circle of friends left, Anne waited for the next goodbye. John Wilding clasped his hands around hers and said, 'It's time for me to go home and start living again.'

'Live well, live happy and live long, Constable John Wilding,' she said, kissing him on the left cheek.

Stepping back, John shook everyone's hand before walking down the tarmac footpath to hear Stuart Pritchard shout, 'Hold on a moment,

John.' He nodded his head at Anne, Simon, Eric, Dotty and Maggie as Anne nodded back, knowing that they would speak again for one final time about his *last* patient, The Adnegveill!

With just five disbanded jury of victims left, each knew what they had to do when Dotty, Maggie and Eric strolled back to the car park and drove back to Hilltop Mansion in Eric's dusty old Estate, leaving Anne and Simon alone to say their final goodbyes to their fathers. Anne walked one way and Simon the other as each spoke the words that they never thought they would.

Staring down at the grand black granite gravestone of her father's grave, Anne kissed her fingertips before leaning down and pressing her hand on the gold-edged words *"Reginald Price beloved husband and father"*. She then said, 'I love you, Father, and now I know that you loved me too, so rest in peace until the day that we meet again.' She smiled and added, 'But hopefully, not *too* soon.'

Wiping the "happy tears" from her eyes, she looked across the cemetery at Simon who was standing over his father James Dodd's plain grey gravestone where he too was smiling when he said, 'You could have saved us both a lot of pain and torment if you just told me that you loved me, Dad. You didn't have to fucking go and get yourself killed by that bastard serial killer to prove it. But just to let you know, I love you back, but I'm not going to die proving it, you old sod. Instead, I'm going to live a long and happy life with Anne, proving that you didn't die for nothing.' Turning away to see Anne walking towards him, the two lovers clasped hands and slowly walked out of Treetop Cemetery for the last time.

Six Weeks Later

Anne stood in the middle of the hallway staring at the last of the boxes piled high on top of each other, waiting to be collected and delivered to their "new home" when the doorbell rang three times and she smiled.

'Do you want me to get that?' shouted Maggie from the kitchen.

'No. I know who it is,' she shouted back. Maggie carried on packing up the last of the crockery and Anne opened the door to see Dr Prichard standing in the porch, holding a file. She smiled again and led

270

him into the lounge that was empty of furniture except for two, fold-away black plastic chairs.

Handing her the file, he said, 'Everything you requested is in here and I've left specific instructions on what the patient's hourly and daily requirements are, including the four clauses:

(1) That every night when the clock strikes midnight, he will hear your recorded bedtime story through the speakers telling him about "The Tree of Eternal Life"

(2) That he must *never* leave the cell

(3) And never see daylight again

(4) That there is to be *no* deviation from those instructions.

'The special bank account to pay for the patient's ongoing treatment has been set up by Jeremy Caine with a holding fund of £3.2 million from the sale of Kay Corporation after deducting the shareholders' final bonus payoff and Mr Caine's extremely generous ongoing retaining fee. You will receive regular six-monthly updates on the patient's care until you state that you no longer wish to.'

Catching his breath, Pritchard concluded his report with a slight smile of satisfaction, 'Hopefully, the patient will live a very long life and with £3.2 million to pay for his ongoing treatment, I see no reason why he shouldn't.'

'Thank you for arranging everything, Dr Pritchard, or may I call you Stuart now that you're officially retired and no longer my doctor, but just a friend doing another friend a favour?'

'I would consider it my privilege to be your friend, Anne, and I thank you from the bottom of my heart for giving me the opportunity to finally fulfil my promise to your father to protect you from *him* and put things right between us before I retire.'

'Enjoy the Caribbean sun and don't forget to send me the occasional postcard like all good absent friends do,' she said, placing the file marked *The Adnegveill* on the plastic chair before escorting him out of the house and into the taxi that was waiting to take him and his housekeeper, Martha Pope, to the airport.

Waving goodbye as the taxi drove out the long, shingled driveway into Hilltop Road, Anne saw the tall, upright, seventy-one-year-old silver-headed and well-dressed outline of her neighbour and new owner of Hilltop Mansion, Mr Henry George, strolling down the driveway towards her with that same, smug smile of satisfaction on his face that, for just moment, sent a shiver of déjà vu through her bones.

He smiled and said, 'I'm so pleased to have caught you, Mrs Kay, and wondered if you had a moment to discuss one tiny little matter before you vacate Hilltop and hand the keys over to my solicitor.'

'Please call me Anne for, as you can appreciate, I no longer wish to be associated with my late husband's name or his past'

'Of course, Anne, and I do apologise for being so insensitive and likewise please call me Thomas, especially now that I am the new owner of Hilltop and your late father's company.'

'Please come in, but I'm afraid there are still a few boxes left to go,' she said, showing him into the kitchen where Maggie was just sealing the last box of crockery.

He smiled at her and said, 'Ah, just the person that I wanted to speak to.'

'Really?' said Maggie, surprised, because in all the years that she had passed him watching Hilltop Mansion from his front door directly opposite in Hilltop Road as she went in and out, he never once smiled or spoke a single word to her until now.

'Yes, I was wondering if you would be interested in staying on as my housekeeper when I move in next week, ah… Maggie? I would pay you well and as you know Hilltop Mansion inside-out and have kept it in tip-top order all these years for the previous owners, you would be the perfect applicant that I require to keep this grand house in the immaculate condition that befits its status in the road and village.'

Trying not "too hard" to hide her pleasure at turning his job opportunity down, Maggie politely smiled when she informed him, 'Thank you for your extremely generous offer, ah… Henry, but I've already been offered and accepted a much better position. I wish you well, though, in your search for that "perfect applicant",' finishing the last seal on the box.

'Oh…?' he said, unable to hid his annoyance at his "extremely generous" offer of continued employment at Hilltop Mansion being rejected.

Anne took the opportunity to ask the question that Simon advised her not to until he had signed all the contracts on the sale of the house and company for fear of appearing intrusive. 'I hope you don't mind my asking, Henry, but I'm curious as to why you wanted to buy both Hilltop and the company when you were obviously living in a very nice house already and enjoying your retirement?'

Stepping out into the large, grand square hallway and looking up the long winding staircase, a dark, crepuscular scowl crept across his face when he told Anne his story of being gazumped by a more ruthless adversary, Reginald Price.

Turning round to see both Anne and Maggie standing transfixed with a mixture of shock and intrigue, Henry George told them how he was originally buying Hilltop when the estate agent telephoned him to say that the seller had received a much higher cash offer and so therefore was selling to someone else. He then threatened legal action against the seller when their solicitor informed him that as no deposits or contracts had been exchanged or signed, the seller wasn't legally obliged to sell to him and so he lost the dream house that he always wanted in the dream village and ended up buying the only other house that ever came up for sale in Hilltop Road when the owner died of a sudden heart attach six months later, just like the previous owner of Hilltop Mansion did barely a year earlier.

He then went on to tell them that three months after he moved in, his wife, Agatha, came running into the house steaming with rage. She'd just been down to the village to do some shopping and overhead the new owner of Hilltop Mansion bragging outside the grocery shop to the pompous village councillor, Bernard Crisp, about how he had "outsmarted" the original purchaser by bribing both the estate agent and seller's solicitor with a cash backhander if they sold the house to him instead of the original purchaser. Laughing, he remarked at how easy it was to buy people with the offer of wads of cash being floated in front of their greedy faces.

Stepping closer to Anne, he said, 'I've watched and waited for years for an opportunity to take back what was always meant to be mine. And now I have, so I win in the end and I didn't bribe anyone with a cash backhander to do it.'

Unmoved by his rather pathetic story of years of wasted envy, Anne asked, 'I don't apologise for my father's sins, that's his cross to bear; although, I would agree that it wasn't the right and honourable thing to do, but why buy the company as well?'

Dipping his head in shame, Henry replied, 'Originally, I was going to chop it up into little pieces and sell them off to secure a quick profit whilst making several hundred employees redundant, hence destroying your father's legacy. That would have been my ultimate revenge, but then I realised that would make me worse than him. Plus, why make hundreds of hardworking innocent people and their families, casualties of my spiteful revenge? So I sat down and looked around at my empty house and life, to see… nothing.

'Agatha died of a rare blood disorder four years ago, aged just sixty-three. We had no children because of her condition so I spent my life working and working while she did voluntary work at the local hospital to fill her long empty days while I was out building an empire. I've no hobbies and no real close friends. All I had was work and my company which I built from nothing, just like your father built his, but then sold it six years ago to be with Agatha. I put all my energy into revenge because I was empty inside, but revenge didn't replace my Agatha and it didn't fill my long lonely days with purpose, only bitterness, but building something from scratch again would. So I've decided to keep the company and make it bigger and better than it was before and at the end of each day of creating something new, I'll come home to Hilltop Mansion where every room won't remind me of my old house and how empty and lonely it was without Agatha, but of a new beginning where I can tell her every evening about my busy, creative day at work just like I used to when I got home from building my first empire.'

The two women looked at each other and knew exactly how Henry felt. The story of their past lives may be different, but the sadness they felt living it was the same.

Anne smiled and said, 'Every house has its dark side and light side. I hope Hilltop shows you its light side, Henry, because, like your old house after Agatha died, I've only ever known its dark side.'

'I hope you find the light in your new home too, Anne,' he said, losing that dark, crepuscular scowl and replacing it with a kinder, softer smile. He then added, 'And good luck in your new job, Maggie.'

Watching Henry walk back up the long, shingled drive, Anne and Maggie felt their hearts lift with a sense of hope when he turned round at the gates and waved a last farewell before disappearing into the morning sunlight.

Back in the house, Anne and Maggie took one last stroll around all the rooms together, remembering both the good and bad times that they shared in each room before returning to the lounge. Maggie saw the The Adnegveill file on the plastic chair and couldn't resist giving a cheeky grin when she asked, 'I trust everything was as it should be?'

'Absolutely,' laughed Anne, grabbing Maggie's hand and dancing around the room, singing the Monty Python song, "Always Look on the Bright Side of Life". '

Simon, Eric and Dotty walked in and shrugged their shoulders, thinking, *What the hell...?* before bursting into the song. The gang of five newly freed spirits sang and danced their way around the room until they had no breath or voices left and slumped down onto the soft cream carpet floor, exhausted from happiness.

Leaning against the wall, the five sat in contented silence, enjoying the quietness of not having to do or say anything because true friends don't need fancy words between them when a loving silence says it all... until one of them breaks it with life's constant reminder that nothing gets done until someone does it.

'Well, I've got some good news and then some betters news,' said Simon, dragging his body off the floor then disappearing out into the hallway, returning with his brown leather briefcase and beaming like the cat who'd just lapped up all the cream.

'Well, don't keep us all in suspense; what's this good news?' demanded Dotty, impatient as ever.

Pulling out two large bundles of paperwork, Simon could barely hold back his excitement when he announced, 'The first document is the Official Annulment by the court of Anne's marriage to Jason Kay, because he used a false name, passport and date of birth; therefore, making the marriage illegal.'

'You mean, I'm no longer Mrs Jason Kay but Miss Anne Price?' asked Anne, leaping up and grabbing the document.

'You were always Miss Anne Price, even when you thought you were Mrs Anne Kay; only now, it's in black and white for all to see,' said Simon, beaming with pride.

Dotty interrupted again, 'And… the second document?'

'It's an application for an emergency marriage certificate at the local registrar's office at Hilltop Village Town Hall in the names of Mr Simon Dodd and Miss Anne Price for tomorrow afternoon at precisely 3.30 p.m., where we will require two witnesses and one bridesmaid to be present.'

'How did you manage all this so quick and without me knowing?' asked Anne, reading the application, but not quiet believing that it was real.

'Because I'm a damn good solicitor and a bloody impatient bridegroom who's been waiting too fucking long to make you Mrs Anne Dodd; so, do you want the fancy wedding or do you want the quick wedding? Because we're moving in two days' time and I want to carry *my wife*, Mrs Anne Dodd, over the threshold of our new home and future life together.'

'Bloody hell! You've gone all macho since selling your father's house and business and becoming a farmer,' joked Eric.

Dotty and Maggie just stood there giggling like a couple of teenage girls as they waited for Anne's reply to Simon's spontaneous marriage proposal.

'I've already done the "fancy wedding", which didn't turn out too well, so I suppose I'd better go for the "quick wedding".' She smiled, slinging her arms around Simon and kissing him when he dropped all the paperwork on the carpet.

Dotty couldn't help adding the last word when she said, 'Some bloody romantic proposal that was… I think I'll stay single and stick to my emporium business.'

Maggie suggested, 'Tea and cake, everyone?'

They all followed her into the kitchen where she pulled out a large picnic basket from underneath the table and they sat around, laughing and arguing about who said what to who and who did what to who when they were younger whilst stuffing their faces with Maggie's homemade sandwiches and chocolate cake.

Ninety minutes later, and a lot fatter, Maggie cleared away the table whilst Eric and Dotty left to finalise packing up their old lives before moving onto the next. Dotty couldn't help having the last word, again, 'I take it that I'm going to be the bridesmaid because I have the perfect outfit and besides, I look good in cream and pink.'

Grinning from ear-to-ear, Anne didn't need to answer when everyone knew that there could be no other choice. As Dotty and Eric disappeared, Simon looked at Anne and knew that she needed to be alone with Maggie. 'I'll wait for you outside in the car,' he said.

She smiled back then looked into the kitchen where Maggie was standing by the back door, waiting for her.

Walking back into the kitchen, Anne clasped Maggie's hands in hers, then cried both tears of joy and sadness as the two clung onto each other.

'I'll miss you so much my sweet, kind, Maggie,' said Anne, afraid to let her go.

Prising her body away, Maggie pressed her hand against Anne's face. 'You don't need me any more now, but there other victims out there that do... and besides, you're only going to Wales, my girl, not the end of the world. Fred and I are looking forward to at least *two* free holidays a year so stop being a cry baby and help me carry this bloody heavy picnic basket out to my bike.'

Wiping away the tears, Anne asked, 'Have you got everything you need?'

'Yes. Simon has sorted out all the legal stuff and the money man, Mr Caine, has set-up the tax-free trust fund and bank account with the one million you donated, plus he's paid up the next five years' rent on the eight-bedroom house in full so I can now officially inform you that both Fred and I are joint managers of "The Sunshine Home for Women",' said Maggie, beaming with pride and a new energy for life that Anne hadn't seen in her beloved face for a long, long time.

'Remember, if you need anything, anything at all, you know where I am and besides, I expect regular updates on the phone because

I know how much you hate paperwork,' she joked. Anne picked up the basket and slowly walked down through the back garden and round to the front of the house via a tiny little gate. She placed the basket into another bigger, wider wire basket at the back of the three-wheeler bike. Maggie climbed up and kissed her goodbye until the next day, when she would witness her finally marry the man she loved.

Standing outside Simon's house, Anne looked at the estate agent's *"Sold"* board outside and asked, 'Will you miss anything about the house and the business?'

Clasping his hand in hers, they walked up to the front door. He turned the key in the lock and she stepped inside for the first and last time with him.

Simon answered, 'Not one bloody thing.' He looked around at the empty hallway and rooms, adding, 'Well, maybe the garden. I always felt happier when outside in the garden,' he said, leading Anne into the study where there were just a few box files filled with documents that he couldn't leave behind; for the future is ultimately bound to the past by paper... because paper is legal and binding, regardless of time until the "expiry date" on it runs out.

'What's in this box?' Anne asked, noting the name *"Hilltop Mansion sale/charities"* on it.

'Documents relating to the other £2.5 million of the five million you received from the sale of Hilltop Mansion which, in accordance with your late father's Legal Addendum, must be split equally between your late mother's favourite charities.'

Smiling, Anne said, 'He was more honourable than I thought, just like your father.'

Simon gave a little smirk. 'Perhaps, or maybe they were just human, like all fathers?' He ran his hand over the other boxes when he added, 'But my father did leave me a good business and house in a desirable road to sell making three million pounds after deductions, just like yours did, which, in a way, was their legacy to our future and our children's future.'

'So with six million pounds from us and £350,000 from Dotty's sale of her flat, what have we left after buying the smallholding and house in Wales?' Anne asked, noting another box marked, *"Wales"*.

Simon pulled her close into his arms and pressed his lips against hers, then whispered, 'You already know, my love, because you no longer have to hide that smart brain inside your head any more. I'm not *him*... and our marriage will be an "equal partnership" in all things, good and bad.'

'I make it just under five million, she whispered, locking their lips together as their bodies floated out of the study and up the stairs into Simon's bedroom, where they collapsed onto the blow-up mattress on the floor, cementing their "equal partnership" without the need for paperwork.

Three Hours Later

Watching Simon drive out of Hilltop from the front porch whilst thinking that tomorrow afternoon, at precisely three thirty p.m., she would officially be Mrs Dodd, Anne looked across at the lodge to see the tall outline of Eric standing inside. A sudden sadness crept over her.

Knocking on the wooden door, she smiled when he opened it. 'I've just brewed up some coffee on the log fire and opened a packet of biscuits,' he said, when they sat together quietly, looking into the flames whilst drinking hot coffee and munching dark chocolate ginger biscuits straight from the fridge. The chocolate and ginger melted into their mouths like bitter sweet nectar.

Without taking her eyes off the flames, Anne asked, 'Will you miss your lodge and life at Hilltop?' She took another swig of coffee and bite of biscuit. 'I've been so happy these last few weeks that I forgot about your dreams. I just assumed that they were the same as mine and you wanted to go to Wales with Simon, Dotty and me, but never actually asked you if you didn't.'

Filling up her mug with more hot coffee from the hot pot hanging over the fire, she said, 'My memories of Hilltop are of being trapped in a tunnel with no light at the end, so I'm overjoyed to see the light, but I never really asked you what your memories are and what kind of future you wished for.'

Watching the flames from fire rise up out of the logs and dance around inside the large brick fireplace, Eric confessed, 'A part me will always love Hilltop but another part will always hate it. When my father was alive and I was a young boy growing up, I hated it because all I felt was the misery of being trapped inside this tiny lodge with a drunken bully, but when he died and your father took me under his wing, I grew to love the peaceful, cosy, safe warmth of the lodge and fire. I loved the freedom of being "my own man" when I was out working on the estate with no one to tell me what to do or where to work. Your father let me be "just me" and I will always love him for that, but when *he* arrived, I became that trapped boy again; only this time, I was a grown man. I could have left, but then told myself who would protect you, my little sister, but if I'm honest, I was too afraid to stay, but even more afraid to leave. I'm not an educated or particularly smart man and used to drink too much like my father, until I stopped. All I know is that I love working and living a simple life where my days are filled with the freedom of the open air and my nights with the smell of damp wood warming up inside the flames of the fire, whilst I breathe in their life-giving energy as I cook my food and drink my coffee, feeling content in my solitary world. I don't want a wife or children. I don't want riches or a fancy lifestyle. All I want is what I have now, but in another place.'

Turning his head away from the dying flames, Eric smiled when he told Anne, 'You are the little sister that my mother never had, so where you go, I go, because like you, my time at Hilltop has come to an end and your dream is *my* dream, so stop worrying about me and eat that last biscuit before I throw you out so that I can get on with packing up my old life and get ready for the new one.'

Running her tongue inside her mouth, Anne lapped up the last few crumbs of the bitter-sweet melted taste of dark chocolate and ginger before slapping a big, fat, wet chocolate-stained kiss on Eric's huge weather-beaten red rosy left cheek when she left him to his warm solitary lodge. She skipped across the grass to her solitary mansion where she opened door and stepped inside, feeling completely content at spending her last night alone in the house that no longer felt like a prison.

Her mobile pinged and she read the text from Dotty. *"Sleep well, single girl, and don't let the bed bugs bite because after tomorrow, you'll be a married woman and have to put up with a big fucking snoring husband sleeping beside you every night whilst I'll still be enjoying sleeping peacefully alone in my king-sized double-bed, LOL. From your very attractive, happily single, best friend and new business partner, xxx."*

Giggling away like a silly teenager, Anne ran up the stairs to her bedroom and threw herself onto the single-framed wired pull-out bed, then texted back, *"Lucky you have a king-sized double bed because you won't be too far away from the big house should I get tired of the snoring and nip over to your cosy little cottage at the front gates for a more peaceful night's sleep... See you tomorrow at three thirty p.m. and don't let the bed bugs bite you either, partner. LOL. xxx."*

Within seconds Anne's mobile pinged, *"Must remember to get those double locks on the Cottage front and back doors fitted, xxx."*

While Anne, Simon and Eric settled down to sleep in their separate beds for the night, Dotty was wide awake, sitting at the kitchen table in her tiny one- and-half-bedroom flat above the beauty salon in the village, tapping away at the laptop whilst listening to classical music on the "Smooth Classics" radio channel. She didn't know anything about the songs or singers except what the radio presenter added in-between playing records. All she knew was that it was a calming, soothing background noise that relaxed her mind and body as she ran her online emporium business buying and selling anything that took her eye whilst making a handsome profit in the process.

She loved the buzz of negotiating a good purchase and sale that would net her a decent profit at the end whilst making two other people very happy with their deal. She loved being her own woman with no man in her life to tell her what to do or say. She didn't need or want a husband or children. She was used to being on her own and creating her own world.

The only child of busy, absent parents who left her with the live-in au pair cum nanny/housekeeper whilst her father enjoyed being away all week at The Houses of Parliament as an MP and her mother played golf and "other bedtime games" with the dishy male golf teacher in-between lunching with girlfriends, she never had any friends or family until Anne.

Two lonely little girls who didn't mix well with the other girls at junior school and yet clicked like two peas in the same pod one day in the playground when they were just five years old.

Dotty still remembered that third day at school when Anne smiled across the playground from the protective shelter of the large black plastic bins by the toilets to the solitary little girl standing on her own at the other end by the front gates, watching all the other little girls and boys playing together and desperate to leave. Anne walked across the playground and said those magic words, 'Would you like to sit with me in my "secret place", because I think we are the same,' The bell rang and they all went back to school.

Sitting in the classroom playing with paint, brushes and paper, Anne drew a picture of "the well" and passed it under the table to her new friend, Dotty, sat opposite while the other children painted clowns and fairies.

Dotty lived three houses down from Hilltop Mansion, so it was easy to sneak out the back gate of the garden and into the woods to the well.

She knew that the au pair had a secret liaison with her builder boyfriend after he finished work in the village at four thirty p.m. every day and that the au pair laced her warm milk with half a sleeping tablet at four p.m. after collecting her from the school at three.

Like all lonely, only children, Dotty saw and watched everything around her because she had all the time in the world to do just that and so would spy on the au pair just because she could.

Some days, she would drink the hot milk because sleep meant an escape from emptiness, but now she had a "special friend" and a "magical wood and well" to share their dreams and secrets with together and so some days when Anne nodded her head three times across the classroom to Dotty, she wouldn't drink the milk and flushed it down the toilet instead.

As they grew older, Dotty and Anne would meet every week at their special place, dreaming about a future that seemed so far away and yet close when they looked down the well, wishing for the impossible.

Then everything changed when Dotty's parents divorced when she was twelve years old and they sold the house, then packed her off to a boarding school where for six long, dark, lonely years, she never saw Anne again because neither parent wanted her home with their new partners and family during the holidays.

Arriving back in the village, aged eighteen, with no home, job, future, money or support from either parent because she wasn't a part of their new lives and families, just a reminder of a past they'd prefer to forget, Dotty took a job as a waitress in the local tearoom where the kindly couple, Mr and Mrs Nettle, who rented the shop space but owned the flat above it which they used for storage, let her stay in the spare bedroom for nothing so long as she worked at the tearoom.

Dotty loved that tearoom. It was cosy, warm, light, bright and cheerful and full of tasty homemade cakes, pies, ice creams and anything that tasted and looked mouth wateringly delicious. Mr and Mrs Nettle would fill the shelves and front window in the tearoom with all sorts of antiquities to make it a more interesting and fun place to eat and chat in when one day, a customer asked to buy the lovely quaint teapot sitting in the window. Dotty negotiated a very handsome price for it on behalf of her bosses who paid her a small "commission" for being so astute.

Yet every day, Dotty thought about her childhood friend Anne and their "secret place", but was too afraid to knock on her door for fear of rejection when four months later, Anne came into the tearoom one afternoon on her own and recognised her friend standing behind the counter. She nodded her head three times before ordering a cream tea for one and sealing their lifelong bond to each other again. They met up at their secret place, the well, hidden in the magical woods.

The next two years passed by quickly; Dotty became manager of the tearoom and hired other waitresses whilst she built up the emporium side of the shop until sadly Mr and Mrs Nettle got old and passed away thirteen years later, within three months of each other, but they never forgot Dotty and left her the tiny one- and-a-half-bedroom flat above the tearoom where she continued to live and manage the tearoom below, until the landlord who owned the shop re-leased it to a new tenant who turned it into a beauty salon six months later.

But Dotty had the flat and all the antiquities from the tearoom which she stored in the box room and sold online until she ran out and then bought and sold more and more, building her online emporium empire from her tiny one- and-a-half-bedroom flat above the beauty salon.

Closing up the laptop for the night, Dotty looked around the tiny flat and smiled. It was no bigger than a large cupboard, but she loved every nook and cranny in it. It was her haven and full of happy memories where she built her emporium business whilst remaining free and protected from the world outside.

She would never forget Mr and Mrs Nettle who gave her what her parents never did; love, happiness and security, and they will always be with her in spirit, but it was time to move on.

She needed a new challenge in a new place and what better time to take up that challenge than now!

The flat may be tiny, but it was in a sought-after location and £350,000 would buy her that dream future that she wished for with Anne when they threw the coin down the well all those years ago, aged just eight years old.

She could be brave and free and yet feel safe and secure with the three people that were and always will be her real family; Anne, Simon and Eric. Each of them protecting the other and yet free to be what they wanted to be. Four separate dreams linked together as one and yet still apart.

The Wedding

The sun was shining and the air was clear when the newly married couple walked out of the local registrar's office at Hilltop Village Town Hall at precisely four p.m. Standing at the top of the long stone steps leading down from the town hall into the main car park, Mr and Mrs

Dodd smiled the biggest, widest, brightest grins possible for any humans to do, without cracking their faces open.

Dotty shouted, 'Hold that look,' before clicking the camera on her mobile. 'Perfect, just perfect,' she said, clicking again and again whilst Maggie and Eric stood aside, watching in happy amusement.

'Did I mention that you look particularly handsome today in your very slick hired grey suit, crisp white shirt, blue silk tie and well-polished slim black shoes, husband,' giggled Anne.

Dotty took yet another picture.

'Only about a million times since we signed the marriage certificate, Mrs Dodd,' laughed Simon, kissing her with a love so passionate that even Dotty, Eric and Maggie were frozen with a mixture of shock and sheer joy. He released her and whispered, 'I could say how beautiful you look in your cream lace dress, but the words wouldn't do justice to the happiness I feel inside.'

Wiping the tears from her eyes, Anne waved Maggie over to her and Eric to Simon as the two witnesses stood on either side of the newlyweds, looking particularly well-turned out with Eric in his rented dark blue suit and Maggie in her pretty two-piece pale blue jacket and matching pleated skirt. Dotty snapped away at the four on her camera until she had only enough battery left to take two more pictures. Anne ran back into the town hall and out again with the receptionist who clicked the final two pictures of the five together with Dotty bent down underneath the newlyweds, moaning, 'Nobody will see how good I look in my cream and pink dress.'

Watching the next happy couple arriving in the car park for their "quick wedding", the five skipped down the steps and into the long black hired limo waiting for them at the bottom. They drove off for a cosy meal together in the local Italian restaurant that Simon had hired just for them for the night where they drank sparkling champaign and ate loads of fresh pasta in a rich tomato sauce until midnight, when the limo dropped Maggie, Eric and Dotty back to their separate homes before driving the newlyweds to the large country hotel just outside the village.

Tipping the driver an extra-large cash bonus, Simon instructed him to collect them at midday tomorrow before collecting the keys to the honeymoon suite at the reception desk.

Gliding up the grand thick plush red and gold edged carpeted circular staircase with his arm around his wife's slim waist, Simon opened the door to their honeymoon suite, then placed the "Do Not Disturb" sign on the outside doorknob before locking the door secure for the night.

Saying Goodbye to Loneliness

While Anne, Simon, Eric and Dotty left their old lives behind and began their new, John Wilding was preparing to say goodbye to loneliness.

It had been over two months since he had returned home from Hilltop Cemetery and yet he still hadn't plucked up the courage to reach out to happiness.

He was still alone, only now he didn't have a purpose any more; just long lonely days and nights in an empty house with pictures of the past to remind him that he had none of the future.

Picking up the telephone for hundredth time since he returned home, his hand shook with a mixture of fear and hope as he dialled the number but didn't hang up this time.

The woman asked, 'Is that you, John?'

Feeling his voice cracking into a faded silence, he finally said, 'Did you get my letter about Freddy?'

Hearing the silent tears in her breath down the phoneline, John waited and waited… when, just as he was about to click off, she said, 'It was a hard letter to read, but a good letter to receive because now our boy is finally at peace, but the living must go on living, John, so are you ready to let go of the dead and embrace the living?'

Feeling the warm tears of hope flowing down his face, John blurted out, 'I've hurt you and our daughter so much, Molly, but if you could forgive me for forgetting that I had a "whole family" and not a just son to love and cherish, then I would very much like to start living and loving again.'

'Emma is holding a fourth birthday party for Daisy, your granddaughter, at my house in four days' time this coming Sunday. It will be full of noisy four-year-olds playing games in the garden, but it would be good for Daisy to finally meet her grandfather,' said Molly, welling up with tears of hope too.

'What present do I buy a four-year-old girl for her birthday?' John asked, excited and terrified at the same time.

Laughing, Molly replied, 'You're an ex-policeman who's tracked down a serial killer, I think that you can manage to work out what a little girl of four likes playing with.'

'What time, and is Emma OK with me coming?'

'Be here at two thirty p.m. sharp and don't worry about Emma, she's read the letter and wants her father back too. Just bring yourself and a pretty plastic doll dressed in pink inside a big bright box with a birthday card marked aged four with Daisy's name inside. Do you think you can manage that, Granddad?' laughed Molly.

'No, but I'll work it out.' He hesitated for a moment before saying, 'I've never stopped loving you, Molly.' The line went silent.

A little while later, she said, 'I know, John, but the past is the past and I've moved on, but we have a daughter and a granddaughter that we can both love together regardless of our separate lives.'

The time was eleven thirty a.m. and John had never felt more panic-stricken in his entire life. He'd checked the present a hundred times, but still wasn't sure that Daisy would like it.

The woman in the toy shop assured him that the birthday card with pink fairies dancing all over it and the pretty doll dressed in a pink dress inside the huge box were the perfect gift for a four-year-old little girl. But it was too late to change it now and besides, the toy shop was closed on a Sunday.

Unlocking the car and carefully placing the present and card on the passenger seat, John sat in the driver's seat staring at the empty road ahead, still not quiet believing that in just three hours' time, he would see his lost family again.

It had been over thirty years since he left the police force, but right now he was more afraid of buying the wrong doll for a four-year-old little girl than he ever was when chasing and bringing down criminals.

Turning the ignition key on the engine, he drove off. The radio came on and the music drifted over him like a warm soothing breeze on a chilling frosty day.

The more the music played, the calmer he became when, just five minutes away from Molly's house, he heard a voice of the past singing a song of the future. The DJ played Helen Shapiro's 1961 chart-topping hit, *Walking back to happiness.*

Parking the car and collecting the present from the front seat, John saw Molly and Emma waiting for him at the front door. A pretty, dark-haired little girl dressed in a bright pink fairy dress came running out of the house towards him, yelling, 'Grandpa, Grandpa.'

Throwing her arms around him, Daisy stripped away John's loneliness and filled him up with happiness.

Coming Home

Diane Moffatt glanced down the long, grey street filled with the same terraced houses she remembered as a child, only now their front doors were painted in an assortment of bright blues, yellows, soft greys, greens and charcoal black.

Smiling, she thought how little things had changed in thirty years and yet in another way were very different.

The road was the same, but the mixture of families living in them wasn't. Some were still rented, but others were now owned by the "up-market" newcomers who had moved into the area and bought cheap, borrowed high, but now owned trendy newly renovated, desirable, terraced houses in a location that was neither too poor nor too rich.

The train network enabled them to travel to work outside the area, meaning no more need for factories to sweat in until you died; just long, long day's travelling to and from work to earn enough money to pay for the large mortgage on the trendy terraced house with the fancy brightly coloured new front door.

Standing at the front door of the two-up-two-down rented red-bricked terraced house, Diane suddenly felt all the fears of that scared six-year-old little girl rushing back as she attempted to ring the doorbell in the centre of the dull, chipped and worn brown wooden door. Her fingers froze.

It had been twenty years and a bit since she last spoke to her mother and father and wasn't even sure if they were still alive or dead.

She could have telephoned to find out, but then just hearing her mother's voice on the phone would have stopped her coming back to the place where all her memories were dark, lonely, sad ones.

But she was not coming home to relive the old memories. No, she was coming home to banish them for good and replace those memories with brightly coloured ones, just like the front doors on the newly renovated terraced houses in the street.

Taking a deep breath, she pressed the bell and waited, and waited... Just as she was about to turn round and run, the door opened. An old, grey-haired, wrinkled-face woman of just fifty-six years of age smiled at her and said, 'Diane, you look wonderful, my dear girl.' She wrapped her arms around her like all loving mothers do when their estranged daughter finally returns home.

Laughing and crying together, mother and daughter drank tea and ate ham sandwiches and homemade coffee and walnut cake in the tiny kitchen that was still the same; only now it was filled with love and laughter instead of fear and sorrow.

The years hadn't been kind to Diane's mother, Elsie, but she was now happy and contented living a widow's life in her little rented terrace house.

She had little money, but enough from her job as a check-out assistant at the local supermarket to feed herself, pay the rent and bills and enjoy not having to wait upon a grumpy, depressed, drunken husband who died of a massive heart attack five years ago, aged just fifty-five, and now rested, alone, in a simple grave in the local church graveyard that Elsie no longer visited because now, she was free to do what she wanted, when she wanted and with whom she wanted without being answerable to anyone.

'I'm sorry I left you behind, Mother. Can you ever forgive me for not being a better daughter?' cried Diane, suddenly realising that they were both the same; two women fighting for their place in a world that is more often cruel than kind.

'There's nothing to forgive. You did what you had to do to survive and live just as I did the same, so stop crying and tell me why you've come back now, because it is not for my wonderful homemade walnut and carrot cake?' laughed Elsie, scooping another extra-large bite.

'First, I must ask if you ever hear from Tony.'

'Your brother left home shortly after you and I've never heard from him since, but unlike you, I never missed him. He was your father's son, whereas you are my very own sweet loving daughter,' smiled Elsie.

Wiping the tears from her eyes, Diane told her mother about her plans to come home for good, buy a house and run a mobile library from the large main library in the centre of town after she completed her first few months of training at college when she can take her exams and finish the rest of her training at the main library.

'But have you enough money to buy your own home?' asked Elsie, proud of how well her daughter had done all by herself without a man to claim ownership of her life.

'Not quite. I thought the terraced houses here would still be cheap, but the old ones need a lot of renovation and the other ones have rocketed in price,' said Diane, sad at not being able to return home to the same street.

'You could buy this one and we could live together, but separately, if you don't mind sharing with an old, clapped-out widow and newly re-united mother?' suggested Elsie.

Looking around her old home, Diane smiled. 'It would be lovely to start both our new lives together here, Mother, but I fear it would cost too much with all the work that I would want to do to it to remove the dark memories and replace them with fresh, new bright ones.'

Placing her hand on her daughter's cheek, Elsie smiled broadly when she told her, 'The landlord has had several offers from various people to buy this house, but apparently he can't get rid of me because

290

I'm what they call "a sitting tenant", which means whoever buys the house gets me with it because I'm not going anywhere.'

Kissing her mother on the cheek, Diane laughed out loud. 'I could buy our old home for a song then legally transfer your name to the deeds of ownership together with mine, making you no longer "a sitting tenant" but joint owner with me, your daughter.'

'You mean, I never have to pay rent again to live in my own home?' asked Elsie, bursting into tears of amazement and happiness.

'Never again, Mother. We will be two independent women doing our own chosen careers and living our own chosen lives in our own fully paid-up mortgage and rent-free home,' cried Diane, suddenly looking around the tiny old-fashioned kitchen, thinking how wonderful it felt to finally realise that six-year-old little girl's dream of living in a happy, bright home with a loving mother who cherished and loved her daughter as much as she cherished and loved her mother back.

'Welcome home, Daughter,' smiled Elsie, making a fresh pot of tea whilst Diane cut another slice of cake to celebrate their new, happy lives together in their old, but new home.

Moving On

Jacky Jones looked into the long wardrobe mirror in his bedroom, wondering who the man dressed in causal light-blue jeans, grey sweatshirt with a bright blue sky imprinted on the front and white sneakers was staring back at him?

All he had ever seen was the dark side of human nature but now that Jason Kay had finally been expelled from his life, he was free at last from the demons inside his head.

He had been the invisible other half of Mr A's secret covert organisation, The Department, for so long that he'd forgotten that there was a whole wide world outside filled with joyous and happy experiences to explore.

Now the man in the mirror staring back him was a "blank canvas", waiting to be filled up with glorious multi-coloured pictures of bright new adventures.

Saluting goodbye to the old Jacky Jones in the mirror, the new Jacky Jones zipped-up the small, soft, black leather holder containing his most precious personal items, including his favourite framed picture of Mr A and him smiling happily together in the sunlight by the sea on one of their rare days away from fighting the malignant underworld of crime down in the basement.

Picking up the holder, Jacky took one last look around the bedroom before closing the door and slowly walking down the stairs into the hall where he stood in silent contemplation, remembering the last thirty years of a life that he was now leaving behind.

Placing the holder by the front door, Jacky walked down the hall and opened the tiny cupboard door under the stairs, leading to the basement where twelve creaky wooden steps down a whole other world invisible to the residents of the leafy tree-lined well-to-do tall Victorian semi-detached houses outside operated.

'Are you all packed up and ready to go?' David Fox asked, hearing Jacky's creaky steps behind him as he swirled the large leather chair around from the computers and the two men locked eyes.

'I'm as ready as I'll ever be, but are you sure that you're fucking ready because this room is going to be your whole life from today.'

Swinging the chair round full-circle, David scanned the low-ceiling eight by six square metre room without windows or any natural light, packed with an assortment of computers, technical equipment and row upon row of filing cabinets protected by thick padded soundproof dark grey walls. 'This will do just fine,' he said.

Jacky smiled. 'Just as well because I've got a boat to pick up.'

Leaping off the chair, David stretched his back and legs when Jacky laughed out loud and David asked, 'What's so funny?'

'Oh, just seeing you dressed in a black hooded sweatshirt, bottoms and sneakers doing what I had done for the last thirty years, attempting to stretch some life back into your bent-up body.'

Smiling, David said, 'While you've been chasing criminals and bad guys from the safety of your large, comfortable house and cosy warm basement, I've been doing the same only from lonely, soulless hotel rooms, dark alleys and airports, all over the world, alone... and while you've been warm and cosy, I've spent years hiding in the shadows in the rain, the snow, the wind, the heat and any fucking shit hole that I was sent to by my "invisible" employers. I've been shot at, stabbed, punched, kicked and even shoved down a well and all for what? I have no wife, family or home of my own. I'm forty-six years old and spend my rare days off drinking in some dingy bar and eating a takeaway in yet another soulless hotel room. I've earned good money over the last twenty odd years, but I spend it faster than I receive it because what's the point of saving for a future when I could be dead the next day or night?'

Stretching his arms out wide, David added, 'I'm more than fucking ready to embrace this room and house as my whole life from today, Jacky, because now I get to fight the bad guys on my terms from my territory and then get to eat a home-cooked meal and sleep in a warm, cosy bed in a real home at the end of a good day's work without wondering whether I'll wake up alive or dead in a dark alley or down some well the next day.'

'I guess were both ready to move on... only I want to embrace having no ties or commitments whereas you want the opposite and so we both get what we want, and hopefully, find a little bit of happiness too,' said Jacky, embracing his new replacement and friend. The two men walked back up the twelve creaky steps to their very different lives.

For the last two months, Jacky had trained and mentored David just like Mr A had done the same to him; only this time both men began with a clean slate. Jacky without his demons and David without his regrets.

'Now you know everything I know about The Department and have all the relevant contacts at your disposal from the list that's in the *file*, but if you ever need my help, then you can reach out to me through the underworld network. I will get back to you unless I'm lost on some desert island somewhere without a signal,' joked Jacky.

'Then I'll just have to send out a fucking plane to find you,' laughed David. He got serious for a moment and asked, 'Are you sure that you're OK with me staying here in your home rent-free for maybe, ever...?'

'Mr A took me in and gave me this home and now I'm doing the same for you, David, only you're not a fifteen-year-old homeless kid, but a forty-six-year-old homeless ex-hired bodyguard/undercover agent. So, here's the deal... If you last five years and still want to carry on, then you can buy the house from me at today's market value of £1.2 million minus another £650,000... maybe that will give a reason to spend less than you receive.'

'That's a fucking deal,' smiled David, reaching out his hand and the two friends shook on it.

Opening the front door, Jacky picked up his black leather holder and walked down the drive to his car.

David shouted, 'I forgot to ask what kind of boat have you bought?'

'A fucking big one,' laughed Jacky, unlocking the car and driving off with the radio playing the chart-topping voices of ABBA, belting out their 1977 hit song "Move On". Watching Jacky driving off to his new life, David closed the door then strolled into the kitchen to fry some eggs and bacon for breakfast. He pressed the button on the radio by the window ledge and heard the same radio channel playing the same Abba song.

26
The Four Rings

Six and half months had elapsed very quickly since the sentence was passed on The Adnegveill when Anne received her first half-yearly report.

Sitting on the massive stone porch at the front entrance of her new home, re-named The Four Rings, Anne rocked back and forth in the large cosy rocking chair, sipping a double vodka and lime in the early evening sunlight whilst listening to her favourite tape "The Road to Freedom" playing softly in the background as she looked out over the huge green lawn perfectly cut and shaped into a maze with its low green hedges and shingle walkways.

It was an idyllic view to and from the nineteenth-century eight-bedroom mansion that was both her home and now an up-market lovingly renovated bed and breakfast.

Every evening, she would sit on the porch listening to the tape whilst sipping a double vodka and lime from the tall glass on the black-wired table beside the chair whilst waiting for Simon, Eric and Dotty to join her on the other three rocking chairs circled around a much large black iron table in the centre of the porch, containing a huge cocktail shaker with three tall glasses.

It had become their little mantra at the end of the day and one that she cherished whilst she filled up her three albums with photographs and postcards sent to her from all their friends.

Each one of them living their new lives like she was whilst The Adnegveill continued his life sentence in a ten by seven square metres cell with no natural light, soft background music or idyllic view to comfort him.

Opening the file whilst taking another sip of her drink, a satisfied grin crept across Anne's lips while she read the report and looked at the enclosed photographs of The Adnegveill's new life. Simon's voice drifted through the breezy warm evening wind, 'Don't drink all the bloody vodka, Mrs Dodd.'

Looking up, Anne laughed at the sight of Simon, Eric and Dotty skipping through the maze like three naughty children.

'Then you'd better get up here fast,' she shouted, pouring another double from the large cocktail shaker when the three kids arrived and plonked themselves down on the rocking chairs before helping themselves to the vodka and lime. 'Is that what I think it is?' asked Simon, noting the large file on her lap.

Placing the file back on the table by the shaker, she said, 'It is.'

Simon asked, 'Is everything good?'

Leaning back into the rocking chair, Anne sighed a contented grin when she answered, 'Everything is exactly as it should be...'

'Excellent,' smiled Simon as the four sat back in their chairs, drinking, whilst perusing their new business adventure and home together, noting that in just seven days' time, The Four Rings would officially be open for business.

The telephone on the large dark wood mahogany hallway table inside the mansion rang again and they listened to another potential customer wanting to reserve an "All-Inclusive" week away at The Four Rings...

Looking down the long shingled drive to the large black iron gates at the entrance, their hearts lifted every time they saw the huge black iron sign hanging above the gate in the shape of four black iron rings depicting the four separate businesses managed and operated by each of them with the help of locally hired staff grateful for the work.

1) Bed and breakfast in the mansion... managed and run by Anne who lives in the mansion with Simon.

2) Tearoom and emporium in the recently converted barn at the other end of the maze... managed and run by Dotty who lives in the cottage just inside the iron gate entrance.

3) Small zoo with sheep, cattle, alpacas, pigs, chickens, horses, miniature ponies, donkeys plus ducks and swans in the lake located in the converted outbuildings at the back of the mansion... managed and run by Simon.

4) A thirty-acre estate and farm with sheep, cattle and a large black bull managed and overseen by the estate manager, Eric... who lives in the newly built wooden lodge on the estate.

The Four Rings:

Each of them protecting the other and yet free to be what they want to be. Four separate dreams linked together as one and yet still apart.

Finishing up the last of the vodka and lime, the four friends and new business partners strolled off to their new homes on the estate.

Dotty asked Anne, 'Why three albums?'

Picking up the albums and the file, Anne replied, 'One album for The Four Rings, and two for the detectives who gave us and our friends in the album the chance to live the dream instead of just dreaming it.'

27
No Regrets

Steal stared into the bedroom mirror, wondering whether it was time to retire.

Every new case brought more darkness and tragedy into his life and maybe he should hand the mantle of saving the world to someone else when there was no one left in his life to save him.

Yes, he enjoyed putting away the bad guys, but at what price? He wasn't a brilliant detective who always got his man for nothing. But to be that brilliant detective took its toll which showed in his face.

For a man touching fifty, he sometimes looked seventy; yet he was too young to retire and too old to begin a new career, and besides, what else could he do? Because, deep down inside his very soul, he still loved his job. Just not today, when he looked and felt seventy. To do what he did required everything you had to give and then more.

But the price paid for such dedication to serving justice to the guilty and protecting the innocent is a lonely man staring at himself in the mirror, wondering whether he had sacrificed too much when at the end and beginning of each day, he only had his own sad and tired reflection in the mirror for company.

Picking up his detective's badge from the bedside chest of drawers, Steal stared at it for ages.

The front door bell rang and he opened it to find the postman stood holding a large brown padded envelope with his name on it. Signing his signature, Steal's curiosity was awakened. The only letters he ever received were bills and more bills.

No one ever sent him a card or present because he had no one in his life to care whether he lived or died, except his work partner Sergeant Liz Wright and his old mentor and friend Tom Millard, who, like him, led solitary lives with only their reflections in the mirror for company at the beginning and end of each day.

Carrying the package into the kitchen, he ripped open the padded envelope to discover a large dark brown leather album inside with an invitation card imprinted with The Four Rings logo on top and a hand-written gold-tipped ink pen message inside the card that read:

"To Detective Steal, the man that gave ALL the victims inside this album a chance to live their dreams instead of just dreaming them... Keep on saving lives, Detective, and if you ever fancy a break away from catching serial killers, then there will always be a room for you here at The Four Rings."

Opening the album, Steal's tired old face melted away as it grew younger and younger with each page that he turned.

Staring at the happy pictures and postcards inside the album, his spirit lifted with a lightness that he hadn't felt in a long, long time. His mobile rang and Wright asked, 'Are you looking at what I'm looking at, Boss?'

Smiling, he answered, 'You know that we can't show these albums to anyone outside our own world, including the team at the office?'

'Everyone has their secrets, Boss, only this secret is a good one, and besides, I won't tell if you don't, so who the fuck is going to know that we spend our spare time flicking through an album that doesn't exist?'

'I'll read you my message if you read me yours?' Steal said, curious to know if it was the same.

Wright read out:

"To the partner of Detective Steal that gave ALL the victims inside this album a chance to live their dreams instead of just dreaming them... Keep on saving lives, Sergeant Wright, and if you ever fancy a break away from catching serial killers, then there will always be a room for you here at The Four Rings..." Grinning, Steal read Wright his message then added, 'How come you get a free holiday too when I'm the boss and the detective who always gets his man?'

'Because we're *Steal and Wright* and together, *we* always get *our* man, Boss,' she said, unable to resist having the last word.

He laughed out loud. 'You said it, Wright, I'm the boss, so don't be bloody late for work and make sure that the coffee is hot and strong when I arrive at precisely eight thirty a.m. to catch some more fucking bad guys, together.' They signed off.

The two detectives sat in their separate kitchens drinking coffee whilst flicking through the photos in their albums.

1.   A photo of Anne stood smiling outside The Four Rings Bed & Breakfast

2.   Simon smiling in front of The Four Rings Zoo

3.   Dotty smiling outside The Nettle Emporium Tearooms

4.   Eric leaning against The Four Rings Lodge holding a baby lamb

5.   Diane Moffatt smiling outside her Mobile Library parked in front of her newly painted bright red front door with her mother, Elsie, and two six-year-old girls stood beside her

6.   Dr Stuart Pritchard and his housekeeper/companion Martha Pope drinking wine at the local restaurant whilst staring out at the bright blue Caribbean Sea

7.   Maggie Frith and her husband Fred stood outside The Sunshine Home for Women refuge shelter with two smiling women in the background

8.   David Fox sitting at his computer in the basement, brandishing a huge grin whilst holding up a large handwritten sign stating, *"Enjoying my job and lovely warm home whilst saving more victims and punishing even more criminals"*

9.   Jacky Jones standing on his yacht taking pictures of flying dolphins in the middle of the ocean whilst his crew snapped pictures of him laughing tears of sheer joy

10.   Maggie Frith placing freshly cut red roses in the silver holed flower pot on Anthony and Sandra Gibb's grave.

11.   John Wilding holding a family dinner at his house for the first time with his ex-wife Molly, daughter Emma and granddaughter Daisy who was wearing a pink party dress and holding her favourite doll

12.   The Adnegveill sitting on a single wooden bed, brandishing a shaven head with his arms locked inside a straightjacket around

his chest, forming the shape of a cross as his pitiful, empty eyes cried out for mercy

Closing the albums and hiding them away in their secret place, Steal and Wright left for work with *no regrets.*

28
The Sentence

The time was six a.m. precisely when the shaven headed inmate heard the shuttle of the steel spy hole being pulled back to see those damn black bulging eyes spying on him, again… followed by the rattle of keys turning in the lock before the scrapping sound of the steel reinforced black cell door being opened when the six-foot-six bulging muscled-bound frame of the shaven-headed male jailer stepped inside.

Clothed top to bottom in a white shirt, trousers, trainers and wearing a white mask with his hands protected by clear white plastic gloves, the jailer carried the tray into the ten by seven metres, white, soundproof padded cell.

Placing the tray on the tiny wooden table with matching wooden chair in the left-hand corner of the cell, the jailer stepped back six paces then clasped his hands in front of him whilst the other identically dressed muscle-bound jailer with a similarly shaven head stood guard outside.

Standing up from the wooden bed with his arms locked inside the straightjacket around his chest, forming the shape of a cross, the Adnegveill straightened his back before walking six paces to the wooden table where he waited. The jailer stepped forward six paces and untied the leather straps from his arms and he sat down.

The Adnegveill didn't know what time it was because his gold Rolex watch sitting on the tiny wooden shelf beside the photograph of his favourite silver sports car high up the padded wall above the table had no battery.

All he knew was that he didn't sleep much because if he did, the demons would visit him… but as time went on, he learnt to count the hours in-between breakfast, lunch and dinner because the routine *never* deviated.

Midnight — Anne's recorded bedtime story "The Tree of Eternal Life" bellows out from the loud speakers, high-up in the ceiling where the demons hide inside waiting for him to fall into a deep sleep.

Breakfast — Six hours from midnight. Six a.m.

Lunch — Six hours from breakfast. Twelve noon

Dinner — Six hours from lunch. Six p.m.

666 — The demons awaken

Midnight — Anne's recorded bedtime story "The Tree of Eternal Life" bellows out from the loud speakers, high-up in the ceiling where the demons hide inside, waiting for him to fall into a deep sleep...

Breakfast was always the same as was lunch and dinner.

Three small hard-boiled eggs, one stained teaspoon, one slightly cracked egg cup and plate containing two slices of thinly buttered brown bread unevenly cut into six slices, one pot of tea in a stained silver teapot with one matching milk jug containing just enough milk for one and half cups of lukewarm tasteless cheap tea.

There was no salt and pepper but the jailer always asked the same question.

'Is everything as it should be?'

He would reply, 'Yes,' because if he said, "No", they would punish him and he'd go hungry... until he'd say, "Yes", and so he ate the food that made him feel sick with vomit and diarrhoea... over and over again... three times a day... everyday... because that was *the sentence*.

While he ate breakfast, the Adnegveill tried desperately *not* to look up at the left-hand corner of the ceiling by his table because if he did, he would see it... the spider's web with the large black spider spinning his silver thread inside.

He can't kill the spider because when the jailer isn't in the cell with him, his arms and body are locked inside the straitjacket.

If he yelled out or complained, the jailer would unlock the door and make him stare at the spider for sixty minutes whilst he stood in the corner, holding a black leather truncheon to beat him around the legs if he turned his eyes away.

It was the fourth black spider since the sentence began.

Every time one died, the jailer replaced it with another identical black spider. And so, the inmate ate the food he hated in silence and kept his eyes low until the jailer looked at his watch, and he knew that his time was up.

Whether he ate breakfast, lunch or dinner, it didn't matter if the plate was empty… because at some point in the day or night, he would be sick or have to take a shit in the bucket/piss pot underneath the table via the hole cut inside his straightjacket and white inmates trousers, where the excrement would stay for days and days stinking out the soundproof padded cell while he screamed in silence inside his head until the jailer finally took the bucket away and emptied it.

There were no mirrors in the cell for him to look at his reflection, but once a fortnight the jailer would unlock the cell when two more shaven-headed jailers would enter with a tin bath, one bar of white soap, two buckets of cold water and an electric razor. He would strip down naked inside the bath and they'd pour the cold water all over him as he washed his shaven head and thin, stringy body with the bar of soap before they shaved his head and face with the electric razor.

When the sentence first began, he would complain about everything. His name, the Adnegveill. The midnight bedtime story, "The Tree of Eternal Life". The straitjacket. The shaven head. The smelly piss/sick bucket. The food. The spider. The cold bath. No battery for his beloved gold Rolex watch, that he couldn't reach. The picture of his favourite silver sports car that he no longer owned to remind him of what he treasured more than a person's life. The soulless soundproof padded cell where *no one* outside could hear his cries for help.

He complained about the cell having no mirrors, clock, windows, light, fresh air, comfortable bed, furniture or visitors except the jailers and the *two* visits from a man dressed in a black suit and shirt who took pictures of him sat on his wooden bed locked inside the straightjacket with a camera.

He complained about the punishment.

Every time the jailer asked him, 'Is everything as it should be?' and he'd yell and shout, 'No, it fucking isn't!' the jailer would sink the black leather truncheon into the back of his legs. The unbearable pain and bruises would travel through his body for days and days.

Now he complained about nothing.

He no longer desired to look at his reflection in mirror for the man he would see staring back him "was not as he had created him."

"Sooner or later, *everybody* dies. And all that really counts is *how you live*" used to be his favourite mantra that made *killing* so easy, because all his victims would have died eventually. And so he lived the life he wanted to live no matter the cost to anyone that got in his way.

Until now…

The sentence had only just begun but already it felt like he was in Hell, until he heard the bedtime story "The Tree of Eternal Life" every night at midnight.

He used to be so good at lying, but guardians of the Tree to Eternal Life can't be fooled and know who The Adnegveill really was…

The Midnight Hour

Lying on the thin mattress, the Adnegveill could feel the uneven wooden slabs of the bed digging into his back.

Whatever way he turned, the pain never went away, but just spread further along his body and so now he stayed still.

Soon, it would be the midnight hour and he would try *not* to listen to her voice, but with his hands locked inside the straightjacket and the speakers turned up loud, the Adnegveill would have no choice…

And so he waited, telling himself that it was just a story…

That it was not real!

But deep down inside his very soul, a part him knew that it was.

Because, sooner or later, *everybody* dies… when all that really counts to the guardians of The Tree to Eternal Life will be *how you lived*!

Closing his eyes, he counted the seconds. 'One, two, three, four, five, six…'

'Hello, Alex,

It's time for your bedtime story…

Listen carefully because one day, you will be really dead…'

The Tree of Eternal Life

The man stood in front of the three wooden steps staring down upon the four guardians that sat on the steps, guarding entry to the Tree of Eternal Life.

There are the three wise monkeys.

Speak No Evil. Hear No Evil. See No Evil.

With the beast of all beasts; the Hound of Hell.

Sat in the middle of the first step was Speak No Evil.

On the second step Hear No Evil sat to the right, with See No Evil to the left.

Guarding the third and final step stood the Hound of Hell at the centre, staring up at the huge oak tree whose branches reached up into the sky and beyond.

'Welcome to The Tree of Eternal Life,' said the first wise monkey, adding, 'To step onto the first step, you must answer the question: "Have you ever *spoken* any evil in your life that would have harmed and caused any harm to anyone?'

'No, absolutely not. I'm a good person and have lived a normal life and harmed no one,' answered the man, confident that his lies would be believed.

He had spent his entire life lying. He was very good at it and could fool and had fooled everyone. What could a stupid insignificant little monkey do to him when he had faced far more dangerous adversaries when alive?

'Are you quite sure that you've never *spoken* any evil in your entire life that would have harmed or caused any harm to anyone?' asked the monkey again.

'I'm sure,' said the man, smiling that open, innocent smile that always hid the lie behind the lie so well when he was alive.

'Then you may step up onto the second step,' said the monkey of Speak No Evil, hissing that sneaky little grin that all monkeys do when planning to pinch what's yours.

Standing on the step, the second wise monkey sitting to the right asked, "Have you ever *heard* any evil in your life that would have benefited you by harming or causing harm to anyone you deemed a threat in any way?'

'No, absolutely not,' replied the man again whilst thinking how boring these stupid questions were.

'Are you quite sure that you've never *heard* any evil in your entire life that would have benefited you by harming or causing harm to anyone you deemed a threat in any way?' asked the monkey again.

'I'm positive,' said the man, smiling that open, innocent smile that always served him so well when the monkey of Hear No Evil hissed that sneaky little grin.

The third wise monkey sat to the left asked, 'Have you ever *seen* any evil in your life that would have benefited you by harming or causing any harm to anyone that you disliked, envied or deemed a threat in any way?'

Hiding his fury at the irritating little monkey's repeated stupid fucking questions, the man gave that same innocent smile for a third time then answered, 'I've never envied another person's life or possessions or disliked anyone even if they were unkind to me because I was too busy living and enjoying my own life.'

'Are you absolutely positive that you've never *seen* any evil in your entire life that would have benefited you by harming or causing any harm to anyone that you disliked, envied or deemed a threat in any way?' repeated the monkey of See No Evil.

Noting that he was just one step away from gaining the prize of eternal life in Heaven, the man was confident that his lies would continue to serve him well, so he answered, 'If I were an evil man, then I would have gone straight to Hell instead of being sent here to join the angels in Heaven. Therefore, I state with all honesty that I have never *spoken, heard* or *seen* any evil in my entire life that would have benefited me in any way by harming or causing harm to any other person or persons and have never disliked, envied, hated or threatened another living soul.'

'Excellent,' said the monkey of See No Evil, hissing that sneaky little grin. The man felt the breath of the beast of all beasts upon him when the Hound of Hell's huge head leaned down from the third step, growling and sniffing.

307

Running his thick, long, slobbery wet tongue over the man's face, the beast grounded his large yellow teeth. 'I can taste your true soul,' he snarled whilst continuing down his prey's body, stretching his neck further and further without moving from the step.

With his legs and body frozen stiff, the man locked away his fear and continued to play the game out to the end confident that even the beast of all beasts wouldn't be able to sniff out the real him. After all, he was smarter than a mere dog, even if it was a fucking big one.

Lifting its head back up, the beast snarled, 'Is there anything else you would like to say before I make my decision?'

Relieved that he's still got a head intact with a mouth to lie through, the man answered, 'Only that God made me what I am and confess that like all imperfect humans, I've made mistakes in both my choices and emotions in life, but I'm not an evil person. I'm just an ordinary man who wishes to spend eternity resting in peaceful sleep.'

'A good answer,' said the beast, raising his head and growling upwards to the sky when the long green branches of the timeless oak tree of eternal life folded down around the man's body, lifting him gently off the step and carried him higher and higher into the air where he saw the white clouds of Heaven open up to welcome him. He laughed and laughed whilst thinking how cleaver his was and how stupid both the living and dead were.

Feeling the touch of the heavenly white clouds upon his laughing face, the man closed his eyes, ready for the angles to take him to his peaceful resting place when the beast raised his huge head high up into the sky and growled, 'You lied!'

Opening his eyes, the man saw the clouds close by when the branches started to curl around him like barbed wire, cutting into his flesh as he screeched out in pain.

The beast howled again, 'You lied!'

Feeling his tortured body being carried down and down by the barbed wire, the man saw the earth open up beneath him. The snarling, growling yellow-toothed huge jaws of the Hound of Hell opened up, swallowing him into the eternal flames of burning agony.

The three wise monkeys and beast of all beasts resumed their guard on the three steps to The Tree of Eternal Life.

The beast turned his head back and growled, 'The guardians of The Tree to Eternal Life can't be fooled and know who The Adnegveill really is.'

Lying on the bed, after hearing the story for the millionth time, the Adnegveill repeated the same mantra inside his head over and over again.

'It's just a stupid fucking story. There is *no* Tree of Eternal Life, three wise fucking monkeys or the Hound of Hell! It's just a stupid fucking story that *she* repeats every night to torment me with dark thoughts so that I can't sleep in peace.'

But deep down inside his very soul, a part of him half believed that it's true.

Because, sooner or later, *everybody* dies, but until you do, you can't be absolutely sure what awaits you at the other end except maybe the consequences of *how you lived*.

Too afraid to fall into a deep sleep just in case he *doesn't* wake up, the Adnegveill cries out inside his head for mercy from the soundproof padded cell deep down in the basement of the secret secure mental hospital hidden deep in the woods amongst the tall rustling trees invisible to the world outside.

29

The man stepped outside his house, smiling that friendly, innocent, open smile.

He was known everywhere he went and disliked by no one. He was not too arrogant, too loud, too pushy or too anything.

He was just an ordinary man with a kind face living an ordinary life, that smiled, chatted and laughed with everyone he saw, greeted or met along the way.

Everybody liked him because he took an interest in who you were and what you had to say and yet wasn't too nosy, too intrusive or too opinionated.

It didn't matter how insignificant you may feel, he would treat you with respect because everyone was equal in his eyes.

Until he turned the key in the lock and stepped inside his house, when the kind face with the friendly, innocent, open smile withered away like black dust... revealing the true face of the beast that everyone behind the locked door feared.

The
Adnegveill

Street Angel... House Devil...

Do you know one?
Or are you one?

30
The Invitation

It was a Monday morning and the sun was shining outside the kitchen window while Steal ate his favourite breakfast of three scrambled eggs with chopped mushrooms and onions spread evenly on lightly buttered thick-sliced white toast with a generous dollop of brown sauce on top.

He rarely cooked his favourite breakfast because his mobile always rang before he finished getting dressed when Wright would inform him of yet another clue or problem to solve/overcome in their latest murder/mystery case.

But today, he felt good because the last few weeks had been pleasantly dull. All the bank robbers and buglers had gone on holiday. No terrorist had gunned down any innocent people. And no one had been reported missing or found dead.

The team at the office had had a chance to catch up on the backlog of years and years of paperwork whilst Wright had had time to pass yet *another* exam; leaving the boss free for the first time in years to simply do *nothing* except sit in his office and watch everyone else beaver away, doing all the boring stuff that they now had no excuses not to do whist he had time to cook and eat his favourite breakfast every morning without interruption. Until today... when the doorbell rang and the postman handed him the *special delivery*; a large white square envelope addressed to Inspector Steal at his *home* address.

Signing for the envelope, Steal had a bad feeling inside his gut. Walking back into the kitchen, he placed the typed written envelope on the table beside his half-eaten breakfast. The normal post would just have had his initials and name on it. Anything to do with work would have been delivered to the office.

Tapping his fingers on the envelope, Steal finally opened it when his face turned to ashen grey as he read he invitation.

"To Inspector Steal,

If you have received this invitation, then I am already dead...

I know that you do not want to solve my murder *but I can trust no one else to bring my killer to justice.*

I did not have time to solve it myself because they were smarter and more devious than I had anticipated.

I leave that task to you even though I know that I don't deserve your help or pity... And even though you have every right to hate me, I know that you are a good man and a brilliant detective, who always got his man, including me.

Will you do what I couldn't and find my killer, Inspector Steal?

If you do decide to solve my murder, then inside the smaller envelope is the invitation to my funeral.

Attached to the invitation, you will see the names of the six *suspects who will also be at my funeral.*

Good luck, Inspector Steal, and if it's any consolation to you after all these years of hating me, you can now take solace in my death being the final justice that you wanted, but couldn't have..."

Reading the attached list of names and then the *invitation* again, Steal knew that he had *no choice* but to accept.

Throwing the half-eaten breakfast in the bin, Steal telephoned Wright. 'I need your help to solve a murder but I can't write it up in the book.'

'When do we start, Boss?' she asked, without questioning the man that she knew had more honour in his little finger than any other detective on the force.

'At the address I'm about to text you...'

To be continued.